BROKEN COUNTRY - BROKEN SOLDIER

FROM FIGHTING FRONT TO HOME FRONT

By

MARY ANNE BUTLER

To Phylis,
Enjoy and learn a bit
of history too!

Mary Anne Butler

First published by AuthorHouse 08/04/04

ISBN: 1-4184-0307-5 (e-book)
ISBN: 1-4184-0306-7 (Paperback)

Library of Congress Control Number: 2004092249

This book is printed on acid free paper.

Printed in the Untied States of America
Bloomington, Indidana

Cover Art: Gettysburg National Military Park.
A portion of the Cyclorama depicting Pickett's Charge by French artist Paul Philippoteaux, first exhibited in 1884. The medal was presented to the author's great grandfather in 1865 upon completion of his two enlistments in the Seventy-Eighth Regiment, Ohio Volunteer Infantry. The man and woman are family photos.

Note: Inscriptions about the Civil War that preceed certain chapters were taken from the
*History of the Seventy-Eighth Regiment,
Ohio Veteran Volunteer Infantry.*
by Reverend Thomas M. Stevenson, chaplain.

To Paul,
Jeff, Anne, Meg,
Katie, Ellen,
and Judy

Acknowledgements

My thanks for helping me with this book go first to my husband, Paul, who stayed with me, reading and editing every word and making invaluable suggestions.

For the Ohio section of the story I visited the Morgan County Historical Society, McConnelsville, and also consulted the historical section of the Zanesville Public Library, and the Putnam Historic Association.

Allen King, Director of The National Road/Zane Grey Museum, Norwich, Ohio, which also exhibits early Ohio pottery, was very informative. The Ohio Ceramic Center, Roseville and the Roseville Historical Society provided leads to other sources as well as substantial information. I am indebted to Steve Blankenbeker, Plant Manager and Ceramic Engineer of Resco Products, Oak Hill, Ohio for explaining the properties of various clays used in pottery making and for descriptions of how it was mined.

My appreciation goes as well to my alma mater, The Pennsylvania State University, and Dr. William Blair, Director of the Civil War Era Center, who not only answered my questions, but also led me to the book *Shook Over Hell: Post–Traumatic Stress, Vietnam, and the Civil War* by Eric T. Dean, Jr., published by Harvard University Press, Concord, Massachusetts 1997.

"The Civil War has sometimes been portrayed as almost gentlemanly, an unfortunate war between brothers in which Union and Confederate soldiers routinely chatted with each other and exchanged newspapers or tobacco for coffee. Yet how quickly in victory atrocity is forgotten."

Shook Over Hell, Post-Traumatic Stress, Vietnam, and the Civil War
Eric T. Dean, Jr., Harvard University Press, Cambridge, Massachusetts, 1997

Prologue

The sun blazed white-hot over the hayfield. Cicadas scratched their mating calls from the dry grasses in shrill high-pitched stridulation that set Adam Springer's head to throbbing. He took off his sweat-stained hat and looked ahead at the endless rows of hay waiting to be rolled up with his pitchfork. At war with the unyielding ground over which he walked, "I hate this," he said aloud to no one, for not a soul was in sight. The land was already tired of the plow and the harrow, yet it was land his now ailing father had wrenched from the wilderness and turned productive. By his own hand he had hauled down a forest, plowed and spaded every inch of soil before even one seed could be set into the ground to sprout a crop.

Adam wanted none of it; yet he was as tied to the earth as his father ever was. And in this harsh end to summer 1865, when the streams ebbed to a trickle and the dry ground split from lack of rain, escape was not possible.

Dan, the horse, was even more perturbed and refused to pull the wagon. He was an obstinate beast in the best of times. "Dammit! I'll show you," Adam shouted, lifting the reins and swatting the horse's rump. Dan whinnied, danced in place, and refused to budge. Adam moved around in front of the horse and tugged at the harness. "Move, you dratted animal, move." The horse jerked his head and curled his lips to expose large yellowed teeth. Another yank. Dan remained where he was. Anger rising, Adam once again slapped the reins in a loud thwack across the horse's rump. Ears back, head thrust high, Dan stayed put. In a fit of frustration at being so defied, Adam picked up the pitchfork and hurled it at the horse's flank. Blood spurted from all four holes left by the prongs. Dan reared and took off, the wagon careening crazily behind him.

Head in his hands, Adam sunk to the ground. Tears mixed with sweat rolled down his bronzed face chiseled by sun and wind, snow and cold. His lean body shook with sobs.

One

The town contained many large and beautiful residences, but now present evidence of the sad desolation of war. The homes of wealth and comfort, where the youth sported in princely grandeur, are deserted and shattered under the tramp of contending armies.

If there was a softer side to the nation's terrible conflict for twenty-two year-old Adam Springer, she was it. A moment was all it was, but the sight of her made a memorable impression. Never before had this lanky, Ohio farm boy seen such a serene and lovely lady as the one he encountered on the spiral staircase in the grand plantation house outside Atlanta. Since that day, she existed in his mind only as an illusive image; someone he should forget as quickly as he conjured the moment.

Ordered to burn such places, the common soldiers of the Seventy-Eighth Regiment, Ohio Volunteer Infantry, Grand Army of the Republic could barely comprehend the lifestyles of Georgia's elite. They lived like kings and queens in palaces with great central hallways that soared three stories to allow the summer heat to rise. Pillars marched along grand verandas the width of the houses. Ornate furnishings no farmer-soldier's family had ever seen, let alone own, furnished the interiors. At first the men stood in wide-eyed disbelief at the grandeur, hesitant to spread the kerosene and drop the matches. Until the order *to get it done boys,* they seemed rooted to their positions. Then like a band of hoodlums, whooping and hollering, they showed the enemy they were losers in more than the defeats their armies suffered on the battlefields.

Adam stood in the vacant house, his ax upraised near the grand winding staircase, a jug of kerosene at his feet. At his superior's shout he let the ax smash onto the mahogany railing until the polished wood split into jagged pieces and the silken balustrade sunk toward the stairs. He viciously attacked the uprights, his heart racing with every whack. It wasn't right to mutilate a thing of such beauty, so lovingly crafted by the hand of a skilled and painstaking artisan. Still, Adam did as commanded. The columns of polished wood that held the railing in its graceful sway from top step to bottom began to break and bend. Adam was chopping furiously when he heard the rustle of skirts on the landing above him.

1

The ax ready to descend again, he held it in midair as he focused on the sedate creature standing ladylike and unperturbed by the desolation she witnessed below. Under her dark wavy hair, her face remained steadfastly angelic but determined, nonetheless, not to crack with emotion amid the ruin. Where had she come from? The men had searched the house before setting it ablaze. They were forbidden to burn an occupied house. General Sherman's orders!

Fires lapped at her possessions in the grand rooms on either side of the staircase where Queen Anne tables burnished to a satiny finish gave in to the ravenous flames. The grandfather clock, its brass pendulum moving from side to side, would count the seconds and minutes it took for the sprawling home to become ashes, for that had been the order issued by the general himself: *burn it, burn it all,* he'd said. The heat of smoldering upholstery warmed Adam's back, but he did not move, so transfixed was he by the lovely woman descending the steps of her home for the last time. She clutched the hands of two small girls, their inexpressive faces stiff and white as china dolls despite the desolation they were witnessing. Both girls wore their bonnets above frilly dresses, colorfully embroidered with intricate flowers in pink, yellow, and lavender, and the smallest held a drooping rag doll. The woman's dress of shimmering gray silk was chosen, he supposed, to show her allegiance to the gray uniforms of the Army of the Confederacy. The fine silk moiré swayed slightly as she set each leather-clad foot on the treads that lead to the grand entrance. As she held Adam's attention, his heart fell into her rapturous embrace, and he ceased desecrating the staircase.

"Throw that kerosene and be quick about it," the shouted voice of a sergeant behind him commanded. Adam picked up the jug and dribbled some on the railing. He did not light and throw the match, but waited while the woman passed him on the staircase. Two soldiers stood guard at the front entrance. She glided toward the open door, remaining unhurried and graceful amidst the confusion of Yankees renting her damask drapes, smashing her belongings, and setting fire to ripped upholstery. As though she possessed some supernatural power that ordered them to do so, the respectfully silent men moved aside to let her pass.

Adam lit a match and threw it onto the splintered wood, lit another and another, then moved away quickly lest his clothing catch fire. He walked closer to the doorway and watched her descend the steps of the portico.

A weary appearing mammy dropped from the seat of a broken down, dirt-spattered wagon, boxes and bedding piled into the back. She helped the woman and her children climb onto the wagon seat. Tears streaming down her face, she crowded in beside them and took the reins.

"You're free now. You don't have to go with her," someone yelled and a few other soldiers picked up the chant. "Let the darkies go, Mam, they don't belong to you no more."

"Where you all think I gonna' go?" The thin black woman, who looked as though she had not eaten in weeks, hurled her answer toward the soldiers.

With their fields burned, storehouses looted, there was little food left for anyone. Had she given her share to her mistress and her children who did not appear deprived? Adam wondered.

"Stop, give us your horse," a soldier shouted. "Let the white folks walk."

"That old nag ain't worth takin'. Leave em go," an officer yelled. "Besides we already took what good horses was left." He turned toward the Negroes gathered to watch the departing women and children. Arms and hands used to field work, planting gardens, tending animals, and washing clothes hung loosely as if they had no place to go. The men and women shuffled about, the children clung to their mothers. Loss of their masters left them aimless, unable to decide what to do next.

"You can all go now. And tell that old black lady to get shut of that wagon and leave with you."

A woman holding a baby, a passel of black children clinging to her skirts, yelled back. "Old Pearlie ain't about to leave Miss Annabelle. She done been wid her since the day she was borned, and Miss Annabelle cain't do nothin' wifout her. She a lady."

Adam wanted to cry. Bad as the shacks they lived in and hard as the daily drudgery in which they found themselves, what would these people do without their masters? Some fifty of them—men, women carrying babies, women without, and children—stood around in their rags, seemingly helpless when faced with making their own decisions. And the lady of the plantation, where would she go? Everything for miles around, every house, shed, and barn was burning or would be. Was she too destined to sleep outside?

Pearlie lifted the reins and swatted the horse's rump. The wagon rumbled off down the tree-shrouded lane. Adam stood riveted, his eyes following the grand lady sitting straight and tall until she disappeared as the wagon rounded the bend. Although he knew he should leave the burning house, Adam stood in the doorway, turning slightly to see the staircase give in to the fire, its steps consumed by flames, the mahogany railing no longer visible.

He had fallen in love, but the feeling was not joyous, only an ache remained to remind him of that beautifully composed woman—a woman with the strength of steel. The likes of him could never command the love of such a gracious, beautiful lady whose inner strength belied her outward appearance of a pampered, indulged wife.

Fighting to lose the memory in Uncle Jake's and Aunt Mary Jane's house, he turned on his side in his grandfather's bed, his head nestled into the down pillow, the first bed he'd slept in since his furlough after Vicksburg. One thing is certain he thought before drifting off, if I pick a woman, she will not be a farm girl; she will be a lady. Oh, perhaps not as grand as the lady of the plantation, but a mannered woman nevertheless. He vowed not to be enticed by one of these lonely farm girls, who lay waiting as eager to pounce after her prey as a lioness in the jungle.

The next morning his aunt prepared a sumptuous breakfast of pancakes, sausages, eggs, and bacon. Adam ate it all as though he might never again see another meal. Soldiers tended to eat like that when food was not guaranteed to arrive anytime soon. They sometimes marched for days with only hardtack and water to sustain them.

"You look like you need some fattening up," Aunt Mary Jane patted his thin shoulder while she poured coffee from the blue enameled pot that Adam remembered from his boyhood.

"I suppose. There were times when we had to make five days of rations do for seventeen, but we ate pretty good on the march to the sea." He poked a slice of sausage into his mouth. "Because by marching across the southland, we could steal our vittles."

"Oh, my." Mary Jane sighed.

When he finished eating, Uncle Jake, who had been fingering a paper while he waited, thrust it toward him. Adam supposed he wanted to hear more war stories, so he was surprised when his uncle changed the subject.

"I've been planning to do this since you first went away," his uncle began.

Adam glanced at the paper. It was a deed, handwritten in spidery black ink. "What's this, and what's it got to do with me?"

"I'm conveying that eighty acres I bought some years ago near Pineville to you. Probably you remember the land where I used to pasture cattle before taking them to the slaughterhouse. The property only has a cattle shed on it, but I thought you needed something to come home to that's yours, especially after all you've been through. Now it's not great cropland, too much clay, but enough of it is all right for pasture. There is a stream with good water, and some timber is left. If you ever need money, you can sell off the wood; a portion is old growth. And if Pineville grows, it might be good land for turning into plats. Or you could simply live there yourself when you acquire a wife, which I suppose you will be doing one of these days." Uncle Jake grinned at his nephew. "I predict it won't be long. A fine looking man like you, Adam, will be fair game for the girls around here. A few of them are fairly panting for husbands, what with the soldiers gone for nigh onto four years."

"I don't know about that." Adam shrugged. "But Uncle Jake, I'm thunderstruck. I'm coming home from nearly four years at hard labor with only a few coins in my pocket and a couple of bills issued by the federal government, so only God knows what they're worth. That's all I have in the world. And not even a decent suit of drawers to cover my privates."

"Adam. Don't talk disrespectful." Prissy Aunt Mary Jane had not changed. She turned away from the stove and sat down at the table. "There's one thing I want to say before you get all fired up about moving to your own place." Her restless fingers pounded on the table in a gesture requiring Adam's complete attention. "Lizzie is going to need some help. Since your Pa came down with the apoplexy, she's had it all on her narrow shoulders. There was nary a young man left around here to help out even if she could afford to pay, which she couldn't, so she's been doing all that field work herself. Jake here helped with the planting this spring, but he's not young either and had this here place to take care of. Thank goodness for old Eligah, the hired man. Without him, I don't know where we'd be."

"How bad is Pa? Ma wrote that he is ailing, but that's all I know."

"Your Pa's pretty lame, laid up a lot of the time, and he walks with a cane. Problem is he has no use of his left arm and very little action in that leg. Hit him all of a sudden."

"No doubt about it," Uncle Jake added his face unsmiling, "your Ma has had a terrible burden placed on her and needs your help. Barn needs boarding up, and that old corncrib was near blown over in the last big wind."

"Sad," Mary Jane said, "for such a lovely woman as your Ma was to end her days like this, when she should be a settin' in a rocker. Why I recall before you were born she was something to see. She had two Sunday meeting dresses when everyone else around here had but one. And just before you were coming on, she fairly blossomed; her face glowed like sunshine. Some folks thought she put on airs the way she dressed and furnished that house."

"Furnished the house? When did she do that?" Adam asked. "It always seemed like pretty old stuff to me."

"Don't forget she used to be the piano teacher around here. Must have had all of six or eight pupils, and she sold pianos too. People said it was no fit business for a woman, but Lizzie said she didn't care and just went on pocketing the money. Folks grumbled about that too. What she earned should have been given right away to her husband they said. She finally spent it on furnishing the house from top to bottom, so that tended to quiet them. Why she even went to the cabinetmaker in Four Corners and had him make those three spool-turned walnut beds, when everyone else wanted store bought shipped out of Zanesville. She's so proud of those beds. You slept in the child-sized one when you were a little boy."

"I remember, almost until my legs grew too long and began to stick out between the spindles."

"She had lots of nice frocks then too; now she wears worn and faded housedresses, but like the German women before us, she insists they only come to mid-calf. She says a woman can't be much use behind a horse and plow or drilling corn with her skirt raking the ground. The English types, who attend the Methodist Church and never go into the fields, criticize her for that too. They say it's unseemly for a woman to let her legs show."

"Well if things are as bad as you say, I guess we'd best get going Uncle."

Adam felt a sudden depletion of energy. Gloom fell over him like fog. It obliterated every image of a pleasant future he might otherwise have found waiting for him, a future devoid of plowing and planting and farm animals with their incessant demand for attention day in and day out, no matter the weather. Adam had no illusions about what awaited him, but then what else could he do? He got up from the table, thanked his uncle again and pocketed the deed. Then kissing his aunt aside her cheek, he threw the haversack over his shoulder, picked up his knapsack and followed his uncle to the buggy.

Two

White flags appeared along the entire Confederate line, and immediately after, the rebel army marched outside their entrenchments with their colors flying and formed line. They stacked arms, laid their colors on the stack, about-faced, and marched back within their entrenchments as prisoners of war. There were ten thousand Union casualties in that fight . . .

Uncle Jacob and Aunt Mary Jane did not exaggerate. When Adam waved his uncle off and turned to walk into the kitchen from the side porch, he felt a terrible bleakness of spirit. His mother, whom he remembered as sweet-faced and amply endowed in breast and hip, seemed as worn as the broken down shoes he wore. Now she was all one size—wiry and thin. When he'd been home after the terrible siege at Vicksburg in July 1863, he hadn't noticed much change in either Pa or Ma. That was sometime before Pa had taken sick.

They had asked him about that Mississippi battle, and seemed eager to know all about it, for they realized it had been a most decisive conflict for the Union. He remembered telling them about its end after days of Yankee bombardment until the rebels became desperate and on July 3rd hoisted a flag of truce. He had recounted how two blindfolded Confederate officers came into camp bearing dispatches from their General Pemberton to General Grant. "Both mannerly young men," he had said remembering their blond good looks, and "once their eyes were unbandaged, they talked freely with the Union officers." Adam told how he heard one of them say "iron enough thrown into Vicksburg to stock a foundry and build monuments for all the fallen citizens and soldiers." His mother, sad faced almost to the point of tears, had remarked "was there no other way? All this killing is shameful."

Now there were no questions about Atlanta or Savannah. His parents seemed drained, two beleaguered spirits broken by life: his father incapacitated to the point of uselessness; his mother worked nearly to death. How was it that house, farm, father, and mother had deteriorated so much in only two years?

After waving his uncle off, Adam, overcome by melancholy, paused on the side porch. From now on everyday sameness would take the place of the excitement and joshing of a fraternity of men facing one of life's worst struggles together. They

7

had a shared purpose, a goal, even if it was killing. For nearly four years, those men had been his family. And when one died or was killed, they came together like brothers. Before opening the screen door to the kitchen, Adam paused a moment to think about his lost friends: Hiram Bush and Thomas Harter, killed at Atlanta; George Coulson died of his wounds at Marietta, Georgia; and James Bailey took sick at Vicksburg and died soon after. He thought of their families. How many like them would never unite with their returning soldiers? How much grief must be spreading across the land while I stand here secure and safe? He had no answers.

In the kitchen, his mother, with a great deal of clatter, was putting away the coffee and remainder of the cakes she'd offered upon their arrival. "Adam," she said, before he could sit down, "I need some help propping up that corncrib. I tried to do it myself yesterday, but I need two more hands. I thought if we did it this afternoon, you could be about repairing the floorboards, making a new door, and have it finished by the time we harvest the corn. There is a bit left from last year, and because the crib is in danger of falling down, I have stacked the corn outside."

He didn't answer, but neither did she notice. His father sat in the rocker by the kitchen fireside, and even in this July weather, wore a knitted shawl over his shoulders. Adam had trouble understanding him, so Ma translated.

He was mumbling something now.

"Oh," his mother glanced quickly in Adam's direction as though noticing him for the first time. "He'll have plenty of time to rest after we get that crib fixed. I've already got the posts. They just need to be tapered from eight inches to about four at the ends to replace the rotted ones. Adam can sit to do that. Then I'll help him get them up."

Adam felt disgust and disappointment. She had not even inquired as to his wellbeing, nor did she ask about his foot. He got up from the table, grabbed his haversack, and with the foot still hobbling him, hastened out of the kitchen. Blood dampened his sock requiring him to walk on his heel so as not to leave red splotches on the rugs. Even as he emphasized his limp, Lizzie paid no mind. Passing through the family parlor, he could tell by the kitchen sounds she was getting out the dishpan to do up the cups, saucers, and plates on which she'd served sweets and tea to her brother. Adam hobbled up the hall steps and into the room where he'd slept as a boy and dropped onto his bed; he felt as tired as his father looked and was soon fast asleep.

"Are you sick or something?" His mother stood in the doorway.

"What time is it?"

"It's dinnertime. You've been sleeping nearly two hours. Didn't you sleep last night?"

"I did, but I have a lot of catching up to do." Adam rose from the bed. "Is there water in the pitcher?"

"I'll get you some." Before he could offer to fetch it himself, she grabbed the pitcher from where it sat on the washstand and went out the door and down the stairs so quickly that Adam was left standing alone. The bedroom window overlooking the cistern was open, but it did little to assuage the heat of the July morning. Flopping onto the bed again, Adam sat up only when he heard his mother's footsteps pounding on the stair treads.

In the kitchen, he helped his father to the table. The old man was able to feed himself with his good right hand, though some of the food dribbled down his chin. While she reached across with her own napkin and wiped Pa's face, Ma never stopped talking. "You're lucky," she said to Adam, "not to have come home with any war scars."

"I'm lucky to be home at all." Adam had lost his appetite. The food looked gray. Had she rustled up a mess of leftovers for her returning soldier son? Or maybe it was the monstrous breakfast he had consumed after going so long on hardtack and embalmed beef.

"Why aren't you eating?" Lizzie looked askance at the plateful of food she had so generously apportioned to him.

"I think I ate too much breakfast. Auntie made more than I needed after going so long on army rations." He had a sudden urge to be by himself. "Ma, do you mind if I go back to bed? I'm really so tired. Just give me a little time. Besides, I can't even think of working on that corncrib until I get me some shoes and my foot heals up a bit."

"That will mean a trip to town. Anyway, what's wrong with your foot?'

"Cut it on the roadway," he said flatly. "I'll go to town in a few days. I have a few dollars to buy some work clothes, and I'd be obliged if you'd make me a few drawers and shirts. If you don't have the goods, I'll buy some. Then I'll go by and see Emma."

"Well, if that's the way it is, I guess that's the way it is. Never mind about the corncrib. If we get another big wind, we'll just let it blow down." She leaned her head closer to her husband. "What did you say, Pa?'

9

He mumbled something to which she replied, "How can you use a drawing knife with only one hand working?"

"I can do it," he said angrily, and Adam understood they were talking about the corncrib.

Three days later Adam, having slept himself out, decided it was time to go to Four Corners, a town four miles distant. His mother entreated him to take along a peck basket of peaches. "Mr. Stansbury is very agreeable to taking produce in exchange for goods, and seeing as how you're a veteran of the war, his prices might not be so dear."

Adam had another reason for going to town that day, a reason wrapped tightly in his kerchief in the bottom of his knapsack. Shortly after arriving home he had removed the wrapping from the small figurine. Not having seen her since he took the statue from the rebel widow woman. He remembered her pointing to a shroud-wrapped portrait over the mantle and pleading that the figurine was a fine French porcelain given to her by her deceased husband. She tearfully begged Adam not to take it. He'd shoved her aside with his rifle butt and ripped the shroud from the portrait to expose the image of a distinguished man of about thirty-five in a gray uniform. Raising his knife, Adam slashed the portrait from head to chest, then grabbed the figurine and headed toward the door. It would be a grand reminder of *his lady on the stairway*. The woman screamed, *may God curse you for this*, and sank to the floor. Adam cared little. She, after all, was the enemy every bit as much as her husband. The name *Limoges/France* was inscribed on the bottom. He daren't give it to Ma: she would know straight off he had stolen it. Why, he wondered, did the figurine remind him of the lady on the stairway? She was much younger and certainly not attired in a mournful gray dress. This tiny lady was wearing a china blue skirt that furled in a bewitching swirl about her legs. A low-cut bodice was tight around her waist. She was painted prettily with dark hair piled above a white, rouged face and red lips. Adam felt foolish now and hated himself for having stolen it. How had he been so heartless? Did he feel nothing for that poor woman, whose husband had met death on some bloody battlefield? Adam wanted to be rid of his stolen goods. Yet it was too valuable to toss away in the backhouse. He decided to give it to Emma. Not knowing its history, his sister would not be burdened by conscience; she would be grateful to Adam for bringing her such a lovely gift.

Adam bought new boots and a pair of Kentucky jeans to replace his government-issue trousers. Ma promised a shirt, said she had enough goods for that and two pairs of drawers. She was already at work knitting him a pair of stockings, but Adam bought a cotton pair anyway. He wore his new jeans, boots, and stockings out of the store, topping them off with his army shirt and suit jacket. He left the general store and walked along Main Street past the hotel, Dr. Kennedy's office, Swingle's piano and organ store, and the apothecary before coming to a group of frame houses, all painted white with the exception of two, turned aged gray. Old Mr. Tucker must have died: his house looked empty. The other housed a family named Cochran, never known to be particular about how they kept the place. A bevy of ragged children spilled out the front door and down the rickety porch steps. They stopped and stared at him like a litter of puppies waiting for a handout. "A stranger," he heard the tallest one say. "Don't never remember seein' him around these parts afore." Adam didn't bother to correct the child. He'd lived within four miles of this place from the time he was born August 25, 1841. Over the years he had been in town often.

He soon came to a well-kept white clapboard house with a side porch, climbed the steps, and slammed the knocker with a loud clap. Emma, as she always did, greeted him warmly. "Look at my little brother," she said standing back for a better view. "Why you've grown two inches. The army must have fed you well."

Adam let the remark pass. He was learning that the homefolk had neither sympathy nor understanding about what the soldiers had gone through. That he had survived seemed in no way remarkable. Only Uncle Jake was curious.

"Tell me, Adam, are the darkies all loose now?"

"Hordes of them appear aimless with no idea where to go or how to feed themselves. After being taken care of by the southern land barons, I'll agree not too well; they seem unable to care for themselves. You would not believe the shacks they live in: dirt floors, no windows, just bare bones, yet the people they served lived like kings and queens, while those poor darkies were treated like animals, lived like them too."

They settled in for tea. Emma announced that the children were in school except for Lucinda. "You may remember Mrs. Kimball. She was childless, and now old age has fallen rather hard upon her. Lucinda goes over every afternoon to see to her. But tell me, my dear Adam, what has become of those poor Negro folks? I have a special reason for asking."

"I don't really know. But from what I've heard they relish their freedom, although most don't have the skills to take care of themselves."

"I'm sure if our Mr. Lincoln had lived he would have found ways to help them, but now that he is gone from us, I can't imagine how they find places to live with no money. Surely President Lincoln would have seen to it that each family had forty acres and a mule."

"He would have sent them to some island, or to that African country, where freed slaves settled back in the fifties. Liberia I think it's called. Despite all we supposedly fought for, I don't think our President cared very much for black folks. Have you ever seen one?"

"A Negro? Oh my yes. Now I can tell. But it was a secret for a very long time. We were a station on the Underground Railroad, right here in little Four Corners. Well, my Reuben helped out at any rate, but I did my share too."

"How's that?" He had never seen a Negro in Morgan County.

"He hid runaways at the blacksmith shop in an old cellar. A pile of iron bars had to be moved whenever anyone went in or out the entrance. It was just a dug hole in the ground with a rickety ladder going down. Place had once been a root cellar for an old cabin on the property before Reuben took it over and built his blacksmith shop. There was just a pipe to let in air, but it was a dim, damp place. We tried to keep the darkies just one night at a time, only sometimes if the Virginia slave catchers were known to be about they had to stay longer. I took care of feeding them, and one day a young girl came with another woman and two men. She was very sick, and it turned out pregnant, so I took her in and hid her in the loft, having no idea at the time she would miscarry that child. She did the next day. It was a light skinned baby, must have had a white father. Reuben took the remains wrapped in a blanket and buried the child behind the blacksmith shop. Then lest he bring attention to the grave, he planted an oak tree on the spot. You should see how beautiful and tall that tree has grown. I kept the mother here for a week while she recovered and let her come to the second floor during the day when the children were in school. Having no way to while the time, I taught her to write her name and cipher from one to five. She took to it and worked so hard that I could have cried watching her, so I got out Lucinda's primer and taught to her to read a bit of it."

"When did all this secret activity take place?"

"I can't remember the exact dates, but the Underground Railroad began about the time you were born. I was still living at home then. It was active right up until the war began—all of twenty years. No one knows how many poor souls we helped to freedom; it was all so secretive. People around here were ingenious when it came to helping the runaways."

"Like, for instance."

"Well, for one thing, there was a man who found two Negroes being closely pursued by the chattel hunters. He started out with them on foot for the National Road traveling at night. The hunters were gaining on them and stopped at Mr. Wolpert's place to inquire if he had seen the Negroes pass. He decoyed the men and kept them engaged for a time to give the runaways a chance to escape. Another time the Negroes were hidden in the Methodist Church, and since it was bitter cold, the man guiding them lit the fire in the stove. But fearing the light in the windows would give them away, he daubed the cracks around the stove door with mud and kept the refugees hidden in the church until the next night when they were safely taken away."

"I had no idea all this was going on. Nobody ever spoke of it."

"It was pretty secretive, because you never knew who might give the project away. Those slave catchers would offer as much as five hundred dollars and sometimes more to get the runaways back."

"Did Ma and Pa know?" Adam could not imagine the resourcefulness of people he had come to think of as rather isolated regarding outsiders.

"I never told. You see they were from Virginia, a slave state, and though they came from The German Settlement and not the Tidewater where the slave owners were more apt to be, we still weren't sure of their allegiance. Of course, no Germans we knew believed in slavery. And besides from Ma's stories about her grandfather, we took for granted he had no prejudice."

"What stories? I don't recall her mentioning a grandfather?"

"When he first came to America from Germany—that was back in 1750, I believe, his name was Heinrich—he had a fight with the ship captain and escaped while the vessel was being repaired in New London, Connecticut. He couldn't speak much English and had no money, since his chest was still on the ship. At first an Englishman, who needed help on his farm, gave him food and a place to sleep, but they had some kind of falling out, and our great grandpa was thrown off the place. An educated, freed, black man named Antoine took him in, and Ma said forever after her Grampa Heinrich would brook no bad talk about Negroes. Antoine taught him to read and write English, and they corresponded for all the years of their lives. Still, we took no chances by spreading more word than was necessary about the Underground Railroad. There was never any reason for Ma

13

and Pa to know; they were too far away from the stations to be involved anyway. From here the trail led to Putnam, thence to Zanesville and finally out the National Road,* but it could be mighty tough getting there."

"I can't believe what I'm hearing. Then where did they go?"

"Most of them were trying to get to Canada."

Adam considered that he was not the only one to court danger in the slaughter that had so recently engulfed the land. Sitting there in his sister's small parlor, he felt more kinship with her knowing how strongly she and Reuben felt about the slave matter.

Emma brought a second pot of tea and another tray of pastries, while continuing to prattle on about the Underground Railroad, but she seemed to have little interest in his experiences. Perhaps she felt it to be a difficult subject, since several boys from Four Corners had returned pretty cut up.

When it was time to leave, only then did Adam proffer the figurine.

At the sight of the china lady, a grand smile came over Emma's face. "Oh, Adam, how kind of you to think of me with such a petite and lovely lady. I'll treasure her always." Emma put the statue on the mantle, then stood back to admire her. "Here I can see my little lady every time I enter the room.

"Thank you, thank you so much." She stood on tiptoes and kissed him on the cheek. "And I'll always think kindly on my little brother." She laughed, "but I guess I can't call you *little* anymore. You're taller than Pa."

Emma was so excited about the gift that Adam felt puffed up with pleasure at having brought it to her. His eyes rested on the tiny figure. I can always be reminded of that beautiful woman on the stairway when I come into this room, he thought, if I can force myself to forget the rest.

*Originally named the National Road, the name was changed in 1835 when the states through which it passed took responsibility for maintaining the first federally financed highway in the United States and turned it into a toll road.

Three

One morning the rebels asked for a cessation of hostilities for two and a half hours. It was granted; our men went up to the fortifications where the rebels stood and mutual conversations took place. Some came over and drank coffee with our men.

Where once he could not get enough sleep, Adam now had trouble making it through the night, not drifting off so much, but half consciousness and nightmares were becoming unbearable. In terribly grotesque ways, he was living the war all over again. Mostly he kept his harrowing dreams to himself until one night when he relived an incident during the siege of Vicksburg. He saw the deep hollows and fragrant groves filled with Yankees within eyesight of the rebels. Sometime during the cessation of fighting, the enemy was near enough to converse. At these times they agreed to be civil and, throwing aside their weapons, would meet between the lines for social chat.

For several nights Adam enjoyed the company of one gray-clad soldier, who, in a gesture of friendship, offered him a Confederate button. Pleased at the boy's generosity, Adam returned the favor and handed him a Yankee button. "Name's Joey." The boy, who could not have been more than eighteen, extended his hand and Adam reciprocated. With a thatch of blond hair falling from beneath his cap, Joey possessed the air of a garrulous youth playing soldier. He laughed and chided Adam for the condition of his uniform. "Looks like you fought a war," he said grinning. But their friendship was short lived, for when the Seventy-Eighth's own General Leggett ordered that a ditch ten feet wide and deep enough to shelter a horseman be dug toward the walls of Fort Hill, where many of the rebels were located, Adam was unprepared for what came next. The Seventy-Eighth and other regiments remained in their rifle pits forty-four days until the Forty-Fifth Illinois Regiment entered the gap and a fight took place at very close quarters. The swarm of blue and gray wrestled so closely they could grasp each other's rifles even pull each other's hair. Finally, both sides fell back and friendly encounters began again until General Leggett ordered that a ton of powder be placed under the fort wall and lit. The explosion buried rebels by the score, and many were thrown high into

15

the air. It never happened that Adam saw his reb friend, Joey, blown up, but his dream implied otherwise.

The young man's freckled face stared down at Adam from the sky while his spread-eagled body dropped toward him like a giant hawk intent on its prey. The boy's bloodied face grew larger and more grotesque the closer it came to Adam. He screamed and tried to get away.

His mother found him in the upstairs hallway. "Wake up, you're dreaming. Wake up now." She turned him over and peered into his eyes. At first, he thought it was Joey's face staring down at him. But then slowly penetrating his view was Lizzie's long narrow face crisscrossed with wrinkles. She helped him up; Adam realized that another deadly nightmare had claimed his sleep.

"I do believe you have put off going to church too long, son." Her face, which usually wore a frown, turned gentle like he remembered her when he was a child. She was pretty then. What had happened? Was it age? At seventy-one she was still working like a young, farmwoman. Her days were so taken up with washing clothes on a washboard, ironing, milking, wringing the necks of chickens to throw into a pot for dinner, and the extra work a farm required that she rarely played her beloved piano. Before he realized the extent of her labors, he had asked her why. Lizzie simply replied sadly, "no time."

The dreams rattled his mind and took away restful sleep, so rather than argue with her, he put on his only suit and went with her to Jerusalem Church to worship with the Lutherans the following Sunday. He soon realized she might have had another motive when he noticed a number of young girls sizing him up. A few he recognized, although some had grown and rounded; others had turned scrawny, anxiety gripping their long faces because no man had yet spoken for them. "Hello, Adam," they said, all smiles. And he knew what they had on their minds and vowed to escape their clutches, even as his mother practically committed him to attending the next church social.

"Why, of course he will go, won't you Adam?" Lizzie left him little room to escape. The giggling girls said they would be sure to make a place for him at the picnic table.

Two weeks later he appeared at the gathering for young people held in the grove beside the Jerusalem Church. Adam greeted several young men he had served with in the Seventy-Eighth. Sam Haugh seemed to have already taken to Cynthia Turner, and the couple remained together laughing and nudging each other playfully the entire evening. Dancing was forbidden but singing was allowed. Adam could barely remember the words, but moved his lips along anyway and joined in heartily when the selection turned to *When Johnny Comes Marching Home Again.* Some of the couples paired up in buggies for the ride home. Adam ducked out early and took his trap alone over the dirt road that connected the Springer farm to the church property. He had not lacked female companionship that night, but to get involved with one of these girls meant certain matrimony, a baby at nine months, another a year later, another and another until the house bustled with sniveling toddlers. Adam congratulated himself on escaping the clutches of the females and vowed not to attend another social.

Tired of hearing his mother's persistent hints about "the corn coming on quickly and the rain that might come before we get it stored," Adam finally gave in and tackled repairs to the corncrib. He concluded that Lizzie would have made a fine general in the army, but he dared not say so. "Set that post in this hole; move that hinge up a bit." And so it went until the tipsy old crib was righted again. Together they set the broomcorn aside for shelling and grinding into feed. Adam carried the cobs off to the woodshed for kindling. The rest of it went into the newly repaired crib.

He soon fell into the rhythm of the farm though not as quickly as his mother would have liked. With the help of a neighboring farmer and his harvester, they brought in the wheat. He cut hay, repaired the ripped screens on the outer doors, plucked peaches from the trees for preserving. And when the pole and lima beans came on so fast they threatened to overwhelm his mother's efforts to can them, he helped her pick them. She washed the vegetables, blanched them, and put them jars before setting them on the stove in the canner to boil. All this activity turned the kitchen steamy as a jungle in summer. When he found Lizzie nearly passed out from the heat, her face red and blotchy, wisps of hair sticking to her forehead, Adam realized he needed to give a hand with the boiling pots.

The work was unrelenting, but both knew they needed the stores to get them through the winter, so they kept on. They dried corn he'd harvested. She cut off the kernels, mixed and boiled them with sugar, course salt, and sweet cream. Spread on shallow trays for baking slowly until the corn turned crispy, the kernels were then poured into paper bags and taken to hang in the loft above the kitchen, not to appear again until winter.

17

Fall approached with a snap to the air that should make a man frisky, but Adam's loneliness and depression only escalated. He longed for interchange with someone other than his family, a companion to confide in, to love. *I should be looking for a wife* he told himself when these moments made him feel hermitlike; but in truth, Adam had not seen a girl who tempted him. At these times he almost wished he had not set his sights so high. *That lovely woman on the staircase in Atlanta will haunt me forever. Maybe I'm odd. None of these farm girls disturb me in the least.* And like a man without a soul, he went on through endless days, like a puppet with his mother pulling the strings. Besides the heavy fieldwork, he plunged into the demands of fall: dug potatoes and turnips, pulled up carrots, and took in the squash for setting in the root cellar. The farm work was unrelenting. His back ached, his hands wore calluses. How, he wondered, had they managed in his absence?

Since his father had suffered the apoplexy, Lizzie spent a good hour each day vigorously massaging the useless left leg and arm with liniments. At least once every week she prepared a concoction of sweet oil, ammonia, and chloroform to rub into his affected parts. The resulting tang hung over the household in a peppery mist that made for labored breathing. At other times, she prepared a bath of boiled valerian root, strained, and poured into the galvanized tub filled with warm water. Even as Pa protested that more than one bath a week will "surely send me to the grave," they lowered him into the tub several times a week.

Finally, the hard work of fall subsided. The days shortened. Cold air blew about the hilly land, and a certain quiet ensued as the weather precluded much visiting back and forth among their few neighbors: Bartholomew and Rachel, his mother's oldest friends in the county, the Longacres and Reisingers each living a half mile or more away. Only the Lutheran Church lay on the westerly side behind the farm. Pastors had a tendency to come and go or not arrive at all, so services on Sunday mornings were not always certain. Few of the itinerant pastors were inclined to visit their parishioners unless invited for a hearty meal, so because they changed so often, Lizzie had long since given up inviting them for Sunday dinner.

Not only did Adam and his mother put away the stores for winter, but he tossed hay into the barn loft and filled the woodlot. He took all the horses to his brother-in-law, Reuben, for shoeing; butchered a calf and a hog. His mother took the hog fat to boil up with lye and ash for soap. Hams and bacon were salted down and cured over smoldering fires for weeks in the smokehouse. Looking over all they had accomplished, Adam felt a sense of pride. He hoped Lizzie did too, but she never said. She was so used to the repetitious work, engendered by spring melding into summer, summer into fall, and fall to winter that she simply took it all for granted. Then one day tiny flakes came to light on the windowpanes, and they knew that winter had arrived. Night descended early, and with the temperatures dropping to zero or below ice flowers grew on the windows. These icy needles made their way across the glass becoming intricate works of art that featured feathers, ferns, starbursts and pinwheels or anything else that excited the imagination.

With fewer sunny days, Adam became despondent again. Work was its own remedy, but now he was tired and listless.

"Church," his mother suggested, might lift his spirits. "There is nothing like a good sermon to stir the soul and wipe away despair. And loneliness," she added, with a wary glance at her son who seemed not to hear.

For a time Adam begged off. He'd gone only twice since his return and had come to question how a benign God could allow such horrible events as those on the battlefields to occur to men so young. Wiping out the southern lifestyle now seemed a terrible evil wrought upon civilians, who might have been brought around peacefully. Perhaps they could have been convinced of the toll slavery took on human beings or encouraged to recognize that secession would only tear the country apart. But men trained in military matters at West Point or toughened by the War of 1812 and the Mexican Wars could see it no other way. They reasoned that gunshot, cannon ball, and fire were the only means by which the Union could be kept together. These tribulations now weighed heavily on Adam.

He had enlisted on Christmas Day 1861; ninety-four boys from Morgan County headed to Camp Gilbert. They were a jovial bunch, sons of religious parents, of good families, and all proud to be putting down treason and rebellion. Among them were schoolteachers, mechanics, farmers, merchants, and clerks. "Just ordinary folk," someone said. None, including Adam, had the slightest idea what they were in for. The boys treated the whole affair as a cheerful trip away from home. Few had traveled more than twenty-five miles from where they were born, so the prospect of train and river travel was exciting. No one thought much about the killing fields.

Invariably thoughts about the war led Adam to wonder what had become of that lovely lady and her two children on the stairway. Where had they gone? Every dwelling in and around Atlanta had been burned; he could not imagine her clad in her gown of rustling silk, probably turned a tattered gray, sleeping in the elements. He'd read that the southerners were having an awful time of it. Ragged as the slaves they had once lorded over, even the gentry were enduring their own deprivations. Was *his lady* reduced to begging for food for her children? Did she find herself widowed when the rebels marched home again? At his lowest, Adam thought about going to find her; then good sense took over, and he banished the thought as quickly as it had come.

He took up reading, starting with the publication in 1865 of an account of the Seventy-Eighth Regiment in the war. He had sent away for the book when notice of its publication in Zanesville arrived in the post. The book was a fine chronicle of every battle, but having been there and seen it all first hand, Adam thought some of it was prettied up. The author had a tendency to treat each company as the finest, the most glorious, the bravest of all the companies from all the states that participated. Little was made of cowardice and other unseemly actions that Adam had experienced first hand.

With a wary eye on his book, Lizzie said, "that's not fit reading for a boy still suffering nightmares from the terrible events down there in the south."

He ignored her and read it anyway. Adam supposed he would always be a *boy* in her eyes and always at an age when she could tell him what to do, even what to read. Never mind that he was now twenty-five.

One afternoon she hitched the horse to the buggy on the pretense of delivering some watermelon pickles to her brother and sister. "I've decided to take the afternoon off and visit Jacob and Mary Jane," she told Adam. "You might see to massaging your father's leg and arm while I'm gone."

The *you might see* he recognized as an order and did as he was told.

She returned some four hours later with a half dozen books in her arms.

"What are those?" Adam asked.

"Books of your grandfather's."

"Gramp read books?"

"Of course, and so did I before the farm work took over every spare minute a body has in this life." She handed him several volumes. "Here you can start with these. I'll put the rest on the piano." She handed him *Two Years before the Mast*, *The Scarlet Letter* and *A Tale of Two Cities*.

He got up from the porch swing and followed her into the house. "Ma, I'm curious. How is it that Grampa had all these books? Most farmers I know around here only read the Bible or maybe *Pilgrim's Progress*."

"Bosh! No one reads *Pilgrim's Progress* anymore. That was old when I was young." She stared at him. "Oh, I keep forgetting you never knew your grandfather.

You came along after he had gone to his heavenly maker." She sat down on the piano stool and sniffled. Her eyes glistened. "He was the most wonderful man, kind and gentle, and he did so much for me. I wonder what he would think seeing me now all broken down."

"Were you his favorite?"

"Well, I was the first, and he was more generous with me than the others. By the time I was ready for book learning, he had become a tyrant about education. When the other farmers were happy enough to have their children learn only German, he insisted we also be taught English."

"But we sometimes speak German here."

"Yes, that's true. We always did off and on, and since your father's taken ill, he seems to have reverted to the old ways. That's part of the reason you have trouble understanding him; he mixes up the two languages. We taught you some German when your were little. Do you remember any of it?"

"A bit. I can generally understand the language, some of the Pennsylvania regiments were made up entirely of German speakers, but why waste time with that now when we're all Americans?"

"I suppose you're right. I tried early on to get rid of that guttural accent. Even though we Germans were born here, some of the English, the old timers at any rate, still think of us as foreigners when we use another language. We learned early on it's best not to go around talking in two languages even if English is one of them."

Four

There was an interim in the work during that fall of 1866 when the leaves on the oaks and maples turned brilliant and hung for dear life to the limbs until they finally gave up and fluttered like a flock of brown birds to the ground. Most of the heavy harvesting was done, and only the last of the butchering remained. Adam was reading in the sitting room; his mother was baking bread; and his father was napping when there was a knock on the front door.

"Now who could that be?" Annoyed at being interrupted in his reading, Adam got up from the rocker and headed toward the hallway. "No one ever comes in this way," he muttered aloud.

Visitors usually drove their buggies into the side yard between the two cedar trees and trooped across the side porch to the kitchen, where they would be invited to sit at the table. Other than members of Lizzie's quilting group, it was rare to entertain in the parlor or welcome anyone to the front hall.

"Yes," Adam said, opening the door while containing his annoyance at being interrupted.

"Good afternoon, sir. I'm Jeremiah Schaffer representing the American Household Hardware and Novelty Company. Here are my credentials." Before Adam could say *not interested*, the young man went on at a rapid pace. "In addition to chamber sets, clocks, kerosene and lard oil lamps, my very latest product is a lamp specially for reading. You look like an educated man. I see you are holding a book. May I show you this lamp? It's very new."

"A reading lamp. That sounds mighty interesting. Come in." Adam motioned to Mr. Schaffer to follow him to the front parlor.

Picking up his black valise, Mr. Schaffer followed Adam. "Is the lady of house in?"

"That would be my mother. She's in the kitchen. I'll go fetch her."

When he returned with Lizzie, whose quizzical look betrayed aggravation at being taken from her bread baking, the sample case lay open on the floor. She quickly perused its contents: cutlery, clocks, pots, and pans. The reading lamp sat on a side table.

"Good afternoon, Mam." Mr. Schaffer bowed and extended his hand.

Lizzie ignored it.

"This is my mother, Mrs. Springer."

"What is your business, sir?"

"Why, Mrs. Springer, I'm a salesman."

"You mean a peddler?"

"Ma, he's got a reading lamp, and I really want to see how it works. I'm spoiling my eyesight with our dim kerosene lamps. Besides they flicker something awful."

Lizzie gave a noisy sigh and sat down on the settee. Mr. Schaffer sat on the straight chair opposite and began to demonstrate how the new lamp worked. "You see here . . . this lamp is of two parts. There is a separate reservoir from which oil flows down a tube into the burner giving the reader a more steady light."

Adam peered at the lamp's two sections while Mr. Schaffer lit a match to the burner. "This is brand new, just developed during the past year. Since the war, in which I served honorably, there have been many new developments to make our lives easier."

Adam's face brightened. "What regiment were you in?"

"I served proudly with the Pennsylvania Volunteer Infantry, One Hundred, Forty-Seventh Regiment." Mr. Schaffer brushed a hand through his sandy hair. His well-formed face appeared more used to grinning than frowning making Adam wonder if this happy-go-lucky fellow ever suffered the melancholy. While Mr. Schaffer kept up a steady patter about his products, the beaming smile never left his face.

"I was with the Ohio Seventy-Eighth Regiment." Adam said, with a grand air of self-regard. "Perhaps we covered the same territory."

"I was at Gettysburg."

"That battle might be comparable to Vicksburg."

"I kind of doubt that."

Ma frowned. "Could we get on with this? My bread is baking."

"Why, of course, Mam." He glanced at Adam. "Please call me Jeremiah. We can talk about our war experiences later. I find most of the ladies are not interested. Now let me show you the latest in potato peelers, Mrs. Springer." He continued through his stash of kitchen gadgets with Lizzie sizing up each critically. Adam said he believed he'd take the lamp and went to get his money, while Lizzie opened a china teapot and came out with enough to pay for a potato peeler. "I generally use a cutting knife for peeling, but I'll try this thing out."

23

When Adam returned, Lizzie was still looking over the remaining contents of the valise. Jeremiah had gone to his buggy to get a newly packaged lamp. When he returned he was carrying another valise, which he opened quickly to display several bolts of cloth.

"Mam," he said. "I'm sure you're a seamstress. I have a special sale today on this fine calico and these trims. You would look lovely with a ruffled tucker around the neckline."

"Don't need one. I have enough dresses for the kind of life I lead."

"Ma, you could use a pretty new dress."

"Adam, we don't need to spend money on frivolity. I've had pretty dresses in my time. But that's over now." She looked away from the two men and seemed to be lost in a memory, then said, "why when I lived in Baltimore I had the loveliest outfits, one given me by the most stylish woman I ever met. Her name was Helena. Another was made just for me. My Aunt Louise in Leesburg, that's in Virginia, had her dressmaker sew it up."

"Ma, I never knew you lived Baltimore. When was that?"

"I was about seventeen. Helena was my piano teacher; well, she wasn't really a teacher, just introduced me to music and the piano. I was staying with my gramma in Frederick, Maryland at the time. She was very old and not well. I was lonely and convinced my uncle to hire a girl two afternoons a week, so I could slip away for a few hours. I met Helena as I passed by her house and stopped to listen to the lovely music coming from inside. She taught me all she could, said I had talent for the piano and suggested I go to Baltimore to study with her esteemed teacher, a strict German woman, Madam Schumann. I was scared to death of her."

"Did your Ma and Pa approve?" He glanced at Jeremiah. "Imagine a young girl going off to a big city alone."

"I dunno about that." Jeremiah winked at Adam.

"Ma didn't approve at all, and I had to wait until Gramma died, but Pa saw that I had the money. And Uncle Christopher, unmarried like yourself, she nodded toward Adam, who lived with Gramma helped too. The money they gave me only provided three months of music lessons, not really enough for a student of my limited ability. Helena made arrangements for me to live in the home of her dearest friend. I took care of the children when I wasn't practicing, but then . . . well, let's forget about all that." She turned her attention to Jeremiah, who seemed eager to get on with closing the sale. "I observe by your evident love for your mother that you would like to see her in a fetching new dress to bring out the color in her eyes." Adam saw his mother's eyes as so faded that nothing would bring up their color. Still, he had never brought her a gift, and now felt bad about giving his sister, Emma, the figurine, while never even considering anything special for his mother. "Ma, I'm going to buy this fabric for you. Please tell Jeremiah here what you prefer and how much you need."

"I don't rightly know anymore. I will have to cut an old dress apart for a pattern and then adjust it. My weight has changed, but I can account for that by taking an inch off here and there in the cutting. That ivory muslin with the green sprigs would be nice."

Adam saw that she was interested, and after she and Jeremiah guessed at the amount of fabric required, he went back upstairs for the money. The old leather purse carried in his army knapsack was gradually becoming lighter.

"What is this one for?" Adam heard Lizzie say when he returned to the parlor. She was holding a pear shaped bottle, and having removed her spectacles, was peering closely at the tiny lettering on the label.

"That's Dr. Kittredges's excellent remedy for rheumatism. People tell me they apply it only once or twice and are cured. I'm not really a medicine man, but I carry a few ointments and elixirs for people who have routine ailments."

Lizzie held the bottle. "You're sure about that—cured after one or two applications?" She sized up Jeremiah's face. Adam recognized that she was taking measure of the man.

"Yes, Mam. Dr. Kittredge runs a noted laboratory in New York City. Best in the business."

"I'd be surprised at that. What's in this?" She shook the bottle up and down in front of a startled Jeremiah.

"Well, I believe there is camphor, skunk oil, and spirits of turpentine, just to mention a few ingredients. There's more, of course. Some is secret."

"I can imagine it is," she answered handing the bottle back to him.

"If you'd like to buy it? I can let you have it for only fifty cents."

"At that rate I'll make my own."

"But Mam this is made by a real doctor."

"I know all about those real doctors. Here take your sham medicine. I've got to be about my bread baking."

Adam was embarrassed at his mother's abrupt leave taking. "Don't let her upset you," he told Jeremiah. "My mother thinks she knows something about everything."

"That's all right. In my business I meet all kinds: pleasant people and mean ones. A salesman learns to take it. Do you still want the dress goods?"

"Yes. Maybe a new dress will change her attitude, though I doubt it."

Jeremiah measured and cut the cloth according to Lizzie's estimate and closed the valises. He picked up one and headed for the front door. Adam carried the other. "I'd like to take the time to share war experiences," Jeremiah said, "but with the days darkening earlier, I've got to finish my route, so I can get back to the hotel in daylight."

"Where are you staying?"

"At the hotel in Four Corners."

"My sister lives right down the street from there."

"It's not a bad place as hotels go, as long as they don't crowd too many into a room. Not too many salesman coming through here though. I usually get a room to myself. I'll spend a couple of days in this area; then I'll move on. I only go to the smaller towns; the larger ones have hardware stores and drugstores, so I have to bring along items that people on the farms can't get easily. Convenience is my big selling point. You can shop in your parlor."

Adam was about to take his leave when Jeremiah called after him. "Say how about meeting me at the hotel later this evening, and we can talk. We'll have supper. I suppose you could stay overnight at your sister's place."

"Well, I guess I could. Truth to tell, I've hardly done anything but work on this farm since I came home July a year ago. Been to church, Ma insists on that every once in awhile, and to a few church socials. Not much fun there. Where will I meet you?"

"In the tavern room say about six."

Five

"Ma, don't fix supper for me tonight. I won't be home, going to be eating at the hotel."

"The what?"

"The hotel. I'm meeting Jeremiah for supper."

"That peddler? Adam, you must be very careful of his kind."

"What do you mean, *his kind?*"

"Traveling men do not always lead exemplary lives; there are temptations."

"Ma, there are temptations everywhere. Besides what would you know about how traveling men conduct themselves? Until today, I never saw any of them darkening our door."

She was peeling potatoes with her new potato peeler. Letting it drop with a clang on the table, she raised her voice, "I'll have you know I haven't always been stuck away on this dratted farm. I once had a life in the city and can assure you traveling men are quite familiar to me. I repeat. They are not to be trusted."

"Sounds to me like you might have known one personally."

"I did, and as I said, they are not to be trusted."

"Ma you can't leave me hanging. How well did you know one?"

"Never mind. But while I was in Baltimore, I worked for one." She picked up the peeler again. "No one in the family ever knew. Ma would have died of horror if she had any idea, but I was determined to get more piano lessons than the money Pa and my uncle paid for and almost did by working for a medicine man. He was charming and an admirable looking fellow too." She stopped peeling, and still holding the utensil, raised her hand to her forehead to brush away a wisp of hair from her damp forehead. Silent for a moment, she added, "though not to be depended upon. He had another girl, while I thought he loved me. But of course, he didn't. Just played me along, because I was such a good worker and could straighten out the mess he called his laboratory. Wasn't a laboratory at all," she sniffed, "just a kitchen in a run-down old house. After I left I found out he had been in all kinds of trouble: robbed, cheated, maybe even murdered. And his elixirs, which he claimed would cure every ailment known to man, were mostly alcohol. So yes, Adam, I know about traveling men, so be careful. I've told you this story

27

only because I want you to be forewarned, but I'd be obliged if you don't mention this to your brother and sisters or anyone else. It's between you and me. I was young and impressionable and a bit lonely, I guess, but I soon learned."

"I never thought of you having any kind of life beyond the time I've been around. How old were you when I was born anyway?"

"Forty-six."

"I guess that gave you a lot of time to live another life." He studied his mother's tired face. "You never wanted to come to Ohio did you? Pioneering wasn't a way you cared to live."

"Not really. But I had no choice. Like all good wives, I went where my husband took me."

The tavern room was dimly lit and further darkened by a haze of smoke. Jeremiah found a table in the corner and they ordered from the menu scribbled in chalk on a black slate over the bar. Adam recognized the waitress as the Wilson girl, the older sister of a boy with whom he'd gone through school. He thought it an indecent place for a young girl to be employed and blurted, "Ida, why are you working here?"

"Gotta' eat and besides, I've got two babes to support and no husband."

"Where's he?"

"Dead in the war, and a body's got to fight the government to get a pittance of any kind. Eight dollars a month don't go far with two young'uns to feed and rent to pay. My folks is gone now too, so it's either take a humiliatin' job or starve. Good to see you again, Adam," she smiled a crooked little smile that did nothing to cover her cracked tooth.

"And two tankards of ale," Jeremiah said. "That all right with you?" He nodded at Adam who nodded back. He wasn't much of a drinker. Hard spirits were frowned upon in his house. "The devil's brew," his mother said. Besides, he'd had one drunken experience during the war and didn't want another.

After Ida left, Jeremiah turned his attention to Adam. "You know that serving girl?"

"I was once sweet on her. I was about fifteen, I guess. She was real pretty then, sixteen or so. Looks somewhat worn now."

"Well, maybe you're missing out on a ready-made family."

"No, thanks."

Ida returned and set down the two tankards. "Your family well, Adam?"

28

"Pa's not too good, but Ma is fine and so are my sisters and brother. John's out in Iowa. Got a big spread out there. How's your brother, Asa?"

"He's married already, has three children. Gone west to some place called Arizony. He writes that it's a territory, nothin' much there, but scrub and cactus. Lands real cheap though. A body can have thousands of acres for what ten would cost here. They're ranchin'. Lots of Indians about. He's mighty fearful of them."

She smiled broadly at Adam. "I'll be back in a jiffy with your suppers."

"Don't hurry," Jeremiah called after her. "We've got talking to do." As Ida swept away, he turned his attention to Adam. "Better watch it," he said.

"You mean me for her? Never. I'm going to marry a lady, or I'm not going to marry at all. Ida comes from a poor coal-mining family. They didn't even have land of their own. Poor as a spent field in winter. What about you?"

"Single. Not too many ladies want a traveling man for a husband. And the others . . . well, they're not hard to find, so who needs to be burdened with a wife and children? Anyway, those fine ladies don't always prove to be much fun, if you know what I mean." Jeremiah winked. "Now tell me about where you were in the war."

Not wishing to recount the battles that were still giving him nightmares, Adam took a long draught of ale and began his tale. He started with an account of the first few days in camp, when the men were occupied in target shooting, making scouts, and learning to hurry out of tents to answer the *long roll*.

"We all went through that," Jeremiah said impatiently. "What about the battles?"

After taking another generous swig of ale, Adam plunged into another version of his story. "We first learned to enclose an enemy in our imaginations. That done, we considered ourselves prepared for war and were mighty eager to get going. When the news came that General Grant was moving up the Cumberland with gunboats and a land force to attack Fort Donelson, we were finally on our way. Our first stop was Paducah, Kentucky. We were a zealous bunch of boys—for that's all we were—I doubt there were many over the age of twenty and some barely seventeen." Adam paused for another sip from his tankard. He wanted to stop his story before he could no longer suppress the images—images that would surface at the slightest noise: a rifle shot, a scream, a crash, a slammed door.

"Yes, go on." Jeremiah urged.

"We were anxious to get on with the fighting. Some of us treated this first battle as a lark, a game; but others, suddenly conscious of what the whole bloody

29

business was about, were restless with dread and trembling. Our boat arrived about an hour before sundown in full view of the enemy's works. Some officers went ashore to assess the rebel strength, and seeing the battlefield strewn with bodies, came back with mighty grave faces. Later we got used to seeing dead and wounded, as we moved through Vicksburg, Champion Hill, Atlanta, and all the rest, but it was that first battle at Fort Donelson that stunned us all." Adam didn't mention his cowardice that caused him to miss the battle. He remembered it now with shame, for when their leaders determined that only by land could they defeat the rebel defenses, he was clutched with dread bordering on terror. They slept that night without tents or fire and within rifle shot of the enemy's works. Night came, dark as pitch, and a cold heavy rain fell, followed by sleet and wintry wind. Adam curled up tight on the edge of the woods, but between the cold and ungodly fear, he did not sleep. When in the morning the fighting resumed, he was nestled in the brush behind a rock, where he stayed secure and unnoticed as his company advanced until the shots came intermittently like popcorn starting to burst over heat. His cowardice had plagued him throughout the war and was the reason, when after three years of incessant fighting and marching through swamps as vicious as any battle attacking the enemy, he re-enlisted the fifth day of January, 1865, one of twenty-seven men from his company to do so. How tempted he had been that day at Fort Donelson to join the deserters by simply rolling away into the woods. It would have been so easy, but duty and the terrible ridicule he might endure were as much to bear as the thought of dying in battle. "What about you?" Adam was anxious to shift the conversation away from a memory that brought him shame.

"Gettysburg was the worst. To this day, I can't forget it. I was with regiment hiding behind some rocks and trees. The rebels thought we were behind our breastworks and opened fire there. We retaliated from our hidden positions, and with my very own eyes, I saw five men drop side by side. It went on like that most of the day. July 3rd it was. The enemy made repeated charges upon our lines but was often swept back. We slaughtered them wholesale. Our men positioned themselves where we could hold our charge until the rebs were nearly upon us; then we let go. They fell down like poisoned birds. We only lost five men, sixteen wounded. God only knows how many really fell that day; the battlefield was littered with gray-clad dead and dying. The screaming and sobbing were awful, some even crying out to the Lord. But that wasn't the worst of it." Jeremiah was silent for a few moments while he took in another long draught of ale. "You know Adam, I'm not sure it's good for us to dwell on all this. I rarely talk about it to anyone, and don't quite know why I am doing so now."

"God knows few of the homefolks care to hear about the war, so who else do we have to talk to but each other. I don't know much about Gettysburg, so I'd like to hear more." Adam was being polite, for even as the words popped out, he really didn't want to know. Battlefields bear similar scars, only the names of surrounding towns and villages, rivers, hills, and distant mountains change. Jeremiah took another swallow from his tankard while Adam waited for the words he dreaded, lest they trigger the demons in his memory.

"Both armies, near exhausted by the hard work of our marches and the three days of battle, soon fell asleep. We were awakened about one-thirty in the afternoon by a signal gun, then a reply from the other side. About three hundred cannons belched forth death and ruin everywhere. The air was filled with screeching, bursting shells. And screaming men. I'll never forget how it felt to witness my fellow man—and I include our enemies—contorted in pain. I hate to say this, but I saw some begging to be shot, and in a few instances our men complied. While all this was going on the rebel, General Pickett, was getting ready for his famous charge. It lasted scarcely an hour and the entire division marching in orderly lines to their deaths was nearly wiped out. By three that afternoon it was over."

"How did they go about getting so many of the dead buried? Where did they put them all?"

"It was gruesome." Jeremiah warmed to his story, his eyes glazing like a pair of wet marbles from the quantity of ale he was rapidly consuming. "Afterward I learned the enemy lost more than thirty-two thousand men; we lost twenty-three thousand. I was in one of the contingents ordered to bury the poor devils. Some went by their own hand to end the pain. One man loaded his gun, placed on a cap, then put the butt between his feet, jammed the ramrod upon the trigger with one hand and held the muzzle under his chin with the other. I could have stopped him. It haunts me to this day that I didn't. You can imagine the rest."

"I don't think I want to. We had some like that too. They were in wretched pain and asked us to do the job, but I never could." Adam looked across the darkened tavern room filling up with other men—farmers mostly, but a few locals too. He felt his stomach clutch and the muscles of his throat tighten. Be damned if he'd cry in front of all these jovial people who, if you mentioned the late conflict, would probably ask *which war you talkin' about?* He recognized an elderly bachelor friend of his father's and waved; the old man did not wave back. Other men now crowding

31

the long walnut bar, their feet on the brass rail, were joshing back and forth as men do in a spirit of shared camaraderie, not generally shared with their womenfolk. Only a few were known to Adam. Some wore parts of military issue clothing. The sight of them unnerved him. A few were veterans known to be ill adjusted to home and hearth, and the conviviality of the barroom provided the comradeship of men at war, which some sorely missed. He waved to one ex-soldier, Vesty Echelberry. What's he doing here? Adam wondered. His family is dirt poor, six kids and a wife in a rundown shack. He's got no money for drink. Vesty took off his slouch hat and waved back. They'd been together in the Seventy-Eighth and had come home on furlough from Vicksburg together.

Jeremiah was speaking again. Adam turned to listen although he was sick of the story already. "I remember it was Sunday, we went out to help bury the dead as best we could. Several were assigned to digging trenches. I was ordered along with about six others to bring in the bodies from the battlefield and close-by woods, which were full of dead men and horses. The weather was a problem." Jeremiah paused long enough to take several more swallows of ale. "Intense heat and heavy thunderstorms raged on the nights of the third and fourth, and by the time we began our grisly work, the sun bore down on us. You'd a thought we were already in hell, and the stench liked to kill us. Some of those men lay there unburied since the first battle three days before. A few got sick and had to quit, so they ordered us to stop until more trenches could be dug." Jeremiah sat back in his chair and tipped the last of his ale to his lips. He banged the empty tankard on the table. "These trenches were about a foot-and-a-half wide and two-and-a-half feet deep. We placed forty-two in one trench and thirty-one in another. The bodies were put in the trenches two deep, side by side. I know because the lieutenant made me count them out, so he could note them down on a paper to turn in to the captain."

Ida approached and Jeremiah sat back while she set down the roasted mutton and squash pies. "Anything else sirs?"

"Another round," Jeremiah raised his empty tankard.

Ida flashed Adam a tentative smile. "You too?"

"I guess." He still had half a tankard, but wanted to appear as worldly as Jeremiah.

Ida moved in close to Adam and reached across to remove the tankard; "I see you still got some." Nodding, he stared at her for a moment, but looked away quickly when she smiled at him. It wouldn't be long until she'd lose a few teeth. Her mouth already had that puckered look of the poor.

When the waitress was gone, Adam said, "Perhaps while we eat we better cease such mournful talk. I don't like to think on the war anyway."

"Nor do I." Jeremiah admitted. "I get a few belts of ale in me, and it all comes back."

Ida returned with a tray on which sat the tankards, a mess of pickled green beans, and a basket of cornbread. "There, that should do you," she said. 'I'll come back later to see if I can interest you in some sweets to top it off."

They thanked her, and Adam noticed that Jeremiah was referring to her as *honey.* He was also downing much of the ale in quick gulps. Adam pretended not to notice. "This place isn't bad," he said. "I've never been here before. What with the liquor, it was kind of off limits when I was coming up. God fearing folks like mine didn't cotton to strong drink. Ma always said there was no quicker way to get sent to hell. And the preachers—they rail against it Sunday after Sunday along with dancing and card playing."

"Well, so anyone can notice, they aren't having as much fun as I am." Jeremiah laughed. "What about you? Get into town much?"

"We go to dinners at my sister's on Thanksgiving and other holidays, unless the family is coming to our place, but they are hardly times to go popping into a tavern. I sometimes come into town for supplies, and I usually stop to see my sister, Emma. She feeds me, so I don't bother with this tavern. It doesn't have much of a reputation among the better people. But tell me about your traveling job. I'm curious about other lines of work that men do. Oh, I know about shopkeepers and doctors, lawyers and such, but salesmen I rarely see. Not too many come around our place."

"It's mostly a lot of places like Four Corners and the surrounding farms. Some of the hotels on my route are pretty poor. This one could be fixed up; the rooms aren't much, crammed with too many beds. You get used to things being dowdy and feel lucky if the rooms are the least bit clean. I hate the ones where we have to share a bed, but since the war, more establishments offer single rooms. My company is out of Pittsburgh, so I cover most of eastern Ohio along with the very western part of Pennsylvania, little river towns mostly: Brownsville on the Monongahela and Charleroi, even Wheeling in West Virginia. Pittsburgh and anything east of there is another man's territory. I like getting out in the fresh air, but winter is something else. When the roads turn difficult, I try to take January and February off and go home to my ma's place in central Pennsylvania. My real dream is to get promoted, so I can use the railroad. These country sales are not where the money is. If I could

33

travel by train, I would be calling on stores and wouldn't have to go along these back roads trying to convince some farmer's wife to search her jar of egg money for a few pennies. But my boss says I've got to start at the bottom, so I have been doing this route for six months."

"Does it pay well?"

Jeremiah laughed. "The route, no, but I do all right. Just like in the army where I used my card playing skills to take the yokels money, I do the same on the road. Bought my old mother a house on what I got in the war."

Seemingly out of the blue another ale arrived. Adam had had enough, but with the conviviality and bantering back and forth with Ida, he drank it anyway. Although Jeremiah kept referring to her as *honey,* Adam sensed her leaning toward him every time she reappeared. And once she placed her hand lightly on his arm then leaned a bit more until her ample breast came close. "You always were a handsome devil," she said, then straightened up and asked if they would like some fresh baked rum cake.

"I'll bet you could have that wench anytime you wanted her," Jeremiah laughed. "She's not bad, and just think while you're living at home with Mama you could have your fun right here in town; why don't you make arrangements?"

Adam knew he could use a good lay, for he was horny a good part of the time. He thought about women often, but he was still of a mind that the girls he saw in church, on the farms, and in town were not to his liking. After one baby those girls turned slovenly. After six they were embittered old women, unhappy with their men who dragged around in stained coveralls and tattered shirts, like as not two days worth of stubble on their chins, and a chaw of tobacco in their toothless mouths.

"I know her kind. She's not for me. She ripened early and is already spoiling."

Jeremiah signaled the waitress for another tankard. Adam placed a hand over his. He was already feeling the effects. Ida returned with the rum cakes and more drink for Jeremiah, who consumed it as fast as he wolfed down the cake. His words slurred, he launched into another tale of the war. "You know, them rebs were just like us. Boys mostly. They engaged us in a skirmish along the old plank road leading toward Fredericksburg in Virginia."

"I know where it's at. Marched there myself."

"Well, after their charge had been repulsed, a Confederate who had been badly wounded on the plank road was left lyin' there all tied up in wretched pain. By God, to this day I feel sorry for the bloke even though he was wearing gray." Jeremiah brought his hand down hard on the table. "That poor bastard called out to God, his mother, prayed to die. I couldn't stand his cries, so me and another soldier from our side crawled out to get him, all the time listening to our officers screaming at us to let him go." Jeremiah's eyes were teary. "We ignored them and dragged the poor bugger back to our side. He was just a sweet-faced kid. A shell had torn all the flesh off his hips. We tried to patch him up, gave him a draught of alcohol. But in the end had to leave him. About midnight we had a very heavy artillery duel lasting several hours. You ever hear of Stonewall Jackson?"

Adam nodded. The room was beginning to swirl, and he found it hard to focus, but when he did, he saw tears streaming down Jeremiah's face.

"Well, the General died that night, but that didn't end the fighting. It was fearful. Bullets came front, flank, and rear. We were in our breastworks when the battle opened and thought we'd won. We gave three cheers and our color bearer; Sergeant Henry—he was a friend of mine—had just taken off his cap and cheered when a rebel shell killed him. His head was shot away and his brains were scattered over the old flag he had carried so long. I wanted out after that and almost left, but another soldier convinced me to stay." Jeremiah wiped his eyes and nose with a large blue kerchief. He said, "I could never stand being called a deserter for the rest of my life."

Adam had heard enough. He rose abruptly and took his leave.

"You going so soon? Let's have another round." Jeremiah called after him. Adam kept on his steady path toward the door not even looking back, but he heard Jeremiah add, "watch out for those female predators. You're mighty fair game, and not all of them are ladies."

Six

They lie scattered broadcast, along the Mississippi Valley, the mountains and plains of Georgia, and by the rivers and swamps of South Carolina; in the burying grounds of the hospitals from Atlanta to Cincinnati; and in the numberless graves in rebel prisons from Alabama to Virginia.

Jeremiah's words echoed as Adam went into the night from the side door of the tavern opening onto the alley. Females on the hunt were everywhere. He'd nodded to them in the shops, greeted them on the streets in Four Corners, and spoke to them politely at church and during socials, but none appealed. Adam still carried the image of *his lady,* but he now regarded her as only a stupid memory to be dwelt upon before falling asleep. Her serene and lovely face relieved him of more tortuous memories of the war, but he could never quite imagine her lying naked in his arms. She had probably produced her two children and might have already retired from wifely duties. He suspected that was why so many southern plantation owners fathered children among their slave women. During the war Adam had seen his share of cocoa and coffee colored people among the blackest of the black. He'd heard it whispered that the white slave owners could have their way with the darky women they owned whenever the urge grabbed them

Some of the girls Adam met were giddy to get married anyway they could. Jeremiah was right; he'd have to be careful. He had taken a girl home from evening church services, and before he knew it, she was all over him. His friend, Lemuel, got caught that way and was now doomed to spend the rest of his life with a woman he loathed. Lem had done his duty, and it was said the robust baby was a seven months child. With Pa ailing and Ma more overbearing than ever, Adam concluded it would be folly to bring another woman into that house. Still he envied Jeremiah's carefree life and wondered briefly what it would be like to travel about selling goods.

His saunter to Emma's house from the tavern was a tipsy one. Unused to strong drink, he counted the houses from the corner, and after carefully assessing the outlines of various porches turned into the familiar white frame dwelling with a side porch. A canvas-draped settee sat against the wall. But instead of curling up quietly on its cushions, with all the audacity of a drunk, he rapped on the door. They were probably all in bed, but the ale hid his ability to care. Pounding on the door again, he fell against it. Emma attired in a white night dress, a shawl over her shoulders opened it hesitantly and Adam stumbled into the hallway.

"What are you doing here at this time of night?"

"I met a friend at the hotel. We had supper together."

"And a goodly amount of ale, I'd say. Better not let Ma know."

"She doesn't have to know if you don't tell her."

"No, I suppose not; you can sleep in the spare room." She motioned to the stairway. "I declare, you're a mess."

Getting to the second floor required concentration on each step to avoid letting Emma know how wobbly he really was. Once in the spare room, barely eight by ten feet, he dropped onto the single bed without undressing. His head spun, the room tilted, his stomach verged on nausea. He sat up and tried to keep from getting sick. Ma was right. Traveling men are dangerous.

The next morning, his condition the night before was ignored; Reuben had already gone to the blacksmith shop, and the children were in school. Emma served Adam a sizeable breakfast of bacon and eggs with corn bread, lots of fresh butter and elderberry jam. Although still somewhat liquored up, the food went down easily, and he felt better for having eaten.

Emma sat a spell talking to him, her face bright with anxiety at the announcement she was about to make. "We've got some good news," she said, "Lucinda has a beau, and we believe it's serious. He's one of the Hoovers. They have a good sized farm, and his father also sells farm implements, so we think she's made a good match."

"That's wonderful. When's the wedding?"

"It's a little early to make those plans, but Lucinda says they've talked about it, so we'll know pretty soon." She eyed him quizzically. "And now that the next generation is old enough for wedlock, I'm thinking it's about time for you. What you need more than anything, now that the nasty old war in behind you, is a good woman. There's this girl, Amy Louise, a lovely person, who lives with her father on the next block. I think you would make a good pair. She's not beautiful, mind you, but a comely girl and very capable."

"I suppose I could take her and her father into Pa's house, and we would live happily ever after. Emma, not now." He cleaned up his plate with a slab of cornbread and got up to leave. "I've really got to go; the horse and trap are at the livery stable by the hotel. And there's plenty of work waiting for me at home, so I'd best be on my way before Ma has a conniption fit."

Adam didn't quite make it home in the time he had planned. He was walking the horse and trap along the lane behind the hotel when he passed by a decrepit shanty, nothing more than a nailed up box with one window in the front and a door. To his surprise, someone called out to him. Turning to look, he saw Ida still in her nightdress. She dumped a pail of washwater to one side of the entryway, and setting the pail aside, waved energetically. Her once auburn hair pinned in a ball at the nape of her neck the night before was loose and fell wildly about her shoulders. But it was still luxuriant, and he had an instant desire to run his fingers through it. Without hesitation, he wrapped the reins over a tree limb and went toward her. "Oh Adam," she said, "It's been such a long time. I hoped you would come. You were my first love."

"Where are the children?"

"They're still at my sisters. I was just about to get dressed to go fetch them, but then I saw you."

Adam took her in his arms but released her quickly when she led him to a small room, where an unmade bed occupied an entire wall. His mind blank, desire on the upswing, he ripped off his shirt, dropped his trousers and lay down upon the still warm crumpled sheet. Laughing as though she expected a glorious romp, Ida slipped out of her nightdress to lay her naked body over his. They remained there among the tumbled blankets for half the morning, doing to each other what they had once only dreamed about as youngsters. When it was over, doubts came at him like wind blowing ashes from a fire. He panicked. Why am I such a fool? He stared at the ceiling of the two-room cabin, a feeling of complete relaxation swept over him, while down deep there was the frightful thought of having fathered a child with a woman he did not want. He could see a table, two chairs and a child's high chair in the kitchen. The two rooms appeared clean but shabby; he supposed the loft overhead was where the children slept. If he had made her a mother again, he would be expected to take her, the two children, and a baby to the farm, a thought too odious to contemplate. He turned to look at her face in repose, her hair curling prettily around her forehead where tiny wrinkles had begun to show. Best get out of here, he thought. Sanity replaced the sexual satisfaction he felt moments before, and he got up to pull on his drawers and trousers.

She stirred and looked up at him. "I suppose you are leaving. Will you be back?"

"Ida, don't count on it. My folks need me. I simply can't take on a woman and two children, if that's what you have in mind. I'm sorry. I shouldn't have stayed."

"No," she breathed one of those long, defeated woman sighs. "I didn't expect that much. Anyway, it wasn't your fault; it was mine too. I'm lonely, but I'm not without men in my life. Your friend, Jeremiah, was here last night. He paid me two dollars."

"You mean you want to be paid? Adam's face turned angry. Any sense of relaxation he had felt moments before left. He was tense with disgust. "Why didn't you tell me that up front?"

"Why indeed? You didn't ask, but that's what I charge when I think I can get it."

He reached into his pocket and threw the bills onto the bed; they were all the money he had left from his night of carousing. "Why would you sell yourself like this? It's degrading."

"Sell myself, I'll tell you why. I've lost a husband. And like I told you last night, the government generously allots me eight dollars a month, hardly enough to feed, clothe, and shelter us. I get work at the hotel only a few days a week. It's not busy enough to be there more. And what else is a woman to do? With my sixth grade schooling, I'm hardly qualified for teaching. I could nurse, I suppose, but I hate taking care of sick people, and deliver me from old ones. In this backward town, the shopkeepers won't even hire a woman to clerk. Of course, some of them don't mind visiting me from time to time, and I make certain I get at least two dollars out of them before I agree to take them on. I do what I have to do in fifteen minutes. When I add that up, that's nearly eight dollars an hour, when I'd be lucky to get twenty cents if they hired me to clerk though I'm not likely to get more than one a day, even counting the peddlers passing through. Oh, they all complain bitterly about the money, telling me that other women charge only a dollar. Usually, they are so charged up by then, they can't fancy leaving, so they pay."

"That's revolting. You spent more time with me than fifteen minutes, so I suppose I owe you more."

"You're different, Adam. I always had a warm spot for you, like most of the other girls, I guess. Still I must have the money if I am to live and keep my children. When I can save enough, I'm going to traipse right out of this dead-end place. I'm sorry about that, but it's simply the way it is. Maybe someday I'll go to a city, but right now I need my sister to help out with the children, and I need to pay her, so I do what I can to earn the money."

"Did you stay at Emma's?" His mother greeted him from the garden, her face angry under the wide brimmed straw hat. She didn't wait for an answer. "I thought you'd get back before noon. This garden needs to be dug up and your Pa took another spell this morning. He's sleeping now, but I don't want to leave him alone too long."

Like a little boy, turned sheepish, after a night and half a day of misbehavior, Adam took the spade from her. "Go see about Pa, I'll finish this." His sins of the last eighteen hours began to weigh. Unless I get a woman of my own, that's the last time. I can't stand this worry over whether they will come after me. He plunged the pick into the ground, then stood up. Of course, with Ida, I could claim the child was some other man's, and what could she do about it? The scandal—could he trust her—but all those other customers gave him an out. After remembering them, he felt better and went about his digging as carefree as a boy who'd been on a lark.

Winter descended with unusual fury that December. A new snowstorm rushed in every week from mid-month blanketing the ground with layer upon layer of new snow, until Adam found it necessary to dig a ditch through the drifts to get to the barn. In case a quick blizzard should blow in to blind him in his trek back and forth to the house, he strung a rope as a guideline from the rear porch to the corn crib, and from there to the barn.

To read, Adam sat near the parlor stove, where his front overheated while his back remained chilly. He sometimes wished that in a fit of modernity they had not closed all the fireplaces. Most of them threw more heat than the stoves, and their lapping orange flames brought cheer to a room doused in winter gloom. But the fireplaces were dirty, and housewives hated the constant mess of ashes to be swept up and dumped. In the Springer parlor, loose fitting, poorly hung windows rattled in the wind and let some of the gale forces spend their energy inside. They hung blankets over the north facing windows leaving only two in front to cope with the room's winter darkness.

Several more *spells* left Pa unable to move without help, so they moved a bed from upstairs to the sitting room. To be alert to his nightly needs, Lizzie slept in the downstairs bedroom. She spent an hour or more each day massaging liniments into his useless limbs, but no matter how she tried, his left leg remained lifeless.

"We've got to keep turning him," she told Adam, "lest he get bedsores." So they moved him from his back to one side or the other every two hours, but tugging and turning him, even as he had thinned, was akin to lifting dead weight. It took both of them to accomplish the task. Adam was now scheduling his life and work by two-hour intervals. In loose thinking moments, he wished the old man was dead, then hated himself for such an unseemly thought.

As it had done the winter before, the gloom brought melancholy leaving Adam with a deadened feeling inside. One night a horrible dream reduced him to sobbing. His screams broke the night silence and brought his mother up the steps to waken him. "What is it this time?" She shook him vigorously. The trenchant tone of her voice betrayed her irritation at having her sleep interrupted.

"Oh, Mama, Mama!" He hadn't called her that since he was a little boy. "It should have been me. I should have taken that ball, not Nicholas. He died because I left where I was sleeping. I went into those stinking woods where a thousand men had defecated before me. And while I was gone, it happened. When I came back to the sleeping space, the ball had ripped open his side; the side that would have been by me. I lived and he died."

"There, there, son. God selects who lives and who dies and decides when to take them. It was not your fault. I'll get you some hot milk. That will soothe you and put you back to sleep in no time."

What had happened was the same as in his dream. Dead was his boyhood friend, Nicholas. They had gone through grammar school together; raced horses through the countryside; gone sled riding down the hill behind his house; and when they were aware of strange interior juices flowing they went to socials together, where if they were lucky they sparked the girls.

Adam, now back in bed, could hear his mother rattling around the kitchen. He could tell by the sounds of the kettle sliding onto the hot lid that she was now at the stove. As though she wanted to make certain the family knew she was slaving for them, she was always noisy in the kitchen, even in the middle of the night. When she returned carrying the steaming mug, Adam was sitting on the edge of the bed. "Is there never going to be any peace for me in this life? We may have won the war, but my heart is sore and aching," he said.

"There, there son, God will take care. Now drink this. It will help you sleep. Sit up straight, so you don't dribble it."

He felt like a child again, and after taking the milk soon drifted into peaceful sleep. The next night, and for several nights afterward, he fixed a cup of hot milk before lying down for the night. For a few hours it helped, but around three or four in the morning, some memory, dream, or more likely a nightmare would waken him. He took to rising before dawn, dressing, and going downstairs, where the old man snored in the sitting room bed. Adam sat in the rocker and watched daylight arrive before heading to the barn, where he fed the animals and milked the cows to relieve his mother of some of the chores. Sometimes after a night of wakefulness or violent dreaming, his hands shook too much to pull on the teats, and when a cow held back her milk he flew into a rage. Once he hit Bessie hard upon the rump, which only served to make her more unruly. Adam stamped back to the house. "Milking is woman's work, you do it," he told Lizzie. "Anyway, I'm sick of those damned animals. They don't like me."

"Of course they don't. You're mean with them. And they give you back just what you deserve. For a farm boy, you don't seem to understand the animals at all."

"Well, let me tell you something about animals, in the war . . ."

"Here we go again."

"As I was about to say . . . we were near Pittsburgh Landing, aroused from our blanket couches by booming cannon. A terrible fight was in progress near Shiloh Church, but our Company E was far off in the rear. There was no transportation to get us to the battleground until we were furnished with forty wild mules. The boys had one devil of a time corralling those beasts, but I grabbed a couple of them and had them trained to the harness before any of the others. And just in time, the first day's fight was already over and the battle was almost decided in favor of the rebels.

"So did you win?" Lizzie was busy washing up the dishes and threw a towel at Adam. "Here dry these plates."

"Are you even listening?"

"I am."

"The enemy in sufficient numbers to relieve each other in the fight had feasted all day on cheeses, cakes, liquors and canned fruits, which the abandoned sutler stores had furnished in great abundance. Flushed with their success, they had maddened themselves with spirits. We, on the other hand, were soaked from the cloudburst the night before and fought all day without breakfast, dinner, or supper. Our artillery saved the day raining a storm of shot, grape, and shell on the hapless enemy. The thunder was deafening. The rebels at first lay flat, but finally retreated.

Captured men told about the effect of our fire. One shell from a Yankee mortar fell among a dense mass and killed or wounded one thousand rebels."

"Adam, I don't want to hear any more. It's sickening. I know you're upset, but don't take it out on our poor beasts . . . or me." She stamped out of the room, her chin set.

"I hate this place," he shouted after her. "How much longer must this agony with him to go on?" He stood in the doorway between the kitchen and family sitting room and thrust his head toward the comatose figure in the bed. "A man injured in the war does not linger for years."

"Adam, watch that mouth of yours. You are very wrong about that. I hear tell there are hospitals—why just this year, I read in the *Herald* that a soldier's home was opened in Washington. Men hurt in the war are confined there; some will nurse their wounds for the rest of their lives, and I suppose a few are sick in the head. But you . . . look at you. You're hale and hearty. Not a scratch. Yet you complain."

Seeing that Sunday church services did nothing to alter Adam's distress, Lizzie suggested that he might go see Dr. Kennedy in Four Corners. "He must have treated people with violent dreams before. Everyone dreams, but yours—well, they do seem extreme. I must waken three or four times a week to stir you out of them, on top of getting up every night with your Pa. And you two are never on the same schedule. I'm in dire need of sleep myself."

Adam gave some thought to taking her advice. He felt himself getting worse. His temper tantrums had increased. The other day he had kicked one of the cats and sent her flying into midair. And when his mother asked him to water the chickens, he yelled at her to do it herself. Wearied from her own endeavors, she snapped right back at him. Like two fighting cocks, their shouts even caused Pa to stir. Hearing his moans brought Adam to his senses. It wasn't fair to burden Pa.

Seven

Two days later Adam went to Four Corners to see Dr. Kennedy. The old doctor, who must be nearing seventy, was showing his years.

"I'm feeling mighty poorly." Adam told him as he followed Dr. Kennedy from the hall into his office. The doctor walked around the desk and sat down in a wooden armchair that tilted him backwards. He motioned for Adam to sit in the chair across the desk opposite him, and with the high back framing the doctor's unruly gray hair and ruddy face, his light blue eyes bored in on Adam. "Now tell me," he asked, "where do you hurt?"

"I don't hurt anywhere, except in my head."

"You have a headache?"

"No. It's the dreams; I can't seem to rid myself of them."

"Dreams, about what?"

"The war. They're all about the war—death, shouting, carnage, young men screaming for relief. I race about trying to get help, and none ever comes."

"Well, you don't seem to be injured. In fact, I'd say you're in good shape."

"Not injured in the true sense, but my mind. I fear it's my mind."

"You mean you're going crazy? There are institutions for people so afflicted. I could set you up in one at Columbus. Lots of crazy veterans there, most with acute mania. Is that what you want?"

"No sir, just some relief."

Dr. Kennedy got up and pulled a ponderous book from a shelf weighted down by learned tomes peculiar to the medical profession. The one he carried bore the title *Anatomy Descriptive and Surgical* by Henry Gray. Above the shelves in the freestanding bookcase were the doctor's various certificates validating his present profession, among them Ohio Medical College in Cincinnati, where it was noted he graduated with honors. Next to that were his memberships in the Zanesville Academy of Medicine and the Perry and Morgan County Medical Societies. Since many physicians had done little more than study with a local doctor, Adam concluded that Dr. Kennedy had more inclusive professional training. He also knew that the doctor had attended to wounded soldiers after the battle of Pittsburg

44

Landing. This alone gave Adam confidence, but his feeling of well being was soon to dissipate.

While the doctor perused the pages of the medical book, Adam looked around the office and concluded that Dr. Kennedy had constructed the bookcase with its several glass-enclosed shelves as well as the desk. Ma had once told him the doctor's earlier trade was cabinetmaking? "Later," she said, "he apprenticed to a doctor in a neighboring town." That he had gone for further study at a university gave Adam an additional sense of trust.

Dr. Kennedy selected another book from behind one of the glass doors, carried it to his desk, sat down, and without saying anything to Adam began going through it, page by page, his spectacles low on his nose. He stopped occasionally to read a passage, his finger gliding over the lines, then moving on through more pages, he looked up. "Nothing here about mind sickness," he said. "Maybe nervousness. Do you consider yourself nervous? No. That's usually a woman's disease." he answered himself without waiting for Adam's reply. "Tell me, do you see rebel soldiers when there is no enemy in sight, like when you're working in your fields?"

"Of course not."

"You haven't committed any crimes, stolen, beaten up, or threatened anybody?"

"I rarely see anybody but Ma. A few neighbors stop by once in awhile, but nobody wants to talk about the war. I'm pretty much a solitary worker."

"Do you ever take your bedding and a few supplies to camp out alone in the woods for days on end?"

"Never." Adam knew he was talking about Vesty Echelberry. Unable to stand home life after nearly four years with his compatriots sleeping in swamps, heat, rain, and freezing snowstorms, Vesty longed for those times. He was known to disappear for weeks. Sometimes when his wife got desperate to find him, a few of the veterans got together to search the woods. Vesty would stay home for a few months and then disappear again. Twice Adam had joined a group of men looking for him.

"Did you ever strike your Ma in a fit of temper?"

"No. She'd wring my neck."

"I don't doubt that," Dr. Kennedy laughed.

Adam decided not to mention kicking the cat, or ramming the horse's flank with the pitchfork. The cat had disappeared. He wondered if he had killed her.

"Now here's something about nightmares. Eat nothing after three o'clock, and restore the healthy action of stomach and bowels." Dr. Kennedy got up from the chair and came around to Adam's side of the desk, his stethoscope dangling from around his neck. He put the plugs into his ears and the other end onto Adam's chest. "Heart seems fine," he said after a moment.

Adam concluded that Dr. Kennedy was unsure about what to do.

"I suppose I could give you a potion of some sort. A tonic maybe." He replaced the book and brought down another. Adam saw that it was labeled *Medicines, Tonics, and Elixirs.* Dr. Kennedy let his finger stop at one entry Adam thought randomly, as if he had not the slightest idea as to its effectiveness. He disappeared from the room and returned moments later carrying a bottle. "That will be seventy-five cents, fifty cents for the consultation and twenty-five cents for the tonic. Take thirty drops a day."

Adam reached into his vest pocket and brought out the coins. "Dr. Kennedy, would you mind telling me what's in this tonic? Ma says you should never take a medicine without knowing what's in it."

"She does, does she? I fail to see how your mother would know whether a tonic was good or bad, but since you ask, laudanum, my boy. It will help banish the nervousness."

On the way home, Adam thought over the effects of laudanum on the human body. He had seen it work its wiles on some of the boys who used it to staunch their physical pains inflicted on the battlefield. Those who could not get the demon off their backs were some of the broken men seen in towns and along the waterfronts, homeless men who never found a place after the war. For them the mixture of opium and alcohol occupied their days and nights and alienated them from their families. No need for them to find occupations; they found solace in the bottle. Adam considered the stuff poison. As he drove the horse and trap over the dusty road on his way back to the farm, he contemplated what it might do to him. At a point where the creek that meandered through the meadow trickled across a low place in the road, he pulled the stopper and dumped the contents into the water, then threw the bottle into the woods. That old doctor hasn't an idea in the world about treating people with mind sickness. All he knows about is mending broken bones and delivering babies.

At home his mother inquired as to what the good doctor had prescribed.

"Laudanum," Adam answered disdainfully, and after a few months on that, I can become like those addicts who roam the streets with sagging faces and bloodshot eyes, announcing to the world that they are drug slaves. I'll stand the dreams, dammit."

"Now don't blaspheme, son. The way I see it, you might as well get aholt of yourself and quit dwelling on that old war."

As it inevitably does, spring finally came opening the roads to more comfortable travel and bringing with it a visit by Uncle Jacob and Aunt Mary Jane, who professed alarm at how dreadfully sick their brother-in-law appeared. "Is there nothing to be done? Did you call Dr. Kennedy?" Mary Jane looked sadly at John, emaciated now from lack of food.

"What good would he do?" Lizzie snapped. "The man is dying and taking a good long time to do so."

"Oh, Lizzie don't talk like that. Pray. I'm sure God will help."

"Bring him back? I doubt that. Leastwise, not as he was in his prime, and I'm not sure I want him any other way."

"Sometimes I despair with you, Lizzie; you've gotten mighty sharp tongued in the past few years. And somewhat godless as well."

"I suppose I have, but that's where life took me. As for your prayers, we all prayed that Adam would come home alive, and he did, but what about Nicholas and Hiram and all the other dead soldiers whose folks prayed every bit as hard as we did? They didn't come home, so what good is prayer? Now let's be about having a bite to eat."

"Lizzie, you blaspheme. You will burn in hell if you are not careful with that mouth of yours. I declare I'm disgusted with you."

"Then let's change the subject."

Emma came the next week, and alarmed at the condition of her father, began staying two days a week, and this afforded Lizzie a much needed night's sleep. Adam welcomed her visits. Emma was a likeable, uplifting person, and she always brought news of Four Corners. In early April she arrived with Lucinda. Adam had only seen his niece three or four times since his return from the war, as she was generally caring for the old lady down the street from Emma's house. Now she was talking of giving up the job when she and Fred Hoover wed. "It wouldn't be fitting for me, a married woman, to work for pay then," she told her uncle. "Oh, I would help out now and then but not for money." Then she added that she and Fred had finally set the wedding date for the next month.

47

"We're going to have it at the house with Pastor Ehrhardt officiating."

Talk of weddings made Adam uneasy. Ma and Emma were always pointing out eligible women or suggesting he attend socials, where he had come to feel like a fish waiting for the bait.

"Fred says we can't take a honeymoon in Zanesville like I wanted. He's very frugal, said there is no use spending on a fancy hotel when we can be in our own home by then. That's why we must wait. He's been saving his money, and is building us our own three-room house on property his father gave him next to his farm. Except with spring planting coming on soon and ground preparation, it's taking a terribly long time to finish the inside.

"Let me know if he needs a hand." Adam felt sorry for Lucinda in her eagerness to lay claim to young Fred. She was an attractive girl with dark curls that hung loosely about her face in contrast to her mother's and Lizzie's more severely pulled back hair. He noticed that her generous curves at hip and bosom threatened the very seams of her dress and decided she might soon run to fat. He hoped she wouldn't turn into a waddling woman with dimpled elbows. "Maybe I can help," he said, wondering when he would find time for such generosity.

"Why that would be very nice, Adam, but I don't think it's wise to take you from Gramma Lizzie while Grampa is so sick. Besides, another lady is already looking in on my charge two days a week, so I'll help Fred then. Sister Clara is with Mrs. Kimball now, but she can't help much during school. The old lady needs someone all the time, nights too, when she's very restless. I don't think she'll be around much longer, but old people do seem to take a long time to die."

Adam concluded Lucinda was anxious to be shut of her old-lady burden and could not blame her. He felt the same way about Pa.

"Anyway," she prattled on, "You're needed here, so even as I'm sure Fred would appreciate your help, I don't think I'll offer it."

"No I suppose it's better if I don't, but I would have liked the change." Adam smiled at his niece and wondered what it would be like to have children of his own.

Lizzie insisted that Adam needed a new suit for Lucinda's wedding. "I declare you are bursting out of that old thing you've had since before the war." She arranged for Mary Jane to stay with Pa while Adam drove them to Pineville, some seven miles from the farm where the stores were larger and the offerings more inclusive. Lizzie needed shoes, and Adam allowed as to how he could use a pair of dress shoes. The ones he had purchased on his return from the war were outdoor boots; now he needed a pair to go with his new suit.

"Son, you should be in business or a profession. You grace that suit beautifully." His mother stood back looking at her transformed son and said, "Yesterday a slouching farmer, now an aristocratic cultured man, or so one would think from your handsome appearance. Now you resemble some of the accomplished men about town I used to see in Frederick when I was young. Why we had to have a downturn just as you got out of grammar school and then that nasty old war, I don't know. Otherwise, we would have sent you off to college. Of course, your Pa never thought that was necessary, even as I was determined for a time. He dreamed of having you take over the farm, and farmers don't generally need college educations."

"I would have had to go to high school first, probably in Zanesville since the schools around here stop at eight grades, and Pa said I was needed on the farm when I tried to talk him into letting me go. Do you remember?"

"Vaguely." His mother changed the subject by remarking on such balmy weather for mid-April.

Adam decided this might be a good time to pursue the matter of his future. "Ma, I've been trying to think of something different to do than farming, but with Pa like he is and the small income the farm brings in, I don't see how I can leave. But I would like to. Maybe I could be a salesman like Jeremiah.

"A common peddler! Well, I should hope not."

"They travel around and are not stuck in the same place like I am."

"And they get into trouble, so banish that thought."

"Not likely I can go away now, anyway. Do you think?" He hoped she would think of some miracle.

"Sometimes I feel sad about that, but what else can we do? We're lucky to have a nice roof over our heads and a bit of a livelihood."

They walked down the street toward where the buggy was parked. Adam decided there was no use in pursuing the matter, at least not now while Pa lived. He took his mother's arm. "Come on, let's have a root beer at Mrs. Sturdivant's tea garden." He steered her across the dusty street to the front porch of a house the widow Sturdivant had turned into a place for people to gather for tea, root beer she made herself, sandwiches, and sweet cakes.

Eight

Lucinda and Frederick were married in early May. Adam supposed Lucinda, desperate to rein in Fred, had decided not to wait a day longer despite the chill in the air. Lizzie arranged for her dearest friend, Rachel, to see to Pa while she and Adam attended the wedding. A friend of long standing, Rachel and her husband, Bartholomew, had lived in a poor cabin two miles from the Springer's place when John and Lizzie came west from Frederick, Maryland in 1818. She was the first woman to befriend Lizzie, who at the time was feeling exceedingly put upon at having to live between a shed and a Conestoga wagon, until they could build their own cabin. Rachel's original one room had all but disappeared into the built-ons put up as their fortunes improved and more children joined the family. People joked that you could always tell another baby was on the way when Bartholomew got out his hammer and saw to add another room. Lizzie taught the unschooled Rachel her letters, for which her student was forever grateful, and the two women maintained their friendship throughout marriages, births, deaths, droughts, rainy days, and blizzards, always helping one another in times of stress.

Lucinda's and Fred's wedding brought out nearly all the family, except brother, John, who wrote to say the trip to Ohio was prohibitive, as it was planting time, and he now had a spread of three-hundred-twenty acres to manage. He was sorry not to see Pa before he died, but since the old man could no longer respond to anyone or anything, he would rather remember him as the robust man he was in his prime.

Wedding guests crowded into the hall of Emma's and Reuben's house, stood on the porch, packed the front and back parlors. Adam was amazed at how large the family had grown since he'd enlisted some six years before. Uncle Jake and Aunt Mary Jane were turned out in their Sunday best, although his aunt's somber costume, a dark blue spattered with tiny yellow polka dots was obviously purchased some ten years before. Adam's sister, Margaret, arrived from Cleveland accompanied by her daughter. It was well known in the family that Margaret had married well, and she dressed the part in a new amethyst colored gown with matching braid, a tight waist, and voluminous skirt. She was seven years older than Adam and his memories were of pleasant times together as they played soldiers or romped across the countryside, until Margaret at fifteen declared herself too old for such foolishness. About that time she began to interest him in books, making certain he could best the other children with his reading skills. Her effort led to her becoming a schoolteacher, a profession in which she remained until she married. Then, as was the custom strictly enforced by male school board members, she was forced to retire. They doggedly stuck to their policy of not hiring married teachers and forced those who secretly tried to break the rule to resign. She continued to encourage Adam in his reading, and from time to time sent him books.

Adam felt like an outsider at the wedding and recognized that he had been so engrossed in farm work and his father's care, he had largely ignored his relatives. He seldom visited his Uncle Sonny and Aunt Nell, both of whom he found unpleasant. Sonny was only a few years younger than Lizzie, but being the oldest boy in a family of seven, tended to lord it over everyone else. He had a flighty wife, who paid little mind to Adam as he grew from boyhood to adolescence and young manhood. Aunt Nell seemed to have trouble placing her nephew, so he learned early to greet her by reminding her straight away of his name. He'd heard Aunt Mary Jane and his mother make whispering remarks about Nell's ineptness in the kitchen and her lack of housekeeping skills, and surmised that they considered her slightly unbalanced. For the wedding she had gotten herself up in a beribboned bombazine dress far too showy for a country ceremony. Two of their children came with their own broods, but they remained outdoors during the reading of the wedding vows and appeared mainly interested in the eats. The families of his dead Aunt Sally, his mother's sister, were there too. He never knew his aunt, so the children being much older than Adam were never around much.

The food was spread outside on long tables made of planks and set up on sawhorses. Recently sewn cotton tablecloths made for a festive atmosphere in spring colors of yellow, orange, and green. That there was a slight chill in the air seemed not to bother any of the guests, who eagerly helped themselves to the bounty that Emma, Lizzie, and Fred's mother had spent days preparing. The groom's large family was there as well, but since they lived some six miles out of Four Corners in the opposite direction, Adam knew none of them.

Hunger soon overtook him, and he joined the crowd pressing toward the food-laden tables; then carrying his overloaded plate, he sat with Margaret and his mother at a table set aside for older folks. He finished the wedding feast and was relaxing before dessert when he saw her. Was this fetching woman, who glided toward the food tables smiling at folks, another relative? She seemed unfamiliar with the guests for she did not tarry to pass the time of day nor remark upon the weather or beauty of the bride. He decided she was probably a friend of Lucinda's. She had an elegant bearing, neither stooped nor untidy; her nearly blond hair was done up in a chignon on the top of her head. She had wide spaced, ice blue eyes and a saucy little nose that in no way dominated her face, like so many German noses. As if her face had been sculptured in ivory marble, a creamy complexion gave her the look of a lady unused to sun, cold, or harsh elements. He wouldn't be surprised if she was using extract of elderflower or some other concoction for her complexion and possibly lip salve made with lard and rosewater. He'd heard that some women resorted to such mixtures to keep their skin supple and their lips from cracking during inclement weather. Adam could barely take his eyes from this wondrous creature, and catching glimpses of her from time to time, considered how he might meet her without seeming overly forward. He managed to sidle up to her by the time she reached the dessert table.

Appearing unable to make a decision, she was standing before the array of honey cakes, chocolate sauerkraut cakes with mile-high frosting, wet-bottom shoofly pies rich with brown sugar and molasses, and cookies of every variety. "Hard to decide," he stood beside her studying the cakes, and he made certain it was the left side of his profile she would notice first, as he knew that to be an aristocratic one. Other girls had told him so.

"Yes," she replied. "I don't know when I've seen such a repast. I guess I'll take the hickory nut cake, or . . ."

"A wise choice. I know it to be a delightfully rich concoction made with buttermilk." Adam moved a bit closer; he could feel the heat of her body.

"Or," she repeated, "maybe the chocolate, but then . . ." She turned toward Adam and laughed. "You decide."

"I believe I would like the chocolate. May I cut you a piece?"

He sliced the cake and placed it on a plate, and as if it were a princely gift, presented it with a slight bow. She thanked him, smiled, and moved off. He quickly cut a slice for himself and hurried to catch up with her. "You from around here?" he asked.

"My no. I'm from Marietta. Lucinda included me today even though I am not family. I came here to care for my aunt who is very poorly. Lucinda used to look in on her, but between the wedding and my aunt's increasingly debilitating condition, it seemed wiser to have someone there night and day. I don't know a soul here except Lucinda and her family. She arranged for a neighbor to look in on Auntie and very kindly invited me today."

"I'm so glad she did." He smiled down at her while trying to see the fourth finger on her left hand to discern a wedding band. But she was still holding the plate, so to see it, he would have to bend down and look underneath, a far too awkward gesture at their first meeting. Instead, in nervous anticipation, he waited for her to finish the cake, then offered to take the empty plate. At the moment she handed it to him, he got a look at her hand. There was no golden band. Nor was the skin roughened. These were the hands of a lady unused to farm work.

"Wait for me. I'll be back," he said. He hadn't meant to be so forward, but risk had its rewards.

"I'm Adam Springer, the bride's uncle," he told her when he returned. "And you?"

"Martha Shipman. I'm pleased to meet you." When she smiled, her deep set, wintry blue eyes were alarmingly penetrating. He imagined they resembled the blue of glacial ice he'd once seen in a painted picture. "I'm going to miss Lucinda, as she is my only friend in this town, and now she will be living six miles away." Miss Shipman hurried on breathlessly. "We had wanted Auntie to come to our house in Marietta, where my mother and I could both see to her care, but she is a stubborn old lady and would have none of it. So here I am." She smiled up at Adam so winsomely that he was immediately overcome. He sensed a certain excitement growing within her as it was in him and strongly suspected he had finally found *his lady*, so before the magic spell was broken, he threw prudence away like an empty poke.

"Come I want to show you something," and taking her by the hand—a real breech of propriety at so recent a meeting—but no longer caring what people might think, he led her toward the front porch.

They arrived in the front parlor of Emma's house, now devoid of wedding guests, where he took her to stand in front of the mantle. "See this, see this little lady. She reminds me of you. I bought her for Emma," he lied, "because she is so lovely." They were alone in the room. He stared down at her with soft eyes, took in the gentle contours of her face, the sparkle in those strange eyes that told him she was as excited as he.

He was holding the figurine in his hand. Inside his heart was racing.

"She is lovely. Now I'm so glad I came. I didn't want to." Martha blurted.

He replaced the figurine on the mantle. Then turned to look at her, their eyes locking.

"Will you come to call?"

"Of course."

"I must go now, I promised to be back in two hours and the time has gone by much too fast. Is Sunday next all right?"

"If I can wait that long, that's a week. May I walk with you to your aunt's house?"

"If you don't mind what people might say."

"For heavens sakes; they're just family and a few neighbors. No one is paying any mind to us anyway; they're so taken with all the eats."

"First, I must take my leave of Lucinda and her groom."

"I'll meet you by the porch steps." Adam's heart was thumping like a hammer pounding hard upon a nail.

But they were wrong; someone was paying attention. Lizzie, her dessert fork halfway to her mouth with a piece of shoofly pie, let it pause in mid-air. When Martha left his side, Adam stood staring after her with a longing that he had felt for no other, except for the lady on the staircase, and that was simply wishful thinking. He came to his senses the instant his mother approached.

"She's not for you Adam," she said, sailing by.

"Now what do you mean by that?" He called to her departing back. "I thought you wanted me to find someone."

Lizzie seemed not to hear.

Nine

"Make sure my best shirt is clean for Sunday." Adam told his mother on washday.

"You going to church?" she asked brightly, her face wreathed in an anticipatory smile. Having decided that her remedy for Adam's melancholy was better than Dr. Kennedy's bottled one, Lizzie had been trying for months to get him back to services

"No, I'm going to be calling on Martha Shipman, Lucinda's friend."

"You mean that girl taking care of Mrs. Kimball."

"That's the one. I think I fancy her."

"Forget her. She's much too elegant for you."

"I'll be the judge of that." Adam answered her in a tone he did not generally use toward his mother. And for the next few days relations between them remained icy.

On Sunday, Martha's aunt, upon hearing that her niece was to have a gentleman come to call, rallied to sit in the parlor with them. Polite conversation regarding the weather, the state of the crops, recent deaths in town, and other mundane subjects soon palled. Only the clink of teacups on saucers broke the frequent silences. Perhaps she was as bored as they were, for Auntie soon drifted off, thus allowing the young lovers to tiptoe out of the room to the hall. Adam boldly took Martha into his arms, even as he knew the rules of courtship prescribed the gesture as premature. He didn't care and apparently neither did she. Martha willingly yielded to his embrace and lay her head upon his chest. "I can't wait another week for you to call," she whispered.

"Then please let me come again on Wednesday. I'll invent an excuse to come to town for something related to the farm and just happen to pass by."

Martha pulled away, and looking up at him, struggled with her answer. "If we could only be alone, but we can't. Auntie will never allow it."

"Maybe your neighbor could take care of her next week, and we could go for a buggy ride."

"No, Auntie wouldn't allow that either. I'm afraid we're doomed to tea and cakes in the parlor on Sundays, at least for a time. She is weakening fast. Just be patient, my dear Adam. Call again next Sunday, and I promise I will hold you in my heart 'til then."

Adam wanted to smother her in kisses but knew that might jeopardize what he instinctively recognized as a tenuous relationship. So with their hands clasped together they remained on the stiff-backed horsehair sofa until he took his leave at four o'clock, a time Martha considered appropriate, should any of the neighbors be watching his departure from their windows.

He visited on four consecutive Sundays. The routine for the next three remained the same with Auntie joining them in the parlor until the last one, when she stayed in her bed unaware of his impending visit or even that it was the Sabbath. "I didn't tell her," Martha smiled up at him, her arms tight around him. "A month is long enough to be so stringently chaperoned." Back again on the hard-cushioned horsehair sofa, they courted more energetically, though it was not the best arrangement for hugging and kissing. He felt the roundness of her breast and when she did not object desire drove him wild, and he blurted, "Martha, my darling, will you marry me?"

"Oh, Adam, yes, yes," then extricating herself from his embrace, she immediately added, her face luminous, "but first you will have to ask Father for my hand."

"I'll have to write to him," Adam said, "now that spring is here, I can't get away from the farm long enough to go to Marietta."

"With your father ill and Auntie going fast, perhaps we should wait a spell," Martha said, as if good sense had suddenly taken over, "but Adam I do love you so. I promise if Auntie doesn't go to her Lord and maker soon, I'll tell Father that someone else will have to be hired to see to her."

He left her that day with a lightness of being he had never before experienced; he felt he was drifting on a cloud of feathers. His melancholy lifted, and in idle moments, it was Martha he dwelt upon. She is a lady, no doubt about that, and she is pretty, not beautiful, but a nicely formed girl with a bright look about her that bespoke a certain intelligence. For a girl she is obviously well schooled, writes a fine hand, and speaks correctly. It seemed that nothing could hinder the weightlessness of his step, the joy he felt at being in love with Martha—so like *his lady*. Best of all, he felt that the incessant despair he'd lived with since the war's end might finally leave him.

John Springer breathed his last in late June 1868, one month after Martha agreed to marry Adam. It was as though the old man, in his comatose state, sensed his son's anxiety, and late in his seventy-fifth year, complied with his wishes. Adam was still in bed when his mother came to tell him of his father's passing. Then without further word, no suggestion of condolence, no sign of her own bereavement, she left him alone. The death had been expected as the old man's declining presence made him nothing more than a part of the sitting room décor, except when it was time to feed, bathe, change, or turn him. It was then that his sickly presence commanded their complete attention. Adam's relief was encompassed in an awesome sense of freedom, not unlike the day he was released from the Union Army for the second and last time.

He dressed quickly and went downstairs to take leave of his father. John Springer had always been somewhat remote from Adam. All of forty-eight when his son and last child was born, he was more like a grandfather than a father. Harsh with his reprimands, he was frequently put off by the mischievous deeds of a growing boy. As Adam stood by his father's deathbed, he thought how his once strong features were now slack and white with ghostly flesh falling from his strong-boned chin. As a younger man he had the indomitable look of his German ancestors with a hard edge to his jaw and flinty Nordic blue eyes that could blaze when anger invaded them. After drawing the sheet over his father's face, Adam said a prayer, albeit a small one, "God, please take him quickly into heaven, into your care." His grieving over in that small moment, he went to the kitchen to comfort his mother and found her at the table sipping tea. She had not, to his knowledge, shed a tear.

"You'd best be about going to the cabinetmaker for a casket, nothing fancy," she said, "also to the grave diggers. When you get back take the news to Jake, Mary Jane, and Sonny. And find out when the cabinetmaker will be ready for the body. Hurry now, because with the heat rising we want him out of here as soon as possible. You will go by Emma's house, of course."

Adam wondered had Lizzie loved him at all—this man who had claimed more than two thirds of her life? Or perhaps before grief set in, she was simply taking charge. He had heard it was different when her father and Adam's four-year-old brother, Sam, died. Aunt Mary Jane told him. "Lizzie mourned for days, sobbed and cried. Lordy, no one thought she would ever get over those two deaths."

Adam was preparing to leave when Lizzie reminded him of the family plot in the Lutheran Cemetery. "It's to the right of Sam's."

He knew that Sam was the small boy who died long before Adam was born. His mother once told him the child was always sickly, but he lived to be four years old. Each spring Lizzie laid fresh flowers over his grave on the anniversary of his birth. He wondered now, would she do the same for his father? For as long as he was a fixture in the parlor with his slop jar, bathing tub, pitcher, and wash basin, there was no way Adam could bring his beloved Martha to the farm. Now he was free to do so, but the more he contemplated that possibility, the more he saw how shabby and poor looking the place was. His mother, once so meticulous, was at seventy-three too worn out to see the torn covering on the rocker or notice the threadbare rug.

Adam made one more stop that morning. He went by the house where Martha was caring for her aunt. "I'd be obliged if you could come to the cemetery day after tomorrow about nine. But if you can't get away, I'll understand."

"I'll do my best; it depends on my neighbor. I'll ask her if she can care for Auntie in my absence. I suppose Emma would take me."

They were standing in the hallway. Time was short so he resisted pulling her down on the sofa, and kissed her lightly on the forehead.

"You can do better than that," she told him throwing her arms around his neck for a long kiss upon the lips.

Ten

The day of the funeral arrived. Emma and her Reuben and the children came with Lucinda and Fred in two buggies. There was room for one more. Glances at the roadway to see if Martha might be coming along late brought nary a sign of her, and she did not arrive at the house for the funeral supper provided by neighbors. Her absence sent a wave of worry through Adam. Could she have lost interest in him? Although he didn't want her to visit while his father was in the throes of death, there were enough mourners in the house to conceal its debilitated condition, what with aunts and cousins in their voluminous Sunday go-to-meeting dresses covering the worn settee and obscuring the soiled wallpaper. The house could discourage Martha's desire to live there. He was wild to have her—all of her—without the accouterments of corsets, petticoats, buttoned up dresses, and long pantaloons. He'd have to be about encouraging Ma to decorate a bit. Maybe put up new wallpaper. Only then would he bring Martha to the farm.

Bartholomew, Rachel's husband, who had gotten the call from the Lord as a young man, preached at the gravesite. Because of its dependence on itinerant preachers, the Jerusalem Church needed Bartholomew to give sermons on certain occasions. He was not an ordained Lutheran minister, but with the congregation's dependence on circuit riding preachers, Bartholomew was a handy substitute. He gave a sermon loud enough and full with what the fires of hell could mean for wrongdoers that parishioners left the church properly chastened for their sins.

Reading from the Bible, he recited the usual prayers that accompany the dead and then digressed. "This man, John, was my great friend, a man I could count on to help me in times of trouble, as I hope I might have helped him. He was strong and honest, a good husband and father, in short a credit to his maker. The day I helped him find his Lord and master, I can tell you, my friends, he was shouting happy. John loved our Lord with all his heart, and now as I commit him to the earth, we ask you dear God to take him personally into heaven to sit by your side for all eternity."

Adam listened uncomprehendingly. He didn't see his father as a religious man at all. Perhaps he had been at one time, but he rarely went to services, no matter how many times Lizzie entreated him to do so. Yet Bartholomew spoke as though

John had been a prayerful icon in his church. Had Adam missed something? True, he rarely paid much attention to his father's comings and goings; their relationship was always distant.

The mention of religion led Adam to think of Martha. What was her faith? So caught up were they in their lovemaking, the touches, kisses, they had never discussed it. He could feel the softness of her neck upon his lips even now, but while witnessing his father's descent into the grave; he abruptly ceased such unseemly ruminations. Still, his mind kept wandering to his own affairs. Now he supposed they could set a date for their nuptials. While Bartholomew intoned the Lord's Prayer at the end of the church service, a terrible thought occurred. Could Martha possibly be Catholic? If that were the case, their wedding would be out of the question. Ma would never live in the same house with a papist. He mused over the name Shipman. It didn't sound the least bit Irish, but one never knew. He'd have to get that settled along with the matter of the visit to her father in Marietta, a two-day trip by stage with an overnight stop at a hostelry each way. A river excursion entailed a ten-mile trip by buggy to Ebensport, overnight livery of several days for the horse and buggy. The stage would be cheaper.

Ma would insist on a time for mourning, and there was the matter of waiting for Mrs. Kimball to pass on. He felt that making Martha his wife was more like an obstacle course with family concerns strewn like thistles in their path. As his mind rambled over his own affairs, he barely noticed when the ceremony ended and the mourners began to move from the church to the gravesite. Gravediggers lingered in the background by the woods that separated the church burying ground from the Springer farm. Reuben and Emma saw to his mother, while Adam lingered to glance at the sandstone markers of other Springers, the stillborn sister, and Sam. He knew his mother had seven children; he must ask her what became of the seventh. There was no grave.

Adam thought of his father's death as the first day of his new life. He was twenty-seven, had found his true love; the farm was thriving as well as could be expected in the hilly, craggy county of Morgan; and the stand of timber on the Pineville property could provide him with extra money. For the first time he felt in a position to begin life as a married man. He had decided against going to Marietta to ask for Martha's hand, so all that remained was to write to her father of his desire to wed his daughter, but before that happened, as it frequently does, another death followed.

"I always say, look for another passing," Emma remarked when she told him Martha's aunt had gone to her maker. "Deaths come in three's."

"That's superstition," Adam said. "When did she pass on?"

"Five days ago. They've already buried her next to her husband in Black Oak Cemetery."

"When I called on Martha just after Pa passed, her aunt was unable to get out of bed, but I had no idea death was so near. With Pa's passing, I've been busy. I thought Martha might come to his funeral."

"I'm sure she was taken up with her own problems. It's not easy to call in a neighbor with death rattling in the loved one's throat." Emma went on with her explanation while Adam was eager to race down the street to claim his bride-to-be. "Mrs. Kimball was just too sick for her to leave, because Martha had asked if she could ride out with us. But then said she didn't dare leave her. Now it's all over for our Pa as well. The two of them had dealt with life long enough." Emma paused and gave her brother an unblinking stare "Do you have designs?"

"Designs?"

"Yes, with Martha."

"If you put it that way, I guess I do."

"Adam, she's a lovely girl, but I wonder, where would you live?"

"On the farm, of course. What else have I got to offer with Ma still around unless you take her in.?"

"I hardly have room."

"Even with Lucinda gone?"

"Clara still occupies that room. The sisters shared it. Maybe later when Clara marries, but she's only fifteen. And that tiny spare room would not be adequate for Ma. Anyway, she would never leave the farmhouse; she has too many years invested there."

"Doesn't make much sense to leave anyway. I've got to earn a living and farming is all I know, so I might as well hang on to the place, keep it running and satisfy Ma."

"That worries me a little. Martha is a city girl. Besides she comes from the monied classes. I doubt she's ever milked a cow, let alone helped with the planting. Anyway, she's English, and they don't do farm work, not like German girls. You never find English girls out in the field working beside their men. That's a well-known fact. Been repeated over and over. Can't you find a nice German girl who would be a helpmate with the farm?"

"But I love Martha, and I believe she loves me."

"Love can only carry a body so far. You're twenty-seven, old enough to know your mind. Martha is just eighteen. Girls her age are blinded by love. Yes, I know she is of marriageable age, but she is still in her girlhood. I doubt she has given any thought to life on that farm. Adam, it's isolated; the nearest neighbor is a half-mile away and the others a mile or more, and I don't think she'd have much in common with those Reisingers anyway. They're farm people; the parents have had no schooling, and that young Maude, the one closest to Martha's age, dropped out after third grade. Who would she have for a friend?"

"Why would she need a friend? She'd have me . . . and Ma."

"You know as well as I do that Ma can be difficult especially now that she is growing older—seventy-four her next birthday. That house she and Pa built will always be her home; her heart and soul are in it, although I don't think she ever liked being there all that much. She'd been off the farm in Virginia where the family once lived for some five years and was willing to leave that life behind in exchange for life in Frederick, but being a good wife had to go where Pa took her. Considering that they built the farmhouse around their original cabin, she does have a certain attachment to it. That place will never be Martha's, at least not until Ma passes. In that regard, she might be slowing, but she's still healthy as a horse."

"I don't see that as a problem." Adam turned to take leave of his sister. He didn't like the direction this conversation was taking, but added, as he went toward the door, "girls are used to living with their mother's-in-law. Speaking of Ma though," he paused, his hand resting on the wrought iron door latch. "I always thought she had seven children, but when we buried Pa there were only two graves in the burying ground, and there are four of us living. Where's the other one?"

"That child never even had a name. Ma was in a family way when they came here over the new National Road. It had just opened, courtesy of the federal government, to encourage pioneers to go west and settle. The roadbed was still very rough in places, and the jostling about must have been too much. She miscarried the child on the side of Laurel Mountain above Uniontown in Pennsylvania not far from Pittsburgh, and they buried the baby next to the roadside near a watering trough."

Adam finally took leave of his sister and went directly to see Martha. Walking along the street past the white frame houses of indeterminate style nailed together by a succession of local carpenters, he reprimanded himself about being hurt, even angry with Martha. Clearly, she had her hands full with her dying aunt. "How foolish of me to think otherwise, to think only of my own loss," he whispered aloud. Then another happy thought possessed him. His intended bride was not Catholic, as he had feared, but Methodist. At least he could assume she was, since the uncle and aunt were laid to rest at Black Oak cemetery. With the weight of these puzzling doubts lifted, he walked jauntily down the street and up the steps to the front door. Before he could lift the knocker, the door flew open so suddenly that he was nearly knocked over as Martha pulled him into the hall and threw her arms around his neck. He bent to kiss her full on the mouth.

"Adam we're alone at last." They fell into each other's arms with a passion that neither could resist. But when he fumbled with the tiny cloth covered buttons on her blouse, she pulled away. "Oh God, we can't," she said. "We musn't sin. We must wait to take our marriage vows. Dear Adam, when can we be married? I can barely wait."

"If I didn't have to ask your father for your hand, and spend time mourning our losses, we could be married in a few months. I don't think Ma is going to make me wait for six months on account of Pa's death. She already thinks I'm past marriageable age. What about you?"

"I've decided I will not mourn six months for my aunt, although my mother would think a year more appropriate. I've had a letter from her and a box containing a black dress, which she says I must wear for the next year. Oh Adam, I don't want to be courting in death weeds. I look awful in black. I don't care what my folks or the neighbors say. I won't wear that ugly old thing after Father leaves."

"He's coming here?"

"Yes, this afternoon by the stage. He's planning to take me back to Marietta. Dear Adam, I can't stand being away from you. What am I to do?"

"I'll ask for your hand and suggest that you stay here in your aunt's house until the mourning is over."

"You don't know my father; he'll never agree to a girl living alone in a strange town."

"Plenty of widows and spinsters do."

"But I'm neither." She smiled up at him fetchingly; "maybe I could get pregnant, now today?"

"God, no. We can't do it that way. That would bring so much shame upon our families, we could never live it down. Many of the farm girls resort to such a method; it's easy enough to do, but Ma still thinks she's someone special, that her family is above all that and would have a tizzy-fit. We would never hear the end of it. We'd have to leave, go far away, and then what would I do?" He studied her beseeching face, her hand fluttered to her collar and to his amazement, she began to unbutton her bodice. "But at the same time I can barely resist," he said, wishing that she would lay open those buttons down past that luscious bustline. Like rusted fasteners, those dratted buttons resisted even her touch.

"I think there is a way we can have each other but not quite," he said fumbling with the button at her waist. Where is the bedroom?"

"We can't go that far today even as I want to; Father will be arriving within the hour when the stage arrives. There's not enough time, and I want our first time to be a long loving. I only wish you had come by sooner."

Adam was now in a frenzy the likes of which he could hardly bear; he tried to calm himself. It would never do to have her father find him there with her alone, let alone naked in bed. "Why is he coming anyway? Just to fetch you?" Reason began to settle in over the passion that permeated his loins.

"He wants to settle matters pertaining to the house and see to his sister's estate, so he will be going to the lawyer in McConnelsville while he's here. There will be ample time for you to speak to him; I'll make certain of that."

"He'll be asking me all kinds of questions: where we will live, and how will I support you?" As the more mundane business of living took over, Martha began to rebutton her bodice and pulled away from him. All at once he noticed that the house was musty smelling; the odor of death lay about like a shroud enveloping the faded upholstery of once loved furnishings. He wanted to leave, to take Martha away before having to face her father. Why did their decisions have to be so caught up in the whims of others? His mother didn't even know of his intentions to marry Martha, and so caught up was he in the gloom that surrounded them that he barely heard her prattling on excitedly.

"I've been wondering if we could build a house on the land your Uncle Jacob gave you, that eighty acres near Pineville. I'd like to live near a larger town. There is a Methodist Church and a number of stores, a tearoom, and better schools. Of course, I'd prefer that you come to Marietta, or at least purchase a farm nearby, even though land near there is very dear. Maybe Father could help out, if farming is what you intend to do. You could sell your farm here. It would be easy, but if you insist on staying, the land near Pineville might do. Could you take me to see it?" When she got through this recitation, she was breathless.

Eleven

When General Grant proceeded to the East to take command in Virginia, he was succeeded in the Southwest by General Sherman who began his forward movement at the head of 98,799 soldiers and 254 guns. Atlanta was the immediate object . . .

Adam met with Martha's father the day before their scheduled trip, and somehow in all this his plan for taking her to the farm was mislaid. There would have been time, but he put the matter off. When he told his mother he intended to ask for Martha's hand, she set her face in a surly mask. Attired in a worn housedress ripped under the arm, her hair pulled back in the tight bun, she looked like somebody's servant. The rents in the curtains were obvious, and the rugs were so thin the floorboards underneath turned footsteps into miniature thunderclaps. Mr. Shipman would be appalled at the shabby appearance of both his mother and the farmhouse, and being a city man, he would not be impressed with the well-planted fields. Sturdy shoots of corn and wheat were already thrusting tender heads above the soil, but he sensed that Martha and her father would be unmoved by how they got there. They would never understand that he had walked every row behind the plow starting at the middle of the field, then back furrowing so not a bit of it was trodden over to be followed the next day by the harrow. Would they know that it was necessary for the ground to warm to just the right temperature before planting to encourage speedy germination of the seeds? Would they care about any of this or have an opinion about planting corn in drills or hills? Would they think him unlearned, because he saw only the rumps of the team for days on end from plowing to planting, and the spreading of manure, lime, and ashes? Did they care if he fought off insects, set traps for varmints, brought down chicken hawks from the end of a shotgun? What kind of work did her father do anyway? Martha never said.

Adam was unprepared for the imperious presence of the man he hoped to call father-in-law. Well spoken with a loud dictatorial voice, Mr. Shipman thrust his hand out and grabbed Adam's with a firm lock, a lock that momentarily stunned him with its ferocity.

"So you want to ask for my daughter's hand?"

"Yes, sir."

"And what, may I ask, can you offer her?" The man's large paunch, a sign of prosperity, featured a wide gold watch fob that rose and fell across the broad expanse with every breath.

Adam wished he had prepared his remarks but managed to utter: "love, respect, a fine farm home. I'm a hard worker."

"Education?"

"Eighth grade."

"That didn't prepare you for much in a state already noted for its large number of colleges."

"No, sir, but I had two enlistments in the Ohio Volunteers with the Grand Army of the Republic, marched under Generals Grant and Sherman."

"And you survived. That must mean you are somewhat wily in being able to preserve yourself. Great generals, both of them."

"Yes, sir."

"Were you with Sherman in Atlanta?"

"I was. We burned it unmercifully."

"And what did you think of the great southland?"

"At first I hated those people for what they were doing to the Union, to break it apart and kill our fine young men in the process; then I began to feel sorry for them in their misguided efforts. They had a lifestyle—at least the wealthiest did—like no other I could imagine, with slaves in their houses and thousands more laboring in the fields. Those darkies were unpaid men and women who worked from dawn until well into nightfall. If they objected, they were whipped. I saw some with heavy scars across their backs. Their homes were lowly shacks with dirt floors, cold in winter, baking in summer. They had no hope of ever getting out of slavery or seeing anything better for their children who could be sold by their masters like calves. I did begin to understand why the southerner hung on so doggedly. If the situation had been reversed, I suppose we would have too. That life was a lot to sacrifice, but you can't hold another man in bondage, even if his skin is black."

"I gather you have a good mind. Pity you didn't do more with it. You speak well. How did you come by such learned English in this farm country, where I see so many people fracturing what the mother country so generously gave us—its language?"

"My mother, sir. She is a well-spoken woman, well-read too, as was her father before her."

"German, I understand."

"Yes sir. My great grandfather emigrated. For his time he was fairly learned too. At least he could read and write."

"Umm. I'll wager you probably are a hard worker."

"I am that."

"And you are not a carouser, given to strong drink, dancing, cards, or cavorting with women?"

"No, sir." Adam now thought it necessary to stretch the truth a bit, although he neither danced nor played cards, which his mother referred to as devil's tools.

"Your faith, my boy?"

"Lutheran."

"Attend church regularly."

"Yes, sir." Another stretch of the truth. He hadn't been to services in six months.

"And how large is your farm?"

"One-hundred-sixty acres, plus I own that eighty acres we are going to see tomorrow near Pineville."

"That's a goodly amount."

Adam hastened to add, lest Mr. Shipman think he was somehow deceiving him, "although I haven't done much with that property. There has been so much farm work with my Pa ailing. He died only a month ago, so I have some catching up to do. But I assure you I will take good care of your daughter. We may have to live a short spell on the farm, but someday I will build her a fine home worthy of her charm and abilities." Adam felt he was rushing to spit it all out before Mr. Shipman took him in some direction he did not want to go, like his mental state. Lately his nightmares had resurfaced and there seemed to be no remedy, no magic potion from Dr. Kennedy that didn't want to rip up his stomach or make him a slave to its enchanting promise. Adam had never mentioned any of this to Martha and guessed she saw him as a tall, handsome young man, generally happy with no flaws. He had tried not to show the ugly side of himself, his temper and sulky disposition. Martha never mentioned the war to him and that was just as well. Like most young girls of her standing, unless a husband or lover had gone off to fight, she had little interest in whether the Union won or lost.

Mr. Shipman began pacing the parlor floor, his ruddy face contorted in thought. He ran his hand over his bald pate. "I'll be honest, Adam, I had hoped for my daughter's marriage to someone of her social class, a lawyer, as I am, perhaps. But she will have none of it. I have tried to reason with her. Her mother is most upset at this turn of events, for she envisioned her Martha in a fine city home with magnificent furnishings, enjoying a life of ease with servants—servants who are paid, to be sure. Sadly, you offer none of these. I've tried to tell Martha that farm life is a hard life, but she is young and cannot see it. I will not cease in trying to persuade her otherwise; however, if I fail, you have my blessing. There are some conditions I expect you to honor. I insist that she be allowed to visit us in Marietta, where she has a brother and two sisters, as well as her mother and me. And I demand that she come at least twice a year. We have no intention of giving her up. You understand?"

"Yes, sir."

"And further, I suggest that you look into becoming a Methodist, as she is, for I do not like to see a house divided, especially when there are children to consider, as I assume there will be."

"Do you promise?"

"I do."

Now there would be another problem. This one with Ma, who would not condone switching over to a faith she related to being English, not German.

Four months later Adam repeated those words, *I do,* not in the country Lutheran Church which he had suggested early in their engagement, but in the parlor of Martha's home in Marietta. No one from his family was present. Emma begged off; she said the trip was too long and too expensive what with four nights in hostelries, two on the road and two in town. His mother said she was not up to the trip. "Besides what money I have needs to be spent on curtain fabric. You can see the rents in our window hangings would be a turnoff for a young bride, especially one used to all manner of frippery and finery," she voiced between gritted teeth.

Mrs. Shipman barely acknowledged his presence after their initial introduction. Adam thought it wise to stay out of her way. He spent most of his time in a rocker on the front porch, where he could observe the large, rather fussy houses across the street set in tight conformity one to another: each with a wrap-around porch and a yard exactly the size of the others in contrast to the large expanses of green around the houses in farm country. Not even Martha came to talk to him, so busy was she preparing for the wedding.

He had left Four Corners for Marietta with a neighboring farmer, who was transporting his corn to market in McConnelsville and slept that night in a local inn, where he picked up the stage to Marietta the next day. The money in his pocket came not from crops but from the timber sold off his Pineville property. Faced with the need to purchase a wedding vest and fancy shirt, Adam decided not to tell Martha about the timber sale. She had a citified attitude toward a forest, while Adam's family saw all those trees as something to be rid of in order to make the land productive.

"I just love those big old trees," she had said when he took Martha and her father to view the Pineville property. They had seen it well timbered. One tree was so large an old timer had said *it must be nigh onto three hunnert years, 'spect it would make plenty o' boards for a house, just itself.* The tree was part of the original stand, a hearty oak, and Adam chose to spare it. Indeed, he treated it like an old gentleman to be forever revered. It gave the small section a settled look with its wide canopy that shaded much of the area near the creek that cut through the property. Martha said it would provide wonderful shade for the house she envisioned.

That day she had run about like a willful child stepping out the confines of the dwelling: "the parlor here, the sitting room behind, and the kitchen over there. Oh Adam, I'm so excited." She chose the upper pasture for the house, "so that we will have a view of the creek, but not be subject to rising water." She had to know that was a possibility for Marietta was situated at the confluence of the Ohio and Muskingum Rivers, both subject to flooding in rainy seasons. A series of locks and dams built in 1836 helped to keep the water controlled while improving navigation. The Shipman home, however, had never been in danger of raging floodwaters, for as happens with better families, their hilltop mansion overlooked the less distinguished houses of the common workers below.

When Adam saw her home the first time, an uneasy panic jarred him. Here was a wedding cake of a house, sparkling white, with porch trim of carved bric-a-brac around the posts and under the roofline, an effect that gave the impression of lace. A mansion—at least he thought it was a mansion—but Martha said it was only a house. There was a wrap-around porch and a bay used as a music room. Martha had told him she played the piano, and Adam thought she and Lizzie would have their music in common. Inside the Shipman house, the furniture, mostly walnut and cherry, was further enhanced by inlays of carved poplar or other exotic woods. There was a mishmash of satin and horsehair settees further enhanced with carved grapes and leaves embellishing the wooden parts. Remembering the fine taste of the English in the south, Adam regarded the embellishments as intrusive reminders of the heavy splendor of the English court; a court presided over these past thirty-one years by Queen Victoria herself. Rugs in a riot of mismatched patterns, here diamonds, there squares, and sometimes flowers and vines in a confusion of colors on burgundy backgrounds, lay about the floors. Knickknacks were everywhere. There were small table rugs of an oriental nature, figurines, bowls of imitation fruit, pictures in ornate golden frames, and gilt tinged dishes for holding tiny cakes. Adam had trouble deciding where to look.

Martha seemed too busily done up as well. In Four Corners, her clothes were simple; there was no profusion of bows, laces, and underpinnings. Now the effect of these accouterments made her seem larger than he remembered. She wore a crocheted flounce with tiny pleats that gathered on a vanilla colored velvet ribbon at her throat. Puffed sleeves and all the horizontal braids and ruffles tended to diminish her already short stature. The memory of *his lady on the stairway* surfaced. She had been statuesque, her clothing simple, more flowing than busy. All this ostentation both on Martha and in the Shipman house brought him more doubts. Adam thought of backing out.

As he rocked back and forth on the porch and looked toward the town below, it occurred to him that it would be easy to board one of the many boats making its way up river toward Ebensport. The rivers, sparkling like streams of crystal, shimmered below him. Both beckoned: the Muskingum would take him home, the Ohio offered access to the new continent and escape from his tortured, ordinary life. He could go west, find a new beginning, maybe ranch, become a cowboy. Since the war, as soon as a territory reached a population of sixty thousand, it became a state. Intrepid pioneers were going west to Iowa, Kansas, Minnesota, Oregon, Nevada, Texas, California—all new states since he was born. Most pioneers were his age or younger, although he'd read about several generations of entire families simply packing up and leaving secure locales in which their ancestors had settled. During nights when sleep would not come, he considered each one as a possible destination and could recite the new states in order of their admittance to the Union. But there was always some obstacle to his leaving: his aging parents, his livelihood, and the roof over his head the farm provided, lack of money.

Twelve

On arriving in Marietta, Adam found he would not be staying overnight at the Shipman house; those rooms were reserved for near relatives from Louisville and Pittsburgh. Mr. Shipman had engaged a room for him at the LaBelle Hotel on Ohio Street, which faced the river and levee. He was pleased not to share a room with an unwashed traveler and grateful for its simple décor with a washstand, single bed, one window, a kerosene lamp on the battered dresser, and a straight backed chair, but he deplored having to spend the money for his night's lodging. At the registration desk, Adam had inquired if the room tariff had been paid.

"No, sir." That will be seventy cents for this evening.''

Adam took the coins from his change purse. When he mounted the stairs and entered the room, he began to tremble, not unlike he felt in going into his first battle at Fort Donelson. Was it the money? His supply would soon run low. Tavern food was dearer than he remembered, and he had been surprised to find that the stagecoach ride from McConnelsville had gone up in price. Or perhaps it was Martha and the prospect of marriage causing his anxiety.

That night in the tavern room he engaged several young men at the table in conversation and soon discovered they were peddlers full of tales of their travels. Ever since dining with Jeremiah, Adam had longed to know more about these knights of the road, still considered low class by the better sorts. One of his table companions sold anvils, another crackers by the barrel, and the third offered a line of sewing goods. When Adam told them he was a farmer, one remarked that after growing up poor in the country he was glad to now be city folk. Envying their lives on the road and their debonair manner, Adam almost asked how he could get a job like theirs, then reality poured over him like a dumped pail of water, and he thought of Martha.

There was much concern among these men over the impeachment proceedings of the nation's president, Andrew Johnson. Several said it was no fit action for a country that had just been through a terrible war to be splitting itself up again. They expressed pleasure over the recent addition of dining cars on trains, and there was considerable indignation over the impending establishment of the Prohibition Party, new to American politics. "If a fellow can't have drink after a long day on the road, I don't know what this country is coming to," one of them offered. Adam remembered the evening with Jeremiah and laughingly agreed.

He slept fitfully and awoke with the knowledge that frequent wakefulness had left him with a mere four hours sleep. Not since he faced the enemy close enough to see their faces had he felt such unease, such terror at what he was about to do. Yet he loved Martha; he was certain of that. And God knows he needed a wife. Ma wouldn't be around forever to see to the washing, cooking and cleaning, the garden, chickens and hogs; he wanted children and someone to share his bed. If it was money or the lack of it that put him into this state, he needn't have worried about the trip back to the farm. Martha told him on his arrival, "Father is handling the travel cost as part of our wedding gift." Still when he awoke the next morning before going to breakfast, hesitation crept over him again: he could turn back, take the stage or find a river boat and go home to his plain bedroom in the plain farmhouse he called home.

Maybe he was one of those men never meant to marry, a man like Uncle Jake, but like many a doubting groom, something held him from fleeing. When he heard a stirring like someone sweeping in the hallway, he opened the door to ask the maid if hot water was available.

"Hot water's in the washroom down the end of the hall." She was a fetching girl, and her smile was less come-hither than a warning *to be careful*; it wouldn't do to get mixed up with the likes of her on his wedding day. Adam stood in the doorway while she swished down the hall, her black skirt swaying invitingly from side to side. She was not more than sixteen, and obviously on the lookout for a husband. At that age, they all are. He closed the door and turned the lock.

After bathing and washing the travel dust from his hair, he breakfasted in his traveling clothes and, in the interest of saving money, decided to forego dinner. Since a sign in the room told him the time for checking out was noon, he took his suit and belongings to the front desk, where the clerk agreed to hold them until time to change. Martha had cautioned that he must not see her until the ceremony, so he walked along the street fronting the river, stopping every so often to look in the windows of stores selling tonics, dry goods, hardware, and clothing among other modern wonders. He bought a penny newspaper and found a place to sit along the levee where boats plied the great Ohio River on their way south to the Mississippi and north on the Ohio to Pittsburgh, or to Zanesville on the Muskingum. He could see why those early pioneers chose this spot for their town, the first in the Northwest Territory.

As a schoolboy, he had learned something about those times, but had not thought much about them in all these years. Now sitting at the very site, upon which the first forty-eight Ohio settlers had landed, he remembered a few facts about the state his stern eighth grade teacher, Miss Blankenbuhler, had voiced to her students. "There were surveyors, boat builders, carpenters, a blacksmith, and several common workmen who had been assembled as far away as Boston in the year of our Lord 1787," she'd said. After all those years, he could still hear Miss Blankenbuhler's firm voice with which she kept control over her class of unruly boys anxious to be shut of school. "The directors of the Ohio Company were meeting at the Bunch of Grapes Tavern," she went on, "when in came the Reverend Mannassah Cutler with the news that a contract for a million acres of land north and west of the Ohio River had been drawn up with the Board of Treasury. This was the initial endeavor to open the vast western lands to settlement," Miss Blankenbuhler told her class. She called on Adam and several other boys and the occasional girl to repeat her words. Then she continued with more facts, which several more students were expected to remember and recite. No one knew which ones would be asked, but none dared to be unprepared. Miss Blankenbuhler wielded a mean paddle. She always ended her speech with, "If it had not been for those intrepid men and farseeing members of the Ohio Company, not one of you would be living here today." That line always told generations of indifferent students that the recitation was over.

The party had arrived at the mouth of the Muskingum to this very place, where Adam sat taking the air and thinking upon his own future. He felt insignificant and wondered why he didn't have the resolve for setting out to the unknown like those men did? From this point beside the river, it would be so easy. Then he thought of Ma and Martha. Both had, with their womanly tentacles, somehow trapped him like a fish in a net.

At three o'clock Adam went back to the hotel to collect his suit and grip. He needed to use the water closet, and it was a pleasant change not to have to go outdoors. Not having seen one indoors before, he wondered how the contraption could possibly work. That morning, unsure of using this newfangled device, he had gone to the hotel outhouse. Now he inspected the water closet closely. There was a wooden tank overhead from which a pull chain dangled. The instructions said to yank the chain. He did so timidly. Nothing happened; he yanked again, harder. A flap valve opened; water splashed into a pipe with such velocity that he jumped back as the bowl filled quickly flushing the contents away.

Believing it was better to have bodily waste taken care of far from the house, he had serious misgivings about the contrivance and hoped Martha, with her citified ways, would not insist on one. Indoors was no place for a water closet with its attendant smells. There was a heavy metal tub in the washroom, but he'd had a bath the past Saturday night, so considered his morning wash sufficient. He donned his new drawers, shirt, wedding vest, and suit, the same one he had worn at Lucinda's wedding, and for the occasional times he went to Lutheran services. He polished his teeth, gave his hair a good comb, rolled up his travel clothes and stuffed them into the grip along with his heavy day boots. Then he added his grandfather's gold pocket watch and heavy chain to his vest. His mother had presented them to him before he set out for Marietta. "I've had them all these many years since Pa died," she told him. "I took the watch to the watchmaker in Pineville to be cleaned and fixed as your wedding present." Lizzie had held the watch by its chain and jiggled it up and down. "He didn't go in for anything cheap," she said, "see it's very heavy gold. Pa always liked nice things. Some people called him a dandy, and Mama acted ashamed when they did. I never quite knew why, but I knew he was never a manly man." He checked his vest pocket for the plain gold band he had bought with money from a timber sale on the Pineville property. Then setting out, leather grip in hand, Adam strode purposely to meet his future as a married man. He passed the hotel's front desk, where the day clerk suggested he might want to summon a hackman to take him to Fourth Avenue. But Adam decided the money he would save by walking precluded arriving at his future in-laws in style. He thanked the clerk and said he needed the exercise.

"I spect you'll get plenty o' that before this night is over." The clerk gave him a knowing grin. Adam could only hope he was right.

Martha's brother, George, whom Adam had never met before they stood together in front of the parlor bay window to await the bride, served as best man, while Martha's sister, fourteen-year-old, Effie, stood as maid of honor. Due to her delicate condition, Martha's pregnant sister, Louisa, was confined to an upstairs bedroom and could not attend. Louisa's husband, Emmet, was present, as were various aunts, uncles, cousins, and the neighbors along with several of Martha's girlfriends. Adam passed pleasantries with one of them before the ceremony and learned that Martha had attended Marietta College for a year before being sent by her father to her aunt in Four Corners.

"She really didn't want any part of that old lady," one of the girls whispered to Adam. "Martha claims she can't stand sick people or old ones either, but her Papa made her go anyway. Was she ever miffed about that, but look what happened! She met you." A little batting of generous dark blond eyelashes followed, but Adam didn't quite know how to interpret what the girl was telling him. Were her words meant to be a compliment? Sister Effie, whom Adam thought, was something of a chatterbox, added, "Martha threw a tizzy-fit, but Father would have none of it. He said a girl doesn't need a college education anyway, so she might as well put in some time taking care of a house, because she'll just get married anyway. And I guess he was right, 'cause here she is marrying you." Adam was not used to coquettish girls who said one thing and obviously thought another. He sensed they saw him as a bumpkin, unwashed, and unread.

Their remarks led him to think that Martha might be using him to get even with her father. Was Martha showing him that she would, henceforth, be the one to decide her future? He noticed she and Mr. Shipman appeared rather distant, and on the day Adam took them to see the Pineville property they had little to say to one another. Martha was obviously closer to her mother, spoke of her more often, and the two could be heard chattering away, as women do, to the exclusion of the men in the family.

A vigorous organ chord silenced the chattering guests and brought Adam to attention as if ordered to do so by a commanding general. Martha entered from the back parlor on her father's arm, and together they moved in measured cadence toward him; her face was radiant—he felt certain it was joy—but looked again and thought it might be paint, so heightened was the color of her cheeks. Certainly no God fearing Methodist girl would resort to procedures used by ladies of the night whose glories faded early. Mr. Shipman was unsmiling; he never once looked at Adam as he escorted his daughter toward the pastor. Pious and stern, Reverend Martin held the Holy Bible open in bony hands that went with his gaunt body. He summoned Adam to stand before him and watched unsmiling as the bride and her father approached. She wore an ivory dress of shimmering embroidered silk, so tight at the waistline that Adam assumed she must have been wearing one of those dreadful boned corsets. Its skirt, widened at the bottom by a crinoline, brushed over the ankles of the guests seated along the aisle. Her luminous smile erased all his previous worries, and he wondered at those foolish doubts he had entertained the day and night before. Adam was, however, still troubled by the few minutes of conversation he had with the pastor prior to the ceremony.

75

"I understand you are a Lutheran," he'd said. "Now, of course, we expect that you will join Martha's church. There is a Methodist Church in Four Corners named Black Oak. You can join that congregation, and the sooner the better once you return to the country." It was more of an order than a request, and Adam hadn't answered, just stared at the floor and let uncertainty wash over him.

The ceremony was over in a matter of minutes. Adam slipped the gold band on Martha's finger; they kissed judiciously, and together led the wedding party, parents, and guests to the dining room where a lavish repast awaited. Martha's father toasted the couple with green tinged, fruited punch amply laced with whipping cream. "To the health and happiness of our bride and groom; may they revere each other and bring forth children in our Lord's image and remain together for all their days in peace and good will."

Adam wondered if he really meant his words, but quickly dismissed his concern and turned his attention to the bountiful table. He didn't recognize some of the food. The resplendent silver trays bore none of the familiar edibles typical of a German celebration—no sauerbraten, wursts, sausages, sauerkraut, or schmeerkasse. Here on the Shipman's gleaming damask-covered mahogany table, stretched to its utmost by added leaves, was a tray of anchovy toasts, an oyster loaf, and jellied chicken, along with squash and peanut pies. There were fried cucumbers and pickled green beans dribbled over with herbs. The bride's cake, aptly named Lady Cake, was a towering affair turned out on a silver platter with rivulets of rich dark chocolate drizzled over fluffy white frosting.

"You look so startled," his new mother-in-law swept by him in a swish of crinoline. "Are you not used to such fine victuals?" Before he could answer she added. "No, I suppose being German you're not."

"I'm sure they are very tasty," he mumbled and felt the vitality he had experienced moments before, when his lips met Martha's, drain from his very soul. He cast a wary eye at the guests to see if he might find one like himself, but the men were standing in little clutches speaking of business affairs. The women gathered in threes and fours; their silk grenadines challenging each other with silken ruffles bound with colorful edgings, some rose-colored, others in yellow and blue attached to billowing skirts. A profusion of bows at the loopings of the overskirts, upon the sleeves, and on the shoulders added to the flamboyance of their attire. And there was not a gown without a bustle. Would Martha wear hers in the country? Not one woman he knew sported such finery, not even in church. Likely Ma and her set would say they were putting on airs, if they did. Martha flitted about among the guests talking animatedly about matters they shared to the exclusion of Adam, who might as well have been a flyspeck on the flocked wallpaper.

After tea and coffee were served, the bride and groom were toasted once more, and amidst much cheering led the guests to the center hallway where they proceeded slowly to the first stair landing. While accompanied by boisterous cheering and hoo-hawing on the part of the guests, much to Adam's embarrassment, they turned and waved to everyone before proceeding up the last dozen steps to the wide center hallway toward Martha's bedroom. Had Martha's brother, George, not summoned Adam to the library midway through the festivities, where he opened a bottle kept hidden behind several large books on a shelf, Adam might have lost his nerve. "Here," George said, "you'll need it before the night is over," and he poured an ample amount into Adam's cup. Adam drank it quickly and returned to the dining room for a second, smaller ration of punch, then retreated to the library for another dollop, generously poured by his new brother-in-law, who gave his own cup a shot as well.

"Methodists are a dour lot," George offered. "Even Father keeps a bottle here. He also keeps it secret." Feeling a strong need to relax for what he was about to undertake, Adam, upon assuring himself that no one was noticing, had a third shot devoid of the punch and soon found himself dwelling even more intently on what was ahead. He was, however, unprepared for the encumbrances he would be obliged to face.

Inside the door to Martha's bedroom, he was overcome with the massiveness of the carved walnut furniture, especially the bed's headboard, which rose three-quarters of the way toward the ten-foot ceiling. Everything in the room matched the bed: chiffonier, dressing table, chair, and all were festooned with carved grapes, intertwining branches and leaves. "Everything matches, but there is no washstand," he commented.

"We have a washroom across the hall with water, soap, and towels, everything a body needs for keeping reasonably clean. There is another commode there as well, but we shall soon be rid of that as Father is looking to install a water closet. Won't that be wonderful? I hate that old outhouse. And if you need a bath, Mary, the servant girl, will fetch water from the cistern, heat it in a bucket, and bring it upstairs to the tub. Afterward, she'll see to emptying it. Just let her know by pulling the cord that rings the kitchen bell." Martha reached her arms out to him, "Oh Adam, I'm so happy. We're alone together at last. You can get ready for bed, while I change in the washroom."

They were now man and wife leading Adam to wonder why the privacy. He would like to have watched her prepare for bed. He was frantic to see what would emerge from under all the finery.

When he was alone in the room Adam removed his wedding suit, and lest the sight of his privates shock her, stripped down to his drawers. The outhouse was at the rear of the property; he had used it several times while at the Shipman home and thought of doing so now, but didn't want to face the guests or a family member who might also be so inclined. Instead, he used the slop jar, a dainty little pot, which he pulled from under the bed. When he was finished, he replaced the lid and shoved the bowl out of sight, where he assumed Martha would find it and empty it in the morning. His mother had always done that for the family as one of her wifely duties. Or in this house was that the job of the maid? Adam crawled into the bed and propped his head on the fat pillow, thick with goose down, reminding him of the thinning pillows at home. He'd have to ask Ma to restuff them with new goose down. Why hadn't he thought of that before? He crossed his hands over his chest and awaited his beloved, and waited, and waited some more. He studied the embroidered borders on the white cotton sheets that had been ironed so crisply; they appeared to have come directly from the store. Why was it taking her so long to get out of her wedding dress: those miniature silk-covered buttons no doubt? It seemed he was always being flummoxed by a set of tiny buttons. He was now in a frenzy to possess her. What was taking so long? She had gone into the washroom across the hall a half-hour ago. If she didn't come soon, he would go and fetch her. Realizing that would be an ungentlemanly thing to do, he snuggled deeper into the pillow and waited.

When she came into the room, she was wearing a filmy affair that hung in folds away from her body with lace at the cuffs and around the collar. She removed it slowly and stood in front of him with only her nightgown between his desire and her body. Falling into bed she gave herself freely as though she had been as anxious as he was. When the petting and lovemaking were over, he lay back as satisfied as he had ever been. She lay on her side, her body shaking, and when he rose up to see why, she was crying.

"What's wrong," he asked.

"Oh, it's nothing, dear Adam, nothing at all. I'm just overwhelmed and so very tired. I didn't know it would hurt so much."

He kissed the side of her face; she did not turn over for more as he expected she might do, so he lay back and considered that she was probably exhausted.

Thirteen

In the morning when Adam awoke, Martha was gone from the bed. He relieved himself in the slop jar, still not emptied from the night before, and after washing up across the hall, dutifully carried it to the privy. After dumping its contents, he washed the jar at the cistern, and returned to the bedroom by way of the back stairs. It was really up to Martha to empty it, but he decided that would be a poor way to introduce her to married life; emptying slop jars and pails would come soon enough. There was considerable chattering in the kitchen as he passed by on the stairway, but no one seemed aware of his presence.

He packed his few clothes in the grip and smoothed his hair before going down the front staircase, where Martha greeted him with a quick kiss and a hug. "Time for breakfast," she took his arm and together they went into the dining room, where another lavish repast greeted them. This was more to his liking: scrambled eggs, a rasher of bacon, crusty hash-browned potatoes, sweet cinnamon rolls, fresh creamery butter, sliced peaches and pears and various cheeses. Martha joined him, and together they ate their first breakfast together. Afterwards, they repaired to the parlor where the array of gifts was waiting to be packed.

Martha sat at a small lady's desk. "Adam, you can begin wrapping the fragile things and putting them in that trunk Father thoughtfully supplied, while I write down the names of the givers, so I can pen them notes of thanks." There were glass candleholders and a silver turkey-dressing spoon. A china lamp in two parts, the bottom for the oil and the top for a matching china shade in the shape of a ball, was half in and out of its box.

"Wrap that carefully in this flannel," Martha handed him the cloth. "It's very fragile. I plan to put it in our bedchamber."

Bedchamber! A quick image materialized in Adam's mind. That room accommodated only a chifforobe and a double bed. There was only one small table beside the rocker in front of the west window. Surveying the array of gifts that sat on every table and chair in the parlor, he wondered where they would put them all at the farmhouse. There was even a china set for twelve with serving dishes, platters, and casseroles. Except for one complete place setting, which had been exhibited on the gift table, it remained in it's own barrel. They were completing the packing when Mr. Shipman, his usual stern face seeming to dismiss Adam as part of the décor, appeared in the doorway. He took his gold watch from his vest pocket and reminded them that they had only four hours before they must leave for the packet boat.

"I thought we were returning to Four Corners by stage." Adam set down a carafe he was wrapping, a bit noisily he realized the moment its bottom touched the tabletop so hard the lid rattled.

"Please be careful." Martha cautioned in a more commanding than entreating tone he had not heard her use before. "No, Father thought the boat would be an easier ride for me than that old stage, which bumps along those dusty roads and jostles one about unmercifully. Oh, I know we will have to take a stage and probably hire a wagon for my trunks at Ebensport, but that's only ten miles, not forty. Anyway, we already have the tickets. We leave this evening."

Adam wondered if his father-in-law was also paying for the ride from Ebensport. It wouldn't be in a stage, but a rough wagon run by an aged former riverboat man, known to be a heavy drinker. If the timing wasn't just right that could mean a night in another inn and the Ebensport offerings weren't that desirable, especially for ladies. Adam concluded these city folk were unaccustomed to country services, which tended to be almost nonexistent. Two trunks filled with gifts, along with the barrel, now sat packed ready for the drayman to take to the dock. When Martha's trunk full of clothes was brought down from the second floor, there was one more plus Adam's grip. The accumulation convinced him that it would be best to go by packet, since no stage could handle all this. Not happy with having to hire a farm wagon at Ebensport, he could barely conceal his displeasure. All he wanted now was to get out of the Shipman house with its cumbersome furnishings where both mother and father avoided him, engaging him only in small talk when they engaged him at all.

Moments before they left in the buggy, Adam saw Mr. Shipman hand Martha an envelope. Watching her thank him with a quick kiss upon the older man's cheek led Adam to think she knew what it contained, but she did not share that knowledge and quickly put the envelope into her reticule. Adam assumed it was money he, as her husband, could use should he run short, a comfortable feeling that erased his anxiety.

Adam spent a frustrating night in the men's quarters of the packet while Martha went to the ladies cabin in the rear. Husband and wife were not to meet again until just after sunrise at the dock in Ebensport, where Martha remained with the luggage while Adam went to find the retired boatman to take them to the farm. When the old fellow saw the number of trunks, he upped his price, because he said, "with all that there stuff, I can't take anyone else." Not that anyone else on the dock appeared to want transportation in their direction.

"The Missus will have to set with me in front, and you'll have to find a place in the back with the trunks. You folks et yet?"

"No, we haven't had even a bite," Adam said. "The boat goes on from here to Zanesville, and they serve breakfast on that portion of the trip."

"Wal, I'll see that my missus feeds you a little something before we start out. That's a long trip, mebbe ten miles."

Adam picked up his grip and walked across the road to the man's house. Martha, wearing an angry expression, stayed put on top of one of her trunks. "I'm not leaving until all this is safely secured in the wagon," she announced in such a resounding voice that Adam had to turn to make certain it was Martha who spoke out so firmly. "Heaven only knows what could happen to my things here. I had expected a decent coach, not some broken down farm wagon, which lately carried pigs or something worse." It hadn't taken long for her to acquire an unfavorable impression of the local terrain; the profusion of taverns, liveries, and tired houses, where boatmen and other people serving the locks and various shipping enterprises lived. "I think this is a mean sort of place," she called to Adam's departing back. "So don't tarry. I don't like being here alone."

To Adam it didn't look mean at all, just typical of a river town in the country. He supposed Martha would, henceforth, judge every place by Marietta's standards. Putting aside the thought, lest it trouble him further, he shouted, "do as you please," the first curt words he had uttered in her presence.

The old man, who was chewing a wad of tobacco, spit into the street and grunted that he'd get the wagon. He tottered unsteadily toward the stable. Adam assumed he must have already had his shot of Old Monongahela. The log cabin was set in the midst of what might once have passed for a lawn, but now it was a confusion of overgrown grasses and just plain dirt.

The look on Martha's face when they returned with the horse and wagon told Adam she was mighty displeased. "Why there is not even a backboard on that seat," she said, staring at the rude conveyance. Adam ignored the remark, and the two men loaded the wagon and parked it in front of the two-room cabin. Martha joined them, but no sooner had they entered the kitchen than Adam wished they had opted for one of the taverns. The woman, wearing a spotted apron that bespoke of the last dozen meals served, was slovenly; her hair turned into a knot on top of her head was greasy gray; and the kitchen table still held the crumbs from a recent sitting. She took down two bowls and heated up the oatmeal on the rear of the stove, slopped in some milk, and after swiping at the table crumbs with a damp rag, thrust the bowls toward them. "That'll be twenty cents, and if'n you want tea and bread, they's extry."

Martha lifted a spoonful of the glutinous mix to her lips and worked at swallowing it. "I'll take the tea and bread, this oatmeal is lumpy; how many days ago did you make it?" She pushed the bowl toward the woman who made no effort to take it.

"That's all right, I might eat it," Adam said, his mind on the ten miles of barely improved roadway ahead, a road he knew well, having taken many a load of grain and corn to the mill and the dock. A look at Martha's outfit, however, gave him pause. On shipboard her traveling ensemble served its purpose by impressing the other ladies, who admired the exquisitely embroidered bolero jacket with its three-quarter sleeves. They remarked favorably about the velvet trim on cuffs and collar, and the braiding they said, "gives it a military look."

"Most appropriate," one said, "especially if your destination is Zanesville." But here in this poor town, her suit and the matching hat with a velvet crown tipped over one eye seemed out of place. The purple fabric on the brim matched the skirt she was forced to fold around her legs due to the narrowness of the wagon seat.

Adam prayed that there had been rain, not too much, for that would have brought splashes into the wagon to dampen their clothes and spatter their faces. A little moisture, however, would hold down the dust. Unfortunately, no rain had fallen recently, and after a few miles, a light dusting appeared on the velvet trim of Martha's traveling dress and over the crown and brim of her hat. They bumped along stopping only once by a creek, where the two men went into the woods to relieve themselves, leaving Martha to remain on the wagon seat, her jaw set in an obstinate manner. Adam wanted to ask if she needed to find a hidden place in the woods, but felt the subject too delicate to mention. He had heard that women were reluctant to make water under adverse conditions, like an outhouse in winter, and also became very constipated unless they made use of a slop jar, which they had a tendency to put off. Little was said the entire trip, only the crunch of wagon wheels broke the silence, interrupted occasionally by the mooing of a cow or the chirp of a bird. Adam was seated on the other side of the trunks too far away to engage either Martha or the old man in conversation.

They arrived at the farm late in the day. In helping her down from the wagon seat, Adam's nerves took over. The old house, which to his knowledge had never had a coat of paint, was a weathered gray. Because it didn't have a proper foundation, it sagged from the middle toward both sides. A fragment of the porch trim had fallen years ago and not been replaced. Why had he never noticed it before? The image of Martha's white confection of a proper Marietta home surfaced in his mind like a queen's palace.

"This is it?" he heard her ask.

At the sound of the wagon, Ma came out the front door. She wore a new ivory muslin dress dotted with green sprigs and a bright yellow grosgrain bow at the neck. Adam recognized the material he had bought from Jeremiah. Lizzie had never bothered to sew it up after he bought it. Her hair was freshly washed and fell in light waves about her forehead—she must have used the heating tongs to crimp it that way. He was used to severity as befit a woman of over seventy and could not remember when she had worn it so fetchingly. Usually, it looked as if she had pasted it against her head. There was high color in her cheeks. Ma, he was certain, never used paint. She must have pinched them up when she heard he wagon approaching. He was gratified with how nice she looked, almost pretty.

When it came time to pay the wagoner, Adam realized he was short of cash and not wishing to let Martha know, he went past his mother and whispered, "Got a dollar?"

"In the teapot," she answered smiling as she hurried past him to reach out to Martha who fell into her arms and immediately started to cry. "It was such a dreadful trip over that uncertain road with all the dust. I feel it has lodged in my throat. And look at my new outfit." She brushed her skirt with her black gloved hand.

"There, there," Lizzie said, "we can shake it out. I'm sure you must be very warm, my dear. Come, I'll get you something cold to drink. She beamed at Martha, "but first, let me welcome you to your new home."

Martha didn't answer, just looked around at the fields on every side, the fenced garden across the road, the corn stalks heavy with ripened ears that reminded Adam he must waste no time in tending to them. Only the Longacre's home down the lane to the east was in view, a tiny dollhouse on the horizon. There were no other houses in sight. He should try to be sympathetic; this must be a shock after Marietta, where the homes marched side by side in close procession down the streets. He brushed past his mother and Martha to pay the wagoner and offer him a drink of water before he began his trip back. "Got any food?" Adam asked. You're welcome to sleep in the barn, since you won't get home until after dark."

"I've got me some cheese and wurst, a couple of apples my Missus put up in that there poke under the seat, and my brother-in-law lives partway. I'll bunk at his place, if darkness rolls around or I get too tired. Ain't as young as I used to be."

The old fellow helped Adam unload the trunks and gave him a hand carrying Martha's to the upstairs bedroom. "We'll put the others in the front parlor until we decide what to do with them," Adam said.

"The Missus seems a mite upset," the wagoner ventured as they set the trunk down in the bedroom, where Adam's mother and father had once slept, but now would be his and Martha's.

"I guess." Adam said. "Coming from Marietta to the farm country is a shock for her."

"More'n likely, 'specially if'n she ain't never seen it afore. She's a pretty little thing though, probably too high-falutin' for farm work."

Adam shrugged, and after bidding the old fellow good-bye went inside the house, where from the front hall he heard Martha and his mother prattling away in the kitchen. The trip had been hard on her what with the jolting wagon and the heat, which had unaccountably come this late in September. Adam joined them in the kitchen where Martha sat sipping lemonade. He was pleased that the two women appeared to be getting along and bent to tell her so, while Ma dashed out the door with a slice of hickory nut cake for the wagoner. "You'll like my mother. She's an educated women, went all the way through eight grades and been around a bit, lived in both Frederick and Baltimore. She plays the piano like you do." He kissed her on the cheek, but Martha barely cocked her head to receive it.

"Really?" she said and burst into tears again.

"Come on now, buck up. Don't let Ma see you crying."

"Is that what I'm supposed to call her? Ma! She isn't my mother." Martha dabbed at her eyes with a lace-trimmed hanky.

"Come on, we'll go upstairs and see how nice the bedroom looks. You can bring your lemonade."

In the bedroom Martha barely noticed the pieced quilt. "Ma's very best, the one she keeps for company," Adam offered. "It's a snowflake pattern; she made it herself, much of it at the ladies quilting bee. They meet every two weeks. You might like to join them."

"I don't quilt." Martha snapped.

"This is a very fine bed," he tried to change the subject. "Made especially for us by a cabinetmaker in Four Corners."

Nothing in the room impressed Martha: not the walnut spool bed, nor the cherry chifferobe that Adam pointed out "was made from lumber right off the place." She seemed equally unimpressed by the new curtains that blew like froth in the gentle breeze. Not even the braided rug Lizzie had brought from the downstairs parlor dazzled his bride. He watched dejectedly as she sank wearily into the rocker.

"This is it? This is where we are to live?" She put her head against the rocker's slatted back. "When will we have our house near Pineville?"

"Sometime, but not right now." He knelt down before her, took her hand and kissed her fingers. "Just bear with me, my dear, my darling Martha. I promise this won't be forever. But isn't this a pretty room?"

"If you like plain, I guess it is. Pa told me just before we left that he would ship my furniture to me, if I only say the word, and I'm saying the word now. If we are to stay here for an indeterminate amount of time, I want my own things."

Adam looked at the simple décor so fitting for a farmhouse room and thought of the ornate high-backed headboard on the bed they shared that first night. He hated its pompous look. It overwhelmed Martha's bedchamber, and this room was even smaller.

"Leave me now, Adam, I want to bathe and change. Will you please bring me some warm water in the pitcher?"

Adam left for the kitchen where a kettle of hot water was kept on the back of the cast iron stove.

"I expected this," Lizzie said, "I tried to warn you."

"Ma stop. It will work out." He carried the pitcher to the bedroom door and lifted the iron latch.

"Leave it outside the door," Martha called. "I'm not dressed."

Fourteen

When Martha finally emerged from the bedroom, it was nearly suppertime. She joined them in the kitchen just as Lizzie was boiling a pot of red cabbage and apples. The tangy mix of vinegar, lemon juice, nutmeg, and onion signaled that one of Adam's best-liked dishes was being served. Martha sat down at the table, and to Adam's horror, her eyes began to tear again. "Are you crying?" He whispered so his mother, who was thrashing the pots around over the cast iron stovetop, wouldn't hear.

"No, I'm not crying, but whatever is she cooking? The concoction is making my eyes water."

"Red cabbage, onions, and apples," Lizzie, who had hearing that could detect a scurrying mouse in an upstairs bedroom, answered before Adam could. "We have it often; the recipe has been in the family for years, probably came over from Germany, along with the kraut stamper handed down in my mother's family. They were old time Frederick people and not poor, I'll have you know. Those two German tavern chairs by the buffet came out with us too. Belonged to my gramma. Easy to travel with; the legs and back come off just like that." Lizzie snapped her fingers.

Adam interpreted the remark as one intended to impress his new bride with the importance of the Mueller family.

Lizzie set a platter of sliced ham on the table and poured the cabbage, onions, and apples into a serving dish, with only the red of the cabbage set off from the rest of the colorless ingredients. She sat down and passed the dish to Martha, who took a tablespoonful. "Is that all you want?" Lizzie wore a scornful look that worried Adam. Gone was the light-hearted welcoming voice. Now she appeared to be controlling herself with fearful determination, setting her jaw so that her lower teeth jutted forward, a look he had known as a child when he had angered her in some way. He complimented her on the tastiness of the dish. "Always one of my favorites," he said, watching Lizzie warily. When his mother got that look, there was no telling what explosion might ensue. They ate in silence until Lizzie asked Martha if she felt better?

"Yes, but the dust is still in my throat."

86

"Then eat up. There's nothing like vinegar to clear a nasty throat."

Martha took another spoonful and grimaced as she swallowed.

"It's not medicine," Lizzie said sharply.

Martha appeared to be using her fork as a plaything, flicking it over and under the cabbage mixture, but rarely bringing it to her mouth. At the moment Adam finished, Lizzie sprang from her chair and hastily removed the dishes including Martha's barely touched mound of cabbage, onions, and apples.

Later that evening when Adam attempted to join Martha in the nuptial bed, she suggested that since her throat was still bothering her he might prefer his own bed across the hall. "Wouldn't do for both of us to come down with colds, and that may be what I have. I have chills. Besides this bed is way too narrow for two people, especially when one is as big as you are."

"Strange, my folks slept in this bed for thirty years. And my Pa in his prime was nearly as big as I am. Ma's right proud of that bed with its turned spools and curved posts. They had to be turned on a lathe, the first one ever brought to this county."

"But it's only a three-quarter bed. At home mine is full sized."

Adam remembered trying not to notice that ornate bed on his wedding night, so eager was he to get to making himself a married man. "I think this bedroom is very pretty," he said reaching toward her. Ma worked hard while I was away in Marietta to make it nice for you. Like she said, this is your room—yours and mine. The furniture fits the room, not too big, not too small, but just right."

"Like Goldilocks!"

Adam ignored the reference. "She even put up new wallpaper so everything would be fresh and new for you."

"Appears she missed the parlor. That room is really dingy."

"There was hardly time for that in the few days I was gone. But look here at the quilt; Ma made it herself, never used it though, just kept it for nice. Lavender sprinkled with tiny yellow flowers is pleasing, don't you think?" And that little pillow there is called Ohio Star. Ma stitched that up too."

Martha sniffed. Adam didn't know if that was because of her cold coming on or her disdain for the plain and simple farm bedroom. When the windows were open, he liked the way the wispy curtains blew in the breeze. Now the windows were tightly closed lest Martha in her debilitated condition find herself in a draft, and everyone knew drafts were bad for the human body, so he couldn't argue with her over that.

Martha picked her nightdress out of one of her trunks and stood with the fluff of white lace and ruffles in her hand. "I'd like to get ready for bed now, if you don't mind."

"Well, I guess then, I'll leave you to get some rest." Adam got up from the rocker and went toward where she stood.

"For heavens sakes, don't kiss me." Martha turned her head. "You'll catch your death."

"I really wasn't going to," he said, miffed that she was so emphatic. He was already at the door when she called after him.

"Adam, I'm going to ask Father to send my bed, chifforobe, and the settee. He said I could have them."

"All that oversized furniture won't fit into this room."

"I'll make it fit."

"Suit yourself," he grumbled and walked out the door. He remembered glancing at the intricately carved furniture while he waited for Martha on their wedding night, and hating what he saw. The wood was dark, almost black, and the carvings were pretentious like all the furnishings in the Shipman house. As long as she didn't want any more of her family's furniture should her folks pass on, he would give in to the bedroom set. But never that dining room. Opening the drawers required putting your hands into the open mouths of carved wooden lion heads that served as drawer pulls. If she might someday decide to bring all that terrible furniture here, he would forbid it.

Seeing that she intended to sleep alone and not wishing to bring attention to the fact, lest Ma have more ammunition to berate him for his choice of a bride, he tiptoed across the hall and settled into his own bed. Adam did not stir until morning light crept over him. Lying there he thought with considerable satisfaction that he'd had only a few nightmares since Martha had agreed to marry him. The war seemed further and further away, but to dwell on the events of the past week could make him tired and cranky again. He must be on guard. There had been wrong turns everywhere: the overly decorated Shipman house; the number of gifts that thwarted plans for returning by stage; the cost of the wagon, hotel, and meals eaten out. He was trying mightily to keep calm in light of his frustration with Martha and the gathering impression that perhaps his choice of a bride had been a bad one. But then, she isn't well, so I should be understanding, he told himself. As morning light stole over him, he thought of animals to be fed, the barn to be mucked out, and the haying, which would require spending all day under a grueling sun. He really should be up and about, but lay there anyway and wondered why the war wounded seemed so grateful for each kindness, no matter which side they represented. He remembered how they struggled to keep going even as their wounds threatened with ungodly pain. Martha has a slight cold or maybe just dust in her throat, but she acts like a demanding sickly invalid.

He mused upon a particularly poignant moment on the battlefield when he stumbled across a young rebel who had lain there since the conflict ended four days before. Adam discovered him when he heard the young man's moans and stooped to comfort him. "Water," took all the energy the boy could muster. "My canteen's empty." Adam opened his own canteen and put it to the soldier's lips. "It's my leg," he muttered.

Adam pulled back the torn pants leg to see a festering hole, dark and slimy and covered with maggots. He felt his stomach clutch. "You take a bullet?"

The boy nodded.

"Let me get the ambulance corps," Adam said, "if I can find them or the surgeon." The words came out authoritatively, but Adam knew full well that he would not likely find either in time.

"Thank yee, thank yee." The soldier was little more than a boy. Adam would never forget the sight of tears welling in his eyes.

"How old are you, lad?" he asked.

"Sixteen, but don't tell. S'posed to be eighteen." He took a deep breath.

"Don't exert yourself." Adam patted the tattered sleeve of the gray uniform, left him, and ran toward camp where medics were caring for the wounded. When he finally found a stretcher, the corpsman yelled, "You crazy, we have all our own men to take care of; we can't stop to go after some damned reb. Let 'em take care of their own, and if they're too late, we'll pick him up when we start gathering up the dead again."

Putting that memory down, Adam sat up and watched the sun peek over the horizon, then got up from the bed, poured water from the pitcher into the bowl, and after splashing his face, put on his work clothes. He did not think to look in on Martha, not that he didn't want to, but deep inside he feared another rejection.

Ma stood over him while he slathered butter, sugar, and milk on his corn meal mush. "Did you sleep well?" she asked.

"I did." He sensed she knew he had slept alone.

"And Martha?"

"I suppose so."

"That's good. I could use a little help with the churning this morning. Those Guernseys are giving so much milk I can barely keep up with the milking. I've got two pails sitting in the cellar, and the cows will have to be milked again this evening. With you gone, I didn't use much."

"I don't think you should involve Martha in the churning or the milking, if that's what you have in mind. I doubt she's done either. The Shipmans had a hired girl."

"Well, I swan. You really did marry up."

When Martha did not appear by nine o'clock, Adam, having already seen to the animals, went to check on her. She was still under the covers. "I fear I now have a terrible cold. I thought it best to remain in bed this morning." Her face was red and her eyes watery. "It took you long enough to look in on me."

"Sorry. I thought you needed your rest. Would you like your breakfast brought up?"

"Oh, Adam, how thoughtful of you. That would be most pleasant."

By noontime Martha had rallied to join Lizzie and Adam at dinner.

"We're having chicken pot pie," Lizzie announced when her new daughter-in-law sat down. "It's got a goodly amount of onions and pepper along with a touch of saffron, grand medicine for a person ailing with the chills and cold. So eat up."

As she had done the night before, Martha only picked. She speared some chicken and potatoes, but largely ignored the potpie squares. Golden brown on top, they had soaked up broth on the bottom which made them soggy.

During the week that Adam waited for Martha's cold to run its course, he tried to maintain his patience. She had done little to help Ma, slept late, and usually spent the afternoons in her room. One day when he went to her room, as he did every afternoon, she had all the items from her trunks on the bed.

"I'll put some things in the in the chifforobe, but I can leave other garments in a trunk so you will have a drawer for your clothes."

"No, you take them all. I'll leave mine in my old bedroom across the hall."

The trunk, now sitting under the west window, was open. A white envelope lay on the lid; the same one Martha's father had handed her in the hall of the Shipman house. He stopped himself before picking it up. "What's in that envelope?" he asked, aching to know how much Mr. Shipman had given them. "I saw your father hand it to you before we left the house in Marietta. A wedding present?"

"Wedding present! Well, I guess of sorts. Go ahead, open it."

He reached for the envelope and lifted the flap. Inside was a legal document having to do with a property; the address was 18 Main Street, Four Corners. It had been conveyed to Martha. "This your aunt's house?" Still holding the official looking document, he looked down to confront Martha sitting on the bed in a ruffled cotton day dress, a knitted shawl over her shoulders. "This only bears your name as owner. Where's mine?"

"Father thought it best that I have something of my own."

"That's unheard of. Tell your father that I am now your husband, and I expect to be included on this deed. We'll go to the courthouse in McConnelsville and have it changed before this month is out."

Martha's wide-spaced blue eyes glared up at him. "No we won't. It's mine and I intend to keep it that way. In a sense I earned it taking care of Auntie all those months. I gave up college to do her bidding, and now it's time for my remuneration."

"You seem to forget I am your husband, and a husband owns what his wife brings to the marriage."

"Am I included on the deed your uncle gave you to that eighty acres no one cares to make productive?"

"No, but that's different. I acquired that property before our marriage, and truth to tell, haven't had time to decide how to use it. The land is too far away for putting into crops. Anyway, the soil's mostly clay, not good for farming."

"Well, my property was given to me before marriage too. See the date."

Adam saw that the house had been conveyed to Martha when her father had come to Four Corners to settle her aunt's estate. He read further and found that any rents accruing were to be paid to her. She would have money of her own to do with as she wished.

"A fine kettle of fish," he shouted. "Why have you kept this from me for so long? As your husband, I am to be informed of all you have and do; you are to keep no secrets from me. Do you understand?"

"I suppose your mother kept no secrets from your father?"

"She had no secrets," he yelled. Martha's demeanor infuriated him. She acted so high and mighty, not at all like the unassuming girl he had asked to marry him. He watched her turn away and saw a slight smile rise about her face. She reached for the deed. Adam held it fast. "As I recall your father found a family to rent the place shortly after your aunt died. Am I right?"

91

"That's right and a fine upstanding man with a wife has rented it. He's a clerk in the drug store, a college man able to mix cures and potions. Came from Zanesville."

"Have you collected any rents?"

"Absolutely. They come to me by post." The tone of her voice had changed to one of extreme self-importance, a fact that left Adam diminished in a way he had not felt before. He could see that she was not going to acquiesce to his commands, but he tried anyway. "Will you see that they are paid to me from now on?"

"No, Adam, Father made it clear that these are to be my own funds to use as I see fit."

"Then what about the money I earn? What about that? Am I not required to support you?"

"Well, I would hope so. After all, I am your wife. Now give me that envelope."

"Women are illogical," Adam raised his voice so even his mother in the downstairs bedroom could hear. He tossed the envelope toward her and stamped out of the room, slamming the door harder than he meant to, and remained sour tempered for nearly a week. He made make no effort to join Martha in their bed at night until nearly three weeks had gone by since they had consummated the marriage. He dwelt on the problem every day, letting it interrupt his sleep and his relationship with her, which had now turned cold as left over fish. No longer did he visit her while she recuperated from her cold, nor did he inquire how she was feeling when they met at mealtimes. As the days progressed he noted that Martha had begun to help Ma with the dishes and was present in the kitchen as she prepared meals. They chattered away like two sisters while Lizzie showed her how to make German food, the recipes for which had been handed down in the family through three generations and were now heading toward the fourth.

While he turned dour and spent more time in the barn, or the fields, or husking corn, and seeing to the animals, Martha and his mother seemed to be connecting. When Martha was over her cold, she asked Lizzie if she would teach her how to dry corn "since Adam seems so fond of it." As she spoke, she turned toward him and patted his hand. At her gentle touch, he felt his inner resolve breaking, and that night after he donned his nightshirt, he sheepishly knocked on her bedroom door. "May I come in?" he asked.

"I'd like that," she called through the door. He went inside, and when he turned back the covers, like some brazen hussy he could only imagine in his dreams, she was naked. How had she known this would be the night they would finally get together in the embrace that would surely make them man and wife forever? Not only are women diabolical, he thought later as he turned over to relax into sleep, but clairvoyant too.

The next morning he awoke beside her, happy, satiated, and energized. He decided not to bring up the matter of the house in Four Corners—at least, not then. But that didn't mean the situation left him completely, rather it continued to annoy like a stone in a shoe for the next several months. He just needed to find the right time to address it: a time when Martha was tired of his advances, for in no way did he want to cut them off.

Fifteen

As the weeks wore on, Adam took his cue from Martha's disinterest and only occasionally approached her for lovemaking. While he considered the act his right, he saw that she was given to angry outbursts, shouted incriminations, and tears. He didn't want to cause more trouble especially in front of Lizzie, who had eyes and ears that could see and hear around corners. He was observing traits in Martha that he had not noticed before: she was headstrong, selfish, and now with the added impediment of having her own money, she could move back to Marietta without asking him. The quandary he felt at this turn of events grew, twisting his mind and building his resentment against her. He wanted her to accept her role as an obedient wife; whether she was happy in that role was of no consequence. Then one morning she awoke before Adam, leaped out of bed, and began heaving into the wash basin.

"What's wrong?" He jumped up and grabbed her. She was barely able to hold herself up over the bowl. Her fingers clutched the washstand.

"I don't know. I'm so sick. Get me back to bed," she wailed.

He wet a washrag, wiped her face and then guided her back to bed. "You must be coming down with something."

"I guess." She closed her eyes; her face was bluish white.

Please God, don't let her die, he thought. "I'll get Ma. She'll know what to do." He dumped the vomit into the slop pail and carried it to the outhouse.

"That didn't take long." Ma remarked on observing the prone body in the bed, her face still drained of color." Martha fluttered her eyelids, but seemed unable to focus on her mother-in-law.

"How far along are you?"

"I dunno. I didn't know it would be like this. I'm so sick," she whimpered. "I don't want any children."

"Well, they come with marriage in the same package. Not much a body can do about it. You'll be all right in a few days. Stay in bed for now. I'll bring you some soda crackers and later some oatmeal. That will help settle you down."

Lizzie followed Adam down the hall steps, "Congratulations," she said.

"I didn't think it would happen so fast. I'm not sure I'm ready." He supposed he should be happy, but wished they could have settled the problem of the house in Four Corners first. It would be nice to have that income now. He surmised the pregnancy must have begun that first night, as they'd had no relations for more than a month after their frolic in the nuptial bed. A baby, a baby of my own, he thought, and try as he might, he could not get excited.

Not so with the two women.

Martha was sick every morning for two weeks. At first light when she began to moan, Adam leaped from the bed and ran downstairs to get his mother who arrived with crackers and soothing words. He hated being around sickness and a pretty bride turned ashen, her hair streaming, heaving the contents of her stomach disgusted him. The sick only brought back images of war. After the battles were over, he heard that most of the dead didn't die because of their injuries; it was sickness and disease that took them. As he listened to Martha, it only served to remind him of the moans of fighting men throwing up their guts.

When Martha was all of three months along, Lizzie thought a trip to the doctor might be in order. With everything snow covered, they could take the sleigh. It would be less jostling for the expectant mother than the wagon. Roads and fields were pillowy white with snow making chalky humps of the bushes and frosting the barren tree limbs.

"Oh wonderful, I've been wanting to go into town ever since I got here, but with the cold and the baby coming on, I fear I have been here too long."

The women bundled up against the chill with their heaviest clothing. Over their knitted hats, both wore fascinators they could pull over their faces against the wintry wind. Adam helped them into the sleigh and tucked the carriage robe tightly around their legs, then got into the front seat. The sleigh moved briskly over the fields.

Adam had gotten up earlier than usual to see to his chores. Several recently shot carcasses of deer and squirrels hung in the smokehouse waiting to be scalded in the trough, the very one his father had scooped out from a log on the family's arrival in Ohio. Adam could have had the fur removed, the animals cut up, and salted down before this day was over. But to keep peace, he gave in to the demands of the women.

They reached Emma's front porch by ten in the morning, and the two women informed him that not only did they intend to see the doctor but would be shopping at the general store and visiting with Emma. "I also plan to call on my tenants," Martha said rather grandly. It was going to be a long day, a day during which he would be largely left out. Other than a visit to his brother-in-law, the blacksmith, with some tools to be repaired, and a stop at the feed store, he had little else to do. Adam considered going to the tavern, but with a pregnant wife and his mother along thought better of it. Lizzie disapproved of strong drink and would be sure to smell it on him. He fought off the urge and continued on to his sister's house.

"Well," Emma said when they were alone, "how does it feel to be an almost father? I understand Martha's in a family way."

"I don't really know. I'm not used to the idea yet. Did you hear that her father gave her that house down the street and my name is not on the deed?"

"No, I've met the young renters, but we didn't discuss that, of course."

"I'm furious. I fear it may come between us."

Emma poured coffee and set one cup down in front of Adam.

"I don't know. Sometimes I wish I had money of my own. It's terrible to be always waiting for a handout, and I don't like having to ask for the wherewithal when the family needs something. My Reuben is very close with a nickel. I think he resents giving me anything with a dollar sign attached." Emma looked down as though studying the flowers on her cup; her eyes, usually animated, were expressionless.

There's a smoldering there, Adam thought, adding aloud, "But that's the way it is for women. They were meant to be dependent, to have a man take care of them."

"Do all you men get that attitude through your mother's milk?" Emma retorted. "Well, let me tell you something: when they freed the slaves they didn't even consider freeing women, and God help the ones who have no man to care for them. There is simply no decent work outside the home, at least not the honorable kind. You probably remember Ida; you were in school with her brother, Asa. Well, her husband died in the war—that late great conflict you remember so well—and the government took forever to give her a picayune eight dollars a month. Seems she had trouble proving she was his wife, so while she waited she turned into a tart working in that hotel tavern. Who could blame her? With two children crying for food, and no money coming in, she had to work. That tavern paid her almost nothing, so I can hardly chastise her if she earns a little on the side, even if her line of work is sinful."

"Emma don't talk like that."

"Those are the facts, like it or not. And another thing, you remember Silas Gebhardt. He came home early, before the war was over, without a leg and a crippled up arm, not to mention he's mental too. And you know what the government so generously allots him for his three years in the war?"

"Can't say that I do considering I don't have those problems."

"All of six dollars a month. And him with a wife and five children. She takes in laundry from the hotel."

"I'd say that's more honorable than wenching."

"Not as lucrative, I'll wager. Speaking of wenching, I hear Ida has left for Cincinnati. She's gone and left her children with her sister."

"Where'd you hear that?" Adam suddenly took interest in what he regarded as a dull subject: women wanting freedoms allotted only to men. All a widow had to do was find another man to marry her.

"One of the traveling men who calls at Reuben's place told him she's working for a classy bordello and living well. Dresses up in finery. And I guess she got that tooth fixed, so she looks pretty good despite the debauchery of her life. She told him soon as she has enough money saved, she's going to put her two children in a fancy private school, so she must be doing quite well with her sinful life."

"I understand there are a lot of really rich businessmen in Cincinnati with fat wives who might pay well for the services of a young wench, so I guess a good bordello is an improvement over that impoverished cabin she lived in here." Adam poured coffee into the saucer and sipped.

"How would you know about that cabin? Or what a bordello looks like?"

"I could see the cabin from the road."

"If you stretched your neck around like a snake's,"

Adam blanched. He hoped his sister wasn't wise to his depravity, which he considered he could use a little of now with Martha indisposed for the rest of her pregnancy. "On eight dollars Ida could have survived."

"Not well."

"I knew her in school. She was a nice girl then; at fifteen she was a pretty little thing."

"I remember, but life seems to take its toll on women first. And she grew up fast."

Adam wished to change the subject before his past sins in that cabin should catch up with him, so he asked about the children.

"They're all fine. I guess you've heard Lucinda is expecting."

97

"I think I heard a mention of that. So you're going to be a grandmother. Congratulations."

"And you'll be a great uncle."

When Lizzie and Martha arrived two hours later, they settled in for talking with Emma. From the moment they sat down, Adam agitated for them to head home. "We should be leaving," he said. "It will soon grow dark, the snow might start again." None of the women paid him mind, but went right on talking about the neighbors, the parson's sermon last week, the quilting club, and other silly subjects Adam found boring. They continued to ignore him until, stamping his foot and pounding the table, he stood up and yelled louder than was necessary, "I'm leaving. You two can stay if you wish."

"How I wish," Martha gave him a wilting smirk; Lizzie went right on telling about Mabel Altman who folks said had run off with the preacher.

Sixteen

Benjamin Duvall Springer arrived in August 1869, a ten pound-six ounce baby, who burdened Martha with two days labor before Dr. Kennedy brought him safely into this world. After driving into Four Corners to summon the doctor, Adam left the house while the birthing took place and remained all day in the north field harvesting barley. Seth had come with his reaper, and Adam welcomed the respite from the groans and screams emanating from the upper bedroom.

"Don't think the barley's in danger of shriveling, do you?" Adam looked at the older man's face, creased into deep indentations by sun and wind. He was still not used to determining when to plant, to harvest, to bind up? Those decisions had always been his father's. But now that the farm was his to run, he wished he had paid more attention growing up, had asked more questions instead of having to depend on local farmers to give him advice he should have acquired at his father's knee.

"Peers to me, it's just about right. If we leave it a couple of days longer, it's liable to crinkle down; them heads would drop off and be lost. I reckon you planted this crop a bit early. It don't usually head until later." Seth reached to snip off a few kernels with his callused fingers, and rubbing them between thumb and forefinger, pronounced the crop ripe. He thrust the grain close to Adam's face. "See this here, if that was to appear milky, we'd of had to let it stand a few days longer."

Adam was grateful that the day would be taken up with reaping the crop. In the house, meanwhile, his firstborn was coming into the world, a bawling, red faced, demanding, little boy who, from the moment his dark hair appeared in the doctor's hands, let it be known he would be a force to be reckoned with. No one came to tell Adam of his son's arrival, so the two men continued to cut barley leaving it lay where it fell from the reaper platform. While Seth drove the horses, Adam walked behind with his barley fork turning and spreading the piles to hasten drying, and only occasionally did he dwell on the events taking place in his farm bedroom.

"You should get at least two bushels out of each acre," Seth said cheerily, when he took leave of Adam after the job was done.

Adam never mentioned the goings on in the house. Birthing babies was not a subject to be discussed, especially not while the process was taking place. One never knew if a healthy child would result, and if there was the slightest abnormality, it would not do to let the fact be known. There were some houses around where odd children were kept out of sight, isolated in a bedroom or attic to forevermore be the subject of conjecture, but never seen lest they bring shame upon the family.

Inside the house, he gave the squalling infant short shrift and went immediately to Martha's bedside to ask how she was feeling. She looked up at him wearily. "It was awful," she said, "I could ever go through it again."

"There, there," Lizzie interjected. "All mothers feel that way, but when you take that child into your arms, those feelings disappear and love—love like nothing you have ever known—pours into your being like a million rays of sunshine."

Though they fully expected Lizzie's predictions to come true, neither Adam nor Martha seemed to feel anything but put upon by the demands of their robust baby. Martha nursed him as instructed by Lizzie, but the child's incessant demands were almost more than she could handle, and Adam found her frequently in tears. To calm the screaming child, Lizzie cooked up oatmeal, strained it through a sieve, and poked some into the infant's mouth. Most of it drooled down his chin, but enough got inside him to quell his hunger and quiet his screaming. Lizzie announced that the new mother needed more rest because her milk was not coming in, as it should. She told Adam to return to his bedroom. "Martha should have complete rest at night."

The situation lasted three months.

Presumably by that time, Martha's milk was rich enough and ample to quiet the child, and he was growing into a vigorous baby. By five months, as though the two were soul mates, he had begun to give Adam a toothless baby smile. Martha fell into the rhythms of the household, and when she did not retire to her bedroom to nurse the infant or take to her bed for her afternoon nap, she began helping Lizzie. The napping improved her disposition. She was less tired and more amenable to having Adam join her in the bed as soon as the kerosene lamps were turned down, with the result that when Ben was nine months old and being weaned, against Lizzie's objections, Martha found herself in a family way again.

The ponderous bed with its tall head and footboards, the overwhelming chifforobe and satin covered settee came by wagon. Since he had not yet told Lizzie about Martha's plans for having her furniture moved to the farm, Adam greeted the arrival with trepidation. The drover helped him carry the bed sections to the upper hallway and take Martha's chifforobe into the bedroom. On hearing the noise, Lizzie came to the hall from the kitchen to ask what was going on. Adam told her. Without a word she turned abruptly and marched back to the kitchen. She had worked hard on that bedroom in preparation for their arrival after the nuptials, put up new wallpaper, made curtains, and laid out her best quilt. Adam watched her stalk to the kitchen and felt torn between Martha and Lizzie. His sympathies lay with his mother. Why couldn't Martha be more understanding, more cooperative? It was, after all, Lizzie's house.

Strangely, his mother never alluded to the matter, but when she helped him carry out her prized spool bed, she said, "This is such a lovely piece. Oh, I know it's kind of plain, but the wood is so pleasing to the touch. Almost satiny now." Adam thought she felt bad at having it relegated to the loft over the kitchen, the gathering place for out-of-date furniture, knickknacks, and old clothing from which his mother pieced her quilts. He remembered hearing his older brothers and sisters tell about sleeping in the loft before the new six-room frame addition was added to the original log cabin. Now it was nothing but a catchall for discards, including the now disassembled spool bed.

"I would have been satisfied with one child, the pain of bringing babies into the world is just too terrible," Martha told him shortly before the second child was due.

"How can you say that? Rachel and Bartholomew, Ma's friends, have eight, Mrs. Chrismann has six, and you grouse about two."

"I'm the one that bears them, not you," Martha flashed back. "What would you know about birthing pain? Well, let me tell you something here and now. When this is over, and this child is brought safely into the world, there will be no more. So make yourself comfortable in that other room. From now on this room is mine."

Adam was stunned. "But I thought you loved me. How can you banish me from your bed?" And then he made the terrible mistake of adding, "that's what wives are for."

"Oh really! Well, not this one. I have no intention of being a brood mare."

He started to raise his voice, but instead stood over her, a menacing look on his face. Lady, you'll do my bidding or else."

"Or else what?"

He didn't quite know, but anger, more terrible than he had felt against the southern agitators gathered in the pit of his stomach. He strode out of the room, slammed the door behind him so hard the metal latch rattled. Let her have her damned room; he couldn't stand the sight of it. Not only did her father send the furniture, but also all manner of figurines and little dishes, even a dresser set, an ugly affair made of ivory. Martha bragged that it took the tusks of two elephants to make all the pieces including the tray. He doubted that but why contradict her over such a minor matter.

As she had done during the first confinement, Martha spent considerable time in her room, not even going to services for which he was grateful because it meant driving her to the Methodist Church in Four Corners. Since he was banished from her bed, he decided that after the baby was born she could get to services anyway she could find. Be damned if he'd take her. The Lutheran Church was less than a mile away. Why drive four? If she wanted religion, why not go where his family worshiped?

The rhythms of the household continued; polite conversation or none at all ensued during mealtimes, until one day shortly before the birth of their second child when Martha confronted him with a question. "Since nothing more has been said about building our own house on that Pineville property, I've been wondering when I might expect a home of my own?"

"Woman . . . are you out of your mind? How can I build another home with this farm to run?"

"No, I am perfectly sane, but sometimes when we were still sharing my bed, I thought you had lost your sanity what with your terrible tossing around in the night and screaming about that dreadful old war. I simply lost track of how many times I had to waken you, because you were dreaming, shouting out, and cursing. It was disgusting. Now, back to the question; when can I have my home?"

"I haven't the slightest idea. How are we to live if I no longer have a farm?"

"You can farm the Pineville place and rent this one out. I already have thought about how. Those rented fields would bring in a smart sum of money, and the house can go to tenants like my house in Four Corners. With two rental properties we should get on fine, and you can farm the rest of those eighty acres. We'll have a garden, of course. And I can have some cultural advantages. There's a woman's literary society in Pineville, and I'm told by members of the circle a very fine Methodist Church. They have Bible study and a circle group. I am dying of mental distress in this place, never see anyone, never go anyplace. I hate it!"

"Like I have told you over and over, that land would make a poor farm. The soil's mostly clay. We'd be lucky to get a garden on the place. Don't see why you have such a need to get away. Probably you're upset because you've been in a family way for – let's see how many months?" He was trying to calculate when she blurted, "almost sixteen, and we've been married less than two years. When this baby comes I won't be able to leave for more than four hours because I'll be nursing. I haven't done anything but go to your mother's quilting society, which I hated—bunch of old biddies cackling away about their uninvited neighbors. I haven't even ridden horseback since I came, and that used to be my greatest pleasure. I have my riding dress, but need a sidesaddle. Your mother said she straddled the horse, but I prefer not to. That's not ladylike."

Adam turned away in disgust. There was no use talking to a woman who had such little understanding of the way things are on a farm.

"What about the house?" he heard her say as once again he slammed the bedroom door.

By the time he was at the bottom of the steps the door had reopened. "And another thing. . ." He looked up at the sound of her voice. Her great bulk disgusted him. Even her face was swollen. "As soon as this baby is six months old, I'll wean the child and take both children to Marietta to see my folks, and I'm not sure how long I will be gone."

"Suit yourself," he muttered.

Sulking became a way of life for Adam. He groused about the haying, the animals, the chores, spent most of his time in the barn, rarely thinking on his predicament and uttering cuss words when he did. "Dratted woman," he'd say to himself and wonder if he loved her at all or ever had. While longing to be away, he tried to maintain a semblance of interest when his mother spoke about farm matters, the garden, the incessant repairs, a sick calf. He thought of visiting his brother in Iowa, but rejected the trip as too expensive, and he really couldn't leave the two women alone anyway.

Neither he nor Martha had given thought to naming the child although when faced with the choice, Adam considered that his wife might select his name. She wanted a girl and seemed disappointed with another boy. The unnamed baby was not as vigorous as his brother, Ben, who was growing into a busy toddler.

"No name yet?" Lizzie asked one morning.

"We can't agree," Martha told her mother-in-law. "Adam wants to call him John after his father, and I would like to name him Isaiah from the Bible. Adam will have none of it. He can't seem to realize that Methodist names are the same as

Lutheran ones if they come from the Bible, and for someone who doesn't even go to church most of the time . . ."

"May I suggest a name then?" Lizzie asked. "We can't go on calling him baby; he's all of three weeks old. How would Edward suit? After all, that is Adam's middle name, and using it would not cause all the confusion caused by two people with the same name in the same house. I used to know an Edward, a handsome man. Oh, he had his foibles, but he was intelligent and personable." At this revelation, Martha studied Lizzie for a few moments and thought she looked a bit dreamy, a rare show of emotion for a woman who was generally hard bitten. She mentioned her thoughts to Adam. "I'll wager your mother once loved an Edward."

"No, she didn't have anyone else. Not serious anyway. Just Pa."

"Umm, I wonder," Martha remarked adding, "I think Edward is a nice enough name. And if it pleases your mother, why not?"

Pleasing Lizzie had always been a trait of Adam's, so he readily agreed. He was especially happy to have pleased her, when two months later she fell ill, and for the first time he worried that she might not be part of his life much longer. His strong-bodied, strong-willed mother was taken down by a tumor that Dr. Kennedy said must be removed, and he recommended a prominent surgeon in Zanesville. The prospect of an operation for the seventy-five-year old matriarch of the Springer family was chilling, for few survived undergoing the knife without contracting another malady. Infections were frequent. Lizzie considered refusing, but Dr. Kennedy convinced her that the operation was her only hope for life. "We're living in advanced times," he told her and Adam, when they went together for a final consultation. "The medical profession learned a great deal in the late war. A patient's chances of being cured are now far superior to what they were before 1861."

Adam had his doubts. Memories of harried surgeons sawing off the limbs of the war ravaged gave him pause, but he kept his counsel and let Lizzie determine her fate. She was more troubled about her first overnight trip since she and her husband visited their eldest son in Iowa before Adam was born. "That trip was marked by a pleasant riverboat voyage as far as St. Louis and then a stage to Iowa." Lizzie had told him. "I felt free for the first time since leaving Frederick years earlier, but the trip home was ghastly. I was sick every morning, so ill that by the time we reached St. Louis we had to stay in a hotel for three days. A doctor was called in, and that's when I found you were on the way, Adam." She smiled at her son. "I remember wailing to your father that I was too old for another baby.

We came home by riverboat, because the doctor warned that a jostling stagecoach could cause a miscarriage." And Adam, her change-of-life baby, became her pride and joy. Now, however, the situation was different. Lizzie knew well the chance she was taking at having an operation. "Perhaps it would be better to just let it go," she told her son. In the end, she accepted her fate and once she decided an operation was unavoidable, met the prospect with her usual stoic determination.

"My greatest concern," she confided to Adam, "is leaving the farm chores to Martha. She tells me she has never even milked a cow. I haven't wanted to force the issue, but I declare that is a mighty strange attitude for a farm wife. Fortunately, I've pickled the beets and beans, dug up potatoes and turnips, and put them in the root cellar along with the hams and bacon. I doubt you'll starve."

"I've been thinking about that," Adam said, "What with two babies and the house to care for, I wonder if Rachel's youngest girl would be willing to stay. I've asked Seth and his oldest boy to look out for the animals."

"That might work, at least Ermajean would be another hand. She is rather slow witted, though, not bad enough to have been laid aside by the midwife, but dull when it comes to book learning. She will have to be told what to do and then checked on to make certain she has done as instructed."

"Martha may lack certain household skills, but never fear she will be good at checking up on her. And," he added grimly, "shouting orders."

Seventeen

Dr. Kennedy made the preparations for their trip and reserved a room for Lizzie at the surgeon's Zanesville hospital. Until the operation was safely over, Adam was to stay in a boarding home near a tavern, where he could take his meals. Then he planned to go home leaving Lizzie to recuperate for three weeks before returning to take her back to the farm.

Martha, however, had another idea, one she kept to herself until the last minute. With baby, Eddie, tucked into his blanket, she had gone to Four Corners shortly before Adam and Lizzie were to leave for Zanesville. She remained the night at Emma's house having told Adam she had some shopping to do and a visit with Emma would be a welcome change. "God only knows how tied up I will be when your ailing mother returns. Besides, I've been cooped up in this house for nearly three years what with my confinements and nursing, and I am sick to death of it. I haven't gone once to see my family, but I assure you that will soon change."

Adam hoped she'd go to Marietta and take the children. He needed some peace. His nightmares had returned, and he was angry a good bit of the time. To be sure, the nightmares were intermittent but disturbing enough to leave him exhausted many mornings. Besides, young Eddie was a squawler, never satisfied, always hungry and his caterwauling screams left the entire household seeking sleep at odd hours of the day. He was also becoming more concerned for his mother. What if she did not get well? What if she was unable to do her work? What if she died? She was seventy-six, not young. He would need Martha, but his wife was still an enigma, intent on being a grand lady on one hand and a shrew on the other. She was still nursing Eddie, so the prospect of her getting with child again was nearly impossible, yet she continued to refuse his advances. Was there anything worse than a confounding woman? He spent more time in the barn and tried to forget the pickle in which he found himself.

"Have you given Martha any instructions about the work here," he asked his mother the day before they were to leave?

"We've had a few sessions with the cows, and I think she is getting the hang of it. I'd say that she's better at it than you are—not so rough with the poor beasts. And yesterday she fed the chickens. Not willingly, but at least she paid attention when it came to deciding how much feed and how often. This evening we see to the pigs."

Adam had a vision of Martha in her ruffles and bows throwing garbage into the pigpen. Although still smarting from the matter of the rental house in Four Corners, he decided to show his appreciation by alluding to her increased interest in work around the place. "Ma says you are taking to the chores." Martha shrugged, said nothing, and went to her bedroom. Ermajean arrived the day before Adam and his mother left.

"I should be back by the end of the week," Adam said while they were at the supper table. Lizzie sat bouncing Ben on her lap. "I'll miss my big boy," she was saying when Martha interrupted. "I've been thinking Mother Springer that Adam should not leave you there in that strange place alone; rather he should stay until you are well enough to come home. That way he can see you every day and make certain you are receiving proper care. I've heard terrible accounts about some of these hospitals, slovenly help, uncaring nurses, and I would feel better if your son could look in on you every day." She paused seeming to appraise Adam's reaction. "I'd go myself except for the boys."

Adam set his teacup with a clatter onto his saucer. He used to pour the tea into the saucer to drink, but Martha had put a stop to that. "No one in town drinks tea from a saucer," she told him. "And I won't have that practice in my house, so you may as well get used to it while you are still in your mothers."

"Staying in town takes money," he said, "livery fees, board and room."

"I'm prepared to handle your staying in Zanesville." Martha said, reaching into her apron pocket. When she removed her hand she was holding a roll of bills. "Here, these are for you. Make sure your mother is comfortable and take a nice room for yourself. Don't share if you can help it. Pay whatever extra is required."

Lizzie stared at the bills crumpled in Adam's open hand. "Where did you come by all that?"

"My rent money. Stuck here, I never had reason to spend it. I thought it would go for the house Adam said he'd build for me, but now I see that won't happen soon. When I went to town a week ago, I withdrew it from the bank."

Adam's eyes turned red, almost teary, but not quite. Tears were the stuff of women with their uncontrolled weaknesses, and he recovered enough to ask her how she got the money from the bank without his signature.

"I forged it; that farm boy clerk never questioned it."

When she saw Adam's face turn red, Lizzie quickly changed the subject. "I don't know what to say. I'm overwhelmed." Lizzie thanked her daughter-in-law adding, "I can't tell you how happy this makes me. I dreaded being sick and unable to speak for myself if some of the terrors I've heard about hospitals were to be my lot."

Adam, though surprised at her generosity, considered the money his due, but did manage an almost inaudible "thank you." He knew his name was on the account along with Martha's but feared the consequences if he ever took one penny of it, although tempted at times. Ermajean arrived early the next day and was given the upstairs bedroom in the rear of the house. Martha told her to keep the door open, "so you can hear Eddie should he cry in the night. Then you are to arise, change him, and bring him to me for feeding. Do you understand?"

"Yes mam."

Adam wanted to remind his wife that Eddie was her responsibility, that a mother is to quiet her son, see that he's changed and clean, but he could see that despite his opinion the child was about to be put into Ermajean's hands.

The hospital was nothing more than a house the surgeon had turned into his workplace. Its former kitchen was fitted out as an operating room, and the front and back parlors were given over to patients. What had been the dining room was kept for those awaiting surgery, and this proximity to the operating room could prove unnerving, should an inadequately sedated patient react with screams to bodily intrusions by the surgeon's scalpel.

While Adam waited in the hallway, Lizzie was taken into a former parlor, now a bedroom, and given a white gown to wear. A prim nurse told her to make herself comfortable in the bed. "Rest," she said ominously, "is what you need now for the ordeal ahead."

"Maybe I don't want to do this," Lizzie's look toward Adam was pleading; her usually busy hands lay helplessly by her side.

"It's your only hope, Ma. I'm sure you'll do just fine, a woman of your determination with nary a sick day in your life."

Her face was as white as the sheets pulled tight across the bed. There was a crisply made-up bed on the other side of the room, but evidently Lizzie was the only patient admitted that day. Between the beds was a large window topped with a panel of stained glass, a tribute to the taste of the couple who built the house before the war, when the area was up and coming. Now the neighborhood was a mite shabby with some of the large homes harboring more than one family.

"You can leave us now," the nurse commanded. She was a tall, hawk-faced martinet probably efficient in what she was about, so despite new misgivings, Adam left his mother certain that she was in capable hands.

He found a room in a private home nearby, where the widow who owned it spoke of earlier times when she and her husband built the house "long before the Great War." She told him her husband had worked in a bank before enlisting and died in Atlanta of the dysentery. "So rather than lose the house, I took in boarders. I used to serve meals but grew too old for all that work."

When Adam mentioned his own service to the country, a bond developed, and the woman brought forth some of her husband's letters. Adam read them eagerly but noted that the Lieutenant had judiciously left out the details of fierce battles in which Adam had also participated. Nor was there any mention of his suffering, but dysentery was known to sweep a man low and inflict him with such excruciating cramping that death was welcome relief.

In a small front room on the second floor, Adam stashed his garments and stood for a moment looking out the window at the roadway below laden with crushed stone. Might cut down the dust in front of our place he thought, wondering where he might get a load of stone that would not be too dear. He was responsible for all the road that fronted his land. Martha and Lizzie were always complaining about the dirt that, except in winter, required them to wield their dusters at least three times a week.

After settling in, he explored the town before stopping off for supper in a tavern recommended by his landlady. His walk took him up and down several streets past small shops where craftsmen were working at various trades: candle making, soap manufacturing, carpentry, dressmaking, and millinery among others. Feeling flush with the money Martha had provided, he stopped in one shop and looked over the display of flowerpots, cooking vessels, and crocks. "Made by a young man who lives in Fultenham. Names Weller," the proprietor said, "does all the work himself: digs the clay, throws the pots, fires them, and brings them here to sell. They sell pretty good too."

Adam said he'd take a flowerpot. It would be a thoughtful gift for Martha and a reward for her generosity. With the package under his arm, he soon found the recommended tavern and sat down with several men who appeared as unattached as Adam. Within a few days, he joined them for all his meals and shared a nightly tankard of ale. He looked in on his mother twice each day, being careful not to do so after the ale, telling himself this was only temporary until he could take his mother home, for no spirits—except for medicinal purposes—were allowed in Lizzie's house. A week after their arrival in Zanesville he wrote to Martha.

November 3, 1871

My dear wife,

Ma survived the operation in good form. The doctor said if she continues to mend, she can return home by mid-month. There was another man here who brought his wife for surgery, but he has taken her home, preferring not to subject her to the uncertainties of cutting out the tumor. He claims another doctor he consulted said the ordinary practice of cutting never cures, so he decided to follow his advice, which uses a caustic treatment to destroy the cancerous germs. He said this results in permanent recovery. So I am somewhat worried about having chosen surgery for Ma, but she wished to follow Dr. Kennedy's advice and now the deed in done.

I am comfortably lodged at the home of an older widow whose children have grown, so she has four rooms to let. Two are occupied permanently by a couple of bachelors. Another bedroom and mine are for transients. I don't get meals here, but there is a tavern two roads away that serves tolerable eats. I am also near the hospital and am able to leave the horse nearby in the public livery. All this is costly so I appreciate the money you provided.

I hope you are well and the children are getting along all right without me and Seth's boy and Ermajean are proving helpful. I will write later about the actual date of our return. I hope it will be before the snow falls, but Dr. Kennedy seems reluctant to tell me when exactly.

Your loving husband,
Adam

As the days wore on and the skies turned cloudy with November threat, Adam approached the doctor about Lizzie's release.

"Not before we are certain the wound is sufficiently healed, so as not to tear apart on that long trip, all of twenty-five miles, you say."

"That's right, sir." Adam almost saluted him. He had learned to pay surgeons respect after seeing them perform on the battlefield and marveled that they could

110

saw through mangled limbs with such assurance while a suffering soldier, whose pain was tempered only by alcohol, screamed obscenities and asked for death. His mother appeared to be in pain a good bit of the time and cried out for an elixir the doctor willingly provided. "I know it is amply laced with morphine and maybe even alcohol," she told Adam. "All these medicines are, but they give me relief."

Adam's anxiety grew with inactivity and concern for worsening weather. Every morning, he awoke in his small bedroom and raced to the window to assess the graying sky, but still the doctor refused to release Lizzie and ordered her to remain very still to give the wound time to heal.

Martha's letter, in answer to his, pleased him for he sensed she was managing quite well.

November 14, 1871

Dear Adam,

I am pleased that Mother Springer is mending and that you will be coming home soon. Little Ben asks for both of you every day, and I assure him you will be here before the snow flies. He sometimes stands in the road looking for the buggy, and then I have to run out and caution him about various conveyances passing by. Of course, on most days there are none at all, which only emphasizes how remote and lonely this place is.

I must admit to some annoyance at Ermajean's slovenly ways. Yesterday, I had to tell her three times to wipe up the table, but she only swipes the cloth. Sometimes I wish she had not come at all. Except for helping to feed the chickens, milk the cows, and slopping the hogs, she needs constant direction. I have showed her several times how to change Eddie's diaper, but she has trouble remembering to bring up warm water first, and leaves his bottom exposed to the cold, while she runs to the kitchen to fetch some—that is when she finally remembers. I asked her why she seems so confused about the procedure when we have talked about it so often. 'I dunno', she invariably answers, "I ain't never changed a baby's diaper before."

I guess that's because she's the youngest. She told me her mother had fourteen children with four in their graves. Isn't that positively awful? I only knew about ten. To have that many children rattles me. I intend to have only the two. Take care of yourself, and we look to your homecoming soon.

Your obedient wife,
Martha

Eighteen

A week after receiving Martha's letter, Adam escorted Lizzie to the buggy. She had been up and about for only two days and was terribly unsteady on her feet, so he carried her from the hospital door and placed her gently on the backseat. About as heavy as a bluebird, her face remained drained of color. So lackluster was she that he concluded the doctor must have cut out her spirit along with the cancer.

Lizzie stretched out as best she could in the confined space with her head propped on a pillow and blankets securely tucked around her. Adam tried to avoid puddles and ruts, but occasionally his mother would cry out. He had to stop the buggy twice, once at a tavern where he carried her to the privy and waited outside the door, and once along the road, where not even bothering to locate a shielding tree, she relieved herself while he turned his back. The going was slow, and they didn't return to the farm until long after dark, the horses finding the way with only a kerosene light to warn travelers coming from the opposite direction.

Lizzie was exhausted. Martha, seeing the state she was in, hustled her right off to bed. "Now don't you worry about a thing; we have matters under control. All you need to do is rest easy and get well soon. Could I get you a bit of broth, some chicken soup maybe, a cold rag for your head?"

"The broth will be fine." Lizzie, tired as she was, sensed a new attitude in her daughter-in-law and mentioned this to Adam, when he stopped by her downstairs bedroom the next morning.

"Maybe all we needed to do was to give her a chance. I always thought she was a capable woman," Adam said. "After all, she did take care of her aunt."

"Yes, Lizzie sighed, "but sometimes I feel sorry for her. She is still a city girl at heart. Other times I become exasperated with her. It's her selfishness."

Adam bristled. "How can you say she is selfish when she gave the money for me to stay in Zanesville throughout the ordeal of your operation?"

"Maybe it was worth it to her to get us both out of here for a spell. Now I doubt that I will ever get my house back."

Adam was furious. "Ma, give it up," he said. "Your reign is over."

Indeed her reign as head of household in the home she and John had practically built by themselves—once the masons and carpenters put up the shell—was now about to end. When they arrived on their land in 1818, she had helped tug down the virgin trees that covered every inch of their property. She had carried water from the spring, cooked over an open fire and when the cabin went up she made the curtains and bedspreads, braided the rugs and put in the garden. Then years later when they got a nice six room house, she wallpapered, painted, spaded the garden, planted, cooked, and cleaned. And now this upstart of a girl was pushing her out. Oh, to be sure, she seemed concerned with Lizzie's health, but the joy of being in charge was evident from the way Martha bustled about the house and issued orders to Ermajean and Adam. Without consulting Lizzie, she decided what she would cook for dinner. Household chores were carried out under her direction, and when Lizzie seemed recovered enough to feed the chickens and gather the eggs, Martha assigned those tasks to her. "You might also dust around the parlor and sitting room," she suggested. "It's better to keep busy than to sit around feeling sorry for yourself."

A place outside the kitchen door was to be set aside for an herb garden, and Martha told Adam to dig up the area near the door to the root cellar. Knowing his mother's disdain for giving over that ground to herbs she'd never heard of when there was a perfectly good garden across the road, he did so reluctantly.

Lizzie complained to Adam. "You would think this is an English household instead of a German one. Who needs tansy or fennel, or even mint? Isn't our garden good enough for Martha's herbs?"

Adam shrugged and did as bidden. He was happy to see that his wife was at last asserting herself. But Lizzie continued her complaints. "I used my earnings as a music teacher to buy furniture, pictures, and nice things for this house only to see her put my possessions away and bring out her own fussy figurines and gilded dishes."

"Don't fret about it," Adam said. Except for the figurine he had bought Emma on his return from the war, he was never much interested in the curios women thought important.

A month after her return from the hospital, Lizzie was still persisting. She took another tack against her daughter-in-law. "I notice a perceptible change in our diet," she told Adam. "Instead of our tried and true old German recipes, Martha is introducing foods her family cooks. When I asked her about that, she said her mother's people were originally from Massachusetts, which explains that terrible brown bread. She went off and bought a pudding steamer to make it in."

"Ma I don't want to hear it."

Lizzie was undeterred. "Last month when I was just beginning to feel poorly, I was sitting at the kitchen table watching her get supper. Oh, I had suggested a dish I thought appropriate, but she ignored my wishes and went about making that terrible mix of greens. Do you remember?" She didn't wait for Adam's answer, but went right on with her tirade. "It was that strange concoction she called herb pie. I remember you said it was good, but did you know it was a mixture of lettuce, parsley, and spinach. I watched her boil them up; then she chopped and chopped 'til they were little more than mush. She sautéed onion in butter, put it in piecrust and topped it off with the greens. And over all this she poured a batter of flour, cream, milk, eggs and spices. I declare I never saw such a mess. Now did you ever hear of such an abysmal combination?"

Adam left his mother's room abruptly and did not answer.

Despite her misgivings about her daughter-in-law, Lizzie was getting her bearings. At her doctor's behest and to keep out of Martha's way, she gave up the heavy work and began spending more time with Ben: reading to him and taking walks along the lane to the church. They would leave by the back door, walk down the hill along the trail made by the farm wagons and buggy. Lizzie pointed out various shrubs and trees to the eager little boy. "See this one," she said, pointing to a leafy bush busy with bright red leaves and berries. "That's poison sumac. Ben does not want to touch it, and never ever put the berries in your mouth. You'll die if you do."

"What's die, Gramma?"

"That's when God takes you to heaven to sit by him for eternity."

"Ma, you're going to scare the boy talking about death and heaven when he's so young." Adam had come down the lane behind them. "Give him a chance to grow bigger first."

"He needs to know about such matters. Your wife takes him off with the Methodists, and we have no idea what they are teaching him. I have in mind telling him about God the Lutheran way before his mother gets wise." Lizzie began reading to Ben from the Bible, alternating with stories from some old children's books, among them *Grimms Fairy Tales*. "Your Grandpa bought this book for your Aunt Margaret when she was a little girl." Lizzie stopped reading and stared out the window toward the grove of fruit trees they had methodically planted in rows so many years ago. She turned back to Ben, her face long and sorrowful, for she had become quite thin and wizened. "I was a pretty lady then."

"You're not a very pretty lady now, Gramma," he answered. "Mama says you got wrinkles."

"That I do," she said. "Now let's read this one. We can probably finish it by the time your Mama calls us for dinner."

With her grandson for company, Lizzie adjusted to the household changes. Following doctor's orders she napped afternoons and did light chores, while Martha bustled about rearranging furniture and generally taking over more and more of the household duties.

Adam took pleasure in the peace that descended on the household. Martha was back to performing her wifely duties in bed as she was still nursing Eddie and confidant that she would not get pregnant. "At least that's what your mother tells me," she told Adam. He felt that their lives had finally reached a kind of steady routine, that Martha was accepting her role as wife and mother. Lizzie seemed to be mending, although she continued to waste away and she tired easily. But with seventy-seven on the horizon, some slowing down was to be expected.

Adam had begun to congratulate himself on fathering two sons and weathering the initial turmoil of their marriage, when one day a screaming Martha confronted him in the barn where he was currying the horses. "Adam, Adam," she yelled, her face twisted and blotched with tears, "Eddie is dead, our baby is dead. Ermajean killed him."

Adam dropped the currycomb, and raced with Martha to the house, his stomach sick with dread. "It can't be," he yelled, "he's just asleep." They tore through the house and up the steps to find Ermajean sobbing in a heap on the floor, the baby lying on his stomach in the crib. A woolen blanket lay on top of the light covers.

"I din't do it; I din't do it," Ermajean shrieked. "Please Mam."

Martha slapped her across the top of her head, "You contemptible idiot. I should have got rid of you months ago."

Adam leaned over the crib and listened for the child's breath. He lay his large hand gently on the little body. "I can't feel anything," he said, turning him over and again leaning over the child, his ear to the tiny chest. With Martha sobbing hysterically and Ermajean lost in her wailing, he couldn't tell for certain. "I'll get Ma," he said, but when he turned to go he saw his mother standing in the doorway, her face masked in shock. "You're not supposed to climb steps," he said.

Ignoring him, Lizzie moved quickly to the crib. "What's this blanket doing here? Was this on top of the baby?"

Ermajean stared wide-eyed at Lizzie, her terrified face expecting another slap. "I found it over his head," she said. "I honest don't know how it got there. I din't do it; I din't do it. I took the cover off and went to get him up, and he was stone cold dead."

Martha gasped and fainted.

Lizzie reached to pick up the tiny body. Cradling it gently in her arms, she said, "I've lost three children to death. It wrenches your heart from your being like no other loss, but this grief will pass. See to Martha here, Adam. I'll take the child to the kitchen."

Nineteen

"We'll need a coffin." Lizzie looked up at Adam. "And bring me the wash basin, the large one and a clean baby blanket."

While Lizzie bathed and wrapped the child in the blanket, Adam went to the barn to construct the casket. Martha, still distraught, remained sobbing in her bedroom. There was no sign of Ermajean. When Adam returned to the house, he was carrying a simple pine box in one hand and a lid, hammer, and nails in the other. Once the body was inside, he planned to nail the coffin shut. Mourning would be confined to the family; there would be no viewing.

"You'd better be about finding the grave diggers," Lizzie told him. "There is a plot beside Sam and your father. After that, go by and tell Mary Jane and Jake what has occurred. Tell them we will have a family-sized service at the gravesite in the Jerusalem Church cemetery. In the meantime, after you get this nailed shut, put the casket in the root cellar. It's too hot to leave it here."

"You'll do nothing of the kind with my baby. I want him." Martha stood in the doorway leading from the kitchen into the family sitting room, her face a blaze of tears and puffy blotches. "Get him out of that ugly box. He's mine. You can't take him away from me like this. I haven't even gazed upon his dear face." Her hair, having fallen to her shoulders, hung limp beside her face. She stood screaming like a crazed spook, "I want my baby. I want my Eddie."

Adam went to her and led her to a chair by the table. As wrung out as a rag doll, she slumped and reached her hands toward Lizzie. "Please?" she said, her voice as wispy as a child's.

"Remove the lid," Lizzie told Adam. "You've only got three nails there so it should loosen easily." When the lid was lifted, Lizzie reached in to get the little bundle, walked around the table, and put the dead child in Martha's arms. She carefully unwrapped his face, which had turned bluish white. "God wanted him more than we did," she said as gently as she could. "Let him go Martha."

"He doesn't look well, does he?" Martha turned her ravaged face to Lizzie.

"No dear," he doesn't." Lizzie pulled the blanket back over the child's face. "Perhaps he was sick all along, and we didn't know it. He never grew very big." She picked up the bundle from Martha's arms and once more laid him in the box.

Then looking at Adam, who was making no move toward his distraught wife, she said, "It's getting late, son, you had better leave the nailing to me and go and see about the gravediggers. That extra grave is right next to Sam's. I don't think the minister is about, so we may have to call on Bartholomew. Seems whenever there is a tragedy, we need him."

At the mention of Bartholomew, Martha tore into a rage. "You will not bring the father of that murderess into this house. I will not have him saying prayers over my child. And my darling Eddie is not going with the Lutherans either. Adam, stop by my church and see if Reverend Chandler is about."

Before he could acquiesce to either woman's request, Lizzie shot back. "This child is a Springer, and Springers go with the Lutherans."

"Over my dead body," Martha stood up, her tear-stained face turned belligerent. "He will be buried in the Methodist cemetery beside my church."

"But his father is Lutheran."

"I haven't seen him going off to church recently."

"And furthermore," Lizzie bent closer to Martha, so close that their faces were less than a foot apart. I'll not have that poor girl, Ermajean, accused when we have no proof." Lizzie sent Martha a look that did not cover the contempt she harbored against her daughter-in-law, even as she had tried with every ounce of resolve she could muster not to let it show.

"Then how did that blanket get over his face?"

"Did you see that blanket over his face?" Lizzie shouted.

Adam winced; the confrontation was heating up.

"When the burial is over—and I assure you it will be in the Methodist Cemetery—I am going to pay a call on the sheriff." Martha addressed her husband. "And you won't stop me."

Adam suddenly came alive. "I'll decide the fate of my son, and he will not go either place. I'll bury him here upon our own land. He sprang from here; he'll go down here." He spoke so sharply that neither woman had the courage or energy to cross him. "And furthermore if you go to the sheriff on the basis of the little information we have about how this happened, you may go back to your precious Marietta tomorrow, but Ben stays here."

The next day, after having used pick, mattock, and shovel to dig into the ground, Adam carried his son's casket down the hill toward the place he had prepared in a grove of trees. "And with good luck, I'll someday come to rest beside you," he said aloud to the box as he began to shovel dirt over the lid. Before he turned to go, he paused to ask God to take his son to heaven. The deed done, the box covered with loose soil and tamped down with several stones, he shuffled up the hill. In spring he would return to the site to erect the gravestone ordered from the stonecutter in Four Corners. The simple white marker only one foot wide and two feet high would read: *Here lies Eddie, son of A.E. and M.J. Springer, Aged 3M, 3D.* To keep the cost down, he held the lettering to a minimum.

To Adam's knowledge, even though he told them both where it was, neither woman ever visited the grave. But he did many times. In early summer he transplanted clumps of violets over the child, watering, and nurturing them through the warm months after their blooming season was over. Those flowers die young just as our Eddie did, Adam thought, and concluded that violets with their purple blooms and diminutive size truly represent mourning for an infant.

When his nightmares returned, the child seemed to be mixed into them. He saw dead and maimed soldiers either cuddle the boy or kick his small body aside. Unsure what these dreams meant, Adam would awaken in his boyhood bed drenched in sweat. Martha refused to speak to him, and when no preacher was asked to say the words from the Bible, his mother's brooding created a house in silence. During mealtimes conversation flowed through Ben, who asked repeatedly for his brother. His parents and grandmother invariably answered, *God took him,* or *he's gone to Heaven.*

"Heaven! What's heaven?"

It fell to Lizzie to answer, "A beautiful place we all go when we die."

"Why did God take away our Eddie away?"

"Don't ask so many questions." Adam commanded.

The child yelled back, "I hate God, he stole our Eddie."

"Be quiet and eat your supper."

Ben bent his head over his plate, and between sniffles began to spoon stew into his mouth. Silence resumed as it did most days during mealtimes to be interrupted only by the rattling of forks on plates, spoons in cups, and shifting chairs that signaled the meal was over.

Once Adam tried knocking on Martha's bedroom door. "Please, let me come in. I need you Martha. He was my son too."

There was no response.

The next time he knocked, she called out. "Go away, I want nothing more to do with you."

He shuffled back to his bed and did not try to reach her again. Then one spring night he awakened to see her standing in the doorway clad in her long white ruffled gown, her dark hair hanging over her breasts. In the moonlight she appeared childlike. He sat up and held out his arms.

"Adam, I want another baby to take our darling Eddie's place."

He was happy to comply and when months passed and finally a year and no child appeared, he found her desperate for his attentions. Ben passed his fourth birthday in 1873, the year his grandmother turned seventy-eight and still no baby appeared imminent.

That was also the year Lizzie took a turn. Adam found himself with two sick women to attend, for Martha was finally coping with morning sickness. Frequently in pain, his mother once again sought Dr. Kennedy's advice, only this time, Adam deemed her too sick to travel and went to fetch the doctor from his office in Four Corners.

With snow on the ground, the doctor arrived the next day in his horse-drawn sleigh and hastened to Lizzie's bedside in the small room behind the front parlor while Adam waited in the sitting room for the doctor's assessment. When it came, he felt a terrible weight. "I thought the surgeon guaranteed that he had gotten all the cancer."

"There are no guarantees, my son. It sometimes happens that when a cancer is removed by the knife minute germs are released to invade organs near the original site. And that may have happened in your mother's case. She has maybe six months at most. I fear the cancer has returned and since she has already undergone an operation, there is not much chance that my remedies will cure. But we can try. Sometimes nature surprises us. If you would like, I'll start now."

Did he need to make the decision, or was such a determination his mother's to make? What does she want?" Adam asked.

"She wants to live, of course."

"Then do what you must."

"I'll need some assistance. Is the Missus about?"

"My wife? She wasn't well this morning. I think she is in a family way again. I'll have to help."

"I warn you, it won't be pleasant."

"If it gives my mother life, I'm ready." Adam got up from the rocker. "Tell me what to do. I doubt it will be any more unpleasant than what I have already witnessed on the battlefield."

"Probably not. First, let me tell you what I'm going to do. Do you have a quantity of ice nearby?"

Adam allowed as to how he did. The creek was iced over and the remains of several loose slabs sat in a galvanized tub in the root cellar

"Pound up a small amount and put the chips in a clean handkerchief; a thin one is preferred. Add some rock salt and bring the mixture to me. Meanwhile, I'll give her laudanum to relieve the pain."

Adam did as he was instructed, and when he had the ice packet in hand, he joined the doctor at his mother's bedside. Her nightdress had been raised to her waist to expose an oozing sore just below and to one side of her navel, where Dr. Kennedy applied the poultice. "I'd prefer that the Missus be here so that she can learn how to do this, for it should be done twice each day. Do you think she's well enough to come down and observe? If it is only morning sickness she is experiencing; the nausea should be over now—it's almost noon. She needs to watch how I press this pad into the wound until the cancer is freezing cold and your mother can barely stand it more."

Adam went to get Martha who arrived reluctantly, but took her place by the bedside regardless.

"Now I'm going to use this caustic." Dr. Kennedy picked a ready-made potion from his black bag and spreading it liberally on gauze inserted it into the wound. Lizzie's cry of pain shattered the stillness like smashed windowpane. Indeed, her cries were more intense than the short intakes of breath they had come to know as *suffering*. "The laudanum will soon take effect, and the pain will be lessened," Dr. Kennedy assured them. "But you must keep this tight upon the wound for at least five hours until it is impossible for her to stand it any longer. Do this for at least five days, after which the cancerous mass should slough off."

"What's in that potion?" Adam inquired.

"Carbide of zinc, carbolic acid, and tannin," was the doctor's reply.

Twenty

One body comes into this world, another leaves, and in the Springer household that is what happened as 1873 came to an end, and a new year with its attendant promises for happier times beckoned. Martha delivered her third son without much fanfare in December just before the new year. They named him Franklin, Frank for short. She showed no disappointment in not producing a girl and seemed to regard the baby as a God-given substitute for the deceased Eddie. Lizzie lingered on until early 1874 when, as she was nearing seventy-nine, the suffering ended. It had been a long siege, and there were times that even as he wished her life, Adam could only pray fervently for her death. And when the end came, they could barely conceal their joy at having the ordeal over. Through it all Martha performed remarkably well from the moment Dr. Kennedy showed her how to apply the poultices to the day she bathed Lizzie's body for the last time and dressed her in the newest dark dress she could find.

Six months before Lizzie passed on, Martha's morning sickness that preceded Frank's birth had ended, and Adam found her in the kitchen early each morning. She set up a schedule for every routine chore, washing, and bathing Lizzie afternoons, changing her nightdress and her sheets daily. Such activity meant that not a day passed without her having to fill the two galvanized tubs with warm water—one for washing, the other for rinsing. She took down the wooden washboard from where it hung on the side porch and scrubbed the soiled clothing. If the spotting did not come out, she set a large boiler on the stove and boiled up the garments until every stain disappeared and she could hang the glistening whites to dry outside on a sunny day or on inside lines crisscrossing the kitchen in winter. Adam hated having the lines inside. They set him to bobbing and weaving to avoid being slapped by the damp and sometimes dripping clothes. No matter how large her abdomen grew Martha did not complain, even as she heated up the six heavy irons on the stovetop and kept ironing into the night after everyone else was in bed.

Adam never liked going into the sickroom. His mother's face was as pale as the white pillowslip on which her snowy hair splayed. Her appearance was ghostly like someone who had already died and come back to haunt him. Mostly he simply stopped by, inquired how she felt when he knew full well she felt as poorly as a body can. He never sat down but remained in the doorway as though waiting for his chance to escape.

"You might read to your mother," Martha said to him at breakfast one morning. "She lies in that bed all day long with barely a conversation from any of us, and Ben acts like he's afraid her. Ben who loved her so much doesn't even want to be near her in the throes of death."

Adam tried reading from the Bible, but after a few psalms and verses, she generally fell asleep, and he could silently close the big book and step from the room. Sometimes after Martha bathed her in the early afternoon, she would go to the piano in the parlor next door to Lizzie's bedroom and play from one of her mother-in-law's songbooks, a respite that Lizzie said was the brightest spot of her day. "I didn't play enough in later years," she told her daughter-in-law. "You should not give up the piano because household and family needs take over your life. I love hearing you play. Is that a new piece? I never heard it before."

"Yes, Mother Springer it is. When I was in town last week, I picked up the music at Swingle's store. I had stopped in to look at the new organs and happened to see this piece prominently featured on the music rack. Mr. Swingle said it's very new, and I thought it appropriate to play for you. The title is *Silver Threads Among the Gold.*

"It's lovely and time we had some new music. My pieces are so old. Nobody wants to hear *Listen to the Mockingbird* and *Tramp, Tramp, Tramp the Boys Are Marching* anymore."

"Or *Jeanie With the Light Brown Hair,*" Martha laughed.

"You play beautifully. You must have had a good instructor as I did for four or five months. I can't remember now exactly how long I was Madame Schumann's student. That was when I lived in Baltimore, just for a short spell, mind you, so I could study piano from an esteemed German teacher."

"Thank you, Mother Springer," Martha said, ignoring the reference to Baltimore. She was inclined to believe that was a figment of her mother-in-law's imagination. Martha doubted that a simple Virginia farm girl could ever have had the nerve to traipse off to Baltimore alone at seventeen. "I'll try to remember not to let home and children interfere too much" Martha indulged Lizzie. "One should always take time for diversions from the cares of the day. And yes, I too had some excellent instruction as I was growing up. I took to it from the start, not like my flighty sister, Effie, who Mother had to command to sit at the piano for the required practice time."

After two days of following Dr. Kennedy's orders Martha decided the cures were barbaric. "I declare they leave your mother more debilitated than when we started them; they are giving her no peace, no rest whatsoever, her pain is only compounded by them."

Lizzie shared her disdain. "I can't stand much more," she looked pleadingly at Martha, her once feisty spirit having already gone to the grave. Please let me go in peace. More laudanum would help"

"Truth to tell, I can't stand to see you suffer like this. Why don't I just try to make you comfortable."

At first Adam thought if the treatments gave his mother longer life, as Dr. Kennedy said they might, he wanted them continued, for he still could not quite imagine life without her. Both women ignored his objections and the applications ceased. On her own Martha made up a stronger mixture of laudanum, having concluded that Dr. Kennedy's was too weak. She went to the apothecary and purchased Turkish opium, which she sliced and soaked in boiling water. When it was sufficiently dissolved she poured the mixture into a half-pint of seventy-six per cent alcohol; and when Lizzie's pains came on, Martha had no qualms about pouring into her as much as she could swallow.

Meals arrived on time with Lizzie's consisting of thin gruel that Martha cooked and sieved separately every morning. Adam marveled at the ease with which Martha took charge even as her stomach rounded. Pregnancy seemed to give her new enthusiasm; he suspected that was because she was eager to replace the lost Eddie with this new life coming on.

Ben, meanwhile, came under his father's care and followed him around as he did his chores, even toddling out to the barn where he helped him divvy up the hay and feed for the animals. Adam welcomed the eager interest of his son, who was growing into a sturdy, talkative four-year-old. "Someday you'll take over when I'm old like your gramma." The boy's presence had the further effect of keeping Adam calm, when he inadvertently hit his thumb with a hammer, or faced a surly animal, or some other event that could set his fragile feelings and temper reeling.

No chore seemed too much for Martha to handle. "My looks are gone anyway," she declared to Adam patting her massive stomach when he complimented her on her efficiency. "Why I don't even have time to make my complexion soap, and I'm nearly out it. I must get to that for I used up mine keeping your mother's skin soft. She wounds easily; her bedsores must be exceedingly painful, but she never complains. We should turn her more often. I put her from side to side, but she can't lay upon that oozing stomach."

A few days later, Martha confronted Adam. "I've gathered a tub of fresh lard for making a new batch of complexion cream. It's resting now in spring water, and after I rinse it at least three more times—God only knows when I have time for that—I'll beat it into a cream and add the rosewater. Adam, I don't like to ask you to do woman's work; I know how you hate it, but I could use a little assistance. If you could do the beating, I'll add the rosewater. Working together we can have it done in no time, and with winter upon us, we need that soothing cream."

Adam was so overwhelmed with her newfound affability he readily agreed. Maybe keeping her pregnant was the answer. She seemed more at peace with herself, he concluded, than when she had few chores to perform, and there was nothing like a baby on the way to keep a woman focused on the future. He saw that in whatever spare time she had—usually at night under the kerosene lamps—she was knitting booties, sweaters, crib blankets, or sewing another quilt. In the evenings with Ben in bed, Lizzie dosed with laudanum, Martha at her needlework, and Adam with his books or the McConnelsville Herald, the family seemed at peace.

That was short lived, for when Martha gave birth household chores fell to Adam. "There's nothing wrong with a man learning to cook," Martha told him, "and as for Lizzie, Emma has agreed to come and help." While Martha remained upstairs in the bedroom, her new son by her side, Emma took charge of both Lizzie and the household, a situation that remained until Lizzie took her final breath.

"A life well lived," the mourners who came to the house agreed. "A fine upstanding woman," others said. "A pillar of our Lutheran Church," was heard from another. And several remembered that it was Lizzie who gave them piano lessons when they were young. "She will be missed," they concluded. And contrary to Eddie's forlorn little burial, neighbors came from miles around to see Lizzie off to her maker. They brought so much food that the kitchen table could barely contain all the casseroles, plates, and platters. "It's the least we could do," many said.

When the last mourner left and Adam and Martha were alone in the sitting room, a new subject came up—not exactly new to Adam, but one he hoped would be put aside.

"Now that your mother is gone and we have two children, it is time for that home of our own. What do you say, Adam?"

He was reading and didn't say anything.

"Adam, I'm speaking to you." Her voice rose to a shrillness she had used early in their marriage, a tone Adam hoped never to hear again.

"What did you say?"

"I said, I feel it is time now with your mother's death and our family grown to four that we have a home of our own. I want to sell this farm and build on that eighty acres. They tell me Pineville is growing. Already it is nearly to the boundary of that property your uncle gave you, land for which you have found no great use. We could build us a fine home, not a house your mother would have liked, but one for me, to my liking. I want a modern house with an indoor water closet that I can use daily at my ease and not when I am finally forced to regardless of the terrible weather. Why sometimes, I wait for days . . . well, never mind that."

"And how do you propose that I earn a living?"

"You could get a job in Pineville. Maybe sell off a few lots, and with the money we would get from this place we could build a fine house."

"I know you loathe this farm? But this is your fate, so I think your idea is humbug," he rose abruptly from his chair, "and furthermore, I want to hear no more about a new house."

"Before we were married, you promised the day Father and I went with you to see the property that I could have a home of my own. Remember, I marked out on the ground where the various rooms might go."

"I remember, but I have rented that land for pasture and have sold off some of the timber, and if things get bad, I'll sell the rest of it. I'm in charge here and don't you forget it. Now cease this idle chatter about a house."

"But I thought you didn't like farming."

"I don't, but with a growing family, I have no choice."

"Adam, you lack nerve; you're still your mother's little boy; afraid to take a chance on something bigger. You're always wrathy about this or that as if that makes you a big man. Well, it doesn't. Father was right, I married out of my class to my everlasting regret."

"Don't you talk to me like that, mere woman that you are." He stepped toward her, his hand raised.

"And don't you ever raise a hand to me," she said defiance flashing in her ice-blue eyes. "I'll kill you, if you ever strike me."

"And go to hell for all time, let alone jail?" He threw down his book and stalked out of the room.

126

"Preferable to living here in this broken down old house with a nasty husband I can't stand."

Adam and Martha spoke to each other only out of necessity for the next eight months. There were no friendly discussions about neighbors or family, and after the children were bedded down at night, Martha repaired to her bedroom to read or knit by kerosene lamp, while Adam contented himself in his favorite sitting room rocker, a book or newspaper in hand. They kept to their own sides of the bed refraining from even the slightest touch until Adam left in disgust and returned to his boyhood bedroom. When Martha ceased nursing Frank, she announced with a new measure of authority that she would be going to Marietta during the fall of 1875 to see her parents. "They are aging, and I feel I am neglecting them."

"Suit yourself, but just remember you are my wife, and I expect you to return after a week's stay."

"I'll be the judge of that," Martha sniffed. "I have talked the matter over with Emma to see if her Clara can stay with you. We can pay her something." "We don't need to pay her anything. We don't need her. I can take care of myself for the short time you will be gone." He left the parlor thus negating any further conversation. She shouted at his back. Adam, as was his custom when faced with a matter he did not care to discuss, stamped off to the barn before he could hear her yell, "you will never tell me what to do." Truth to tell he welcomed ten days of his own company; he was tired of being beholden, first to his mother and father, then to Martha and the children.

Twenty-one

Martha must have recognized that leaving before spring planting and summer's harvest would only cause another flare up. So she waited until the stoneware crocks were filled with sauerkraut, dried corn was hanging in brown bags in the loft, root vegetables were in the cellar, and the preserves cooked up and put in jars. All that remained before winter set in was salting down the newly butchered meat. "Adam, you can certainly manage that without me," she told him when setting her departure date for mid-October. "The weather will be chilly then, but still clear." Her plans took into account Adam's trip to and from the Ebensport dock, where she would board the packet for the excursion to Marietta. Adam had tried several times unsuccessfully to return to her bed but was barred during the interim months, a fact that further added to his discontent. "I do not plan to arrive in Marietta with another child on the way, and now that I've stopped nursing that could happen. In fact, I have no intention of ever again being in a family way, so you had better get used to it."

Once more Adam shuffled off to his boyhood bedroom, even as he felt he should assert his manly rights. *Get them out of the house in peace. I'll be damned if I'll allow her to continue rejecting me.*

By the time they left for Ebensport, Martha had perused the weekly newspaper for boat schedules to Marietta, but was vague about the time of her return. "I'll write," she told him.

"What about Ben and his schooling? "

"That school is terrible; the school board doesn't pay enough for an adequate teacher; she only gets thirty dollars for three months work and has to take part of that in food for her parents in Pineville. That new one doesn't even have a high school education, and her English is countrified, *southern speak* I call it. For the short time I will be gone, I'll teach him myself using my old McGuffey Reader and Ray's Arithmetic from my own school days."

She was well on her way when he noticed she had not addressed the date of her return. He had ordered her back after a week's stay, and his anger grew as October ended and the wintry winds of November blasted the bleak Ohio countryside. Ice gathered on the river, snow arrived, but still she did not return. She had been away six weeks when she finally wrote to tell him she would be coming by stage in mid-December. Anger welled in him like hell-fire and brimstone. The woman needed taming. He had repeatedly told her, "you would have been a happier wife and mother without all that education. These colleges must be crazy enrolling women." She had simply given him a saucy look and slammed the bedroom door. He remembered that his sister, Margaret, had gone to Oberlin as soon as the college broke the barrier and let women in. Now more were following suit. Where would it end? Even Lizzie had said girls should be educated.

The barren weeks without his family left him so lonely that he forgot his determination to teach her a lesson and greeted her and the children with hugs when they arrived in Four Corners.

"I'm going back every year," Martha told him. "I feel so refreshed. I dressed for dinner every night, saw my old friends, partied, and did not neglect Ben's education, even enrolled him in my old grammar school, so now he has a good start."

Adam couldn't find words to refute all this exuberance and listened intently as Ben read from his primer with all the self-assurance of a scholar.

"See Papa, these here are letters: A,B,C . . . and here is where I can use them, that's a *A*. Ben pointed his finger at the page. "And it says *ax*. See this is a picture of a ax and over on this page is a girl and that's what the word next to her says."

"I remember, I had this book when I was a boy your age."

"We all did." Martha joined the conversation. "I think our Ben reads very well, don't you?"

"Certainly does, for such a little fellow."

Martha seemed so vigorous that he decided not to break the spell; he would beg her kindly to bend to his wishes. But her refusals continued. It was soon necessary to use force and by the following year, she was burdened with another babe in arms. Swearing that the additional child would not stop her from going to Marietta, she left Ben in the care of his father to attend the local school. "There is a new teacher this year, who has had a year of college." Martha told him. "She seems engaging and proficient enough, but living with that stern-faced president of the school board, Mr. Schmidt, and his family may deter her from returning. I hear they don't allow any gentlemen callers, so not only is she expected to teach in school but also to help Mrs. Schmidt with the chores and the children. That poor girl can't be more than nineteen. People around here don't seem to mind that she has no social life; they claim that means she can concentrate fully on educating the children rather than mooning over some sweetheart."

On Martha's trip to Marietta that fall of 1876, she took along four-year-old Frank and the baby they named William. From Martha's point of view, the new baby was unexpected and unappreciated even as her motherly instincts took over. She reminded Adam often that the circumstances of his birth "are most troubling to me and always will be. Don't you ever force yourself on me again, or I will take the children and leave. I may be a wife, but I don't relish being raped."

He too had bitter memories of that night; she had fought and clawed him, refused to let him on top of her, but in the end by mere brute strength he prevailed.

"No, Adam, I don't want it." Her shriek still pierced his mind like the scrape of diamond on glass.

"You are my wife, and I will have at you whenever I want; you will not again reject me. Do you understand?" And for the next year her protestations went unheeded until they finally ended. Adam had, at last, begun to assert himself, not only in the matter of having his wife whenever he wanted but also in matters having to do with the farm. He had been lackluster about these issues over the years, seemingly content to get along, to do whatever his mother wished and later his wife. His nightly dreams and depression were close to taking over his life in those years, and when during a few sessions with Dr. Kennedy, he was told to "buck up, take charge of your life, and quit dwelling on that damnable war," he finally had the courage to try. Since he and Dr. Kennedy were talking man to man, Adam got up his nerve to ask how one could prevent the onset of more children and still remain a man.

"Why that's easy," Dr. Kennedy responded. "Tell Martha to go to the apothecary and ask for a female preventative; its called a pessary in medical terms. She will need to insert it—you know where—just prior to relations. The directions are on the package, and the device costs a dollar."

He would talk one-to-one with Martha, he reasoned, explaining how she could get over her fear of having more children. Then he thought better of that and decided to ask Emma to talk to her. Surely Emma must know about these matters; she has only three children. He needed to trod a fine line. Martha's anger at him seemed to be escalating, but she still carried out her household duties, as a good wife should. She hurled her energies into fixing up the house: painting, wallpapering, and scrubbing. She put Ben to work, so the boy rarely had time to be a boy, to frolic with the other children.

She confined her household improvements to the winter months after her annual return from Marietta, which seemed to give her new impetus for keeping matters on an even keel. Each spring she planted pansies along the front walk; iris and salvia grew on the south side. Occupants of wagons passing by saw a pleasant well cared for house with a profusion of inviting flowers, shrubbery, and rose bushes. She wore the pessary and endured his advances without so much as moving a muscle for his or her own enjoyment. And no more children appeared.

Seeing his wife's endeavors gave Adam new purpose, and he rebuilt the old barn with the help of Seth's boy. Leaving the log uprights and cross beams hewn so long ago by his father, they enlarged the building and added new siding. Now he had room for more cattle, which would result in more calves to sell. And not once did he ask Martha for money. Instead, he went to the bank and took out a small loan. The tenants still occupied the house in Four Corners, but he would not put it past her to oust them and move in herself. He knew of no wife leaving her husband, not for any reason. Homer Parkin, it was said, abused his wife, and she was frequently seen with her hat pulled low, her scarf wrapped high, but even she would never leave her husband and eight children. Besides where would she go with no money, her family long dead? It simply was not done. Divorce was considered the devil's work. In the Great War, he'd known Homer as an unruly buzzard given to strong drink when he could get it, but they had never been close.

Martha, however, remained a puzzle to Adam. There were times when she appeared loving. She would pat him on the shoulder or take his hand when they walked, but still he felt she wasn't happy with him or the way they lived. Even with three children, the work of the farm and garden, she didn't have enough to keep her interested. Ben and Frank helped with the chores leading Adam to conclude that had Martha been a man, she would have been a meritorious master sergeant or perhaps a general. Indeed, there was little in the house the boys could not do, for Martha made no lines of demarcation between women's work and men's. Mercifully she had quit talking about a home of her own design, but Adam knew her well enough to recognize the thought still simmered. She appeared amiable. This new attitude had been unexpected, for as soon as she learned he would not be pushed around she quit being disagreeable. No doubt about it, he had been a dunce during those early years of their marriage.

Martha's and Adam's twelfth wedding anniversary passed without much fanfare in September 1880. They could look to significant accomplishment, if not much money, and they now had three healthy boys: Ben, eleven; Frank, seven; and Will, an even-tempered, sweet four-year-old. Martha had passed her thirtieth birthday the year before and seemed to Adam as restless as ever. She still went to Marietta every year, but now left both the older boys at home to attend school and help their father. During the lonely evenings, Adam had reason to resent his wife's independence. What kind of wife goes off and leaves her husband and children simply to nourish her own desires? Confounded woman! When she returns this time I'll put my foot down, tell her the trips have to end. Did she have no concern for how they were eating, doing the wash, keeping up the house? That was woman's work and here were the three of them doing it all themselves. True, she had done the preserving, the putting up and putting down of the winter foodstuffs before she left, but Martha's place was in this house, and she'd better get used to it. He'd tell that when she got back; put his foot down and forbid these annual trips to Marietta.

He was further annoyed when she arrived home and inquired hardly at all as to their wellbeing. Instead, she was full of chatter about the goings on in Marietta: the clothes fashionable ladies wore, the musicals in the town, visits with her friends. Clearly, these trips are worth it, Adam thought, as he listened again for another recounting of *who said what, when, and to whom.* But he could not bring himself to mention that the trips must end, although he had to admit they seemed to sustain her for what she called "the rest of the boring year." When she returned in the winter of 1881, she was off on another tack. "While I was there, my sister and I had such great fun riding horseback like we did when we were young girls. Father always had horses. In the early days we straddled them, but now we go sidesaddle. It's more ladylike, and once you get used to it—well, it's not so bad."

She told this tale often, and Adam began to suspect there was more to it. Indeed, he was right. "It's a riding horse, I want," she finally told him. "If I had a horse I could go over the countryside and smell the grand outdoors in all its purity. Please, Adam, I so want a sprightly horse of my own. You've already taught the boys to ride that old mare, but I want a stylish horse, a two-year old, perhaps—one that would be my companion for many years to come. I promise if you buy me a riding horse, I will take care of it myself. I'll need a saddle too—a sidesaddle."

She cast him a crooked smile as though taking measure of his opposition, if that should come.

Adam simply grumped and walked away.

In all this talk of a horse, which went on throughout the winter, she never once mentioned having money to purchase her own. He conceded it wasn't such a bad idea to have an honest-to-God riding horse, one too grand to pull a buggy. The boys would enjoy such an animal. By the time his conjecture became reality, Martha had passed her thirty-first birthday, and they were about to celebrate thirteen years together. Adam decided that a horse would be a fine present and made an excuse to go to the auction in Pineville to buy one as a surprise. Since placing the plain gold band upon her finger, he had never bought her a present. Birthdays went unnoticed and Christmas brought forth oranges for the boys ordered by mail, but nothing for Martha, although she generally provided knitted scarves or mittens all around.

The little filly they named Daisy was a spirited animal. She had been broken and seemed well cared for. Adam carefully examined her legs for signs of sprain and blistering. Detecting no scars, he noted her fine straight back, her well-shaped head, full eye and long neck—all signs of a good horse. Her four middle teeth were still in place, so Adam was certain that the colt was only two years old as the owner claimed.

With some careful maneuvering, he and a hired hand at the auction house managed to get Daisy into the wagon, where she was closely penned by high wooden slats. Although she fought the confinement by kicking and bucking in place, once she discovered the oats and carrots in the feed bucket she settled down for the seven-mile trip to the Springer farm.

Martha bounced across the porch to greet them. She was as pleased as he had ever seen her and held her hands together under her chin as if she were praying. "Oh Adam," she said, "this is the nicest thing you have ever done for me." Then she hugged him, the first in a long time. The boys were thrilled and each one asked to have a ride. While they all stood around admiring Daisy, Adam went to the barn and when he returned he was carrying a saddle, a small one fit for a woman.

"Did you buy that too?" Martha stared, but her look was incredulous. "That's not a sidesaddle," she said.

"No. Ma never rode sidesaddle. This was hers. I found it in the loft in the old barn."

"But Adam, I want a sidesaddle, one fit for a lady."

"This will do for now. I cleaned it and polished it real good. The leather is a bit dry and cracked here and there, but given all the years it's been around, it's in pretty good shape. If you confine your riding to our farm, no one need see you." He threw the saddle over Daisy's back, tightened the cinch, and invited the boys to ride.

Martha turned abruptly and went back into the house. "I have to get dinner," she said.

"Don't you want to ride too, Mama? Papa says Daisy is really your horse." Ben's face was as animated as she had ever seen it.

"Later, dear. I'm not dressed for a ride now. But I will be soon enough."

She fed and cared for the horse, but she never rode her. Adam knew why. Martha would not ride on that saddle. He had bought the horse, now let her loosen up her own purse strings for the sidesaddle. Before long she did, and although Adam was somewhat appalled that she had also purchased a store-bought riding outfit, he did not question what she spent or where the money came from. She became a familiar figure in her black derby hat dashing about the countryside as regal as a queen in her brown gabardine riding costume with its black velveteen collar.

"People say Mama thinks she's better'n anybody else around here when they see her dressed up on Daisy," fourteen-year-old Ben told his father.

"Well, that's the way your mother is," Adam said. "But don't you think she makes a fine picture?"

"I guess, but Joey Pfeister says she's real stuck up. I said, she is not and he hit me."

"Well, I hope you hit him back."

"I did. Balled up my fist and let him have it right across the nose."

"What'd he do?"

"Ran home to tell his Ma."

After she purchased the riding outfit and sidesaddle, Martha rode every day in mid-afternoon. Sometimes her jaunts lasted no more than a half-hour; other times she was gone two or more. Adam never worried about her. She seemed skillful enough and had established a good rapport with Daisy. Never mind what people were saying, he was proud of the way she looked.

A good six months passed during which Martha ceased to ride in winter, but as soon as the first crocus poked its pert head above ground, she and Daisy were back on the road again. That is, until one day when the riderless horse came trotting home. It was Ben who saw her. At first sight, he ran to the field where his father was working. "Papa, Papa, come quick. Daisy came home without Mama."

Adam told Ben to take the team to the barn and hitch one horse to the buggy while he ran onto the roadway and looked in each direction. There was no sign of Martha there or in the neighbor's lane. He took the buggy down the church road at the rear of the property, anxiety and fear growing inside him, and was nearly halfway to the church when he heard Ben's cracking voice, neither that of a boy nor a man. "She's coming, Papa, come back." Adam turned the buggy abruptly and trotted to the barn where he saw Ben waving his hand in the direction of the south field. "She's walking way off in the distance. See her. She's stumbling. Let's go. I think she's hurt."

Bruised, but not seriously hurt, Martha trudged toward them as they ran to greet her. Hatless, her hair streamed across her face. "Dratted horse threw me. If it weren't for that sidesaddle, I could have managed her. She's frisky in this chilly weather."

Adam went toward her. "You all right?"

"Just shaken up. But I need to find Daisy. She went galloping off with no more concern for me than for that post over there."

"Daisy's back in the barn," Ben said, his wide spaced blue eyes, so like his mother's, wore a tender look of concern. "Maybe you shouldn't go riding alone."

"Maybe I should not be galloping on that sidesaddle is more like it. Adam, where is that saddle of your mothers? I'm going to show that horse she can't treat me like this."

"It's in the tack room, but what do you want it for?"

"I'm going to ride her and show her once and for all whose boss."

"Now?"

"Now!"

In the days and weeks that followed Martha rode Daisy as though possessed by a driving force over which she had no control. Perched solidly, legs straddling the western saddle that had been her mother-in-law's, she took command of the horse. "To be truthful about it, that English sidesaddle gave me a backache; you never have the feeling you're secure if the horse goes for more than a trot." she told Adam. "When I rode with my sister, we sat sedately like two ladies out for the air. Now I want to have rides I can remember, rides that hurl me across the countryside. I want to savor the wind on my face, feel myself leaping through the air at great speeds. Makes me feel alive and alert."

Twenty-two

When news came of her father's death, Martha returned to Marietta in March 1884. "No matter the weather, I'm going," she told Adam. She made the entire trip by stagecoach, "a disastrous journey," she said on her return. "The coach nearly turned over twice. I was frightened out of my senses. "Why we have to live so far away, I'll never know, especially now that Mother Springer is gone. And all I have to look forward to here is more planting, plucking, and preserving."

"You're going to get through the planting, plucking, and preserving a good many more years," Adam countered.

Martha glared. "Does that mean I will never have a home of my own?"

"That seems about right, considering there are five mouths to feed here plus the animals. Let me remind you that I need to make a living and farming is all I know."

"If you had any nerve, you would go to town and look for more suitable work. Maybe something where you could wear a suit. When did you last put on a clean pair of overalls? Seems to me you've worn that shirt for weeks as well. A man in a suit is respected. He has the incentive to look refined."

"I have no qualifications for being a professional man. Pa needed me here when I came of an age to get more schooling, apprentice to a lawyer or doctor, or anybody in a position to wear a suit."

Martha seemed to know better than to suggest another trip that fall and remained on the farm during the time she would normally have been in Marietta. She seemed grumpier than usual thereby sending Adam into a blue funk of his own. On the few occasions they spoke, other than in matters dealing with the farm or the children, both snarled like two warring cats. They were also enduring another long winter with gloom and cold with drafts darting about the uninsulated farmhouse that forced everyone into scratchy woolen clothing.

Adam took the sleigh to town in mid-December. He needed to go to the blacksmith shop and purchase supplies at the general store, then went by the post box in the apothecary and picked up a letter addressed to Martha.

Dearest Sister,

This is to inform you of our dear mother's death, November 30th last. She had been ill only a few days, but, as you know, never quite recovered from Father's death and so now they are together again in heaven.

We had the funeral two days later. Sorry, but there was not time to let you know. Anyway, after your terrible trip last time, we felt it best not to make you feel you should be here. There was another reason too. Our brother was anxious to be about settling the estate; said he needed the money. You know how that wife of his can spend. That's what he gets for marrying a Pittsburgh girl. He's seeing to the estate now so you should be hearing from him soon.

I hope you and yours are well.

With fond remembrances,

Your sister,

Effie

"Died of a broken heart," Martha said when she put down the letter. "Mother was never anything without him." Tears streaming down her face, she left the kitchen and went to her bedroom.

Adam decided it was best if she mourned alone.

Shortly thereafter the house in Marietta was sold, the proceeds divided among the four children, all of whom were surprised to learn there was little left of what they expected to be a grand estate. Debts and taxes along with lawyer's fees took their toll, for Mr. Shipman had invested in several failed land ventures. Now Adam learned that Martha had been simply marking time, patiently awaiting her inheritance, which proved to be less than expected, but evidently was ample enough to give her new found independence.

"He was getting even with me for marrying you," she told Adam. "Father never approved of my being a farmer's wife; he said I should have remained in Marietta, where I might have had a future as a gentleman's wife. At least that's what my sisters told me, so in the end he got even. Of course, he did give me that house in Four Corners, but my brother got the family home, my sisters divvied up their possessions, even Mother's jewelry and other expensive gewgaws that even if I had been included in their distribution would look out of place here. Father noted in his will that I had been previously taken care of. I guess this means my greedy brother didn't get as much money as he expected either. At least he left me something." She quoted from the copy of the will in her hand, but made no effort to hand it to Adam, a fact that further irritated him. "And my sisters are not inclined to make an even division of spoils," she went on. "I can't believe that I didn't get even one piece of Mother's jewelry. Father was so generous to her; not one birthday or holiday passed that he didn't go to the jeweler and buy her another bracelet, or a necklace. Well, I'll show them. I'll show you all. I consider the house in Four Corners as payment for staying with Auntie all those months. Certainly not a substitute for my proper inheritance."

"How much did you get from the money left?"

"That is my business!"

At this affront, Adam did not have the energy to get up from his rocker but sat staring into the molding on the pot bellied, cast iron stove. I marry into money but get not a penny of it for me he thought. Weariness settled over him like a worn out coat leaving him too tired to argue. The early winter had been hard on all of them, and the attendant recriminations left him listless.

After notification of her share of the estate, Martha took up her duties in a sour mood, unhappy that her sisters and brother seemed to have been given more than she had. And for the next year, Martha never let up on the subject of another house. "I have enough money now, between my savings and the inheritance that we can leave here." Adam continued to turn a deaf ear, not even answering her entreaties. As the months passed and she ceased her haranguing, they rarely spoke to one another and used the boys as conduits for information. After daily rides on Daisy palled, she let the boys exercise the horse, and to fill up winter afternoons, she took up china painting.

"All the ladies are doing it," she told the family as they watched her apply the delicate pinks, roses, greens, and gold to the white ware plates she had bought mail order from a pottery in Cincinnati, along with a set of china paints made in Germany.

Ben asked, "Why do you want to do that when you can buy dishes already painted up in the store? Anyway, we got all the plates we need."

"Son, you have such a limited view of matters, comes from being stuck on this old farm. This is artwork, same as painting a picture, but I am painting little flowers around this rim—see." Still holding the pink tipped brush in one hand, she

138

thrust the plate at Ben. He studied it closely and then picked up another she had completed.

"They don't match," he said. "See here, the roses on this here plate are bigger and the painted rim is wider."

"That's what makes them special. Each one is different, but alike enough to be used as a set, which shows they were done by hand not by some machine in a factory."

Ben looked doubtful. "Who would buy plates that don't match?"

"I don't intend to sell them. I'll hand them down to you someday. You and your wife can give them to your children, and they will give them to their children. These plates will become family heirlooms to be treasured."

"I ain't never gettin' married."

"I declare Ben you are beginning to talk just like these country people. The word is *am* as in *I am never getting married*, but you will. Some pretty girl will come along and entice you."

"Nope, when I'm older, I'm going west. Maybe all the way to Californy."

"Cal-i-forn-ya. There are girls in the west too. But you will do no such thing until you get a decent education."

"No, Mama, school's done for me. We ain't—I mean we don't have no more grades in the country school."

"We don't have any more grades."

"Oh, Ma."

She continued dabbing pink paint, mixing it with red to effect the petals of a rose, then held the plate at arm's length. "When I'm done we will have dessert plates that are special, like painted pictures in a museum done by famous artists. Only in this case I'm the artist."

"What's a museum, Mama?"

"It's a place where curios are put out for people to see; sometimes they are about history or geology, sculpture and painting. Doesn't your teacher ever tell you about such matters?"

"Nope, only readin', writin', spellin', and rithmatic."

Martha sighed. "Nothing about the country or the world."

"Nope, just readin', writin' . . ."

"That's enough Ben, I see clearly that it is time we did something about this miserable schooling your brothers and you are receiving. How many teachers have you had since first grade anyway?"

"Let's see! There was Miss Taylor, Mr. Woodward, Miss Weir . . ."

"Too many," his mother interrupted. "It's time we do something about this sorry country education, or you'll end up like your father—a poor farmer."

"I heard that," Adam bellowed from the family sitting room.

"I'm glad you did," Martha shouted back from the downstairs bedroom, where she kept her paints and plates. Getting up from her chair, she capped the tubes, and still carrying the half-painted plate, walked into the sitting room. "Just thought you should know that I'm making plans to remedy the school situation." Her eyes narrowed and her jaw was set.

"What situation?"

"The poor schooling our children are receiving."

"It was good enough for me. Anyway Ben will be done with school this year. He's fourteen, going on fifteen. Now he can finally be of some help to me. I'll teach him all I know about the farm. Someday it will be his, and he might as well know how to run it."

"Not if I have anything to say about it will he run this place. My no!"

"What then do you have in mind? Painting plates like you do. How many have you painted so far anyway?"

"Four, and I may do eight before I'm through, then I'll do vases. This is art, I'll have you know, and if I become good enough, maybe I will get a job." She wiggled the plate close to his face—since you can't, or won't."

"What do you talk?" He pushed the plate away. "Women who are wives and mothers don't get jobs."

"Oh, yes they do. Why Henrietta Porter told me at circle just the other day that a pottery in Cincinnati, I think it's called Rookwood or some such, hires women, and it's considered respectable work."

"Not for my wife, so don't get any ideas. What do they do anyway?"

"Just what I'm doing. They paint flowers, birds, insects, all manner of pictures, even people, on bowls, plates, and vases; indeed, on anything made of clay and fired. A woman started the pottery in Cincinnati, so there; not every woman is slave to husband and family. They tell me that Ohio is rich in clay and that the pottery business will soon become big all over the state."

"Like I said, don't get any ideas."

"You mean about painting pottery?"

"Don't get wrathy with me; lower your voice."

"Adam, I guess the time is ripe to tell you that I have already gotten ideas that have nothing to do with pottery in the strict sense of the word but rather have to do with a change I am about to make."

He turned back to reading the *Herald.* "I see here the price of pork has gone up; should make for a good year," he said, rattling the newspaper.

"Adam, did you hear me?"

"What change? Another set of curtains?" He rattled the paper again and turned it inside out to the next page.

"No not curtains. I'm buying the hotel in Four Corners."

"You're what?" The newspaper dropped to the floor, and he tipped forward on the rocker, his face reddened in a look of horror.

"I said, the hotel in Four Corners is for sale. The owner is not well, and he's offering it at a good price. I've already talked to the attorney. But there is just one catch. I need your signature on the deed, because they will not let a married woman handle such a transaction without her husband's approval. So I'm asking you to sign for me."

"Well, I won't. How can you possibly run a hotel from here?"

"Not from here, I assure you. The hotel is my ticket out of here. I have already inspected the place. There is a room upstairs in the rear, the boys can sleep there, and a private parlor outside the kitchen downstairs. I'll keep a day bed in there for me. You can have the boys here on weekends; they will stay with me in town Monday through Thursday nights to attend school."

"You've gone mad, woman."

"My name is Martha. I am using my own money, which for the past fourteen years I saved from the rent on Auntie's place in Four Corners. And since you reneged on your promise of a home of my own and have left me here against my wishes, I intend to move into town. It's not quite what I had in mind, but the hotel will give me an interest. I'll meet people while the children get halfway decent schooling, and if I'm lucky and work hard, I'll fix that place up and begin to make it profitable. You can supply eggs, milk, butter, meat, and fresh vegetables in season. I'll pay, so you can benefit too."

"You will not run a hotel while you are my wife. What would people think? It's not like you're a widow, though you may be if you keep driving on me like you do. To my knowledge only widows take over taverns and inns that their husbands owned—never a married woman, unless her husband decides to buy such an establishment, and I assure I have no intention of running a place that serves the public. What are you going to do about the liquor anyway? Last I heard you and your Methodist friends don't approve."

"We don't. I don't have to drink, but if I can make money . . ."

"Sounds a bit two-faced to me. Your preacher will get after you."

"No matter, the bartender stays, but I will separate the eating from the bar, so that respectable people can eat in a nice restaurant."

"No one around here will do that. People prefer to eat in their own kitchens and dining rooms. You will end up serving a bunch of traveling men who drink too much, curse, and carouse well into the night; some might even bring in girls. Those church people who frown on alcohol won't have anything to do with your business? Or you either. Likely, they'll consider you a fallen woman."

"Once the children are through with their schooling, I'll sell the place and move on, building my own house, if need be. Or, I suppose I could move into Auntie's place. I thought of that, but in that little house I would need something more to do than simply wait for the children to come home from school. The hotel presents that opportunity, and if I can turn it into a lively hostelry and make some money, so be it. However, if I find the living quarters are too cramped, we can move into the house, but I'm afraid to cut off that rental income just yet, until I see how I make out with the hotel. I'm going to advertise in some of the papers. That way traveling men will know about my refurbished place. Ben and Frank will help me paint and clean it up."

Adam got up from the rocker and towered over his five-foot-three inch wife. She stood her ground looking up at him, an indignant, irate look upon her face. He was no match for her determination built up over years of frustration with a farm she disliked and rage at what she considered unfulfilled promises. Defeat coursed over him like a flood in spring.

"I'm going through with this," was her tart reminder, "so you may as well sign. Otherwise, I will return to Marietta and take the boys with me. You won't see much of them after that."

His face masked in rage, Adam's hand swung upward, but he caught himself before he let it land, stamped out of the room, and went to the barn.

She got through the summer, while the owner of the hotel wound up his affairs and made arrangements to move to Cleveland. Martha finally won her argument with Adam by refusing to plant the garden ever again or having anything to do with putting up the harvest or putting down the meat unless he signed the deed to the hotel.

He signed.

In early September, Martha and the boys moved to Four Corners. She engaged a wagoner to take her Marietta furniture to the hotel and had it placed in one of the front bedrooms. "I'm going to advertise that room as a bridal suite," she told Adam. The satin settee went into the wide upstairs hallway to replace a half dozen wooden straight back chairs.

Adam made no offer to help, but stood alone in the rooms of his parent's house. "What am I going to do now?" he said in the silence that encircled him. Despite the rancor in their lives, he still loved Martha and wanted her by his side, but he seemed incapable of warm words or promises of a better life, which meant, of course, a house. His was still a subsistence farm. True it supplied a livelihood, a roof over their heads, and food in their stomachs. He silently cursed his grandfather for settling in this unlikely place with its mediocre farmland, when other more successful pioneers had gone further west or into northern Ohio where the flat land was fertile and well watered. His mother had told him her father intended to move there, but at the time he bought his land, hostile Indians were still claiming that land. He slumped into the rocker, his head in his hands, and mumbled to the empty room. "What will the neighbors think, Aunt Mary Jane, Uncle Jake, Sonny, Nell? Do I tell them my wife has left me?" He could think of no similar situation, certainly not where a wife earned her own livelihood. How had Martha come to this scandalous idea? She lived well, had a good husband, and had mothered three sons. What more did she need?

Twenty-three

Certain that she would see the error of her ways, put the hotel up for sale, and return home, Adam made no effort to see his family. But whenever the familiar crunch of wheels on the roadway signaled another buggy or wagon passing, he ran to the window to see if, perchance, it was Martha. Finally, his heart aching, his pride shattered, he went to Four Corners.

He rounded the bend past the Methodist Cemetery and drove toward the corner where the hotel sat like an immense white box overpowering the small shops and houses surrounding it. Immediately, he caught sight of Ben and Frank standing on a board between two ladders painting the clapboards on the top floor of the three-story hotel. What in God's name is she thinking? Adam dropped in a run from the wagon seat and called out, "Come down from there this minute. You'll kill yourselves" Martha had mere boys doing men's work. She had promised they would spend weekends with him, but they had not appeared on Friday last. Already she had broken her promise. Well, I'll see about that. Dratted woman! He called to the boys again. "That's no job for two youngsters, and besides that board is not wide enough to be safe."

Frank shouted back, his face rosy with excitement, "Papa we're fine. We already done the other side. This here side is all we got left to do." He was laughing and waving the paintbrush like a baton.

The commotion brought Martha to the backdoor and onto the stoop. Upon seeing Adam, she shouted, "I wondered when your curiosity would get the better of you. The boys are fine. They know what they're about. Come inside and let me show you how much we've accomplished in just two weeks."

Furious at his wife, Adam hesitated, but the heated words he harbored inside refused to surface.

"At the rate we're going, we will reopen in another week. I've been painting the inside rooms. See I still have paint under my finger nails." She spread her fingers toward him. Her childlike hands were roughened and red. "The bar has stayed open," she went on, "since it is wood paneled, it doesn't need paint, so we have a little money coming in from that. Never knew how many men like a drink, now and again, even as their wives and the preachers are lecturing against it."

"And what does Preacher Chandler think of your bar?"

"Oh, he's against it. Already paid me a visit, but I told him business is business, and when I bought the hotel, it came with a bar. If I'm going to attract traveling men, I need it. Doesn't mean me and mine have to drink."

"Just make certain to keep the boys out of there. Ben's getting to a dangerous age . . ."

"Don't worry; McGinty, the bartender, locks it up at night and takes the key. The only other key is in my safe." She led him rapidly through the kitchen where there was a six-burner wood cook stove and a dry sink that could be drained outside through the window. They were soon in a narrow hall with a stairway on their right. Before ascending the steps, she opened a door opposite the barroom where a few tables of varying sizes and some chairs were pushed to one side of the room. "This is going to be the restaurant. It was a bedroom. I want to encourage people in the town to come here for meals. We'll still serve food in the tavern, but in here families won't be exposed to traveling men and other unsavory types."

"With a woman to cook, families aren't going to spend money on eats outside the home." Adam could see no earthly purpose in giving up a rentable room to a few families who might want a meal in a restaurant. "Now I can see a bachelor or widower maybe. Didn't old Hendrick take all his meals in the tavern before he passed on? But how many widowers are around? Most of them remarry as soon as the wife is cold in the graveyard."

"Women like to get away from the cook stove." Martha eyed him critically. "Of course, you'd never think of that. In Marietta, it was common for the better type couples to eat in places a woman would not be ashamed to frequent."

"I hasten to remind you, Four Corners is a far cry from Marietta."

"Maybe I can expose these country folk to something better. I'm going to hang wallpaper in here, cabbage roses, pink, would be nice, don't you think?"

Then I'll purchase a sideboard for showing off my painted plates and the milk glass we got for wedding presents. We never displayed them, because your mother had all her Virginia and Maryland knickknacks cluttering up the shelves."

Upstairs all four of the second floor rooms had been newly painted and smelled of linseed oil and turpentine. The beds were dressed in quilts she had brought from the farm or Marietta. A memory of those long winter evenings when she sat beside him and occasionally tried to involve him in some inane conversation crossed his mind. He remembered her stitching together the small cloth cutouts—remnants of clothing from another time. Perhaps instead of burying his head in the newspaper or a book, he should have talked to her more, inquired about her day, asked about her health, the children. "The men will make a mess of those quilts in short order, what with their muddy boots and dirty ways." he said. "Few even take their boots off when they fall into bed; sometimes sharing it with two others, and if they're drunk no telling what will happen to those fine coverings."

"I'm advertising these rooms as only suitable for one person, or two if they are a married couple. No more unrelated people to a bed, at least not on this floor. And if they're drunk, I will hand back their money and tell them to leave, even if the snow is three feet deep. There is a sign in the bar to that effect. I do have room for the lowlier types to bed down upstairs." She turned toward another flight of steps, narrower than those from the first floor to the second. Adam followed her to the third floor, where there were two large bedrooms, one on each side of the landing.

"I let more than one man sleep in these beds; they will be cheaper. I can accommodate eight people up here."

Adam ducked his head; the ceiling was lower, but the building's flat roof allowed for standing if a person was less than six feet tall. From the outside the building had no amenities. No columns or portico graced the exterior, just a simple front door to the street with a second opening onto the alleyway outside the tavern. Adam glanced again at two of the second floor bedrooms. Not large, they each accommodated a chair and dresser, washstand with pitcher and bowl, and a commode under a chairlike contraption with a hole in the seat.

"Mighty comfortable looking," he said of the rooms. He thought of putting his arm around her, but she was already hastening down the steps to the first floor. He followed her, never catching up until she stopped in front of the inside door to the barroom. "Here let me show you," she said.

He almost blurted that he had seen it before. The sight of the room with its long bar across the rear reminded him of the dinner he shared with Jeremiah. And once more he thought about his happy-go-lucky friend and felt a measure of envy for his traveling life.

During the next several months, at Adam's insistence the boys showed up at the farm every Friday night after school. They returned to Four Corners early Sunday morning when they were obliged to meet their mother at the Methodist Church, leaving Saturday the only day he could count on their help. The house quickly took on a shabby look: nothing picked up, beds unmade, dirty dishes in the dishpan. The boys, released from the stern strictures of their mother, seemed to revel in the mess.

Adam stumbled blindly through the days too ashamed to announce his predicament to the neighbors or his family. Troubled nights followed and the grimness of the war returned in nightmares that left him sluggish by morning. He no longer had the will or enthusiasm to work. He rented the big field south of the barn to Seth and his oldest boy, Amos, and sold off some of his cattle.

The garden went in as usual. Providing produce for the hotel would pay enough to put a few bills in his pocket. Usually, she was so busy with the chores—bed making, cooking, and greeting guests—that there was little time for communication. Martha did say the boys were doing well in school and that "Ben is even talking about college. I don't know what I will do when he leaves. I depend on him to help, and he's a good worker. Now, Frank here"—she turned to observe her middle son who sat sullenly spooning the last of a bowl of ginger apple custard into his mouth—"I have to keep on him, else he will sneak away."

"Goin' to Californy when I'm old enough."

"Don't talk foolishness," his mother glared at him.

"I'm goin'."

Adam decided not to join the argument. Disciplining his sons had always fallen to Martha; he'd been disinterested in their scrapes and foibles unless they took place on his time when she was not around.

It was during one of these visits on an unusually chilly morning in early October that he felt a bit of quinsy coming on. Wracked by chills, he decided that to allay the effects of his impending illness, he should stop by the bar in Martha's hotel and down a hefty shot of whiskey. After a few moments of banter with McGinty, the bartender suggested he take a pint home in case his symptoms worsened. Adam agreed and watched him take a pint of Old Monongahela from behind the bar. "Good for the soul too," McGinty offered, as he thrust the pint toward Adam. "Just add hot water and a bit of sugar and take to your bed—best medicine in the world for the quinsy or a cough. Good for relaxing stiffened muscles too. And a onion on a slab of white bread ain't bad either. I like it with sharp cheese. That's the way my old pappy back in the old country ate it, swore onions kept him healthy, and he lived to be ninety-five, so there must be something to it."

"I'll try both your remedies," Adam said. "My Ma always boiled up flaxseed, licorice root, and raisins, but since I'm alone now, I can't see bothering with that. Just don't let the Missus know I bought this bottle."

"Shame she's took off like that, but she is doing a good job with this here hotel and claims the school is better for the boys."

Twenty-four

During the summer Ben, Frank, and Willie kept to the winter schedule, since their mother needed them to help with the hotel weekdays. Adam soon learned that the two older boys could cook and put them to work in the kitchen each weekend, so he dined on leftovers for the first few days of each week. Somehow the horrible year 1885 passed with Adam adjusting slowly to his single state. He continued to miss Martha more than he wanted to admit, and concluded that anger mixed with love made poor bedfellows. He vowed that if he could win her back, he would try mightily to curtail his temper.

It hadn't take long for the neighbors, Aunt Mary Jane, and Uncle Jake to find out about his dilemma. "I always knew that citified woman would make you a poor wife; her with all her finery and fancy ways," Mary Jane sniffed, her pinched face taut and her dark eyes mere slits. "A farmer needs a farm wife, not a lady. When I think back on it, she reminds me of your mother. Lizzie was but a simple farm girl, until she came back from whatever it was she was into in Baltimore—I know it was supposed to be piano lessons—she took on airs you would not believe. Dressed up all the time until she got the babies. Then she became like every other wife, dowdy, especially after coming out here. And a good thing, if you ask me. Then when she started selling pianos and giving music lessons to the young girls around here, she got uppity again. As for you, heaven knows there were plenty of young girls around here just waiting for your return from that unpleasantness in the south. Why, Chestoria Souderbaugh used to come 'round every few days to ask if I'd heard from you. I knew what she was about. Didn't fool me. She wanted to trap you before the prettier girls got aholt of you. She married Herman Harkin, and a good housewife she is, good mother too—seven babies already."

A sudden need to defend Martha rose in Adam. "I wouldn't have married Chestoria if I never had a woman." He remembered Chestoria as flat as a board in the chest despite her unduly large hips and fat legs that caused her to clump along like an old war horse. He noticed in church the last time he attended that she had fleshy upper arms that filled the sleeves of her dress like two sausage shaped balloons. Raising his voice slightly he told his aunt, "Martha is a beautiful accomplished person and a hard worker. She is single handedly running that hotel and making a success of it. Of course, the boys help. I have to say she really has them well trained."

"They're afraid of her, if you ask me."

Adam wanted to say he hadn't asked, but kept his counsel. Mary Jane was set in her ways, certain of everything. Black was black, white was white; shades of gray did not exist in her mind. According to his aunt, people needed to follow certain rules of behavior set up by their elders, the church, and their teachers. Not to do so was to sin. In Mary Jane's eyes, Martha on leaving her husband became a sinner of the worst kind. "I'll have nothing more to do with her," she announced haughtily, then added, as she looked around the parlor with a gaze that indicated disgust. "This place needs a good cleaning. Since you no longer have a wife, you better do it yourself or put the boys to work." She stared at the windows and let out an enormous sigh. "If you take down those curtains before I leave, I'll see that they're washed and ironed. I note a brownish tinge to them from the dirt coming in off the road. You'd think that wife of yours could come out here once in a while and give you a hand."

"She's not going to be my wife much longer. Her lawyer has already served me with divorce papers."

"Oh, my Lord. God save us. Divorce!" Mary Jane's slender hand flew to her face, her brow creased. "No Springer or Mueller has ever been divorced. What will the church people think of us now? That woman is to be condemned. I can't believe the Methodists will keep on with her."

"Well, times are changing, I'm afraid. Some of the soldiers—and I suppose me included—do not make the best husbands."

"That's no excuse for a woman to leave her man. Anyway, the war is long over with. No need to be dwelling on that now. Time those men got aholt of themselves."

Adam knew that no commentary about his fellow soldiers would make its mark. Strange how a war to save the Union had receded in everybody's mind. After the welcoming was over and the bands quit playing, the home folks preferred to lay it aside and never think upon it again. He glanced at the curtains that irritated Mary Jane. Neither their dinginess nor the sloppiness of the sitting room had commanded his attention. Jackets and sweaters hung carelessly on chairs; his boots—mud and all—were tossed beside his favorite rocker. His go-to-meeting coat dropped in a rumpled muddle from a hook behind the hall door. Month old newspapers lay about on tables.

After Mary Jane left, Adam set about straightening his possessions. He found a duster in the hall closet and cleaned the table tops and chair backs. But except for changing the sheets on his bed and washing up the dishes, he did little to the rest of the house.

By the fall of 1885, he had recovered enough from his heartbreak to rustle some interest in the farm, even as he momentarily thought of selling it. But images of his mother and father would surface along with their struggle to wrest the farm from the reluctant wilderness, and he didn't have the heart. Anyway what could he do? Already forty-four, he still possessed only the skills and abilities of a farmer. On trips to the dock with grain or corn to be shipped to market, he fell into the habit of picking up a quart or two of Old Monongahela. The influenza long gone, he looked forward to a draught each night before bedtime, telling himself that it banished nightmares and helped him sleep. Martha had been gone a year, and in the late summer of 1886, he was as lonely and agitated as he had ever been. The divorce left him so distraught that, although he didn't have a cold or any sign of one, on his next visit to the hotel he went into the bar and bought a quart of whiskey. "Don't mention this to Martha," he entreated McGinty.

"Why should she care now?" McGinty countered. "She ain't married to you no more."

"I don't know, just habit I guess." By the time night rolled around Adam had finished off a good portion of the bottle and the next morning had no memory of stumbling off to bed. In the morning his stomach burned, but an ample dish of oatmeal allayed the nagging pain and two teaspoons of powdered charcoal in a half glass of water gave him some relief from the headache. The ache in his heart remained, however. There seemed to be no cure for love lost but drunken oblivion; only that remedy never lasts.

On his next visit to the hotel Martha told him since the divorce was now final she was making plans for her future. "I will, of course, go back to Marietta. Meanwhile, I recognize that until the boys are older and ready to leave home, it would be unfair to take them from you. They'll grow up soon enough. Then I can return to my roots."

When she spoke like this Adam's heart wrenched. He couldn't seem to get along with her but wanted her back. At church, he glanced over the available women while the preacher intoned his dark words about the fiery fate allotted sinners: fornicators, bastardizers, the divorced, liars, and cheats. Adam supposed his reference to the divorced was to him, a failed husband. Square windowpanes of colored glass allowed the sun to dance across the dour faces and plain dress of the parishioners giving the women the only tinge of color in their bland faces, for the use of paint and powder was also considered sinful. Few spoke to him or looked his direction. There were a number of spinsters about. Some as young as twenty-five already wore anxiety on their faces, for no man had yet spoken for them. Several stole sly glances his way. He supposed they considered him their last hope. The older ones appeared as dried and withered as the brown leaves dropping from the towering oaks outside the church, but they kept their faces set in stony disapproval, not even speaking as they passed by him. Solace came nightly from his bottle of Old Monongahela, although he had ceased purchasing his supply from Martha's hotel lest she become suspicious of his new found obsession. Soon he was having a bit of whiskey mornings just to get his day started.

Ben and Frank stopped their weekly visits only arriving occasionally and using the excuse that business at the hotel was expanding, but Adam knew they had more interesting activities to pursue with the young lads in town. Besides he had Old Monongahela for his companion, and when the boys were there, he had to give up his nightly brew lest he set a bad example.

One morning shortly before Thanksgiving, he was mopping up oatmeal spilled when he stumbled from the stove to the table and fell over his own feet. He was mopping up the mess when there was an insistent knocking at the front door. Leaving the pail of water and mop, he went to the hall muttering under his breath.

"Yes," he said irritably upon opening the door to a well-dressed gentleman in a sack suit with a multi-colored brocade vest, so unlike the dark suits worn by local farmers. While smoothing his hair with his hand, Adam glanced at his own dirty overalls and wrinkled shirt. Had he put a comb to his hair that morning? He couldn't remember, but the stubble on his chin told him he had not shaved.

"Are you Mr. Springer?" The caller, whom Adam perceived to be about thirty-five, removed his black bowler with a flourish.

"Last time I looked, I was." Adam made an attempt at humor, but there was no similar response from his visitor.

"My name is Kurt Anderson. I represent the Pineville Pottery. We just opened last year. Our operation is similar to that of Mr. Weller's in Zanesville. I'm sure you have heard of that enterprise, have you not? Weller Pottery has been around since 1873."

"I have. Matter of fact, we own a flowerpot purchased in Zanesville a few years back. Mostly my mother dealt with local potters—Bluebird and like that—there being more than forty around these parts. "And my wife" . . . his voice trailed, but he managed to say, "she went, I mean, goes in more for English china."

"May I come in." Mr. Anderson removed his hat. "There is a matter I would like to discuss with you."

Adam moved aside and invited the man into the front parlor, where to his horror, the furniture was tawny with road dust. One look and he hastily closed the door. They went across the hall to the sitting room where newly washed curtains, courtesy of Aunt Mary Jane, hung at the windows. He motioned for his guest to sit in what had been Martha's rocker.

"I'll get right to my business," Mr. Anderson said. He looked quizzically at Adam. "Nasty bruise there on your head."

"Walked into a door in the middle of the night."

"Too bad. It will probably turn yellow before it heals up. But getting down to business, Mr. Springer, I understand you own a parcel of ground near Pineville. Is that correct?" The man was brusque.

"Yes, sir. It once had a stand of timber on it, but I've sold off much of it."

"I know. And without that cover of trees, we have made a discovery. Not knowing who owned the place, and eager to test our hunch, I must confess my men went onto the property without your permission. They did some test borings and discovered a considerable amount of clay thereabouts. Do you know much about clay deposits?"

"No," Adam answered, "only that the land there is not the best for farming because of its abundance in the soil. I know my uncle, who owned it previously, used some of the clay for his kiln. He made inexpensive food containers and tableware to supply the family over the years. That would have been from about 1830-something, up until the war. I remember he had two kickwheels in a log building where he kept a sandstone kiln. I used to play around it when it wasn't fired up. As I recall it had two fireboxes with one door and the flue was sort of moon shaped. We were a large family, and when Jake learned the art of pottery making, he supplied all the family. Don't believe he ever sold any of it though."

"And the clay came from this Pineville plot?"

"That's what I understand. By the time I came on, I was born much later than my brother and sisters, he wasn't making it anymore, though my Ma told me whenever a niece or nephew married he made them a set of stoneware. Some of it is around here too. Old now and not inclined to do much farming, let alone pottery making, he's given away some of his land. That particular plot he gave to me when I returned from fighting in the Great War."

Adam expected that his visitor might make some congratulatory comment about his service to the country, but his guest rushed on. "Well, Mr. Springer, we have a proposition for you. How would you like to lease that land for a clay mine? We would pay you a royalty since clay falls under the category of mineral rights. Your property appears to be somewhat unique for it contains two kinds of clay. The first is Tionesta, a very sticky clay, which lies in the lower depths. The second seam is Lower Kittaning locally known as top clay, because it is mined near the crest of the hills. The two are usually separated by about one hundred feet. Tionesta matures at low temperature and has a nice golden buff color when fired. Lower Kittaning is sandier and turns whiter during firing. The normal mixture we use is two parts Tionesta to one part Lower Kittaning. As you can imagine from my description, obtaining the clays requires underground mining, a considerable operation."

"I'm puzzled as to why anyone would need anything but practical pots, which we already have from local potters."

"Times are changing, Mr. Springer. Finely decorated ware has been made in Europe for centuries, but now we need to be making our own here in America. Have you noticed the trend among more genteel ladies for hand painting lovely pictures on china?"

Adam had a momentary vision of Martha at her paints. He nodded.

"Maybe living here in the country as you do," Mr. Anderson went on, "you are not aware that many wealthier families are moving to the cities. And as they obtain more riches, they want their homes to reflect their newfound affluence. With valuable deposits of coal, fire clay, and natural gas, this is an ideal area for our growing industry."

"If I agree to this proposal, what does it mean for me?"

"I think we should meet at the property, and I'll tell you more about what our project entails. I can assure you this proposal is an attractive one. We are moving away from the familiar Bluebird potters: Possum Hollow, Poverty Hollow, and Henpeck." To be sure, those products are functional and practical and needed by every household. But modern housewives now lean toward more beauty in their pottery."

Like Martha who was so different from farmwomen that she wanted to surround herself with elegance in furnishings and clothing, all of which emphasized his farm boy image as opposed to her more elegant one. He remembered that she had even brought along a china potty from Marietta. Adam thought that was the silliest thing he had seen. Country folk were satisfied with tin slop pails or unadorned ceramic ones. Always fashionable, she even referred to her dainty pot as a commode.

Satisfied that the proposal was one to be considered, Adam agreed, and they made arrangements to meet the week following Thanksgiving.

Twenty-five

Except for one old widower, who had sold his farm and now lived off the mortgage income, Martha's hotel was not occupied during the Thanksgiving holiday. She invited Adam and the widower to join her and the boys for the festive dinner. Adam looked forward to the family meal, for he knew Martha would set out a grand turkey stuffed with fresh country sausage, celery, onions, parsley, and sage. She would likely serve dried corn, creamed onions and mashed potatoes with plenty of deep brown gravy and top it all off with pumpkin and mince pies. The mincemeat had been working in the earthen jar on the back stoop for several months and the beef was the best. Adam had supplied it along with plenty of lard for the crusts from the fall butchering. Martha made the fluffiest crust—not even his mother could equal it. To Adam's way of thinking, when it came to custard pies, German cooks produced soggy crusts, but Martha had a secret. She brought the mashed pumpkin, brown sugar, brandy, freshly grated nutmeg and ginger, and the cream and eggs to a boil before putting it all into the half-backed crust just before baking.

He avoided his nightly communion with the bottle and dressed carefully for his visit hoping the occasion would lead to a softening of her heart. It did not. Adam returned home after the meal satiated but sad as ever. Ben had come home from Ohio Northern in Ada full of college boy spirit and bravado, although he was no closer to deciding what to do with the rest of his life. When Adam approached him on the subject, suggesting he might take some agricultural courses that would better prepare him for taking over the farm, he was met with disdain.

"Never, Pa. I would rather die an early death than be a farmer like you, dependent on the vagaries of the weather, the ups and downs of the markets. I spent enough time at it to know it's a dog's life."

To which, young Frank piped up, "and don't look at me neither, Papa. I ain't never going to be no farmer."

"What then are you going to do?"

"I'm goin' to Californy, like I told you before. By the time I'm eighteen, I'm outta' here, far away from this dumb place as I can get. I promised Mama I'd stay 'til then."

"If you don't do something about your farmer English you'll never amount to anything," Martha snapped, obviously upset at the demeanor of her middle son with whom she seemed at constant odds. "My father would never have become a lawyer if he had talked like you do. Ain't isn't even a word."

"Here we go again," Frank said. "I'm not planning to be no lawyer neither."

All this talk of jobs and future got Adam to thinking about his own. The day away from his liquor had cleared his head somewhat and being in the hotel reminded him of his dinner with Jeremiah. Might like to do something like that too, go into sales, he mused, but then dismissed the thought as quickly as it came.

Adam perceived a certain lassitude about Martha: she seemed less energetic and less determined. She made no mention of changing her ways, and the hotel remained her constant interest despite the lethargy of her two older boys, now fifteen and nineteen. Twelve-year-old Willie couldn't be much help. He was a quiet lad, somewhat tightly coiled, and to Adam's thinking, not very ambitious.

To counter Ben's departure, Martha had hired a young girl to help with the cleaning and bedmaking, but Adam had seen her at work and decided she was not wise to the ways of finer folk. Her bright red tresses marked her as neither German nor English. She was the daughter of a coal miner—coal having recently been discovered in the southern hills of Ohio bringing in miners from Pennsylvania. They were unschooled for the most part and foreign-born Irish and Welsh along with a few Scots, all common folk used to living on very little. It was rumored that some were even Catholics.

The coal, containing a substantial amount of sulfur, which when burned leaves abundant ashes and clinkers, was scattered about in thin veins.

The hired girl, Maggie, came from Manchester Township, where the best coal, alleged to be some twenty inches thick, was being mined. A newspaper article reported that much of it had been cut away by creeks and in some townships appears to have been mixed with shale and limestone. Adam imagined that Maggie, who lived in a room carved out of what was once a windowless first floor storeroom, considered herself in heaven, for it was well known that imported miners were content to live in shacks little better than those of southern Negroes.

Her presence in such close proximity to his growing boys, who were probably on the prowl for willing maidens, unnerved Adam and brought memories of his own raging desires at their ages. He took the matter up with Martha who retorted, "I've thought of that and warned them that I would be on the lookout for any wenching, and if I find them dallying with her, they and she would be sent packing."

"What about the men sleeping here? Does that bode well for the kind of place you keep? Won't she be thinking about making a bit of income on the side? That storeroom is far enough away from your sleeping quarters that she could ply her trade and you would never be the wiser."

"Adam, I can't be everybody's keeper. I've warned her of the dangers, given her a key to her room, and told her she must remain inside late at night no matter who comes knocking on her door. Besides which, she is a religious girl, walks to mass every Sunday to that little wooden church the Catholics frequent in the hollow near Mommy's Bottom, you know the place the Longacres came from. It's where Mr. Longacre's mother still lives."

"That's a mighty long walk."

"She takes along her rosary and says her beads while she goes along the road. Frank offered to drive her, but I know better than to chance that."

At home that night Adam came face to face with his dilemma. He had gone to Four Corners with a grip packed for an overnight stay in case Martha invited him. He assumed no one would be in the bridal suite, and he was right, but he was wrong about receiving an invitation for a tumble on the feather tick. The spool bed belonging to his parents was now back in the upstairs bedroom at the farmhouse. As Adam prepared for another night in it alone, he was sorely depressed, and for the first time gave serious thought to finding another woman. I don't want another woman; I only want Martha, he told himself. Tears gathered in his eyes as they had done when he faced the deaths of the boys on the battlefields, all young men with whom he had been especially close, and some he had to admit, he had not known at all. He felt so sad, that before going off to his lonely bed, he poured himself a generous shot of Old Monongahela and then topped it off with another before he dropped into half consciousness only vaguely aware that by morning he must make some changes, but what kind? He had no idea.

Adam approached the day like all the others: up at five to feed the chickens, clean the horse stalls, milk the cows, slop the pigs, and finally fry himself some breakfast. It was bitter cold outside, and he spent the morning by the fire in lonely isolation. Martha had sent home some turkey and fixings, but he had little stomach for any of it and instead poured himself a hefty Old Monongahela. His noontime dinner was a half bowl of bean soup. Afterwards he fetched the mail, still in his suit coat pocket, and sat down in the rocker to read. There was nothing much except for one letter from the Pineville Pottery. Almost forgotten in his quandary over his unhappy existence was his forthcoming appointment with the pottery people. Adam wrote himself a note so he would not forget and stuck it in his mirror, where he shaved of a morning when he bothered at all. The shaggy haired stranger peering back gave him a momentary start. His eyes were bloodshot, his usually honey-colored skin was red and somewhat blotchy, bloated even. Must be the cold, he thought. Or—he felt a sudden terror—the drink. How much had he taken? He couldn't remember and wondered if he had appeared so unkempt to Martha. The sight gave him such concern that right then and there he decided to dump the contents of his faithful friend, Old Monongahela. The next day, he sorely regretted his action, so on the pretext of needing a haircut, went to Four Corners, not to the hotel, but to the general store, where he purchased another bottle. The rest of the week progressed the same as every other winter week, marked by a heavy snow that roared in on Sunday to blanket everything in white. No one came to call, few buggies and sleighs passed by, and Adam felt secluded and lost. Only the brown bottle offered comfort and companionship, and one night between barn and porch, he fell into the snow and didn't awaken until sometime after midnight, nearly frozen. To thaw out, he downed several shots before toddling off to bed and to sleep the rest of the night in his clothes.

Four days before his scheduled appointment with the pottery people, Adam had a terrible thought. What if they intended to cheat him; what if they took his land in some nefarious way? That Kurt Anderson was a flashily dressed dandy. The morning he called, Adam must have appeared like an ignorant coot, someone who could be easily hornswoggled. He would have to slick himself up and be as shrewd as they were to ferret out their tricks. Right then and there he swore off the bottle. I'll wait until the negotiations are over, he told himself, and hid the bottle in the root cellar behind a bushel basket of potatoes, then thought better of that and dumped the contents in the brush behind the house. He took down his old suit coat and best trousers, then located several irons, which he put on the stove to heat. Getting out the ironing board, he tried his hand at pressing his coat, trousers, and shirt. He scorched the shirt, but with his coat over it no one need notice. A quick trim of his hair and a close shave with his straight razor, which he honed on his razor strop, and he decided he looked presentable enough to meet with the men he now considered his adversaries.

The meeting with the pottery people interrupted his hermit-like existence. By then, he had not touched a drop of his faithful friend in four days. At the last minute, he threw his grip into the buggy in case he should have to stay overnight in Pineville, then rode over to Seth's place to ask Amos to care for the animals.

158

The boy eagerly accepted for Adam said he'd pay him. It was rumored that Amos planned to marry soon even though he was only seventeen. The baby would be a six-months child.

At his Pineville property Adam was met by Kurt Anderson who, he learned, had come from Cincinnati to advise the local pottery. With him was a Mr. John Forsythe. "We'll lease the property at a modest fee, but we're obligated to pay for every load of clay extracted. However, we will need to take over the entire property, build a bunkhouse yonder and a small cabin for the mine chief and his family over there closer to the road." Adam peered closely at Mr. Forsythe as he spoke, to ascertain if he appeared to be the cheating sort. He was the man in charge of the Pineville Pottery, the man with whom Adam would be dealing in future negotiations. Well dressed, his boiled shirt was dazzling white. Over that he wore a frock coat barely visible under his great coat left slightly open. Although it had been pressed, Adam was wearing the suit purchased for Lucinda's and his own wedding. He assumed it was out of date, and his great coat was probably a dozen years old. His gallowses were frayed, but since they held up his trousers under his suit coat they remained hidden. Even so, Adam was so conscious of his shabby appearance that he wanted to run from these finely dressed gentlemen. Good sense told him to stay the course; he needed whatever money he could get out of his Pineville property. The three men walked toward a hill at the rear of the plot where a large stand of timber had been systematically cut as Adam ran short of money during the bad years.

"Our geologists tell us the mine should go here." Kurt Anderson spoke knowledgeably, "We will begin with a horizontal shaft and excavate back into the hill until the ground over the seam proves stable, then start a tunnel. Once we make certain the seam is solid, so that the roof will not cave in, we'll shore it up with timbers and build a tramway to move small cars in and out. Depending on the mine height, these cars will be pulled by ponies or even dogs. Later we may bring in a small locomotive."

"How do you know if there is that much clay here?" Adam felt flummoxed by the knowledgeable discourse of these two men.

"Usually the Tionesta clay has a layer of sandrock on top, and we've determined there is an appreciable amount here. The sandrock provides a very stable roof. The Lower Kittaning clay does not have this attribute. I have seen tunnels so shallow— two feet, for example—that the miners had to shimmy in on their sides or bellies to work the seams. So even if we are confronted with a shallow mine, we will use timbers to hold up the roof. We may have to drill into the clay seam with a hand auger, insert dynamite, and shoot the clay to break it up. Shallow cover clay is best for thrown pottery; for what we produce the deeper coving clay is best."

Adam, feeling overwhelmed, ventured a comment. "I suppose you'll want to use the rest of that timber over there for shoring up purposes. Will you purchase that?"

"We will."

"I'd been saving that for emergencies," he mumbled. Adam was confused by all this talk of burrowing and tunneling, shoring up and building, and could barely imagine the ruin to his property. He needed to think. Why didn't they purchase it outright? He concluded that if the seams of clay were not forthcoming, they could walk away after having torn up the property to such an extent that it would be useless for any other purpose. Adam felt the need to consult a lawyer. Not wishing to appear too eager, neither did he want to discourage the project, lest some other farmer get wind of it and offer land. There was plenty of clay about. "I plan to stay the night in Pineville," he told them, "so let me have the evening to think all this over, and I'll come to your place of business on the morrow."

Twenty-six

In the hope that a house on the Pineville property would bring Martha back, Adam had considered selling the farm, so when he entered the lawyer's office, he half hoped some legal tangle would quell the mine project. This new pottery had no history; it could fail and leave him with torn up land of little use for anything else.

In the law office of the Honorable Chauncey L. Davis, Adam touched a bell announcing his arrival and sat down to wait. Framed diplomas lined the walls. One indicated that Attorney Davis had taken an A.B. degree from Ohio Agricultural and Mechanical College in Columbus. Another announced his graduation from the Cincinnati Law School with an LL.B degree. Adam's wait was interrupted when a portly, rumpled man in his late fifties came into the waiting room. After greeting Adam effusively and listening attentively while the case was presented, he nodded his tousled head in a display of understanding. With his large jowls moving like flapping bellows, he asked if any other use could be made of the property.

"Only to build a house on it so that my wife and I could live closer to Pineville."

The attorney's pudgy hands came together under his chin. "With a proposal such as this, I think you would be wise to consider complying. You can always find another—perhaps even more suitable—plot on which to build your wife a house. I know of several desirable locations, and since I'm in the real estate business as well as the law, I will gladly show them to you."

"I can't consider them right now," Adam hedged, "but your suggestion does make sense."

"And furthermore, I would be happy to represent you in your dealings with the pottery people. I happen to have met Mr. Forsythe and determined him to be an honorable man, so I think we could do business."

Adam hesitated. All he wanted to be told was that the deal was good or bad. Other than paying for Attorney Davis's immediate advice, he had not planned on hiring him. Now confronted with issues of deeds and legal documents, contracts, and the like, Adam thought of walking away from the entire matter. When his mother died, he had simply taken over the farm.

"I'll need to check the county records to make certain the land is clear of debt and garnishments before we can proceed," Mr. Davis rushed on as though there was no question as to his being engaged.

Adam had expected to merely shake the hands of the Messrs. Anderson and Forsythe and the deal would be struck. Now Attorney Davis was babbling about protection, and before he had a chance to think further, Adam agreed to let the man represent him. A perfect stranger would now be into his business, a stranger who presented terrible scenarios of what could happen if Adam were to proceed alone.

After leaving the law office, a new feeling akin to rising self-worth came over him. Having consulted an attorney, Adam felt important. He was dealing with businessmen like a man of the world who had something of value they wanted. Other than the few crops and the occasional meat from the butchering he sold, Adam never had much that anyone wanted. No doubt about it, the lawyer's advice gave him confidence and provided an arm to lean on should trouble with the pottery owners occur. That night he asked Amos to stay permanently on the farm and offered him Ben's old bed. Excited at the prospect of leasing his land and getting paid for each load of clay taken from the mine, he began to think of ways to use his money. First off, he thought, I won't put it in only one bank. Banks can fail. "I'll open one account in McConnelsville for the lease money and another in Pineville to keep track of income from the loads of clay. But I'll remain in town frequently to count the loads until I know these people are honest.

"First time I ever slept alone," Amos told Adam after a night in Ben's old bed. "We boys got to share, there's so many of us."

"What are you going to do when you acquire a wife? What's her name, Tildy?"

"Yes sir. She's one of the Bagley girls, Matilda is her God-given name, but there ain't no room for us at her place neither. Like I said, too many kids already. Her Maw ain't much interested in having another around neither."

"So what are you planning to do?"

"Look for a room somewheres. Baby's coming on in four months."

This set Adam to thinking. Frank and Willy were still coming out occasionally on Friday nights, but he reckoned not too eagerly. They hadn't been there in over a month. He pondered this matter for several days before deciding to offer his bedroom upstairs to the newlyweds. He would move downstairs into his mother's old room and use the front parlor.

A few days later, Adam invited the young couple to move in with the proviso that Amos take over caring for the animals and help Adam with the general farm work. He offered them the use of the entire house except for the downstairs bedroom and parlor and one bedroom for his sons. In return Tildy was to manage the kitchen and keep the house tidy. They would receive five dollars a month, to Adam's mind a princely sum.

Now he was free to spend more time in Pineville, but soon learned his presence on the mine property was not appreciated, and he began to feel in the way. He watched the mine timbers go up and found that the clay removed was of good quality. "Tionesta," they told him, and Adam responded like a man who had always known its value. The mine itself seemed barely high enough for a worker to enter. A narrow track was laid, and a group of miners from nearby farms worked the pit. Satisfied that the work was going as promised, Adam ceased his weekly visits. He had not had a drink of spirits since the enterprise began and vowed never to touch the stuff again. A person needed a clear head and an astute mind to deal with these educated people, and strong drink just addled the brain. He envied Mr. Forsythe for his gentlemanly appearance, his mastery of his position. Adam had begun to recognize that he wasn't even a very good farmer. We're simply existing—the farm and me—and he longed all the more for something else to do with his life. The thought boiled inside, twisting his mind with possibilities, most of which he rejected as soon as he thought them up. On a chance meeting with Mr. Forsythe at the mine site and with no forethought whatsoever, Adam asked, "who sells your pots for you?"

"First off, they are not pots. Pineville makes high class pottery, not run of the mill." Mr. Forsythe had a haughty tone to his voice as though he was dismissing Adam as a bumpkin.

"How do you get rid of the stu . . .art pottery," Adam hastened to correct himself."

"Right now, we have a few peddlers who carry several lines of household gadgets, but we're looking to set up our own sales force."

And right then and there before he had a chance to think on it further, lest he change his mind, Adam blurted, "I've never sold anything but corn, oats, wheat, and calves, but maybe I could try my hand at selling pottery." He wished he could take back the words the moment they fell from his mouth.

Mr. Forsythe paused, seemingly studying Adam's face. "That's selling, I guess. We might consider your proposition, but we'd have to test you first."

"I'd surely like to give it a try. And if it doesn't work out from either side, we can call it quits. No questions asked."

"We'll give you a month to see how it goes. Can you be away from your farm that long?"

"Might need a couple of weekends to check up on my hired man."

"We can keep your route close by in the beginning, but if it works out you'll have to be gone over weekends. Up to this we've let our wares be pushed by a legion of indifferent peddlers who make regular rounds with our canvasser's outfit from which they take orders. They eke out a living by providing housewives with everyday necessities and cheap trinkets, but the image they project is a poor one, so we really don't like having them represent us. We hired a young man last year, but he was inclined to get into mischief on the road—if you know what I mean." Mr. Forsythe winked. Adam concluded it was either women or drink, or most likely both. Like Jeremiah, traveling men were noted for finding ways to dissipate. Such comments gave Adam increased reason to resist Old Monongahela. A man in his cups could be easily lured by the wiles of a comely woman, and despite the divorce, he was still hopeful that Martha would come back. He would need to lure her with that dratted house she was so intent upon. Then maybe if he dressed up a bit, had a real job making money, he could begin his campaign to get her back in earnest. He'd ask Attorney Davis to show him some of the local real estate. Still attempting to be shrewd where the Pineville Pottery folks were involved, he was sorely tempted by Mr. Forsythe's offer, but hesitated nevertheless. "Mr. Forsythe, I appreciate your faith in me, but I would have to give that idea some serious thought." Though he had brought up the subject himself, Adam could not imagine living such a life. He had envied Jeremiah. But now faced with being a salesman himself, fear rose in him to supplant the expansiveness he felt as the recipient of money for his clay without having to raise a finger. At the Pineville Pottery the following week, Mr. Forsythe began pleasantly enough, "before we get into details, may I ask the status of your farm?"

Adam was about to reply that his personal affairs were no concern of his, but caught himself in time. "I have a hired man who takes care of the livestock, and I have one leased field."

"And your hotel?"

"It's in good hands."

164

"So you are not as busy as you once were?"

"No, my oldest boy, who I thought might take over the farm, is going west to work in the Bakersfield, California oilfields. He says the future of the country is in oil, so I've been cutting back, reduced my herd of cattle and now own only three horses. My middle son is hankering to follow his brother west too, so that will leave only one boy, a thirteen-year-old at home. I'm interested in doing something else, but I'm afraid I don't know the first thing about making pottery on a grand scale or selling it either."

"To sell products, you don't have to know how they are made," Mr. Forsythe said, "but I think a tour of our factory might be in order. Right now we produce flowerpots, cuspidors, painted ware, pitchers, and vases mostly, but with a steady supply of clay we intend to branch out. Most potteries specialize. Over there along the Ohio River in West Virginia, Homer Laughlin makes dinnerware and common vessels used everyday. We would like to keep to art pottery. Since our wares are more precious our current canvassers are provided with a dozen or so miniature outfits for order taking, but the samples are also good sellers. Mothers will pay a dollar for the collection to give to their children as toys, and a good salesman can bring in four dollars a day just from the canvasser's outfits. Our new wagon will allow us to stock some full size items too, so you would be traveling with products you can sell immediately."

The next day Adam met Mr. Forsythe at the Pineville Pottery reception area where shelves lined the walls on which sat an array of fine vases, pitchers, and flowerpots. There was a curved tankard with a golden handle that resembled a vine. Molded grapes spilled down the sides of an ivory pitcher. Another bore the likeness of an owl. Among the miniatures was a green umbrella stand no more than three by seven inches, a brown-glazed cuspidor some three inches in diameter, and small replicas of apple and orange banks. The least interesting was an ochre cooking pot. Adam thought this might be a good seller, but the other products appeared to be too rich for unschooled farm women, few of whom expected much elegance in their lives made stoic by numerous children, lackluster husbands, and endless work.

"We'll soon have more products," Mr. Forsythe interrupted Adam's musings, which were already into the negative aspects of being a pottery salesman. He could not imagine himself going up to total strangers and asking them to buy. Mr. Forsythe chattered on, jerking him out of his reverie. "Up to this we have relied on local farmers to bring us clay, but much of it is contaminated with seedline iron minerals, which tend to make the ware specky. Clay varies greatly in quality, but what we get from your mine is quite uniform, so I have visions of branching into another line maybe even tableware of the better sort. We need you to call on the small town general stores and farmhouses. And with the new wagon we've ordered, you will be a traveling advertisement as well." Mr. Forsythe beamed a forced smile on Adam as though taking his measure. Adam was again deep into thoughts of his own. He would become a traveling advertisement, an object of jest among his neighbors; people at the church who already disapproved of a divorced man would think even less of him.

Adam was about to tell Mr. Forsythe there was no point in going on when he found himself being ushered into a room where mounds of clay lay about on tables in front of two men and one woman. The sight of the woman surprised him. Why was she here working among men? Could one be her husband? Mr. Forsythe didn't say but went on with his spiel, which seemed so rote that Adam was certain he had gone through it many times.

"This is the modeling room. No product leaves here until the master artist— that man seated by the window—passes on it." The three modelers were forming clay into various shapes already identifiable as the beginnings of tankards and vases. "Sometimes these modelers work for days or even weeks until they obtain a truly exquisite design." Mr. Forsythe whispered. Adam was not introduced to any of the modelers who barely looked up from their work. Mr. Forsythe moved on quickly, and like a schoolboy, Adam hurried along behind him to the casting room. A door opened and all at once he was assaulted by chalky white air that clawed at his throat. The entire room was filled with a white cloud. There was no place to turn short of leaving the premises to get a fresh breath.

"Out here we make casts of what the modelers have produced, but first the clay must be ground in a blunger mill after which, to insure a smooth consistency, it is passed through a fine screen. Water is added until a slip of the proper thickness is formed, then it is poured into the molds to reproduce the patterns."

Adam wanted to be on his way out of the dusty environs and looked for a door to the outside while stifling the urge to cough. Here and there he spotted a young lad or two who could not have been more than twelve or thirteen. There were women too. Why did their husbands allow this? As though reading his thoughts, Mr. Forsythe hastened to tell him. "Whole families work here. See that group over there: that's the mother, father, and three children. Using the children helps keep our costs low, and God knows those poor families need all the money they can get."

Adam continued to have trouble breathing; he was used to clean country air, but nothing stopped Mr. Forsythe's version of life in the pottery. "See over there," he said. "That person throwing clay into the mold is a jiggerman. The other man is a mold runner; his job is to walk the clay from one place to another. Before his twelve-hour shift is over, he'll travel a good fifteen or sixteen miles." This made Adam wonder how many miles he had walked daily behind a plow.

"Why all the women?" Adam asked between hard-earned breaths.

"They're finishers, smaller hands and tiny fingers are best to round off the edges and sponge down the pieces. Don't need ham-fisted men for those jobs. We save them for the really heavy work like toting that raw clay over there. It can weigh as much as a hundred pounds, no job for mere women." They moved to another table where a woman was patiently attaching feet, pedestals, and handles to various pieces. And all this work done in the foulest air Adam had ever endured, except for the gunsmoke on the battlefield. Mr. Forsythe went right on with his patter, evidently unaware that Adam, still intent on finding a door to the outside, was loosing interest. "The art ware remains here for twenty-four hours before being taken to be sponged." Adam's disinterest was growing to the point of simply getting the tour over with. They were soon into the steam-drying room where a fully laden table of white vases in various shapes and sizes dominated the room. Mr. Forsythe prattled on, "our inspector, Ezra—Ezra this is Mr. Springer who is coming to work for us in sales—carefully examines each piece for blemishes or flaws before it goes to the blending area where the delicate tints and tones are applied." Ezra extended his hand to Adam, who was now considering how he would tell Mr. Forsythe that he was not interested in his proposal. Before he could form the words, they moved on again. "In the damp room," Mr. Forsythe explained that "each piece is placed here until it is sent to the finishing room where painters apply the decorations: sprays of pink roses here, colorful poppies there, autumn leaves on another."

Adam was considering why they would not wish to consign these fine pieces to some peddler passing through when Mr. Forsythe stopped his running narrative long enough to ask, "ever hear of Rookwood?"

"I might have," Adam answered vaguely remembering Martha's reference to the Cincinnati pottery. "Founded by a woman," he remembered her saying.

"We hope to begin giving them some competition. They tend toward Japanese luster, but mostly their artists like to copy living flowers and people, Indians, for example. We hope to get into really fine art ware ourselves. We've got some good artists too." Mr. Forsythe stopped long enough to smile warmly at Adam. "By joining forces with us, you will be in on the ground floor." He kept up his steady patter into the firing room, where the extreme heat from two kilns reminded Adam of what the heat of hell must be like.

"Here is where we carry out the last stage in our process by subjecting each piece to a fierce eighteen hundred degrees." Mr. Forsythe went on enthusiastically. They watched a workman, his head wrapped in cloth, his hand in gauze, plunge a delicate vase into a solution of glaze before setting it on a tray for firing. "That gives each piece its beautiful gloss," Mr. Forsythe said, "and makes the decorations permanent before the final firing."

Adam's head was swimming as he tried to keep in mind each phase of the processes he had seen. He had never even wondered how all those beautiful items were made and experienced another moment of guilt when he remembered the recklessness of the soldiers in the Great War, who gleefully smashed similar objects in those grand southern houses.

Adam lost his nerve when it came to telling Mr. Forsythe that he was not interested and decided instead to write him a note and tell him so. They parted, and Adam said he'd think about the proposition and get back to Mr. Forsythe within the week.

He retrieved the horse, where he had stabled him behind the hotel, saw that he had water before hitching him to the buggy, and went inside to gather his belongings and pay for his night's lodging. He gave no further thought to Mr. Forsythe's proposal. It didn't interest him. With Seth's help, he would resume his farm work, maybe increase his herd of cattle, even find a wife. He'd go to church and check out some of the younger girls coming up. Twenty plus years difference in age would not matter to them if they saw a tolerable farm in the offing, and a man to look out for them, give them children. Yes, that's what he would do. He wondered if he should purchase a new suit. He'd been wearing this one since his wedding. It hadn't really been worn that much so wasn't threadbare, except for the edges of the jacket sleeves which he had inked before calling on Mr. Forsythe. But was it in style? He had no idea.

At home, he drifted peacefully to sleep that night secure in the thought that he would not have to tackle something new and different. But sometime around midnight he encountered a nightmare so frightening that he wondered if God himself had devised it. That face in the mirror, the drunken sop with reddened eyes and swollen face loomed in Adam's shaving mirror. And there was another face behind his, the accusing countenance of Martha, her blue eyes blazing in that terrible way she had of upbraiding him, sometimes without words. She shouted, her voice sharp as a scalpel: "bummer, failure, nerveless nothing." These words and more foamed out of her mouth in a steady stream of invective. He wakened, sat up on the side of the bed. Inside he ached. She was right, what Martha said was true. He lacked the grit to take on something new, feared finding himself in the company of strangers, maybe even to fail in front of them. On the farm he would be a lonely, shuffling, lost soul. Old Monongahela would again beckon him with its siren's call. And Martha would be lost to him forever.

The next morning at breakfast he dwelt on Mr. Forsythe's words. The man had not been forthcoming about details: how far would he travel; where would he sleep nights; and how often he would return home? What was this special wagon he kept mentioning? And most important of all—what would he be paid?

Twenty-seven

"You will have your own red wagon." Mr. Forsythe told him. "It will have gold lettering, and our artists will paint some representative vases and other products on each side."

This news gave Adam another moment of misgiving; he saw himself as a circus clown quite comfortable in a red wagon with gold lettering and painted pictures on the sides. What's wrong with plain black?

"We've ordered the wagon from an eastern Pennsylvania body works and expect delivery in about a month." Mr. Forsythe was exuberant.

Adam had trouble sharing his enthusiasm, but listened in respectful silence while once again considering how to get out of the arrangement.

"We will build shelves of varying heights to accommodate our wares packed in boxes." Mr. Forsythe warmed to his presentation "You will be paid a twenty-percent commission on the amount you sell. You sell a pot for three dollars that's sixty cents for you. Fair, don't you think?"

Adam had no idea if it was or wasn't. What if he went for days and sold nothing? "And my expenses on the road?"

"After the first month, they will come out of your commissions. How often you get home is up to you; more time at home, the less for making sales."

All this gave Adam the feeling of entrapment. Except for his time in the Union army, he had always been master of his own universe, even if that was only a marginal farm. Now the Pineville Pottery would own him, direct every aspect of his life, dictate his earnings. And if he didn't produce according to its standards, what then? He remembered how as a young man he had admired Jeremiah's life on the road, the freedom, and relief from the strictures of home, be they imposed by parents or a wife and children. Now that life didn't seem so appealing. Rejection! How would he handle that? Adam did not like being refused anything he wanted.

In his more sane moments, he had to admit it was not likely after a span of four years that Martha was ever coming back. He'd need Amos and his bride to live in for a considerable period, since it would be foolish to sell the farm before he determined how he felt about his new job. Being in trade, especially as a peddler, had always seemed a reckless occupation. He'd heard it was a tough life: rejection at every turn; doors slammed in your face; signs that said solicitors not wanted.

But if I stay alone in that house, will Old Monongahela become my friend again? Adam envisioned the broken down veterans he had seen on the streets in Pineville, Zanesville, and McConnelsville. And the thought sickened him. Even his old friend, Vesty, was still taking to the woods in an attempt to recreate his army life. Unable to adjust to home, wife, and children, Vesty was lost, confused, incapable of finishing a task. Adam and the other farmers were frequently called upon to tramp the woods looking for him. Men like Vesty had been stalwart soldiers once. Now they were broken men. Too many had already given in to opiates and the devil's brew. Vesty seemed not to be dependent on either, but his mind had gone as surely as an amputated leg on an injured veteran.

Adam tried to jolly himself into seeing the good side of what he was about to undertake. Ma had always talked about there being two sides of a story and "one should be man enough to look at both," she once told him.

Amos accepted Adam's proposition. "Now we can get to settin' the weddin' date. I been holdin' off 'til I could figure where we might plunk ourselves, and this solves our problems. Will I still get that five dollars a month?"

Already feeling like a newly anointed businessman, Adam told him, "for the first year until you get established and the crops are producing. Then we will work out a percentage of the crop for you and the five dollars will cease."

On the following Wednesday, Adam went to Four Corners to tell his family his plans. "I won't be coming here to deliver vegetables anymore, but will drop in from time to time. Amos can deliver your produce; he and his new wife, Tildy, will be staying at the farm. But for the next month until I establish my route, you won't see me at all." Frank's disinterest was apparent. He was still pleading to be allowed to quit school and go west while Martha was adamant that he stay, so not much else mattered to him. Adam no longer cared what his grumpy middle son did. Will too seemed indifferent. He had seen little of his father, so communication was always strained.

"I'll be picking up my new wagon in about a month." Adam went on.

Martha was dubious. "You are going to be a traveling man? I've seen more than my share these past four years, and you hardly fit that kind of life. Most are poor shabby sorts who barely make a living. God only knows when they see their families. Are you sure this is the direction you want to take?"

"It's a change."

"You will be out in searing heat and freezing cold, sometimes with rain and snow smacking your face. You'll drive on terrible roads talking day in and day out to unlettered people, who probably haven't got a cent to pay for anything extra, let alone a fancy pot. If you're going to sell products, make it anvils or plows or something big, something worth selling. You'll starve carrying around flowered chamber sets and decorated water pitchers."

Adam allowed as to how that might be the case, but he reminded her that he would have an income regardless, and went on to explain somewhat hesitantly what he had done with the Pineville property.

"I really didn't want to live there anyway; just tried to make the most of a bad situation. I'm going back to Marietta when I'm done here and the boys are out of school. Now if you'll excuse me, Adam, I have work to do."

Once more she dismissed him in that terribly superior way she had that left him feeling like an annoying bug to be squashed underfoot. Well, he would show her. Looking down at his shabby trousers, he decided that very day to buy a fashionable suit. He left the hotel for the haberdashery in Pineville where he bought not only the suit, but also a snappy vest. Adam also bought shiny new boots, a bowler hat, a black bow tie, and two white shirts, the first store-bought, except for Army issue, he ever owned. With his old clothes in the package under his arm, he walked down the street toward the empty lot where he had tethered the horse. A look at himself in the full-length mirror at the haberdashery had shocked him. No longer a tired looking, disheveled farmer, the new clothes gave him stature, not unlike the day he first donned his Civil War uniform. That had been such a proud day. Four years later the uniform was faded and tattered. He had mended and packed it away in a box in the loft and hadn't seen it in years.

The new clothes made Adam feel like a man of means with newfound gentility, a feeling that certainly called for celebration. A little nip couldn't hurt. He could control the amount. There were taverns here and there all along the street; he passed one, then another, and somehow resisted going inside any of them. Finally he came to the general store where he could buy a pint, take it home, and have as much as he wanted. Once the pint was gone, he'd stop imbibing. His hand on the store's entry door, Adam paused before swinging it open, then passed inside and stood hesitantly near the entrance. The clerk looked up. "Can I help you, sir."

"A pint, I mean a quart of Old . . . no forget it. I'll pick it up another time." Outside, he was horrified at how tempted he had been to take home a bottle and replicate the warm, gentle feeling of the drink. He remembered how it took him away from his worries and his unhappy, lonely life. He knew the drink could kill him. Once I start, I can't stop. I've got to face that, he decided. Still the demons fought him, and he nearly turned back to push the door open again. A nicely attired woman passed him and nodded politely. She reminded him of Martha in her better days. I can't go through this again, he thought, and vowed that not even in the taverns would he take another drink. Ma was right; alcohol is poison.

In the three weeks that followed his sartorial purchases, while he awaited the new wagon and kept to his vow about avoiding the dreadful drink, he grew a mustache. It came in gray, although his hair was still dark with only a smattering of salt and pepper about his sideburns. The redness and bloat in his face were gone now. A look in his shaving mirror left him pleased. He shaved every morning and kept his hair neatly trimmed. As a farmer he hadn't really cared how sloppy he appeared. It was hard to care when the only people who saw him were his family and the occasional neighbor. Now he took considerable pride in the image looking back at him.

"You're a changed man," John Forsythe greeted him when Amos drove him to Pineville to collect the wagon.

"I thought I had better look the part of a successful salesman."

"You look fine; the mustache adds years and gives you a more distinguished appearance so you should impress the women, but let me warn you"—Mr. Forsythe raised a cautionary finger—"never, ever, follow one into the bedroom. Some women are mighty lonely, and a fine looking man might give them notions—notions no God fearing wife should ever entertain—so don't venture from their kitchens and parlors. Heard of one man, a randy sort, who took liberties with a pretty housewife and got himself chased off a farm by a shotgun. Just remember no matter how slovenly or how old they look, they are never without the need for a kind entreaty from a handsome man."

Mr. Forsythe's demeanor had changed abruptly from genial friend to the man in charge, making Adam feel like an underling who would now be dictated to by his employer. Other than his stint in the war, he had always been his own man. But there were compensations. He was taken with the fine new wagon, even its golden lettering. Wagons were generally sturdy and lumbering, and open to the elements. Here was a wagon made to move rapidly over the countryside like a nimble filly. Mercifully they had left off the painted pictures of pots and vases.

Adam decided not to mention the fact; he needn't look flashier than the image the red wagon itself purveyed. Bending to finger the wheels, he said. "Aren't these a mite spindly for the roads I'm expected to travel? Isn't an extra wheel in order in case one breaks."

Mr. Forsythe fingered his chin for a moment, then reaching out to test the thickness of the wagon wheel replied, "I guess you're right. We'll order another one today."

"Order two while you're at it," Adam said, "for I notice the front wheels are smaller than those in the rear. In the meantime, I'll try to stay on the better roads." Adam thought the wagon more suitable for city streets, but accepted that he had no choice in the matter. Time would tell how well the wagon handled the rough roads. There were other advantages. The wagon sported an extension top and canvas storm curtains could be attached and drawn down on both sides to protect the driver in inclement weather. The front of the wagon came up high enough so a person's legs could be tucked underneath. With a lap robe, it was possible to be quite cozy in the otherwise open conveyance. The space between the shelves was two feet wide and only about six feet long ending at the rear, where there were two doors with oval frosted windows. The shelves were filled with boxes. Adam knelt to examine the undercarriage and saw that it sat on three elliptical springs with a reach connecting them to the axles, an arrangement that would make for a gentler ride. "Best to know something about the wagon lest I get stranded in the countryside," he said, untangling himself from the undercarriage.

A man sauntered out of the pottery stable with a roan horse. "Name's Nancy," he said, patting her head, as he began to harness her to the wagon, while Mr. Forsythe showed Adam how to mark the order pads and keep track of the items sold and the amount and numbers of the styles ordered.

Adam put his valise, a blanket, and work boots under the seat and climbed into the wagon. Saying good-bye, he switched the horse, and together they went forth to what Adam considered the great unknown. Remembering his history of hostility with animals, he felt some trepidation about what he was doing and hoped Nancy would prove a good companion. Just in case, he had some sugar cubes in his pocket. Troubling feelings dissipated when a look at the countryside, as the horse trotted them out of Pineville, presented a peaceful scene of hills and meadows. The sun was brilliant, the sky pale blue, and the clouds as fluffy white as angel's wings. Adam considered these cheerful signs for the endeavor he was about to undertake.

Twenty-eight

That cheerful optimism soon turned to despair when Adam began calling at weathered farmhouses set back from the main roads on lanes that sorely tested the springs and tender wheels of his wagon.

"Get outta' here," one grizzled farmer called from an adjacent field where he was walking behind a plow and a team. "We don't want no fancy peddler on our place. Now skedaddle." At the next house, he managed to greet the housewife, but one look at the red wagon and she yelled, "we don't have no truck with the devil here." She slammed the door before Adam could begin his spiel. He did no better at the third house where he was told by the woman, "we ain't got no money for such fripperies." He was holding the miniature kit and asked if she would like to have it—"only a dollar," he said, "the kiddies will like it."

"You think I'm made of money?" And another door slammed.

By this time it was noon. Thoroughly soured on his new occupation, he decided to return home to the comfort of what he knew best, his farm. But because hunger had set in, he switched the horse toward the nearest town where he could eat his dinner. Close by the town center a general store caught his attention; he pulled on the reins, parked at the side of the street and fought off tempting thoughts that told him to forget it. Ignoring the stares of passersby who looked curiously at him and the red wagon, he grabbed his sample case and went inside before he could change his mind. The proprietor, who evidently thought Adam was a customer, looked up from rice he was weighing and asked in a pleasant voice "what can I do for you?" Adam swung his sample case onto the counter and opened it before the storekeeper could dismiss him.

"Notice how artfully painted these chamber pots are and these banks—the kiddies all want them—encourages the little tykes to save. We have them in larger sizes; these are only miniatures." The words tumbled out of Adam's mouth like froth splashing over a dam. The man perused the items, but said nothing. He was a dour sort apparently upset at being interrupted. No matter, Adam rushed on. "Would you like to see some of my other wares? My wagon is right out front."

"That red vehicle out there, that a wagon? Kind of gaudy if you ask me. Looks more like an advertisement for a bawdy house."

"Certainly is. A wagon, I mean." Adam paid no mind to the reference. "May I show you some of my offerings?" he went on rapidly. "We have tankards, pitchers, flowerpots—like this little one here—and cuspidors no woman will object to having in her parlor. Would you like me to fetch a few to show you?"

"If you want," the proprietor said halfheartedly and went back to measuring rice. Adam considered he was only entertainment for the clerk who was bored with what he was doing. Half tempted to leave for the tavern, he took a moment to calm himself, and returned to the store with two of Pineville Pottery's most precious vases. When he was done extolling their hand painted beauty, the clerk, who never stopped measuring the rice, said, "them containers are nice, but way too fancy for the folks around here. And those prices—three dollars is outrageous for that there pitcher, even if'n it does have that fancy gold handle."

Adam felt his spirits sink and practically begged the storekeeper to take the set of miniatures, "just in case people want to order similar items. If your customers prefer them plain, we can supply our wares without decorations." He wasn't at all certain of that. It was just an idea that popped into his head.

"They'd be cheaper, I expect." The shopkeeper gave Adam a hard, unsmiling look. But in the end—perhaps, recognizing the eagerness of a new man on the road—he said he'd take the set of miniatures.

Adam took the dollar almost greedily, thanked him, gathered up the fancy ware, loaded his wagon, and went to find a tavern, where his dinner took twenty-cents just what he had earned that day.

Nights followed days that varied little from the first one with rejection at every store and at the end of every lane. Few shopkeepers had much interest in his fancy wares. Lodging and food and feed for the horse took most of his share of the few piddling sales he made. Even though this first month's expenses were on the company, Adam felt he should be making ends meet. By Friday night, he slept in his wagon in a wooded area, stretched out on his side, the horse blanket beneath him, his valise as a pillow, the lap robe covering him. By morning he was so stiff and dejected he turned the wagon around and headed home.

He spent a troubled weekend determined to call off his bargain with Mr. Forsythe. Except for the miniatures, nothing was sold out of the wagon to warrant a trip to Pineville for replacements. He would have to quit. To replenish his broken spirits, he went to Lutheran services Sunday morning, and on the way prayed there would be another new minister—one who did not know he had not attended in nearly a year—or was it two? That wasn't too much to ask.

The preacher was really worked up over sin that morning, and the congregation already overheated by the heavy stale air inside the tiny church got more so when thoughts of hell's flaming heat took over. Fans the ladies carried went back and forth faster and faster as they contemplated what lay ahead should they wander from their appointed mission in life.

"Hell," the preacher yelled, "burns you ever so slowly. It never stops. You twist and simmer forever; there is no escape. And sin, my friends is what puts you there." He went on to enumerate every sin known to man. Adam soon turned off and dwelled instead on the sin of quitting, not finishing a task taken up. Hadn't Ma warned that God expected man to complete whatever job he is assigned? She had no qualms about applying that sin theory to gathering eggs or feeding chickens. When as a boy Adam had tried to get out of doing some chore or other, guilt always brought him back to the job she set out for him. Ma and the preacher were right. It was a sin to give up without trying. Tomorrow is Monday. I'll be out and about again, he decided. Strangely, once the decision was made, he felt better about himself. And before leaving the pew to shake the preacher's hand, he remembered once again to ask God to encourage Martha to come back to him. But just in case God chose to ignore his request, he had given the girls a cursory glance, but none of the newly grown up ones appealed.

On his next trip he stayed out for two weeks, and while he met with little success, he did sell a few tankards and pitchers to eager housewives. Several seemed very grateful for his company, leading him to remember John Forsythe's cautionary words. Still he found that flattery did wonders for sales. He commented on the attractiveness of the various parlors in which he found himself and began to bow low with a sweep of his hat as the ladies greeted him. Most had faces of granite, wore dirty aprons, and shuffled about in long dresses that suffered from too many washings, or in some cases not enough. "I know you are a busy woman, but underneath that apron, you appear to be a person of taste and refinement," became his opening pitch. That usually elicited a smile and broke the ice. Where the ruse did not work, he learned to accept the slammed door. One woman thoroughly misinterpreted his benign remark and called him a cad for mentioning what was under her apron. After that he left out the reference and said instead that he could tell each woman was a person of style whose good taste was reflected in the décor of her living room. Even the most slovenly reacted with a flutter of eyelids or at the least a trace of a smile.

He continued to sleep in his wagon several nights a week finding it preferable to bunking with others in the dusky rooms of cheap hostelries, where smoke from cigars, curling through floorboards from noisy bar rooms below, made every breath an effort. By sleeping in his wagon on occasion, he could afford to stay overnight in better inns.

By Adam's sixth week on the road, his sales were still faltering. He sold a few umbrella stands to women in the better-looking farmhouses and came to see that some did aspire to beautifying their homes. His wares fit with their desires, but he was still doubtful about making a living. Were it not for spending nights in the wagon, sometimes parked in the lots of the taverns where could wash up and take his meals, he would not be earning enough to cover his expenses.

It was in a general store where the proprietor ordered several cuspidors and a few crocks that he got his first break. "I can't sell that fancy stuff," the man told him, "but I think you might find a ready outlet at the White Dove. That's an emporium up the street run by a lady, a widow lady—lost her husband in the war—so she's accepted, even though her man fought on the wrong side, and she's a Jewess. Local ladies of means shop there for dress goods and knickyknacks for their homes."

Adam thanked the man for the lead and went immediately to the White Dove, just a house with the downstairs turned into a store. When he opened the door, a bell tingled invitingly, and he could hear movement up above. Glassware, porcelains, bookends, and other household gewgaws were placed decoratively on tables and shelves along with golden picture frames and milk glass with its telltale hobnail pattern. The pungent odor of cinnamon brought his attention to a glass case where pastries caused his stomach to growl and his mouth to water at the sight of flaky chocolate-laced confections, lemon cakes, and small cookies. A tall woman dressed in a long black skirt and ruffled white blouse with leg o'mutton sleeves approached him from the stairwell. She wore a lacy jabot at her neck and dainty pearl eardrops. Her skin was dark with heavy eyebrows over flashing black eyes. Nothing about her appeared to resemble any other women he knew. Adam had only seen a few Jews in the war. Generally they were swarthy types, quick of wit, but not to be trusted, at least that's what the other men told him. He would have to be careful lest she cheat him.

"Good morning, sir. May I help you?" she addressed him with a smile as wide as a great blue sea.

"I represent the Pineville Pottery," he stammered, "and I thought you might like to see what I have to offer. We make decorative pieces. I think you will find them very beautiful."

"That sounds interesting. I'm always in the market for unique things. I have heard of the Pineville Pottery, but no one has ever called on me." Her voice was lyrical, and her words came out so pleasantly that Adam felt a slight lurch in his heart. She was not a young woman; there were tiny wrinkles in the skin beside her eyes, matched by a few on her upper lip, but nonetheless she was beautiful in an oriental way.

Adam rushed out to the wagon, took down what he considered his best pieces and carried them into the store.

She gave him another enormous smile. "Come out here on the porch where there is more room to spread out." Adam moved behind her to the rear porch passing by what once must have been a dining room. He could see shelves containing bolts of fabric along the walls. Two pretentiously dressed women, one in a mauve silk outfit with matching hat and the other in ruffled midnight blue, were examining laces and trims.

"Let me know if you need help," the proprietress called out as she paused at the door. "I'll be on the porch."

Outside were three tables of varying sizes set out with wire chairs, like those in an apothecary where phosphates and sweets are served. "Here, we'll use this table," the woman motioned for him to set his pottery on the largest.

"Let me introduce myself, I'm Adam Springer," he reached to shake her hand.

"And I am Mrs. Lazarus."

"I assume you own this shop."

"I do."

Her reaction to his line of goods was like that at a lover's first glance at his beloved. She exclaimed over every vase and tankard. "My customers will adore these." She leaned in close to Adam, so close, in fact, that he discerned the faint scent of perfume. No God-fearing woman of his acquaintance wore anything but rosewater. This was something stronger, but enticing.

Mrs. Lazarus lowered her voice to a whisper. "That taller woman examining the trims is the wife of the local mine owner, and the other is married to the president of our bank. Mark my words, they will be my first customers for these marvelous vases." She got up abruptly and called to the two women who came out to the porch. Adam stood, bowed and momentarily thought of his mother's efforts to teach him gentlemanly manners, which he had resisted adamantly but now appreciated.

"Oh," they exclaimed in unison. "Have you ever? That tankard is exactly what I've been looking for. Mrs. Lazarus, I hope you are going to order several of these," the woman in blue said excitedly. "I'm in the market for wedding gifts, so don't be stingy with the order." She smiled broadly at Adam who got the thought out of nowhere and suddenly blurted. "You will not make any mistake buying art ware from the Pineville Pottery. These pieces can only go up in value. Someday, they will turn up in the antique trade for they are among the earliest to be made." Martha was always chattering about antiques, but he never thought he would.

While the women prattled on, Adam went to his wagon and brought in samples of every item he carried. And by the end of the day, he had sold thirty-two dollars worth and left order forms and a catalog for additional orders, which Mrs. Lazarus guaranteed would be forthcoming.

That night he stayed at the best inn in town and took his supper with another traveling man whose line was fine fabrics: "woolens, silks and satins, cambric and dimities," the man recounted proudly.

"You must sell to Mrs. Lazarus." Adam took a draught of root beer in celebration of his good fortune.

"Indeed I do. She is one of my best customers."

Adam leaned forward somewhat conspiratorially, "tell me is it true; is she really a Jew?"

"Yep, can't you tell?"

"I've never seen a Jewess. Whatever brings her to this town? Her kind usually go to cities, don't they?"

"Her brother-in-law was a peddler, came in here before the war with a pack on his back. At first he carried only trinkets and notions: needles, pins—that sort of thing. Later he got a wagon, which he pulled himself and offered fabrics, simple stuff like calicos. When the war came, he realized he'd have to settle in somewhere. He'd come up from the south and claimed not to be sympathetic to their cause—objected to slavery—so he bought that plot of ground where the store is for five dollars, and set about erecting a cabin. A clever bloke and never one to shirk community responsibility; he even gave to the Methodists when they were raising money to put a steeple on their church. Some folks said they shouldn't accept filthy lucre from a Jew, but most got cross-eyed over the money—more than anyone else had given. So even though they disagreed with his religion—not being Christian and all—his neighbors pitched in to help add to the cabin. As years went on and his business prospered, he put on that second floor and made the entire downstairs into a store. Then he brought in a wife from Pittsburgh, I think it was. They lived upstairs, but she was anxious to move on and every bit as ambitious as he was, so they went to Columbus and opened what is now a fine emporium. This Mrs. Lazarus, who owns the White Dove, was married to his brother. He worked for her Pa in the dress goods business in Richmond, but when the war came he was taken as a soldier by the southern cause and died at Gettysburg. She struggled on for awhile in Richmond, but it was pretty burned out in the Great War."

"I was there, saw it all," Adam said. "Shame we had no feeling for those poor folks."

"Her Pa's place was nothing but ashes, so when her brother-in-law offered her this house, she accepted. The word is he gave it to her. People around here are surprised that she's stayed this long, but some say she doesn't get on with her Columbus sister-in-law who has grown quite hoity-toity as their business has improved and the money rolls in."

Adam had trouble sleeping that night. Mrs. Lazarus was an unusual woman who wouldn't leave his mind alone. He was also troubled about the orders. Certain she would order more merchandise, could he be sure the factory would credit him, or would they take over the account and deal with her directly? He'd heard from other salesmen that companies did that when accounts got really big.

The next day he went to the stationers and bought a dozen envelopes, addressed them to himself, and pasted a one-cent stamp on each one. The envelopes were for his protection, of course, but they also gave him an excuse to call on Mrs. Lazarus again. She greeted him warmly and invited him to sit for a cup of tea and a pastry. When he offered to pay, she declined his money with an airy "That will not be necessary." They chatted amiably, mostly about the merchandise. He explained that when she sent an order to the pottery, he would appreciate her filling out duplicate order forms to be mailed to him in the preaddressed envelopes, "so that not only the pottery will have one, but I will too. That way I can hasten delivery." He was learning that salesmen say all manner of things despite whether they can back them up. She appealed to him, but a Jew—never. Martha had fulfilled his need for a lady, a woman of stature, and she was very much like this Mrs. Lazarus who ran her own affairs. There was apparently no man around, and by her zeal for what she was doing, she evidently didn't need one. They parted as friends while Adam tried to ignore his growing excitement at the thought of calling upon her again. "I'll be back sometime in the spring when we expect to have an additional line of merchandise," he told her, holding her hand in parting a bit longer than necessary. He reluctantly took his leave, temptation boiling inside like a forgotten pot on the stove.

His wagon was nearly empty, and that afternoon he headed home. It was only Thursday, but he decided to take Friday and the weekend to check on matters at the farm and to see Martha and the boys. School would be starting soon; she probably needed his help keeping Frank enrolled.

Twenty-nine

Marked by new enthusiasm for what he was doing and elated by his pocketful of orders, Adam sat tall on the wagon seat as he entered Four Corners. He intended to stay that night with his sister, Emma, but so buoyant were his spirits that instead he went to the hotel registration desk where Martha greeted him. "I'd like a room," he told her in his most authoritative manner.

"You're not going to the farm or to your sisters?"

"Not this time. I've been away so long that I need to spend more time with the boys. Besides, I can barely stand the thought of Tildy's meals. Her idea of cooking is to throw everything in one pot: meat, vegetables, potatoes, and turnips. She cooks it all at once and so long the peas and beans are likely to be mush and the meat gray as gunmetal."

"Like your mother."

"Don't start, Martha."

"How much do you want to spend for your night's lodging?"

"I'm not spending. My name is on the deed and after four years of bending to you, I plan to stay in that front bedroom. And I don't expect to pay a dime for a night in my own bed, that is unless some local bride-to-be has spoken for it. Like before, I'll take my meals with you and the boys."

Martha seemed flustered. "As you like," she said.

"I will be going to the farm tomorrow afternoon to check on Amos, and Monday I will go to Pineville. I've sold everything out of my wagon and need to replenish my stock," he said grandly.

"You're looking well," she turned slightly to look at him as they went up the stairs. Indeed he was: new suit, clean shirt, and shined shoes, hair and mustache neatly trimmed. His ruddy cheeks were glowing attesting to his sturdy good health, which was more than he could say for her: she was looking mighty tired. Her hair was slightly disheveled, and she was thin, thinner than he remembered or liked her to be. A woman of her age should sport an ample waist and bustline.

At the top of the stairs she scurried along ahead of him to the front bedroom, as though she was so busy she could only allot a scrap of time toward getting him settled. Adam had not been in that front bedroom since their first walk through. Now he saw that it was truly grand with a fluffy down comforter on the bed. Martha's furniture from Marietta fit into the large airy room brightened by windows on two sides. Crocheted doilies of her own making graced the nightstand and dresser. A decorated chamber set including a basin, large-mouthed pitcher, and tooth cup was set out on the washstand. He picked up the pitcher to see the identifying mark on the bottom. They were not from the Pineville Pottery, but a company in Wheeling unknown to Adam.

"I'll expect you to remove this quilt and hang it on that rack when you repair to the bed for the night. You can replace it with the comforter."

"I thought you might take care of that," Adam said.

"No, I leave it to the men, or in this case the brides as one never knows when someone else is ready to sleep."

"When can I see Frank and Willy? Are they about?"

"They'll be along shortly, or if you wish to see them sooner, you can go to the garden, where they are collecting vegetables for tonight's dinner."

"So you now have a garden of your own."

"It's small, we couldn't always count on Amos delivering every week or you either, for that matter."

"I'll see them in the garden then." He eyed her critically. "You've lost weight, you're not the ample matron you once were."

She stared up at him, look of wide-eyed wonder crossed her face. "How could I be heavy with all the work I'm expected to do here."

"Nobody asked you to do it."

"Yes, but I did get Ben through his schooling with a year in college, and with God's help, Frank will finish his last year in high school. I'm working mightily to convince him to improve his manner of speech. If I had let them stay on that farm, they would be like all the rest of those yokels out there in the country who are done with school by eighth grade. And I so want them to have better futures than what eight years of education can provide. I'm sorry now that I fought Father when he made me come here to care for Auntie, for all I accomplished was a hardening of his attitude toward me. Had I been more cooperative and gone back to Marietta like he wanted me to, I might have had two years at Marietta College instead of only one. I might have become a teacher. Now it's too late. I've given up on getting Frank to college, but maybe Will . . ." Her voice trailed off in a weary sigh, and she turned to leave. "Dinner's at six," she said.

"One more thing, what do you hear from Ben?"

"Not much," she said closing the door.

He unpacked his grip and went immediately to greet his sons. They passed pleasantries in the awkward manner of nearly grown men and a mostly absent father. Immediately after pleasantries, Frank approached him about leaving for California before school started. "I don't want to go back, Pa. I've had enough school, more than enough. I hate it. My grades were not that good last year, so why do I have to go on with it. I ain't—I mean I don't have any use for Latin and Algebra. Most of the blokes I know have already quit."

"You don't know what you might do in the future, so best be prepared for whatever the future holds. Son, let me tell you something." Adam put a hand on Frank's shoulder. "There are times when we all hate what we have to do; I hated the war, but I spent three and a half years in those places of killing and despair, where boys just like me met their bloody ends. They never had a chance at life, never married, no children. Many times, I wanted to run away, to desert, but fighting is what I was called upon to do at that particular time in my life. So I stayed where others did not. Those who deserted must be bearing their pain even now. I almost died of fright when I found myself at the first dreadful battle. I was so scared, I wanted to run, but I didn't. Now I'm proud of that decision. Deserting is a terrible blight on a person's character, and that goes for quitting school as well." He glared at his son. "And the farm . . . do you think I ever wanted to be a farmer? No, but I was not trained to do anything else, and when you boys came along, I realized I had no choice, but to provide so I stayed on. Now your mother provides, because she wants you both to finish school here in town as Ben did. I don't believe it is easy for her either. Even with the help you boys give her, it cannot be a frolic, for I see she wears the struggle in her strained face and around her thinning waist."

"But Papa."

Adam raised a hand in a gesture that said to stop resisting. "You have no choice at this stage of your life, Frank, but to stay and finish your last year. If you complete your schooling, I will see that you have the train fare to go west. Now let's hear no more about it." Adam turned to leave. "And one more thing, I thank my mother every day that she made me speak correctly, just as your mother is trying to do for you. Right now your speech labels you as a country bumpkin. Of course, if that's all you want, so be it. But she has greater hopes for you."

Frank responded with a sullen expression. Annoyed by the encounter, Adam left his sons and went to the house and into the bedroom, where he washed up for dinner. They all ate heartily; Frank had little to say, but Will babbled on about his friends, helping Ma, and baseball, a new team some of the local lads had organized. He seemed to be filling in for the silences that ensued as Martha, Adam, and Frank appeared occupied with their own worries and thoughts.

That night Adam lay alone in the great, carved bed, further enhanced by a new fluffier feather tick. One by one the street lamps outside were being snuffed out, and darkness soon settled over the town. He was nearly asleep when he heard a faint knocking at the door. "Yes," he called, "who is it?"

"It's me, Martha." Her voice was soft.

"Come in, the door's not locked."

She opened it and came toward him. He could see in the faint light of the moon outside his window that she was wearing her fanciest nightclothes. Her robe was the frilly one he had not seen in years.

"Aren't you worried that your other guests might think ill of you coming to my room like this? Traveling men are used to adventurous ladies, many of whom claim to be widows, who make their unsavory living doing favors for men. And some seem to enjoy it, amazing given that women's real role in life is to be housewives and mothers not expected to find pleasure in the act."

"I suppose you've learned all this by experience now that you are also a traveling man."

"No, I hear it from the other men. You might not want to believe this, Martha, but I still consider myself married to you. That document your lawyer served me I regard as wasted paper. I do not believe in divorce."

"To answer your question. Only two travelers are in the third floor bedrooms and the other one is still in the taproom. We're alone on this floor."

"Now that I am a traveling man, I am more aware of the temptations men face than I ever was before; comely women are everywhere. I've wondered, since I began this salesman's job, if you are at all concerned about the reputation you might have gained by taking on this hotel."

"I assure you I have not engaged in any promiscuous activity. Even though you and I are divorced, I too consider myself a married woman in the eyes of God, and I shall never take another husband as long as you live." She moved closer to the bed; her hand rested on the coverlet as though she was about to pull it back. "Adam, I want to return to you, feel your arms around me again, snuggle against you, that is if you'll have me."

It had been four long years since he had had a wife or a woman. While other men on the road were frequently visited by girls of the night, Adam had avoided them. Still considering himself married, he had not the will—even though desire was always with him—to take up with one of those fancy women. He had been sorely tempted by the lovely Mrs. Lazurus and thought of her often—but a Jewess? There was no way, even though children would not be a problem at their ages. Although he longed for Martha and a semblance of family life, he told himself over and over that she would never come back. He felt certain she had married him on a young girl's whim, probably to defy her father and to assure herself a husband, but she had done so with no idea as to the life they would live together. She was undoubtedly smitten as young girls easily are. But she was unable to see beyond the man to recognize she also married the trappings of his life, appendages he takes for granted and she sees as impediments: an overbearing mother-in-law, a run-down house and farm in which she had not the least interest. Perhaps he had never been sympathetic enough considering her unhappiness with her fate. During those times she exhibited frustration, he had simply tossed it off with a grunt or a walk out the door. When she threw her tantrums, he told her she was crazy; when in reality, he now thought of himself as the crazy one, scarred by war, his brain seared with memories of it all even now.

With their trials behind them, he could not believe his good fortune. Martha seemed as eager as he was to consummate the marriage again and the next day she told the boys that Adam, when he was not on the road, would be staying at the hotel and sharing the bedroom in the family quarters. Will and Frank would henceforth take one of the third floor bedrooms. The boys, their faces sullen, left the table as though what their parents did was of no concern of theirs, yet at the time of the Springer's separation they appeared to be embarrassed by it.

So eager were Martha and Adam for each other now they shared themselves each weekend with reckless enthusiasm, and only when Martha found herself in a family way again did they realize the consequences of their frenzied actions. Adam at age forty-nine was overjoyed at the prospect of another child, and Martha, while at first angry at being a new mother at the age of forty, finally accepted her changed situation by convincing herself that the baby would be the daughter she had always wanted.

Thirty

The people looked indignant and sullen. The colored people seemed to welcome us, and crowded the streets and public square. They said they did not believe we were Yankees, because they thought Yankees had horns and cloven feet.

Buoyed by his wife's return to his bed, Adam acquired a lightness of step he had not known since he was a boy. His sales were taking hold, and at the Pineville Pottery, Mr. Forsythe invited him to share a meal at a neighboring tavern. "I want to congratulate you on a job well done," he told him

"There were times I wanted to quit," Adam said honestly, "but now I'm glad I persevered. Some days are not grand, and I tire of those lackluster meals in greasy taverns and accommodations that are frequently dreary, even dirty, but then I make a sale and all is forgotten."

Mr. Forsythe smiled and hinted that if he kept on at his present pace there might be something better in the offing. Adam wanted to pursue that subject, but Mr. Forsythe quickly dropped it by suggesting he call him *John.* Then he added, "by the way do you belong to a church?"

"The Lutherans," Adam answered.

"Do you think they would have any use for a few vases and pitchers? We have some that are not good enough to sell—they have defects—so we are giving them to various churches hereabouts."

"I'm sure the ladies of the Jerusalem Church would be pleased to have them. They mostly use their own things for picnics and the like, so the church could use some supplies. We like to have flowers on the altar, especially on holidays." Adam left the Pineville Pottery that day with a new load of merchandise and a box of vases and pitchers for the church. On his way, he stopped by a parishioner's home to obtain the key. He was rounding the bend toward the church when he spied what appeared to be a dark and rumpled body dropping from a tree limb. On closer inspection, he saw a man dangling by a rope, his head lolling toward one shoulder, his arms hanging loosely by his sides. Horrified, Adam switched the horse and quickly turned the wagon toward the hanging man. He felt into his bag of supplies for his best knife, stood unsteadily on the wagon seat and began sawing through the rope. A good ten minutes passed before the tightly twisted hemp gave way and the body, with its grossly swollen face, fell to the ground. "Good God, it's Vesty," he said aloud. There was no pulse.

Covering the body with his lap robe, he drove the buggy back to Mrs. Schumacher's. "Is your man about?"

"In the barn, you going to give me back the key?"

"Later," Adam said. "Got something else to do first. I'll need your husband and a wagon."

Schumacher agreed to haul the body to the undertaker in Four Corners. Said he'd rather do that than break the news to Vesty's wife. "Poor soul, he never was much of a provider, and all them kids running loose."

After helping to lift Vesty's body into the wagon, Adam took the vases and pitchers into the church where he placed the box on the altar with a hastily written note, locked up, and gave the key to Schumacher.

"Tell your wife much obliged," Adam said. "I'll go on now to Vesty's place and tell the news. Don't much relish carrying my message, but somebody has to do it." Adam mulled over several conversations he'd had with Vesty. They served together in the Great War. Vesty was a good soldier. He'd tell the wife that. He'd mention the time that Company E, along with parts of the Illinois Twenty-Ninth, were ordered to proceed up the railroad and open it for transportation as far as Jackson, Tennessee. He'd let her know how some seven hundred Yankees took the inhabitants by surprise.

Slowing the wagon he began rehearsing the speech aloud. I'll tell her "the inhabitants were just about to burn the bridges to prevent our entrance to the place, but we beat them to it and marched through their streets triumphantly. And it was your Vesty who bore the flag of the Seventy-Eighth to the top of the courthouse and fastened it to the cupola while we all watched from below. That should make her proud."

Adam decided not to mention how demoralized Vesty was at returning home, how he hated everything about domestic life. He'd married while on furlough from Vicksburg. "I shouldn't a done it," he told Adam. "We got to sparking and went too far; then she told me we had to marry up; we went to the Justice of the Peace and done it. But there waren't no baby; didn't get no kids until a year after I got back; then we got half a dozen. "Ádam," Vesty had said, "I want to be back with the boys agin, eatin' hardtack and crackers, and tellin' stories, sleepin'out. Member the chuckles we had?"

189

"That's all over" Adam recalled telling him. "We're family men now."

And once again he had taken Vesty home. But there was no happiness in that house. It was little more than a three-room shack, the wife as desolate looking as Vesty. She was scrawny little woman, tired beyond endurance, for whatever happened on that forty acres to keep the family fed and clothed fell to her.

She greeted Adam in her usual resigned manner, evidently thinking he was going to tell her he had brought Vesty home again. Adam asked her to scoot the children outdoors before he began, and when the true words rolled out of his mouth, there was no reaction. Her spectacles slid down her nose, but no tears rose in her eyes. She listened unmoved to the news of her husband's death and the terrible manner in which he chose eternity. Adam forced a smile when he told her of the flag and how Vesty climbed to the courthouse cupola. "We all cheered him that day. Vesty came down from his perch, and every man saluted him. None of the rest of us boys had the courage to climb that high."

She sat studying her callused hands, while Adam waited for some kind of reaction. Tears, maybe.

"Want some tea?" she finally asked.

Adam said he'd best be getting back to the farm as he had been away awhile. But before he left, he went to the wagon and took down one of his best-glazed pitchers and gave it to her. He would pay for it himself. The poor woman had not one item of beauty in her house. Several chairs had broken backs; the children's clothes were raggedy. They all looked like they needed a good tub dunking. When Adam passed by the eldest on his way to the buggy, the boy asked, "you bring Pa back agin?"

"No, son, you had better go and see to your mother. You're the man of the house now."

Thirty-one

Adam rarely went to the farm after Martha announced her pregnancy. He traveled for the pottery, and as long as her condition did not show, she ran the hotel. Frank and Willy helped, even though they seemed somewhat ashamed as their mother's appearance began to change, heralded by the gathered waistline of her voluminous skirt. Adam thought his brother and sisters must have felt the same about his impending birth when his mother was forty-six.

"We'd better be making some changes in our living arrangements," he told Martha on one of their winter evenings in the family quarters. "I've been thinking of coming in off the road. Traveling by wagon is hard day after day, and I'm beginning to feel my age. Most of the peddlers I meet are young men. But to prove myself to the company, I'll go out again in the spring even though I know there's not enough money to be made in these small towns, especially with art ware. If I carried a cheap line, that might be different."

"You're making a commendable start, though I hope you will go on to bigger and better things." Martha laid aside the book she was reading. "And I agree, I'm tired of this hotel; it's getting to be a daily grind and not as lucrative as I had hoped. Maybe we should sell it."

"It's your decision. I'll back whatever you choose to do. As for me, I think when I have put in a year, I might ask for something new. I could visit larger towns in the state by rail, far easier than dragging that horse and wagon through the countryside in snow and mud. I've had to dig myself out of foot deep ruts and maneuver over ice with a wagon not fit for bad weather. Regardless, I've got to make a change."

"And if they refuse you?"

"I doubt they will, but if they do, I'll find another supplier. We could buy a house in Pineville, and Willy could go to school there. It's a bigger town and probably the schools are better."

"Best if we stay until after the baby comes," Martha said. "I might get into too much heavy lifting if we move now, and I don't want anything to happen to this precious child; she is really God's unique gift to us. She has brought us closer together than we ever were." She reached over and tenderly placed her hand on the back of his neck. He turned to look at her, patted her hand, and saw that her complexion had turned to a pale pink that made her wide spaced blue eyes glisten, not unlike the little figurine he had given Emma so long ago. At last, he thought, I have my lady.

"Meanwhile, we'd better go about finding a buyer for the hotel. We don't have to rush, but I would like you done with this place. It's a lot of work."

"Truthfully, I'm tired of dealing with some of the unsavory characters who come through here." Martha let out a deep breath. "Men willing to share beds pay cheap, but they are also of inferior character."

By the time their baby son was born, the winter of 1889 had passed, and Adam was back on the road in early spring 1890. Since old Dr. Kennedy had retired and no doctor had taken his place, women in a family way relied on the midwife who lived in Four Corners. She came with excellent credentials, so Martha was satisfied that she would see to her needs. "Get along with your calls," she told Adam, "I'll be fine." She may have been put off somewhat by the arrival of another son, but once she took the child into her arms, it seemed not to matter, and she never mentioned wishing for a daughter again. Adam was simply happy that the baby appeared to be healthy.

Frank graduated from high school soon after, and as promised, Adam went to the bank and took money from his clay account for his son's trip west. Frank stayed around long enough to help out at the hotel during his mother's confinement. He had been eager to leave Ohio, indeed had nagged to go ever since his fourteenth year, but when the time came he lingered. Adam recognized that Frank's dreams were perhaps more beckoning than the reality. By late August when Adam drove him to the train station in Zanesville, the boy doggedly set out to pursue those dreams, even as his father realized he was forcing himself to get on the train with an assemblage of strangers. Although Frank was not shy like Willy, Adam wondered how he would handle a trip across the country with people he did not know and probably would never see again. "Work hard at whatever you choose to do, never cheat your employer or your fellow man, and pay your bills on time," Adam told him. "If you follow my advice, you should do well. Since the gold rush back in forty-nine, that country is growing like no other part of these great United States. Besides, thanks to your mother, you are well armed with a high school diploma, more than some young men have to offer."

Frank smiled at his father, breaking the harsh reality of leaving his home and family. "Hope you are right, Pa, and I guess it's good that I'm now eighteen—more of a man than a boy." He moved jauntily, his valise swinging importantly, to board the train. When he was gone, the family settled in with the new baby they named Ralph, but everybody called Ralphy. Fifteen-year old Willy took over his brother's chores until they had a buyer for the hotel.

Meanwhile, Adam was not without new plans of his own. He visited John Forsythe and proposed that he be given several Ohio cities to cover. "I've worked long enough to know that this art pottery is more suitable for folks in larger towns who have a hankering to beautify their homes. Country folk, for the most part, don't care. They seem too taken up with struggling for necessities with little money left over for the finer things life offers."

The factory was busy and Mr. Forsythe said he thought Adam's plan a good one. "But rather than living in Pineville, I think you should go to Zanesville where you'll have easier access to the railroad, and will not be that far away. Putnam might be a good place to settle. What do you think?"

Adam agreed and shortly thereafter began looking for a house to buy in the small community across the Muskingum River from Zanesville. With considerable enthusiasm for his new endeavor he told Martha, "I can go by packet boat to McConnelsville and Marietta, and you and Ralphy can go along to visit your sisters and brother. The railroad will take me to Columbus, Cincinnati, and points east. No more wagons over bumpy bad roads," he said, taking her into his arms. She laughed and snuggled her head against him.

"Oh Adam, I'm so proud of you," she said. "And I must confess I never was before, but seeing you dressed up like a gentleman and acting like a business person, you are the man I always dreamed about. To think that all those years on that dreary farm, I only thought of you as person of no ambition, willing to stay with the comfortable and only way of life you knew. Now that you have stepped out, you are much more interesting. Then, seeming to hesitate about what was really on her mind, she added, "there is just one more thing. We must see about remarrying; we don't want to make this child a bastard by tenets of the law."

Adam thought it unnecessary given that the divorce was not legitimate in the eyes of God. "Where do we do that?"

"At my church, of course. Reverend Chandler could perform the ceremony."

193

"Better we go to Pineville to the justice of the peace. Reverends don't like performing ceremonies for legally divorced people."

For a moment his ex-wife wore a pensive look. Adam knew her well enough to know that a religious ceremony would, for Martha, make the union more authentic, but he also knew she would be embarrassed at approaching Reverend Chandler with the baby already bouncing in his new basket. Tearfully, she agreed, and the next day, Adam set off for Pineville to make arrangements. Seeing it would be less embarrassing for Martha, he planned to ask the justice to come to the hotel.

The wedding ceremony was performed in the restaurant Martha had set up. Not many families used the facility, saying they could not imagine eating outside their homes unless on a trip. So the room had stayed much as Martha had designed it with little wear and tear. It was a pretty place with its cabbage rose wallpaper and sideboard that featured a plate channel where Martha displayed the china she had painted so long ago. Cloth covered tables in a cheerful red-checked pattern further brightened the room. Martha made little of the ceremony, seemingly mortified at the procedure. She had sent Willy on some errand or other, so he was not in attendance. Only the maid, Maggie, and the bartender, McGinty, stood up for them. Afterwards, she served them tea and cake and tried to make a pleasant face on the matter, even though Adam knew she must be dying of shame inside. Neither ever mentioned their divorce or the paltry wedding ceremony again.

In the hope that a new home would soothe her hurt feelings, two weeks later he went to Putnam. He found a two-story frame house with side and front porches located on a corner lot with space for a garden in the rear between the back stoop and the carriage barn. There was a real basement not just a dugout as existed under the farm kitchen. After paying earnest money, Adam planned to use the proceeds from the sale of the hotel to pay the rest, as his cash was still limited. Martha with her new found congeniality did not object and signed the papers in her neat school girl hand. He signed with a gentlemanly flourish.

When Martha said she was sufficiently recovered from Ralphy's birth to undertake the move, Adam took several weeks away from work to prepare the house. There were some porch repairs, and every room had to be cleaned and painted. He did all the work himself over two long weekends. Martha had never seen the house, and Adam had a few misgivings about his choice, which he managed to brush from his mind as quickly as he brushed on the paint.

The movers drove their wagon to the farmhouse to load up a few pieces of furniture, including a dresser, several washstands and two spool beds. He left most of it for Tildy and Amos. The parlor, which he continued to think of as Lizzie's where her piano sat, he left as it was. Adam expected to stay over at the farm from time to time to check on Amos and Tildy. After some light conversation with his tenants to ascertain that all was going well with the farm, Adam and the movers headed to the hotel. Martha had packed all of her knickknacks and she instructed the movers "to take the furniture from that front bedroom."

Adam had been under the impression that the massive furniture would have been sold to the new owners. He planned to use the larger spool bed and the child's bed in the Putnam house. The other double bed was left in Lizzie's old bedroom should they ever decide to stay there overnight.

Ralphy's new basket, a fancy white affair, had been kept in the bridal suite of the hotel where Adam and Martha slept. None of the baby equipment provided for his brothers was used for Ralphy. Adam insisted that everything, even the coverlets, must be new. Some neighbors and friends and his sister, Emma, were already remarking about how possessed Adam appeared with his new son. "We never noticed him making over the other boys like he does Ralph," Emma said. "An appealing child, I'll admit, but really," she told Martha, "I think there are times when Adam seems half mad over him."

Adam ignored their comments while Martha smiled with obvious pleasure. Ralphy was the most appealing baby Adam had ever seen, although he barely remembered the others at this age. When the older boys were born, he was simply existing, intent on the hated farm work and his animosity toward Martha. If he did take time to notice the babies, he considered their needs woman's work and rarely picked one up. But now each weekend, on coming in off the road, it was to Ralphy's basket that Adam went first. "How's my big boy today?" he'd say, then waggle his long finger in the baby's face and Ralphy would smile. Adam strolled around the hotel or down the street with the child perched on his arm to make certain everyone he passed saw and admired his newest son. At four months Ralphy could return their smiles with a toothless grin of his own.

When the day of the move approached, Adam's worries grew about Martha's bedroom furniture being too ostentatious for the modest rooms in the new house. His mother's spool bed and a simple dresser were more suited to the moderate dimensions of the bedroom. Once the movers placed the huge bed in the largest upstairs room there was no space for the dresser. Martha showed her annoyance when it was put in the hallway. Adam recognized a bit of the old Martha surfacing, as she began her steady chatter about needing a larger house.

"A new house will come in time," Adam told her on one of their nights together in the parlor of the Putnam house. "Just let me get my business established. You'll see I am going to make something of myself. I know I am. And we will have the means for the house of your dreams."

Martha gave him a quizzical look. "I won't hold my breath."

"This time I'll keep my promise."

Thirty-two

Adam now turned his attention to business affairs traveling first to Columbus, a growing city and the state capital some fifty miles west of Zanesville. While traveling by train, he pondered the changes in his life since he had ridden over the same tracks on his way home from the terrible hostilities in the south. Soon after the war, the country was plunged into turbulence with the assassination of President Abraham Lincoln on April 14, 1865. Thus, the President never learned how the country had finally come together and was now prospering and peaceful in this last decade of the old century. Sitting aboard the train, his valises in the overhead bin, the verdant fields sliding by, Adam remembered that dejected, confused young man coming home from battle to face a future as a farmer. Now he was a businessman headed, he felt certain, for success. One valise carried clothes suitable for a gentleman bound to make calls on the leading tradespeople. The other carried small samples of pottery together with catalog sheets listing all manner of art ware the company produced.

For so many years he felt beaten, first by the war, then by the struggle of tending to the farm and livestock, and by the meager earnings his efforts brought forth. When he hitched the horses to the plow in early spring, it was always with the feeling that this was only the beginning of the long siege ahead before a crop would emerge and he could realize a few coins and bills. The next year would be the same as this one and a repeat of the last. Perhaps it was his time in the war when life was tenuous but always exciting that had left him so bored with life on the land where seasons dictated life's changes that rarely altered from one year to the next. There was more rain one year, less in succeeding years, followed by freezing cold or summer-like conditions in January, and the overbearing heat of summer. Adam's life in those years had achieved a deadening sameness with only the elements changing.

With a pleasant memory of the woman who had turned the tide for him, Adam made plans to call on the Lazarus Department Store in Columbus, reputed to be a growing emporium that catered to leading citizens with a dizzying array of clothing, household goods, jewelry, and furnishings. Perhaps I'll meet her brother-in-law, Adam thought, as he rehearsed how he would greet the esteemed merchant.

197

He found the store bearing the Lazarus name, but did not see the venerable Mr. Lazarus. Instead he was directed to the buyer of pottery, a knomelike man who had a sharp eye for design and detail. Mr. Goldman spoke with an accent brought from the old country, and after questions about delivery times, handling of complaints, and other matters associated with buying and selling wares in this modern age, he gave Adam a large order and a handshake. Once again he considered that Lazarus was turning out to be a lucky name.

Adam worked long hours and was home only on weekends with the result that his business was going better than expected. Times were changing. Many people were leaving the farms for jobs and homes in the cities. In the Victorian era women of means set the pace in home furnishings with ornate and colorful objects, which to Adam's orderly mind tended to clutter more than enhance. Ordinary women had a desire to emulate their betters and sought home décor, hairstyles, fashions, and other trappings the rich thought necessary to establish their importance. The changes were very good for Adam's business, and he traveled to more distant cities and villages until there was barely an Ohio town he had not visited. By 1892, he had gone north to Cleveland and south to Cincinnati, where he met considerable competition from the Rookwood Pottery. Founded ten years before and already well established in the better markets, Rookwood artists copied living flowers and images of Indians, birds, and even insects. Their art ware was noted for its sculptured beauty, the use of strong colors, and metallic accents.

To look the part of a man of means, Adam avoided the shabby appearance of some peddlers by paying special mind to his attire, made even more impressive by his lanky frame, mustache, and mane of snowy hair. When, as a distinguished man, he entered a store people noticed—women especially glanced his way—and buyers rarely refused his entreaties with the result that Pinewood's art ware soon found a place on shelves next to Rookwood's.

His frequent visits to these larger markets made him aware of new lines of toys, and he never went home of a Friday without a trinket for Ralphy. Some of his choices were too advanced for such a small tyke, and Martha frequently remarked upon the fact. Adam invariably countered with, "he'll soon grow into them." The shelf in the little boy's room became crowded with all manner of miniature wagons pulled by high stepping horses, a mechanical drummer boy, and even a horse-drawn fire engine that could be wound up, not to mention a menagerie of stuffed animals. Ralphy watched these purchases arrive with great wonder and every Friday ran toward the buggy bringing his father from the station. "What did you bring me this time, Papa? Let me see."

"You are giving that child entirely too many toys," Martha protested. "If you persist, you will make him a very selfish little boy. Why the other three together never had a quarter of what he has."

"I like bringing him presents, and these new stores are a wonder with all the merchandise to be bought today. Not just clothing and furnishings, but jewelry, toys, and baubles of every variety. You should see their finely crafted showcases, just like really expensive furniture. I can't believe how times have changed."

"Well that's all fine and good, but let's don't make a mollycoddle of our son by destroying his will to learn that he must work for life's rewards."

"Awe, let him enjoy what we can give him."

As for Martha's life at home while Adam was on the road, she managed to make new friends. She joined the Methodist Church in Zanesville and became a circle member. The other matrons in the neighborhood with children Ralphy's age were considerably younger than Martha, and one day she told Adam, "I just don't feel comfortable with women twenty years my junior. I think it's time we thought of moving. I have in mind the Terrace; I hear that is going to be the town's most prestigious location, and besides, it would be closer to the rail station. Can't we finally afford to build our own house?"

"Of course we can, my dear. I've been thinking on that myself. My business is doing well, clay is still being taken from the Pineville mine, and Amos is very good about paying one-fifth of what the farm produces. I'm doing so well that I've decided not to sell this house but to rent it out and buy the new property with the money built up in the clay account, that is if I can get a mortgage. It pains me to have to deal with the bank for a mortgage, but even with my many resources, I can't pay for the kind of house you have in mind. Pa and Ma would never approve of my going so deeply into debt, but to please you I'll do it anyway."

She kissed him lightly on the mouth, then smiled up at him, "Don't you think, since this is my house bought with my money, I should have some say about that?"

"Now Martha, let's not go back to those old days. You know as well as I do that what is yours is mine. You are my wife, remember?"

"Fortunately, I tend to agree with you regarding the house, even as I resent your feeling that what's mine is yours. However, I won't make an issue of the matter."

Adam found a property on the southern edge of Zanesville where other commodious homes were either being built or were already sitting heavily on half-acre plots. The homes constructed in Gothic and Victorian styles featured gabled roofs in the attic rooms. On the first floors of these venerable mansions were two parlors: the larger front room for entertaining and the other for family use.

"In our new neighborhood," Martha told Adam gleefully, "we will surely make friends among neighbors who will see that we are as affluent as they are, so I expect we will be entertaining on a regular basis, just like home in Marietta. How I have longed for those days."

Adam wasn't so sure how well they would be accepted. The men who owned these grand houses were lawyers, doctors, bankers, and men who owned their own businesses. When word got out that he was merely a crockery peddler, although some was fine art ware, he felt certain Martha would be in for a letdown. Adam had located the property and found an architect, but it was Martha who took charge during Adam's absences.

"I have given the new house considerable thought, and my experience with that hotel has provided ideas about efficiency that you, having never cooked more than a pot of oatmeal, can't possibly imagine."

He wondered if she thought he existed on only pots of oatmeal during their estrangement.

"You picked out the lot, and I said nothing. You set up the basic design of the house, and I went along, but I intend to plan its interior."

The planning took six months, and when Ralphy celebrated his third birthday, the family took the buggy to the property for a picnic under the towering trees left after the ground was made ready for the foundation. Due to be poured the following week, the foundation would support a red brick house of some five-thousand square feet. A maid's room would be on the third floor along with one for the cook, should they ever hire one, and both reached by a narrow back stairwell leading to the kitchen. Plans called for five bedrooms, front and back parlors, a library where Adam could keep a desk and bookshelves, as well as a music room in which Martha could have her piano. "Not that old upright of your mothers," she made clear, "but a real piano—a baby grand."

Stunned that she thought so little of his mother's piano, which had stood almost as a shrine in the front parlor at the farm during all his growing up years, Adam merely grumbled and said, "I'll think about it."

The pouty look on Martha's face when she abruptly turned away led him to quickly reconsider. "Buy the best one you can find." Still amazed at having Martha back, he could deny her nothing. Besides, he was feeling generous. Of late much of his new business came from reorders sent to him by mail, and his bank account was growing. Nevertheless, his expenses made him greedy for more. He decided to add offerings from other potteries in Ohio, West Virginia, and western Pennsylvania. There were so many that he could afford to be choosy about which lines to offer. No longer would he be dependent on only those items offered by Pineville. "Might as well make a stop in each town more productive," one salesman told him as they sat together one evening discussing their lines in a Cleveland hotel lobby after a gratifyingly sumptuous dinner

He soon added a less expensive line from the Joe McCoy Pottery that proved popular. Encouraged, he added another line from a larger pottery, Home Laughlin, out of West Virginia, pleasing to younger married women who could buy an initial set—usually for four—and add to it as their families grew. Some had as many as a dozen of each dinner plate, cup and saucer, along with platters and tureens, creamers, sugar bowls, coffee and teapots.

By the time the family moved into the new house, Adam, who had not paid much attention to Martha's chattering about what she had bought, was overwhelmed. She had indulged in a spending spree that replaced much of their old parlor furniture. Heavy draperies graced the windows throughout the downstairs rooms. Each boy had his own bedroom, while Martha and Adam shared a large suite in the front. Off this master bedroom was a small washroom equipped with a washstand and the latest most decorative pitcher and basin—and the most expensive—from the Pineville Pottery. Martha was thrilled with the new water closet and appreciated not having to use a potty or a privy. "I never lived long enough in Father's house, after he installed one, to get used to it."

"All the better hotels have these up-to-date contraptions, so I know they work," Adam said, insisting on the latest bathroom conveniences.

It was in the kitchen that Martha's ideas flourished. She insisted on a sink with a drain and a pump that brought cold water into a lone spigot. Though it was still the wood burning variety, the new stove featured a tank in the back for keeping water hot. There was an icebox kept in a small room near the backdoor, which doubled as a pantry. The room was unheated which it was thought would keep the twice-weekly delivery of ice from melting as quickly as it might if the icebox was in the kitchen. A drain pan underneath caught the melting run-off.

Martha professed to be uneasy at the thought of central heating, so fireplaces were installed in the bedrooms and the downstairs rooms with the exception of the kitchen. The attic rooms remained dependent on whatever heat made it up the steps to the top floor.

In the basement were laundry facilities with a small wood burning stove for boiling white clothes. Two laundry tubs were set next to each other for washing and rinsing. In good weather wet clothes were carried up the outdoor cellar steps to dry on the line. In bad weather they were hung on clothesline to dry by heat from the furnace.

The family, consisting of Will, when he was home on vacation from college, the toddler, Ralphy, Martha, and Adam moved in on a fair spring day and were immediately overwhelmed with the size and pomposity of their new possession. Soon after settling in, a letter arrived from Ben telling them he would be visiting soon.

July 10, 1894

My Dear Mother and Papa,

Although I like my new place near the great Sequoia National Park, which I visited with some friends a few weeks ago, I now need to see my little brother. I intended to go back to Ohio last year, but felt it best to wait until you were in the new house. I will arrive in about two weeks, so make sure my bed is made up. I'll probably stay a month. I want to return here to be in on the growth that's surely coming from the oil business. While Bakersfield is very flat and dry, you should see the number of new rigs going up almost daily. My employer has agreed to let me take off six weeks, at no pay, of course. But I do look forward to seeing all of you again, so it will be worth it.

With warmest regards,

Ben

P.S. I wish you could see the giant trees in the park. Two men cannot reach all the way round their trunks. It's nice to know they can't be chopped down as the place has been made into a national park.

Martha was thrilled to have her family together again and secretly hoped Ben could be persuaded to return to Ohio permanently. She also encouraged him to ask Frank to come home too. Although the new house gave Adam a feeling of supreme accomplishment, he was somewhat perplexed by its size and was pleased that his eldest son's presence would make it seem more utilized. With only Ralphy there, or Will, when he arrived on his vacations from college, the house felt like more of an edifice to impress than to enjoy.

Constant acquisitions threatened to crush Adam with expenses, but he still wished to satisfy Martha's incessant urges to buy and thus said nothing. She was quite eager to have his embraces and seemed to understand that to deny him each weekend might undermine his desire to satisfy her every material want, so she gave herself to him freely. He rarely let himself think of it in that way, even as he suspected that each time she wanted set of drapes, andirons, a new chair or settee, she reinforced her request with lavish loving. She was becoming heavier, more matronly, as befit a woman of means and was more attractive to him as he too began to expand in the waistline. He applauded each gain in her weight, which she further enhanced by the shapely fashions of the day. Bustles were out at last, although Martha had never favored them. "They look out of place in the simple homes we live in," she once told Adam. Now that they were in a home among the richer folks of the town, she followed the current fashion dictates with their big puffed sleeves, tight waistlines and curving skirts. Her wardrobe began to burgeon with day dresses, afternoon tea gowns, and at home dresses.

Will was graduated from high school in 1892 and had left home in September for Ohio State University at Columbus. Ralphy, now approaching four, continued to be the frosting on Adam's cake. He was convinced the boy was special, smarter than other boys his age, more appealing, livelier. Adam began thinking of the child's future. Perhaps he could afford to send him to school in the east: Princeton or Harvard. There seemed to be no end to the dreams Adam had for his son; he would have to begin a savings account toward supplying funds that would bring his dreams to fruition. Although every cent he made from his multiple sources of income went to sustain the family lifestyle, he was more content than he had ever been. Memories of the war had largely receded leaving him finally at peace. And somehow he would begin supplying the means to give Ralphy a splendid life.

Thirty-three

To get ready for Ben's arrival, Martha worked for days preparing his favorite foods. She went to the greengrocers and ordered pineapple to make chutney, baked a chocolate sauerkraut cake, insisted that the kraut be made with cabbages from the farm. On her annual fall trip to collect root vegetables, which they then kept through the winter in the cellar of the Zanesville house, she had salted and soaked the cut up cabbages in water, so they could begin working. When Adam pointed out that she could now buy canned sauerkraut, she told him that would not be good enough for Ben.

Reasoning that he needed to talk to Amos anyway, Adam drove the buggy to the farm, not only to collect a crock of the fermenting cabbages, but also to check on the progress of the spring planting. He still kept the front parlor and Lizzie's old room in the rear for his own use. Amos needed looking after from time to time, and Adam liked to get away to enjoy the freshness and grand expanses of his fields and forest and take in the earthy fragrances that only the country meadows provided. The fresh air cleared his mind, taken up now with pottery orders, household demands, and the complications that arise from handling innumerable details regarding the mine, rental house, and the growing expenses of his new home.

Each time he visited, Adam walked toward the old spring past where the deep purple heads of elderberries pointed him toward baby Eddie's grave. After clearing away brush and weeds threatening to blot out the small tombstone, he sat a spell on a nearby rock and invariable wondered who will clear this when I'm gone. Even in his darkest days with Old Monongahela as his companion, he kept the grave clear of brush and worried that someday nobody would care or even remember the baby boy taken before life gave him a chance. Like Eddie, the violets he had planted so many years ago had not survived.

Not having to work it anymore, Adam appreciated the farm's slower pace, away from clanging trains and noisy wagons with their horses that choked and befouled city streets. His infrequent trips to the country sharpened his energies. I could never sell this place. Ma's spirit would not allow it, he thought. Sometimes he felt her presence when sitting of an evening in the parlor still furnished with her piano brought so long ago from Frederick. Poor Ma. This place had dashed her dreams, but in the end, even in death, she remained part of it. Memories of her came to him often, especially when roaming around the farm or sitting in his rocker set close by her piano and imagining he could hear her playing the old tunes like *Barbara Allen*. People around here said Lizzie gave them an interest in music, "elsewise we wouldn't have nothin' special in our lives," old Auntie Rachel used to say. And then she'd add, "your Ma taught me readin' and writin' too. Smart lady! I was just a girl, mebbe fifteen, when she found me. I already had one baby." Adam remembered the tears that glistened in the old lady's eyes whenever she spoke of Lizzie.

While Bridget, the new maid, normally cooked for the family, Martha took over cooking for her son. And on the Sunday after Ben's arrival, she prepared roasted pork stuffed with dried apples. "I just know you haven't been eating right," she told him. "Just look at you. You're much too skinny." And she proceeded to stuff him with sugar cakes and gingerbread, and a deep-dish pie made with chicken and country ham, along with fresh baked rolls and breads.

At first Ralphy seemed put off by the new presence in his life, but Ben was soon trundling his little brother around like a proud father. Indeed, many people thought he was, thereby thrusting Adam into a grandfatherly role whenever the three appeared together. Ben cut a fine figure about town. He arrived in a new suit with a straight-cut jacket, his vest draped with a gold fob that led to his great grandfather, Henry's, gold watch tucked into its pocket. A silk cravat was clipped in place by a square golden stickpin. His boots were shined, and he was clean-shaven with his hair parted slightly off center. Martha wondered how he became so sophisticated, given that he had been living in a dusty, oil-driven town of no importance to her way of thinking. When she remarked on this, Ben said, "Bakersfield is growing; there are stores, a photographer's studio, and a grand hotel. Not like yours. This one must have twenty rooms. The building is a block long with a porch going clean across the front on both the first and second stories. And there are even a few girls about."

Martha frowned.

Ben took no notice of his mother's reaction and hastened to add, "Now take the Jewett sisters, they came to Bakersfield from San Francisco with their father. They live like girls of taste. When I take out one of them, it's Elsa I fancy, I have to look the part of a San Francisco sport. Otherwise, these fine ladies would have nothing to do with me. I know she likes me. Why the sisters even made red checked curtains for the house I share with two other boys. They said it looked like nobody cared about us. After they hung the curtains, the boys and I cleaned the place, and we try to keep it up."

"They come to your house?"

"Well not so anybody can notice." Ben raced on, his handsome face growing more animated. "I even bought a rocker to put on the front porch, and one of my friends and I got us a buggy and a horse we named Dick. Girls don't like it if you don't have a buggy. But none of that seems to make much difference to old man Jewett; he owns the rigs, but he doesn't do much of the dirty work."

"Who's he?" Martha asked, now somewhat suspicious of the life her eldest son had chosen.

"Their father. He's a rough old tyrant with lots of money and a hankering to get even richer. He'll probably make it too. The place isn't much to look at. It's desert mostly with barely a thing growing, but it sprouts oil well rigs like trees amidst the dirt. And that's going to make him and me rich someday."

Martha began to think she was losing her son and remarked on the fact to Adam. "I think Ben fancies this girl, Elsa."

"Only natural," Adam said. "You can't expect him to stick around here, if he's got a girl out there."

"But there are plenty of nice girls here. Why in my church I see that daughter of the Morrison's. She's a pleasant sort and rather pretty when she takes off her spectacles. And then there's Betsy Aiken and those girls up the street, the daughters of Dr. McAuliffe. If Ben married one of them, he wouldn't be so lost to us."

"Let the boy find his own way," Adam counseled.

After a few days in Zanesville, Ben announced, "Since I don't know any of the boys around town, I would like to borrow the buggy, that is if you don't mind. I want to drive out to Four Corners to meet up with some of my old friends. I'm sure Aunt Emma would take me in for a night or two."

"Of course, you can have the buggy," Adam said. "Take it and have a good time."

"I thought you would be staying around with us," Martha remarked. "After all, you just got here, and we haven't seen you in more than three years."

"Don't worry. I'll be back in a few days." He kissed his mother lightly on the cheek.

"Ralphy seems so fond of you." Martha went on. "He'll be disappointed if you leave so soon."

"Ma, I've been meaning to talk to you about him. That little fellow doesn't have a soul to play with around here. Except for Bridget, who must be all of seventeen, there are no youngsters. Since she's the maid you can hardly count her, but I notice she does spend time with him."

"She comes from a huge family. They're Irish, so they never know when to stop having children. She's used to babies, but she doesn't know anything about the finer ways of living. I've had a terrible time trying to teach her. And she's positively awful at cooking. Like the farm people, she throws everything into a pot and boils it until it's pure mush. You should see what she tried to serve us for breakfast when she first came. It was nothing more than white bread stewed up in milk. Pure slop. I told her to throw it out. She said it was something called bruiss and in Ireland they eat it all the time."

"Poor girl, she probably thought she was doing a good thing."

"She did. The bread was left over. But I told her we're not that poor. Then she began taking the stale bread she doesn't use for Brown Betty, stuffing, or breading home to her family."

Ben left the next morning. As Martha and Adam waved him off, she remembered to tell him that Will would be home the next weekend for the summer, "so you'd better get back by then."

"That I will, Ma." He maneuvered the buggy down the curving driveway onto Orchard Avenue, so named because it had once been an orchard. There were several peach and apple trees left, but most had been taken out to make room for the new homes and streets.

Martha spent a lonely week without Adam and Ben. With no buggy to get her to town, she decided to ride old Daisy. There was a small fenced pasture beside the carriage shed where the horse was stabled, and since Daisy was none too spirited these days, she seemed not to mind the lack of a larger pasture. Even so the horse needed exercising from time to time. Martha had not ridden recently and realized the horse was gaining weight. Having decided the saddle she often straddled in the country was not suitable for a lady of her stature to ride into town, she selected her sidesaddle; then dug out her old riding frock from an attic trunk. It looked a bit shabby, and when she tried it on, the jacket was too tight. Deciding right then and there to order another, she made plans to stop by the dressmaker that very day.

So it was that she was fashionably attired when two weeks later Adam arrived home. Ben and Will drove the buggy to the train station to collect him, and they all reached the house just as Daisy, with Martha on the sidesaddle, trotted up

Orchard Avenue. She had been riding in the country through pastures and woods. Martha's face glowed and the horse was panting. Nevertheless, she greeted Adam by telling him how slow Daisy had become. "I think we should put her out to pasture somewhere and get another horse."

"In time, Mother, in time." He stood looking up at her. "You're looking well, the new riding dress becomes you," he said. But to Adam's mind the family's expenses had reached alarming proportions, and here she was in a new habit, when she had an old one she could wear if she let out a few seams. He said, "there will not be another horse, at least not now."

Martha was not listening. She had dismounted and was ushering her sons into the house while Adam lingered behind to take Daisy to the stable. "A slow horse is preferable for someone intent on riding sidesaddle," he muttered.

On Monday morning, Will decided to go to Four Corners with Ben, so the boys stay at the Orchard Avenue house was brief.

"What is it with grown children," Martha complained, "that they barely greet you and then can't wait to get away? You'd think after being gone so long Ben would sit of an evening with us, not to mention that Will has been gone three months at college."

"Now Mother, young people in this modern age have more exciting things to do than we ever did, and sitting with us does not qualify as exciting."

But Martha did not let up. When the boys arrived home, she greeted them with "I declare I don't know why you boys are so anxious to get away. Four Corners is behind all of us now. Why don't you stay around here and make some higher type friends?"

"For someone who hassled pots and pans, cleaned hotel rooms, and washed a ton of linen every week, you've sure gotten high and mighty."

"Don't talk to your Mother like that, Will." Adam glared at his son.

"We had maids. I didn't do it all." Martha snapped.

"You did a good part of it. Didn't she, Ben?"

Ben laughed, but said nothing. He knew he was his mother's favorite; no need to diminish his standing.

"I no longer care to be reminded of those days and don't you dare mention I was a hotel keeper among our new friends, who are coming to tea Sunday. And I expect you both to be here and dressed in your best."

"I guess we're not supposed to mention that you and Papa were separated. Or was it divorced?"

"Stop that!" Martha's blue eyes turned to slate. "Since you have gone off to college, Will, you have become quite sassy, and two years at Ohio State does not a gentleman make, or you would not be speaking to your mother so disrespectfully."

With Adam's blessing and against Martha's wishes, five days later, the boys took the buggy and once again headed toward Four Corners. They said little upon their return about what transpired there, but as promised they were properly attired and polite at the afternoon tea their mother had been planning for the past month. She had baked small apple tarts and charlottes, a mixture of walnuts and dates dipped in granulated sugar before baking. There were soft molasses cakes, and pound cake, and all of it more than the guests, could possibly consume even as the women with their overstuffed bodies seemed eager to stuff them more. Small cakes were placed decoratively on Martha's hand painted china plates. A new buffet held a silver tea service atop a candle flame. Cups and saucers from their wedding gift, which had been packed away during most of the twenty-six years of the Springer marriage, were set out on the massive table. A hand painted pink bowl filled with fruits and nuts further added to the impressive décor. The guests seemed properly dazzled as they moved around the table with its glistening white damask cloth embroidered in white with a scrolling *S* on each corner. "You have such lovely taste," Mrs. Morrison said grandly, while Martha beamed.

Adam concluded that Martha's efforts had made their mark, and henceforth she would be more appreciated by her neighbors who might invite her into their social circle. Or might not. One never knew about these people. Martha was at her best. She was attired in a soft blue gown with paler blue ruffling about the low cut bodice. Bead embroidery sparkled on its front further embellishing her bosom. He had not seen the dress before, and the sight of her in yet another new costume made him determined to speak with her about her spending. Then he thought about another night of bliss with his attractive wife and put off the speech.

The following day he left for Chillicothe where he hoped to sell his lower priced dinnerware. While he traveled toward the town, he thought of Ben's remarks about Ralphy. Around his elders most of the time, the boy did seem lonesome. Perhaps another toy would help, but this time Adam ignored the trinkets and treasures in the stores, having already decided his son was ready for a wagon, a fine wooden one.

Trouble loomed before Adam could carry out his plan, for upon returning to the Orchard Avenue house several days later, he found a very agitated Ben. Thrusting a letter toward his father, Ben raised his voice, "It's from Mr. Jewett?"

"Who?"

"My employer. And I need your advice as to how to answer it."

"Calm down and come into the library." Adam sat down at his grand oak desk and gestured to Adam to sit opposite in the leather chair.

"Pa, he doesn't want me to return."

"Shush now while I read this." Adam took his pince-nez eyeglasses from his coat pocket and perused the letter while Ben chattered on.

"Oh, I know why he's doing this, but I'm wondering do I have any rights? He told me I could be gone for six weeks, that he could get along without me, and now I find I've been replaced."

"Well you said you know why. Was your work not satisfactory?" Adam took a draw on his Marsh Wheeling stogie. Martha did not allow him to smoke in the rest of the house, so after dinner he liked to retire to the library to indulge in a habit he found most relaxing. He blew out the smoke and through its haze waited for his eldest son to answer.

"I believe my work was exemplary. Once I learned the procedures, Mr. Jewett seemed appreciative and even promoted me. I know in his eyes, I was little more than a roustabout, but I had a crew of three men under me at the end. The real reason he doesn't want me back is Elsa, his daughter. He doesn't consider me suitable for her. I always sensed it, but I thought I could overcome his objection.

"This letter says he has sent her and her sister back to San Francisco, so even if you went back she wouldn't be there. I suppose you could go on to San Francisco, but what would you do for employment?"

"I don't know, Pa. The old man objected to my taking her buggy riding with no chaperone. But out there in that raw country it hardly seemed to matter. It's nothing but desert, not even a tree to hide behind if I wanted to take advantage of her, which I did, but didn't. So there was no sparking in that buggy," he stole a look at the still half-empty floor-to-ceiling bookcases and added, "course, I can't say the same for the times she sneaked into my cabin."

He looked so downhearted Adam did not have the heart to berate him. "There are plenty of other girls about. I'm sure you will find somebody. It took me a bit of time to find your mother."

"I suppose, but now I've got to get me a job. I spent most of my money coming back here. I don't quite have enough for a trip west, and I really would like to go back to California. I think I could have a good future there. As you know, Frank is working for a rancher and writes that he's doing well. I've not seen the spread, but he says it's thousands of acres. He loves California, says it's the purest state in the whole United States with a thrashing ocean and mountains all around. Bakersfield is mostly desert, not much water about, but plenty of oil. I'm certain of that. Maybe I could write to him, and he could help me find a ranching job, although I really think oil is the future. In the meantime, I guess I'll have to stick around here for a spell. Maybe find a job in town. The haberdasher was looking for someone to clerk the last time I stopped to buy a hat. But really, Pa, do you think I have any rights where Mr. Jewett is concerned?"

"No, son, I don't. You are just a common employee, so put the prospect of going back out of your mind for now." Adam knew Ben accepted his advice with a heavy heart. "Your mother will be pleased to have you around awhile, and if you save your money, perhaps you can return to California." He made no mention of Ben's paying either rent or board, although he would have welcomed both. His expenses continued to mount. Yet the various members of the household, including Adam himself, seemed to go on as if the finances were unlimited. Clearly, something had to give. But as he had done a dozen times before, Adam decided to think about it later.

211

Thirty-four

Summer gave way to fall. Will returned to college, and Ben went off daily to his job as a clerk in a Zanesville men's clothing store. He still made frequent trips to Four Corners "to be with my old friends," he told his mother, but it soon became apparent there was something, or someone, luring him there. While at the farm Ben used the rooms his father occupied. He left Zanesville every Sunday morning and returned Monday evenings on a day he was not required to be at the haberdashery. Because he never said much about his Aunt Emma, Martha suspected he was no longer staying in town. She mentioned this to Adam. "I thought he hated the farm."

"I gather that not too many of his old friends—married and family men now—have much time to carouse with a young dandy, lately from California. So he stays at the farm. It's nice out there: quiet, tree shaded, peaceful."

"Doesn't seem to me that's of much interest to a young man looking for excitement."

A month later, Ben returned with a note from Amos.

Dear Mr. Springer,
On account we's moving to our own place, we will leave this here farm come Satiday next. The crops is all in, corn's sold off, so we's taken our share and goin'.
Much obliged.
Amos

In late October when Ben announced his betrothal to one of the neighbor girls, Adam's heart sank. "I suspect he's been trapped," he told Martha whose face turned ashen when he told her the news. "Those country girls are fiendish. I know, I avoided their wiles for years. Mothers breed it into them with their breast milk *get a man, get a man,* and they set their wily female traps at fourteen."

Martha sat down heavily on one of the straight-backed chairs and took a linen hanky from her sleeve. Sniffling, she dabbed her eyes. "I thought by getting him away from there and exposing him to finer things he would aspire to more. Oh,

I know it was just an old hotel in a dinky town, but he did get a better education, good enough to get him to Ohio Northern for a year. Whatever is he thinking? Mark my words that girl will never move off that place, and if we sell it, she'll simply find another close to her Ma. Those country people are settled in like moles in their hideaways, and I'll wager when the next millenium hits—and I'm not talking about 1900, but 2000—their descendents will still be trying to scratch out a living on that indifferent land. I thought he was worldly."

Adam turned away wondering, but he did not pose the question aloud: *is this girl, whoever she is, with child?*

Later that day after Ben identified the girl as one of the Longacre's, Adam called his son into the library. "Are you certain you want to do this? I know the family. The Longacres are good people. I vaguely remember they have four children, youngsters when we lived in the country. How old is this girl?"

"Her name is Alma, Pa. And she's just twenty."

"Getting on."

"I love her, so it's all right."

"What about your big plans for going west?"

"I'll take her with me, but for the time being, I have another idea. How would you like it if we move into the farmhouse? It's vacant now and I think I can handle it. I spent most of my growing up years helping you. And Alma, having been reared on a neighboring farm, will have no trouble with the household chores, the chickens, milking, and such. Why she can wring a chicken's neck faster than you can say 'dinner's ready.' She's already told me she would love to live in that house. Of course, it would just be for a short spell. Then you should either sell the place or find a new tenant. It needs a lot of fixing up, and Alma and I can take care of that for the short time we'll be living there, just until I get on my feet. I know there is no point in trying to bring her here. Ma would never hear of it, and Alma would be uncomfortable among these citified folks. Then when the place is painted and papered, you can probably get a better price. After the first crop, I'll make plans with Frank to head west or maybe even go back to Bakersfield. Jewett might take me on again once he sees I'm wed."

"Son, I have to say it straight out. You're going to get ambushed like a bear in a trap. To be sure, there was a time when I wanted nothing more than for you to take the place over, but I see now what a dead end it is for any man of ambition. The soil is not the best, the pastures and fields are hilly, so much so that a good deal of it is not even tillable. You can barely get enough hay out of that north meadow to feed the animals over a harsh winter. I know I tried. Had to sell off six head of cattle to keep them from starving during the winter of '86. Looking back, I think my family made a mistake settling there. They could have gone north at the time to the flatlands of Ohio, but Ma said the Indians were still about, so they decided southeastern Ohio was safer. I sometimes wish they had endured the Indians, now that I have seen the lush lands to the north, flat as tabletops they are. But farming was never really for me anyway."

"That why you took to strong drink?"

Adam reared back in the great leather chair avoiding his son's steady gaze. "I didn't know you knew."

"It was common knowledge, though, like most drunks you thought you were doing a pretty good job of hiding it."

"In truth I hated the place, but that's no excuse, and I was lonely, pining for your mother and you boys, so Old Monongahela became my friend." He paused, studied his son. "And later my enemy. I guess I realized then that I would have to quit the farm. Only when I got out did I recognize how a man is finally drained by the sameness from one year to the next with nothing changing, the work unending and harsh. You fight the elements, the insects, poor soil, an unhappy wife, dying children, and there's never enough money. And all this coupled with memories of war that continued to plague me made it a mighty unhappy existence. You have already seen much of this glorious country. Surely you also see its opportunities."

"I do and I will get there—eventually."

Adam went on. "I had only been to the southern lands in wartime, and what I saw was sickening, so staying among those peaceful hills at the farm didn't seem so bad after a time. I suppose they helped me forget the dreadful desolation, death, and injuries I saw when I was away." He took a long draw on his stogie. "Now I guess enough time has passed for all of us old veterans—it's nearly thirty years—to put the war behind us. I still have horrible dreams from time to time, but I don't like to mention them. Upsets your mother. She used to say I was thrashing around in bed of a night just to keep her from sleeping. I guess I've finally learned to manage them. Making a change and earning a measure of success with my new endeavors helped to banish the worst of those memories." He dropped an ash from his stogie onto the tray and glanced again at his son. "But that has nothing to do with what we speak of here. Just be certain, Ben, that this marriage is what you want."

"She's a lovely girl, Papa. Not sophisticated or educated like Elsa, mind you, but probably she will be easier to manage. I see it here in Zanesville. Girls from moneyed families are very headstrong."

"Like your mother."

"Like Ma." Ben shot Adam a steady stare.

Adam looked away again and wondered how much the boys had taken in during those years at the farm when he and Martha were simply enduring each other in razor-edged compromise.

The wedding took place on a Sunday in late November 1893 in the parlor at the bride's home. Adam and Martha were heartsick, but maintained their most pleasant demeanors as they saw their son and Alma stand before the preacher. He's dashing his dreams, Adam thought, when he heard Ben repeat the required *I do*. True, Alma was an attractive girl and somewhat accomplished. Her mother, a hefty woman, who reminded Adam of an oversized dumpling, mentioned Alma's kitchen skills. "She's an excellent baker, sews a steady stitch," she told Martha. "And she finished all her grades in school right through eight." Her family seemed thrilled at such a catch as Ben. Tall and handsome, surely he would make a wonderful husband for their daughter, "who has always been a dutiful child," Mrs. Longacre hastened to make clear.

Martha told Adam she would have been happy with a marriage if the bride had been from Zanesville, but to go back to that farm country to find a bride was almost more than she could stand. Adam was glad to see that in spite of her displeasure she soldiered on through the ceremony and the wedding supper. "A passable meal, but nothing fancy," she later remarked to Adam. Aunt Mary Jane, frail now with the passage of years, and Emma and her husband joined the groom's parents as guests. There were numerous relatives on the bride's side including her two younger sisters and a brother, who kept questioning Adam every chance he got to tell him about selling pottery. "Might like to do that myself. Would get me outta here," the boy whose name was Howard said. And every chance he got to sidle up to Adam, he had another question about the pottery business. Adam answered patiently for he saw himself in the boy, a lad eager to get away to bigger and better things.

The house was crowded. All the chairs had been removed from the front parlor, where the ceremony took place so the standing guests could witness the proceedings. After the nuptials, the men moved the chairs back into the room to allow the guests to sit and chat while partaking of the wedding repast.

Alma's mother and Martha had met at a quilting party several years before. Not impressed then, Martha was not impressed now. "Simply a local farmer's wife, and that is all I expect of that daughter of hers," she lamented to Adam, as the two got ready for a night's sleep in their old bedchamber.

Martha had maintained a gracious smile while the happy bride and groom ascended the interior staircase to the bridal suite—in reality the bride's bedroom. Emma and Reuben left with Aunt Mary Jane, when the old lady said she was tired. Shortly thereafter Martha and Adam exchanged pleasantries with the rest of the guests and, as hastily as was polite, left in their buggy.

The farmhouse was shabby. Wallpaper had loosened from the walls, and the furniture was scuffed. By the time Tildy and Amos left, they had four children and another expected, so the house showed wear and tear as well as neglect. Martha said, "I am only spending one night in this place, so don't ask me to stay another day. We'll see the children tomorrow and then be on our way home."

"We'll stay two nights," Adam said. "We don't need to seem standoffish simply because we don't agree with what has taken place here. We should spend some time with the children going over needs for the house and farm. I wonder what Ben and Alma will do with the place. It needs a thorough overhaul."

Martha shrugged and said nothing.

He supposed he would be asked for money.

Ralphy had charmed the wedding guests with his guileful ways and continual chatter. "He has the most appealing little face, so full of wonder," a guest remarked to a beaming Adam.

At the farmhouse they had to keep a watchful eye on their small son. There were so many perils for an unsuspecting four-year-old. He was fascinated with the well, the cistern, and the barn. He wanted to crawl up into the hayloft, but lest he fall, his father grabbed him as he scrambled upward from the bottom rail of the ladder. Adam recalled the boisterous shouts of his older sons during the many times they frolicked in that hayloft, but could not remember telling them to cease their fun, nor did he remember having any fear for them.

The day after the wedding, Ben and Alma arrived to take up life in their own house—albeit Adam's house. He had no intention of turning it over to his son lest it become one more impediment to Ben's leaving the area. The prospect of the life Ben had settled for now seemed a dreary one. Was a night of frolic so much on Ben's mind that he had thrown away a lifetime of dreams? Was he so depressed about losing Elsa and his job that he simply settled? He could farm elsewhere.

Thirty-five

Adam put Ben out of his mind to concentrate on his youngest son. Ben's words about the lack of children for Ralphy to play with worried Adam, so he began walking the avenues with the little boy hoping to locate other children who might make suitable playmates. He enjoyed the walks. Ralphy was outgoing and greeted strangers and neighbors as they passed by. "Hello, man, hello, lady," he'd say. Most passersby responded with smiles and welcoming words as they stopped and bent over the charming little fellow. In the evening Adam read stories to his son, and Ralphy, his finger moving confidently over the sentences, was soon mouthing the words *dog, cat, and cow.*

Martha said, "He simply sees drawings of those animals and matches the words. I don't think he's actually reading."

But Adam was convinced his son was very intelligent and told Martha, "we must see that he studies the law; I'm convinced this child has special abilities."

"What if Ralphy doesn't want to study the law?"

"Then he can study something that will make him a professional man, a person to be looked up to in the community, not like me, a simple peddler. People dismiss salesmen as nobodies; I suppose that's why we haven't been asked to join that new club in town."

"I'd say you've done mighty well as a peddler." Martha looked up from her tatting and smiled.

"Only because I've been willing to handle several lines at once. And I have products people not only need, but want; some customers think they can't live without frivolous vases, pitchers, and pots that don't serve much purpose. I'm learning that decorating one's house is very important, in some cases, over decorating."

"Do you think ours is over decorated?"

Adam hesitated. Ever since their reconciliation he had tried not to rile her in any way, but the matter must be discussed. "As a matter of fact, I do. All these paintings—that Orientalist scene with those Arabs or whatever they are in their flowing gilded robes—seem totally out of place in an Ohio parlor. And that ornate porcelain powder box painted with the three graces in all those romantic poses

217

was made in Vienna. That's in Austria, for God's sakes. I don't understand why you bought it when you could have had a more suitable design made by an Ohio pottery. I carry two kinds of powder boxes."

"Without the three graces, I'll wager."

"And the furniture. We have Ohio cabinetmakers. Good ones! Did you have to order from some out-of-state company? I think it was Michigan. Didn't I see a mention of a Grand Rapids Chair Company on those labels? Plenty of chairs can be had right here in Ohio, and you don't have to pay all those shipping charges."

"I didn't just get chairs from them. They also make upholstered and case pieces, and I didn't order direct, but from a local store, so why are you so huffy about it. You certainly didn't expect me to furnish this lovely house with that old furniture of your mother's. Really Adam . . ."

"Since you bring it up, there is something I've been meaning to mention ever since we moved into this house. We have to stop this incessant spending. I may be making a decent income, but I can barely cover our expenses, and some months I don't cover them at all. The clay mine is not producing like it did; wouldn't surprise me if the pottery soon closes it down. The farm will give us nothing as long as Ben lives there, so I must either double my efforts, and that would mean being on the road even more, perhaps two or more weeks at a time—or we must cut down."

Martha's face turned to a pout. "Just when I was going to make a very special request."

"For what?"

"A horse to replace Daisy."

"Not now!"

"You didn't hesitate to buy Ralphy that wagon."

"You can hardly equate a child's wagon to the cost of a horse."

"If you add everything else you've given that boy, it probably adds up to the same." Martha got up from her chair, gathered her tatting, and headed to the doorway, but stopped before she went through it. "After all I've done, running that dratted hotel, you deny me the greatest pleasure I have in life. A ride on old Daisy these days is a very sedate affair. I'd like a more spirited animal. And let me remind you that the money we got from the hotel went into the Putnam house, which continues to bring us income, and I do believe some of it was left over for this place—if memory serves." She slammed the door leaving Adam staring once more into the mostly empty bookshelves that lined his library office.

The pleasure Ralphy got from the wagon soothed Adam's anger at his wife. The child filled it with stuffed animals, trucks, trains, lead soldiers, and building blocks. He dragged the wagon across the lawn to the willow tree, where he built houses and barns and marched his soldiers up and down over ground made bare by the lack of sunshine penetrating the willow's drooping branches. Sometimes Adam showed him how to set up his regiments and battalions in proper order, and when he saw that a section was missing, he'd buy more soldiers. While Ralphy listened, his round face beaming, Adam explained, "a battalion is made up of three or more companies. In the Great War, I was in Company E." Adam grouped a dozen soldiers together and set them apart from the next group. He repeated this until he had four groups. "Of course, there were more men in each company, and in a real army as many as eleven companies in all. We don't have enough soldiers to show it exactly, but these few will do."

"Will you bring me some more, Papa, so we can make us a whole big army with both rebels and Yankees?"

"Maybe, but for right now let's group these four companies into a battalion. Then we'll make a second battalion, and put together they will make a regiment."

"What was your regiment's name, Papa? You told me once, but I forgot."

"The Ohio Seventy-Eighth." As if he was about to salute, Adam sat up straight. "And son, a finer regiment never existed."

"We're gonna' need more soldiers to really fight a war," Ralphy said. "And I don't have any wearing gray. I need me some rebels. All I have is Yankees."

"On my next trip, I'll see if I can find some. Up here in the north it's easier to come by Yankees, but I'll look around when I'm on the road again."

After a time their preoccupation with the Civil War armies took the project indoors, where Adam claimed the attic room set aside for the never-hired cook. He made saw horses and put boards on top to construct a large table painted green and brown. He built hills and valleys out of clay and soon recreated a few miniature battlegrounds where the Seventy-Eighth had fought: Missionary Ridge, Vicksburg, Shiloh. The number of toy soldiers wearing blue and gray soon doubled and tripled until at least two hundred lead men dressed in battle clothes set apart sergeants from privates, lieutenants from sergeants, right up to the diminutive Generals Ulysses S. Grant and the aristocratic Robert E. Lee. After a time there were cannons and horses with mounted men, as each week, much to Martha's disgust, Adam searched the stores for more soldiers. The project afforded father and son hours of entertainment, so she managed to swallow her feelings and let the matter pass. She decided it was pleasurable to see the two so close and lamented those early years on the farm when the older boys seemed more an impediment to Adam's daily life than pleasure.

In January 1895, Martha and Adam were blessed with their first grandchild, a boy. Ben and Alma named their son Edward Charles. They took his first name from Adam's middle name, which had also been given to Ben's brother, Eddie, dead these many years. Ben and Alma had been married fourteen months, and to Adam's dismay, showed no sign of leaving the farm. When they went to see the baby, Adam inquired of Ben when their move might take place. His son tossed off the question lightly, his face devoid of expression that might give his father a clue as to how he really felt. "Now that the baby is here, we may have to put that off a bit, but we'll get there eventually, I'm sure of it." Ben kicked at a stray stone lofting it toward the road. "Truth to tell, I don't like farming any better now than I did when I was a boy. I do it rather routinely, not giving it much thought."

Adam remembered those spring days behind the plow, the cicadas screeching from the meadow in August as he harvested wheat on sweat-drenched summer days. He almost shivered as he thought about winter's wrenching cold when blizzards accompanied his going to the barn or pasture to minister to the needs of his animals. He mentioned Ben's remarks to Martha who sniffed disdainfully, "that girl has no intention of leaving her *Paw* and *Maw*, as she calls them. I could have told you that the day I met her. Girls like her are afraid of anything new. She's got her man; her mother is just across the way, and now this baby completes her rosy, if somewhat limited idea of domesticity. Ben can say good-bye to his dreams of being an oilman on the cusp of a new industry. Why I read just the other day that in the future we will be heating our homes with oil and powering motors that will do all kinds of laborious jobs. At least Frank got away."

"I didn't think you wanted either of them to leave."

"At first I didn't, but I see now that opportunity for young men lies elsewhere. It's just a shame that Ben took on that woman. Oh, she's not a bad sort, keeps a nice house, but she'll probably insist our grandson and all her children stay close by just as her grandparents did to her parents and they have done to her. We should have rid ourselves of that farm years ago; it's going to drag everyone down. There is no future there. Farms are middling and always will be; education is brief, and there haven't been any new families moving to the township in years. Cousins will soon be marrying cousins; there's just not enough new blood to go around."

"I can't sell it now. What would Ben and Alma and now little Eddie do without a roof over their heads?"

"I don't want to think about it. I only want to be rid of the place. And I do wish they hadn't named their child Edward, the memory is too painful. I know Ben thought he was doing a commendable thing to honor his dead brother, but it provides me with a reminder of the saddest time in my life. Whenever I hear someone say that baby's name, I feel a stab in my heart."

"Maybe we can convince them to use the child's middle name. Charles is a strong sounding name, *Charles Springer*, nothing wrong with that."

Thirty-six

On the 23rd, we camped near the Long Bridge across the Potomac. From our camp the capital and the surrounding country presented and indescribably grand appearance. On the 24th, we marched into the city and passed in review before all the great ones of the nation.

When 1895 began some of the veterans in the counties of Muskingum and Morgan decided a parade was needed to commemorate thirty years since the Great War's end. Old uniforms were dusted off and pressed, some needed mending, and most men required let out waistlines. The women, nearly as excited as their husbands, did what was required to make them fit. Where a cap or a jacket was missing, a milliner or tailor was available to stitch up another. Adam's uniform was intact, but the waistline was tight. Martha let out the seams, put an inset into the belt, moved the buttons on the jacket, and he managed to struggle into it. Admiring his soldierly, if somewhat expanded, reflection in the mirror with Ralphy looking on, he heard the child say, "Wish I had me a uniform, then I could march in the parade with you, Papa."

Adam looked down at the appealing, little face and pleading blue eyes. He brushed a hand over the child's fine hair parted in the middle and cut in a Dutch boy bob. "Well, son, I think we could manage that. How about if we go to the tailor and see about having one made in your size?"

"Oh Papa, could we, could we go now?"

"Next week we'll go. Don't tell your Mama though. We'll keep it a secret between us. Can you do that? Can you keep our secret?"

"I won't tell, Papa, I promise."

But as secrets are wont to do, especially in the heads of small boys, the plan became too much for Ralphy to keep to himself. First he told Bridget, remembering to add, "but don't tell Mama."

"I would never do that Ralphy. When you promise to keep a secret God expects that you will never let it go. If you tell the secret, you commit a sin."

"What's a sin, Bridgy?"

"Sins are really bad like when you take something that doesn't belong to you or don't mind your Mama. You never want to die with a sin on your soul, for then you burn in hell."

Ralphy said he'd never heard of hell.

"You will some day when you start going to Sunday school. That would be at the Methodist Church, I suspect, but I'm sure they know about hell too."

"Is that where you go Sundays?"

"No, I'm Catholic. I belong to the one true church."

"Never heard tell of it," Ralphy said, skipping out of the room.

By that afternoon, having forgotten all about hell, he told his mother that he and Papa had a secret—"a really, really big one!"

Martha, who was stitching a ruffle for a dress she was making over, since Adam was being so mean about expenses, said, "then you mustn't tell."

"But I want to Mama, it's about the parade. Papa is going to take me to the tailor and get me my very own uniform. He's going to take me Saturday."

Martha stopped working her needle and glared at her son, "I'm sitting here restitching an old dress, and he's going to take you to the tailors? He's going to buy you a uniform you will wear only once? Well, never mind. I'll discuss the matter with your Papa when he comes home. Now run along and play. Mama has to concentrate on this ruffling."

Jaws set, eyes mean, Martha met Adam at the end of the driveway when the buggy arrived from the train station Friday night. Ralphy was in the kitchen with Bridget; Martha saw to that. She intended to have words with his father There were no warm greetings, no swift kisses, or welcoming touches.

"I understand you are going to the tailors tomorrow."

"So he told you?"

"He did. And I forbid your having that uniform made. You can tell me that we need to keep expenses in line while you go out and buy him—God only knows— how many toy soldiers to recreate that dumb old war, and now this nonsense about a miniature Civil War uniform he'll wear only once."

"We can't disappoint him now."

"I can, if you can't. You are making a fool of that child by satisfying his every whim as well as some he doesn't know he has."

Now it was Adam's turn to set his jaw. "Martha, I forbid you to say one negative word to him. He is my son, and I am the breadwinner in this family. If I want to get

223

him a uniform, I'll get him a uniform, and I advise you to say no more about it to me and most especially to him." Adam picked up his grip and moved past her in a huff, leaving Martha to watch him ascend the front steps alone.

Martha's fit of anger didn't leave her, but smoldered inside. She went over and over the perceived injustice done to her by Adam's stubborn insistence on showering Ralphy with possessions to the exclusion of her needs and desires. But by the time the child stood before her in the soft blue uniform with its ornamental braiding and matching frog fasteners, all she could say was "you look mighty handsome." She avoided comments on the uniform.

"Now we're going to get my picture took with Ted."

"Taken," Martha retorted.

Ted was the dog Adam bought his son shortly after Ben's remark that the child was lonesome. On the farm they had mongrels of indeterminate ancestry, ugly short-haired mutts that lived out of doors or in the barn. Ted, on the other hand, came from a breeder of collies with papers that noted his prestigious ancestry. The dog was a gentle sort, playful but not too rough, and beautiful too with his long pointed nose and lustrous silky coat of black and white fur. "The ideal companion for a four-and-a-half year old," Adam said. And when Martha objected to the dog hair, Adam pointed out that the dog would keep a watchful eye on Ralphy, and thus, "is not a frivolous purchase but a needed addition to the family."

That year, the Fourth of July fell on Thursday. Adam took Wednesday and Friday off, and before the big parade, he met with his compatriots to put the last minute flourishes on the plans. Red, white, and blue bunting went up on buildings lining the parade route that would take the marching veterans to the courthouse for the ceremonies. Adam enjoyed meeting with his fellow veterans, some for the first time since the war's end. Over the years, he had seen one or two surviving members of Company E, but now more of them were together joshing about old times and telling stories. Men who had for thirty years avoided thinking upon their wartime experiences now gushed forth with remembrances long forgotten and rarely discussed. Some still bore the scars of battle. Abram Wood marched on his peg leg, not well, but he marched; Albert Pletcher marched with a flapping blue sleeve. Adam remembered the day he lost that arm. He had stopped to drink a cup of coffee before joining the march ordered by General Grant to evacuate the post at Holly Springs. The regiment, made up of the Sixty-Eighth, Seventy-Eighth, and Twentieth, Ohio, was surrounded by the enemy, but followed the General's order to march on to Bolivar, Tennessee, twenty-two miles north of Grand Junction. The bullet tore at the young private's arm; the hot coffee splashed over his uniform and he fell. The rebels moved in and captured him before the Yankee medics could go to his aid. Eventually Albert escaped and rejoined the company.

Zachariah Nolon, one of the later recruits in Company E, got the talk rolling at the assembly ground when he reminisced, "Remember when the enemy expected to meet no obstruction from the rear and came through that gap between the left of the Seventeenth and the right of the Sixteenth?"

"Yeah, I remember," someone said, "the forest was so dense Claiborne's Division passed through undiscovered."

"It was the advance of that force that shot our beloved McPherson," Adam offered.

"But we retaliated," another man said. "Our generals put their men over their works, and we met the enemy's mad charge with a terrible volley of musketry. Why they were within just a few feet of our works, but we repulsed those graybacks with a slaughter unparalleled. Never saw so much blood and guts in my life."

"Didn't stop them though. Them rebs fell back, reformed their lines and came up again. Why at the end, we was fighting hand to hand."

Adam felt his stomach clutch. The talk brought memories of a battle he had fought as hard to forget as he had fought that day to win. With his bayonet, he alone had severed three men—or was it four, then watched them writhe on the ground before stabbing them again and again. Eyes welling uncontrollably, Adam blinked and sniffed several times, but his watery eyes betrayed him.

"Whatsa matter?" Nolon said. "You don't like thinking on it? We won didn't we, so what do we care? They got what they deserved."

"They were young men just like us," Adam shot back. He was still trying to console himself when someone else said. "We left that ground carpeted with the dead and wounded. I can hear their screams even now."

"We didn't get off so easy either," Adam tried to change the subject. I seem to remember our own Captain McCarty was taken prisoner.

"McCarty was a brave man. Why I heard six rebels came on him yelling to shoot the damned Yankee rascal," another veteran said.

"He thought of resisting, but knew that meant instant death, so he surrendered his sword. Later he wrote up his experience. I read about it in a book written by our chaplain, Reverend Stevenson. That book was all about the Seventy-Eighth, Adam said. "Surprised you didn't get a copy."

"I ain't much of a reader, but what happened to McCarty after that? I never heard, didn't see no book."

"Tossed him into a stockade with about two-thousand other prisoners near Atlanta, I think it was. Supposed to march some twenty miles to Macon, but McCarty—he was a clever one—feigned injury, said he was unable to go that far, so they sent him to the surgeon, who excused him and another man. They ended up spending the day with the Confederate commander of the post, who invited them to dine that night in his headquarters."

"Dine! Imagine that. Helps to be an officer. Hard to believe the enemy bothered with them."

"That's what the book said." Adam went on, "but the story didn't end so happily. They were thrown in with a bunch of old prisoners; some were wandering around in their drawers, lice covered, shabby, barefoot. Not much food either. The rebel officers guarding them were tyrannical, shot a man found bathing in a spring. McCarty was later moved to another prison camp near Charleston, where he was taken down by some kind of fever, but he claimed to have good medical attention. Then he was shipped off to a convalescent hospital. A man by the name of Todd, an ardent rebel, and the brother-in-law of President Lincoln, was in charge."

"I heard about that place. That's where a Negro was given thirty lashes upon his bare back for spitting. He wasn't even a slave, educated, born, and raised in a free state. But them dumb rebel rascals didn't know the difference."

"After that they sent McCarty to some camp outside of Columbia, South Carolina, where the only ration was sorghum molasses, worse than at Andersonville. McCarty and three other officers escaped. Walked nearly two hundred miles mostly at night but got caught and sent back to Charleston, where they were locked up and had to subsist on a pot of mush a day for the four of them."

The conversation ceased when a bugle call summoned the old soldiers to the assembly area at the beginning of Zanesville's Market Street. Here they were to practice getting into the proper order for marching to the courthouse the following day. Adam turned to look for Ralphy, who had been with some of the veterans' grandsons and noticed that the child was not joining them in play, but was sitting idly alone, his face impassive, hands lying idly in his lap. To hurry the child along, Adam picked him up and carried him to the assembly field.

While the men practiced marching, the women prepared picnic lunches of potato salad, sandwiches, casseroles, cakes, and cookies. That night on arriving home from practice Ralphy seemed unusually subdued, so much so that Bridget remarked upon his lethargy to Adam. "I do believe the child is overly anxious. There has been such a build up with the uniform and all. But then again he might be scared about the marching, a little fellow among all those towering men. When he came home from practice today all he wanted to do was take a nap, and he's not awake yet."

Adam was unperturbed. Women are always looking for trouble even if there is none. "He'll be fine by tomorrow. Ralphy is just caught up with boyish excitement."

Bridget's plain face, that even in summer sun looked drained except for the freckles that dotted her white skin, appeared doubtful. "I think we might as well let him sleep rather than waking him for dinner. That way he will be refreshed for tomorrow. If he wakes and wants something to eat, I'll take it to him in the night."

Morning dawned on the Fourth, and when Bridget came to get him up for breakfast, a dazed Ralphy fluttered his eyelids, but couldn't seem to keep them open. "You have been sleeping far too long," she told him. "Get up now; today's the big day. I have breakfast waiting for you in the kitchen."

Ralphy sat up, stretched and lay back down. "I'm not hungry," he told her.

"Don't you want to get into your uniform?"

"I guess."

"Then breakfast comes first."

Ralphy hauled himself out of bed, as if it took every muscle he had.

"Now go into the washroom and clean your face and hands while I see about heating your oatmeal." Bridget was used to moving quickly, so without further words, she dashed out of the room, leaving Ralphy alone. He arrived at the table about ten minutes later, sat down, and stared listlessly into his bowl of oatmeal, only touching his tongue to the warm cereal before dropping the spoon back into the bowl. When Adam came into the kitchen to see how soon he would be donning his uniform, Ralphy studied his father a moment and said, "I don't want to go."

"What to you mean, you don't want to go? We've been planning to have you march in the parade for weeks. Now run along and get into your uniform. Bridget go help him; I have to see about getting into mine."

Adam had the buggy in the driveway when Bridget appeared with the uniformed Ralphy. "He's still resisting," she told Adam.

"Son, I hope you haven't been crying. You're eyes are red rimmed."

"No, sir."

"Then, you're just scared. Now be a good little soldier and get into the buggy. Soldiers do whatever they have to do no matter how frightened they are, how sick, how sad, or how terrible the weather. That's the difference between a soldier and a sissy. And you don't want to be a sissy, do you?"

"No, Papa."

Thirty-seven

At the parade assembly ground, Adam was too busy to pay much attention to Ralphy until he heard the whistle that ordered the men to get in line. With his large hand clenching Ralphy's small one, Adam assumed his appointed position, shoulders rigid, head thrust high, chin uplifted. And when the band struck up *Tramp, Tramp, Tramp the Boys are Marching,* the two set off with the little boy taking three steps to Adam's one. Ralphy was soon stumbling so much that Adam swept him up in his arms and carried him the rest of the way to the courthouse. With Ralphy's head on his shoulder, the child's body turned limp, but Adam, keyed up by the day's excitement, augmented by seeing his veteran friends, paid little mind. So when he spotted Martha in the crowd, he took the opportunity to rid himself of his burden and deposited the child on her lap. She was seated on a blanket chatting with some other ladies who had come for the speeches and musical renditions that marked the holiday. Despite the blasting brass bands, the shouts of children having fun, and the general laughter that surrounded the festive spectators, Ralphy fell asleep and did not awaken until after the speeches.

Martha and her friends gathered their baskets for the move to the picnic grounds. "Come Ralphy, it's time to eat. You've slept long enough."

"No-o-o-o Mama. I'm not." He dug his face into the blanket.

"Get up son, I have to take this blanket." Ralphy didn't move. She picked him up and set him firmly on his feet, but the listless child refused to walk. Put off by his stubbornness, she set down the basket and swept him and the blanket into her arms. Her friends carried the picnic basket.

"I could use Will about now," she told one of the ladies, "but he is probably off somewhere with his chums. A college boy does not stay around long with his parents," she thought to add, knowing that having a son attending college reflected on her stature in the community. "And Ben, who said he would meet us at the picnic ground, is nowhere to be seen."

She set Ralphy down on the blanket, where he immediately slumped over while she smoothed the blanket edges.

"Is he not well?" her friend asked.

"No I think he's simply tired out with the excitement of it all. And to think Adam had that uniform made, and the child didn't march at all."

When Ralphy remained sleeping, not even waking for a piece of chocolate cake, Martha became alarmed. Adam, still joshing with his friends while scooping chicken salad from his plate, was well within Martha's vision. She called to one of the children nearby. "Would you please go ask that very tall man with the mustache over there to come here. Tell him his wife needs him." She went on talking to her friend, now settled on a neighboring blanket.

"Does seem strange that the boy has slept so long with all this noise going on around him," her friend ventured.

Martha nudged Ralphy to wake up. He opened his eyes as though the very action took all the effort he could muster, then let his lids droop again. Martha felt his forehead. "Doesn't seem feverish, but he certainly acts like he is coming down with something."

Adam stood over her. "What do you want?" he asked impatiently.

"I think Ralphy is sick. We should probably take him home."

"If that's the case, he'll just sleep at home as he's sleeping here, so I see no need to hurry." He didn't even wait for a response from his wife, but quickly returned to the clutch of men with whom he had been talking, leaving Martha to cover the sleeping boy with her shawl. As she did so, she noticed a rash blossoming on his face. Like freckles, the red spots dotted his nose and spread across his round cheeks. She assumed it was sunburn for Ralphy was light skinned like Martha; "an English complexion," she once told Adam. The other boys were more bronzed like their Germanic father.

Evening brought another more serious diagnosis, so serious that Alma refused to join the family. She clutched her baby son, Edward, to her bosom and rushed off to the bedroom, where she and Ben slept while visiting over the Fourth. "Until we know what he has, I will not let my son be exposed," she told Ben, "and I don't care a whit what your mother thinks."

The family was becoming alarmed at Ralphy's behavior. Adam had not yet arrived from helping to clean up after the day's festivities, so Martha sent Ben for the doctor. Will was not around either. Martha feared he might be sparking some girl. Her last glimpse of her son confirmed that giggling young women were all around him leading her to think that Will, with his dark hair and long dark eyelashes over brilliant blue eyes, is just too handsome for his own good. She turned her attention from Ralphy when Bridget, having already heard from Alma that Ralphy was sick, came bounding into the room. After a quick look at the little boy, she too agreed it was time for the doctor.

Within a half-hour of his arrival, Dr. McAuliffe confirmed that the child was seriously ill. "Has all the signs of meningitis," he told Martha who turned white with fear, but managed to stay on her feet. Bridget put her hand to her mouth, "Oh no doctor, not meningitis. He won't live." Her words came out as a shout loud enough to catch Adam's ear as he came into the downstairs hallway. He dashed upstairs taking the steps two at a time.

"Who won't live? His horrified face took in the scene: the doctor beside the child's bed; stethoscope dangling from its plugs still in his ears and his hand resting lightly on Ralphy's forehead; Martha ghostly white and immobilized; Bridget in tears. "What's going on here?" he shouted.

"I fear he has spinal meningitis, we must get him to the hospital immediately." Dr. McAuliffe's face was serene, but serious.

"Am I going to die, Papa? Am I going to hell?" Ralphy suddenly came alive. "Do I got sins upon my soul?"

"No, son. Where did you hear such talk?"

"Bridgy told me some bad people who die go to hell, specially if they got sins upon their souls."

Adam shot Bridget a withering glance. Ben, who was standing to the rear, broke into the uncomfortable moment. "Come on doctor, let us not waste time, I'll carry him."

"No, I will." Adam was sobbing, tears streaming down his flushed face, his eyes wild with fright."

"No you won't, Pa, you're too upset." And before Adam could move, Ben scooped up his brother and followed the doctor down the steps with Martha tearing along behind.

"He can't die, he can't die," Adam screamed from the top of the stairs. "You let him die doctor, and I will hold you responsible."

"Mr. Springer, get a grip on yourself," Bridget held his arm, but Adam wrenched away and ran down the steps.

Sometime after midnight, the family returned from the hospital without Ralphy. By this time Will was also with the family. Martha had fainted at the news of Ralphy's death and, on their return, was lolling against Will in the buggy. Adam, lost in grief, sat in impenetrable silence. Will assisted his mother from the buggy while Adam, letting out a whoop that could be heard all over the neighborhood, scrambled up the steps and pushed open the front door. As he tore up two flights of stairs to the attic room, where the battle of Shiloh was being fought by the silent lead men, Adam's sobs came amidst loud bursts of breath. There arose such crashing and banging that Bridget, who had been waiting for news in her attic room, rushed into the hallway and opened the door to what had been the elaborate reenactment. As though the battle had been hard fought and was now over, the soldiers lay scattered in heaps on the floor, blue clad mixed with gray done in by a final horrific act of war. Adam stood hurling cannons and horses through the windows and into the corners. Bridget had never witnessed such a scene when death occurred. Children had died in her family, but never had she seen such a terrible display of grief. Mostly family and friends dropped to their knees and prayed the rosary over and over until it became a chant. She ran toward Adam, reached to grab his arm just as he stumbled and fell backwards onto the array of miniature men. His head banged the wall, but he didn't appear to feel his bodily hurts, only the ache inside. "My son is dead," he yelled, "Ralphy is gone from me forever."

"You upset the board where the soldiers were marching?" Bridget knelt beside him. "You did this to Ralphy's soldiers? Please Mr. Springer, get hold of yourself. Ralphy is with God now. He was such an appealing child that God wanted him too." Her eyes glistened and with trembling chin, she blessed herself repeating aloud, *Name of the Father, Son, and Holy Ghost.*

Adam's eyes blazed, "Cut that out! There is no God, else he would not have taken the one person who made my life worth living."

"Please, don't let your sons or the Missus hear you say that. They are suffering too. We all loved Ralphy." Bridget couldn't hold her tears back. They streamed down her face and dropped onto Adam's uniform in great dark blue splotches. "Come sir, come with me; I'll help you to your room. She reached toward him, but he shook her off.

"Get out of here, leave me alone. That bloody war! That's what took my son. If I had not insisted he go to the parade, had not bought him that damnable uniform, had made myself forget those wretched years, he might still be with us."

"Somehow your son got a disease, a terrible disease."

"But I made him go. If I had let him stay home, he might have got well."

"We don't know that Mr. Springer. Meningitis is a terrible disease, it affects the brain, and I've heard tell there is no cure."

Adam continued to sob; his body shook, and when he raised his eyes to her, Bridget thought he had aged a dozen years. She reached to help him up, but again he shook her off. "Leave me alone," he shouted.

Bridget soon gave up her entreaties and left Adam to mourn alone. He remained in the room the rest of the night and the next day, and when Bridget brought him breakfast, she found the door locked.

"Don't bother me," he shouted.

"I'll leave the tray outside the door," she called softly.

There was no answer, and when she brought lunch, the breakfast tray remained where she had left it. Bridget knocked on the door. Please sir, open up or I will call Will and Ben, and they will force it open. After a small silence, the lock turned, then the knob, and the door moved slowly.

A disheveled old man, his white hair unruly, uniform wrinkled, his face reddened and splotchy, stood before her.

"Oh sir," Bridget said. "This will pass. That's what my Ma always said when a young one of hers passed. My Ma and Pa lost four; one as old as Ralphy died of the measles, but we take heart that he is at peace in heaven seated at the right hand of God. I pray for my dead brothers and sisters every day of my life, and now I'll pray for our little Ralphy."

"Save your damned Catholic prayers, it's over."

"I think you should go to the washroom and fix up before the Missus sees you. And please be strong. She is suffering too, keeps talking about a baby, Eddie, and saying this can't happen twice to one mother. I don't think she means Ben's Eddie, do you?"

"No, the child she speaks of died a long time ago. He was just a baby." Adam, unsteady on his feet, seemed to need someone to lead him.

"I'll wait here for you if you'd like."

He half stumbled into the washroom while Bridget waited, and when he came out, she led him to the back stairway toward the kitchen. "You need to eat something before you go to comfort Mrs. Springer," she said. Having lost all sense of self-determination, Adam followed Bridget to the kitchen, but he barely ate his breakfast toast and drank only a half-cup of tea.

Ralphy's body was returned to the Springer parlor in a small white box, which the undertaker suggested should remain closed. He smiled one of those benevolent

233

smiles undertakers use in times of condolence and added, "since the boy died of a terrible disease, it's safer for the mourners."

Adam nodded. He was dressed in his best suit, his hair slicked. Martha, all in black, sat in a wing chair, her face bland. She appeared to have aged. Only forty-five, she had lost the color in her cheeks, and her eyes were hooded as if she didn't want anyone to see into them. She said little but occasionally dabbed at her eyes with a lacy handkerchief. Bridget was right. Adam glanced at his grieving wife. He must try to gather strength. After all he had seen more death in a lifetime than most men, but this . . . this was different.

The lavender ribboned wreath of purple iris went up on the door; the mourners came and whispered their condolences: *we're sorry for your loss; we'll pray for you; he was a darling boy,* and on and on. Then it was time for the Methodist preacher to lead the mourners in prayer. Adam barely heard the words, while keeping his eyes on the undertakers poised to move forward to take his son away forever. They carried the white box to the waiting hearse with its glass windows on both sides, so anyone observing the funeral procession would know that a child was being carried off. The white coffin lay in shocking contrast to the black exterior of the hearse where only the gleaming brass side lamps broke the dismal effect. Even the seat where the black-clad driver sat in anticipation of carrying the child to the cemetery was black. A pair of golden braces secured Ralphy's small white coffin holding it steadfast in the black interior of the hearse.

Adam sat with Martha, Ben, and Will in a black buggy, the first in the funeral procession of carriages that carried family and friends to the cemetery. In keeping with the solemnity of the occasion, both the carriages carrying the immediate family and the funeral coach were drawn by high stepping black horses. People along the streets stopped and stared at the passing procession. Some, on seeing that a child was being conveyed to eternity, dabbed their eyes. Even grown men seemed struck with the sadness of the occasion. No one spoke inside the buggy carrying the immediate family, but Adam saw the saddened expressions on the faces of people going about their business and thought children in death are surely the saddest scene of all.

Thirty-eight

In the days and weeks that followed, Will put aside his plans for going back to college. Seeing the inconsolable sadness of his distraught parents, he decided to stay on a spell; maybe when the grieving subsided he'd go west to join his brother, Frank. Neither Martha nor Adam remarked about his not returning to college. Both seemed numb to the goings on around them, and the house took on an air of ghostly quiet. Will despaired about when he might get away, so when a local haberdashery had a job open as assistant manager, he applied.

Will and Bridget were especially worried about Martha who, while she didn't spend much time in tears, slept a great deal. "She's trying to forget she's living," Bridget said. "She naps mornings and late afternoons and goes to bed early. Sometimes I hear her prowling around the house in the middle of the night. I'm afraid she might do something drastic to herself, so I get up to keep an eye on her. I've tried to get her to pray, but she just waves me off."

Will gave her a knowing look. He too feared that Martha, who appeared unable to cope with consciousness, might take her life. Meanwhile, Adam shuffled around the house, speaking to no one, and rarely coming out of the library, leading Will to worry that he might be drinking again. Desperate to get the family back on track, Will insisted that his father go back to work. "Get on the road again. Keep busy, and while business matters take over, your loss will recede in your head."

"What do you know about loss? You've been coddled and babied from the day you were born, food and shelter provided, a good education that even took you to Ohio State University. You know nothing about deprivation and the loss of love ones."

"You're right. I've had a good life, no war, no scenes of death on the battlefield, no children to disappoint or die. And certainly you have seen and felt more than your share during the war with death all around you."

"Never like this." Adam slumped in his big leather chair. "I felt bad about Eddie, but this . . ." His voice drifted away in sobs. He lay his head on his desk, his body shook.

Will came around the desk and patted his father. "Come on Papa, we have to get over this. Mama needs us."

And so the son became the parent. Adam knew Will spoke wisely, and as the days moved on and boredom set in, he harnessed the horse to the buggy and visited the Pineville Pottery. Mr. Forsythe had been most patient with him during his bereavement, but when he came to pay his respects, casually mentioned a new canvassers' kit.

The canvasser's outfit included a stork umbrella stand finished in blended colors. It retailed in full size at one dollar twenty five cents. Also new in the line were samples of a Venetian cooking crock, jardinieres, and pedestals selling retail for four to six dollars. Larger jardinieres featuring female heads went for fifteen and twenty dollars. After picking up his canvassers' outfit and catalog sheets, Adam visited the two other potteries he represented, and called on another. It was difficult to choose among nearly a hundred such establishments now crowded about eastern Ohio, West Virginia, and western Pennsylvania. Needed was a line for middle-of-the-road buyers, so he chose an old manufacturer located in Zanesville. The Weller pottery sold a line of garden pots and crockery leading Adam to wonder what had happened to the Weller flower vase he had bought Martha so long ago.

On the few nights he was home, Adam tried to comfort his wife, but she remained lackadaisical, interested in nothing, a poor conversationalist. He worried about her but judged she was best left to her own method of dealing with their loss. Each week on his return she seemed smaller. They were not close anymore, which puzzled him. Didn't tragedy and death bring couples together? Martha seemed to glide about the room like some ethereal spirit rarely speaking to anyone. She let Bridget manage the house and decide on the meals. Poor Bridget, Adam thought, the entire burden of the house was on her. She seemed to have no other life except on Sundays when she went to mass and visited her family in the poor section, where the Irish lived apart from everyone else, meaning Protestants.

Adam saw a way to help one Saturday morning when he chanced to meet a society woman on the street. Mrs. Chadwick, only a distant acquaintance, lived several blocks away and had been one of the mourners at Ralphy's funeral. She inquired about his wife. When Adam told her sadly, "not well," the woman said with great authority, for she was a blustery sort, "she needs to be doing something of interest. I would not like to interrupt her mourning, but do you mind if I call upon her? A woman in grief must pull herself up. No one else can do it for her." Adam agreed and was about to tip his hat to Mrs. Chadwick and move on when she appeared to have an afterthought. "Some of us are organizing a current events club for ladies to discuss the happenings of the day and help the less fortunate among us. Perhaps Mrs. Springer would like to join us."

Already moving on down the block, Adam turned around to address Mrs. Chadwick again, "I'd be so pleased if you would call on her and invite her to join. And I know Martha would be too." He knew there was no question about that, but whether Martha was interested in worldly events or helping the poor, he wasn't at all certain. The country in the 1890's brought a particular kind of frustration to its citizens. There were periodic economic depressions and many were leaving their rural lives to work in the great factories, which to Adam's mind paid little heed to the welfare of their workers. So women's groups began to take an interest in helping beleaguered citizens. Adam thought this might be good for Martha; perhaps to better appreciate her own fortunate existence she should become acquainted with the lives of the poverty stricken.

Adam knew that Martha had been trying to ingratiate herself with Mrs. Chadwick's social clique for some time, so that alone might engender her interest in political affairs and in other happenings of the day. But he had trouble imagining women interested in such manly activities, however, if that is what the leading socialites about town had decided to do, he would encourage Martha to join. Adam thought her lack of success with more prominent ladies was due to his low position in the community. They were German, at least Adam was, and the English held the powerful positions in this and other communities throughout the country. He knew that the bankers, lawyers, and merchants referred to him as a peddler, even as the Springers were living among them in the big house on Orchard Avenue. Their multiple sources of income provided an ample living, but their neighbors saw him only as a peddler of pottery.

By the latter part of the decade, President William McKinley was facing a severe crisis as the country girded for war with Spain over Cuba. And this gave the women considerable grist to discuss at their bimonthly meetings. Attitudes were split on the matter, and Martha related to Adam how arguments had arisen among her friends over U.S. involvement. Aging veterans, including the president, urged caution. But a new generation was taking over. With a strong Navy bent on showing muscle, and urged on by a strident press, the nation determined that it was time to rid the hemisphere of Spanish influence once and for all. War finally erupted in April 1898. By then the new president was dead from an assassin's bullet, and Vice President Theodore Roosevelt had taken over.

About a year after Ralphy's death, Adam suggested that Martha take Daisy for a ride. "A brisk ride—and not on that sidesaddle. It might do you worlds of good, even increase your appetite. You're still looking mighty thin."

"That pokey old thing. Even on the sidesaddle she gives too quiet a ride. There's nothing in that for me. No, I'm not riding any more."

"Adam suspected this meant she'd like a new horse—before Ralphy died she frequently mentioned it—but he was curious about Daisy, and so for the first time in more than a year he saddled her and went for a ride himself. Out among the lush grasses, not yet disturbed by development, he experienced a sense of freedom as he trotted the mare through the late July afternoon with the clear air of summer stirring about his face. Soon the horse was cantering, then trotting, and finally taking off in a short gallop down a country lane amid towering trees that afforded welcome shelter from the blazing sun. And for those fleeting moments, as he sat the horse, all thoughts of Ralphy left him. Yes, this is what Martha needs; she must soon quit that dreary, overly festooned house with its dark furniture full of inlays and carving.

As he brought Daisy to the carriage barn, he recognized that Martha had not been quite honest about the slowness of the horse. He'd had a good ride, but Adam was so intimidated by his wife's continued sadness that he said nothing. He asked Bridget to turn Daisy into the pasture every day. Still the horse needed an occasional ride. Will said he could manage that.

His business was on the upswing again. Adam was gone now about two weeks at a time, as he went further and further into the country mostly by rail. A trunk stocked with the latest samples, carefully wrapped in excelsior, was checked in the baggage compartments of the trains and removed to the local hotels in each town in which he stopped. These hotels were always in close proximity to the train stations and were usually well appointed hostelries. Adam relished these trips away from that house with its memories of a little boy at play with his lead soldiers, his red wagon, and the stuffed bears he dragged everywhere. As far as Adam knew the soldiers still lay in disarray on the floor of the attic room, but he would never go to see for himself. He didn't care what happened to Ralphy's uniform, nor did he ask Bridget, who knew full well that it had been buried with the child. The next day after hearing the terrible news of Ralphy's death, she had carried it to the undertaker, where she dressed the boy for his last journey.

Adam decided to survey Indiana and Illinois as well as points further west; after all he was a free agent and could go anywhere in the country to sell his products. Travel would now become his cure for unhappiness. He would see the country and was soon enjoying the variety of hostelries, some rather elegant as befit the Victorian age, but most rather humdrum commercial hotels. Still, they were clean and accommodating to the armies of salesmen crisscrossing the country. At all times of the day and night, these intrepid men could be seen detraining and marching across streets and down town and city blocks, grips and sample cases in hand. Usually, there was a redcap or bellboy to help trundle the heavier luggage to and from the hotels. They were friendly places for traveling men who ate together and talked after dinner while enjoying cigars in the lounges. Adam found the camaraderie pleasant. Desk clerks were discreet when girls of the night stopped for the room numbers of men who enjoyed feminine company. Adam had not even been tempted. Since getting Martha back he'd had no need, although with Ralphy's death, she was not at all affectionate. He wondered if she blamed him for the child's demise. Many of the girls who flounced in and out of these establishments seemed little more than children to Adam, who was now nearing fifty-nine. Indeed some, although painted up to look older, were only youngsters. Usually from poor families, they generally plied their trade with an eye for snagging husbands.

With the additional products to sell and longer distances to cover, Adam began traveling more than ever. He arranged for Will to process the orders he sent in. The plan worked well, and after the first year when Will married and brought his wife to the Orchard Avenue house, he continued to handle his father's records in return for free lodging. This took a load off Adam, and he was soon traveling as far away as Pennsylvania, Michigan, Indiana, and Illinois—even venturing into Chicago. His travels kept him away from home for longer periods, but Martha seemed not to mind. She was deep into affairs of the current events club, her church circle, and the local women's club with luncheons and socials to keep her occupied.

Will's new wife, a beautiful belle, kept her company and the two appeared to have become fast friends. Nellie, it seemed to Adam, was fulfilling the role of a daughter Martha had always wanted, but which Alma was not about to provide. There had always been a distance between the two, and from the beginning Martha and Alma regarded each other like two warring felines. Ben and Alma were still on the farm in 1899, six years after they wed. They now had a daughter, May, a hefty child, whom Adam concluded was never going to be a beauty. To his father, Ben seemed morose, lost sometimes in regret for what might have been a bright future as an oilman with a rich and loving wife.

As for Nellie, her beauty was legendary. A fine figured woman with long dark hair worn in a fetching twist at the back of her head, she was always attired in gowns with leg o'mutton sleeves and ruffled bodices. Drawn tight at the waistline, the configuration of these dresses gave her an added grace. Her dark eyes were inquisitive, and she never failed to ask after Adam's days on the road when they met for meals or quiet chitchat. With his dark hair and finely cut features, Will was the most like his father at a young age and the handsomest of Adam's sons, so it was natural that he could attract such a woman. She came from a good family, and in time seemed to take over the affairs of the house leaving Martha to her clubs and meetings.

Even Bridget had a steady beau, but seemed in no rush to take her marriage vows. "I understand you've been keeping company," Adam said to her one day. "I suppose we will be losing you."

Bridget smiled shyly. "Not in the near future, Mr. Springer. I know what's ahead of me when I marry, so I'll not be wanting to get into that too soon."

"What do you mean, what's ahead of you? Isn't he a nice young man?"

"A fine lad, goes to mass every Sunday, treats my family well—and I do believe he loves me. But neither of us is anxious to have so many children, and if we marry we know that's likely, so we'll put off awhile and save our money for a nice house. I see quite a bit of him anyway; don't know whether you know this or not, Mr. Springer, but Tim is our milkman."

Thirty-nine

The passing of five years softened the memory of Ralphy, but not the ache in Adam's heart. All that remained was a small picture in a gilded frame taken in his miniature Civil War uniform with his collie dog, Ted. The child and dog look directly at the camera as if beseeching the viewer to never forget them. The picture sat on a lace-covered table in the front parlor where Bridget had placed it the day Ralphy's white coffin was carried into the house. No one in the family ever mentioned the picture, and it had remained on the table ever since. Only Bridget touched it when she moved it for dusting. At first, Ted spent days and nights sleeping in the boy's room, until Bridget decided outdoors was the best place for a grieving dog. "I declare I spend half my time cleaning up those long hairs; they look nice on a collie but awful draped over the upholstery and carpets," she told Adam. "I have to use this Bissell on these carpets every day," she said, furiously pushing the sweeper.

"Whatever suits," he replied, his voice weary. He had no interest in affairs of the household and would have liked to rid himself of the place but lacked the will to make the move.

Since no one else was much interested in the dog anymore, Ted became Bridget's pet. She fed him, bathed him once a month in the big galvanized tub, and although he was free to run, she took him for walks in the neighborhood every afternoon between finishing morning chores, cleaning up after luncheon, and beginning supper. She asked her beau, Tim, to build a doghouse. When it was completed they placed it close by the back door. In cold weather, she let Ted into the pantry and supplied a blanket on which he could curl up out of the wind and snow.

Daisy came down with the glanders that winter, causing considerable dismay about what to do with the aging animal. But when the discharge of matter from her nose became so frequent, Adam decided the most humane course would be to put her down rather than continue experimenting with sulfates of copper and iron, arsenic and the like. Although Martha had rarely ridden since Ralphy's death, she took the loss quite hard, and began chattering once more about how "it would be nice to have a horse of my own."

Just before the century turned Adam acquiesced and went to a local breeder, where he selected a two-year old chestnut with white feet, legs, and face, said to be marks of kindness. Her head was well shaped, neck long, and the distance between her eyes broad and full. Her coat was shiny and her legs were well shaped. Adam concluded these were signs of an intelligent, healthy animal. The only thing he didn't like was her name. Dixie seemed an odd moniker for the horse of a former Union infantryman, but the seller said she had been sired in Kentucky. A border state they called it during the war, but in Adam's time there, he recalled being spat upon by some of the inhabitants as his unit passed through after the conflict was over.

He planned to present his gift as a surprise to Martha on her upcoming fiftieth birthday. On the afternoon that he brought the horse to the front driveway, Martha came out the front door and, dumbfounded that he had finally given in to her request, ran down the front steps to pat the animal's head. Immediately, the horse danced about and threw her ears back. Adam interpreted this as a sign of viciousness, but Martha, who may not have been as familiar as Adam on picking a good horse, seemed not to notice. He considered returning Dixie to her previous owner when Martha exclaimed, "What a lovely animal. I think she is prettier than Daisy. Oh Adam, thank you, thank you so much." And when she stood on tiptoes and kissed him on the cheek, he shoved his concerns from his mind; it would be a nuisance to try to get his money back anyway.

Dixie was soon settled into the stable where clean straw had been laid down with fine shavings from the planing mill added to further soften the ground beneath her hooves. Due to the infectious disease that took Daisy, the stall had been thoroughly washed down and a new blanket purchased for those times when Dixie might be tethered outside on a cold day. "Otherwise," Adam told Martha, "it is better to keep her uncovered in the stall so she doesn't become too delicate. Pampered horses tend to take cold more easily."

Martha attributed her lack of weight gain to Ralphy's death, which had caused her appetite to wane, and she no longer filled her old riding costume. It could be taken in, but another would be more up to date, a black one, perhaps. That would make a more noble impression when she sat the horse. Martha fancied herself a fine lady riding about the English countryside like those she'd seen painted in oil portraits hanging on the walls in the homes of her friends. And this gave rise to the thought that she might have her own portrait painted astride Dixie. With the elegance of the horse, her new outfit, and her regained figure, she could not wait to have it done even though winter weather precluded her riding.

There was a young painter being talked about among her set, who was born in Morgan County where the farm was located. He later moved with his family closer to Zanesville in Muskingum County just south of Duncan Falls, a small settlement the Springers passed through on their infrequent visits to the farm. She could ask him to do the painting. The thought burned in her mind for weeks. How could she manage it without Adam's knowledge? How would she pay for it? Since selling the house in Four Corners, she no longer had her rent money and only a few dollars tucked away in the bottom of her bureau drawer. So obsessed was Martha with the idea of her portrait astride the horse that she let nothing—not even money or the lack of it—deflect her plan. The painting would be a surprise for Adam on his sixtieth birthday the following August. Will would have to be consulted to arrange for whatever additional money she would need from Adam's account, but hers would be enough to start the project.

On a day in February, when the weather had unaccountably warmed, she took the buggy and called on the painter Howard Christy. To her dismay he was no longer in residence, having gone to New York to become an illustrator of novels and popular magazine fiction. "However," his mother told her, "I will mention your interest, and when he returns home for a visit, I'll have him contact you. Young artists always need money, and he might like a local commission to make his two weeks here worthwhile."

True to his mother's word, the young man came around in mid-March and Martha commissioned the portrait. He returned a few days later to begin work. Martha, still fearing that the cold weather would make the horse too frisky, had not yet ridden Dixie. Dressed in her new riding habit and black derby, they went to the carriage barn. Mr. Christy set up his easel and arranged the horse with Martha mounted, but she had trouble reining in Dixie until she remembered the sugar cubes in her pocket. These settled the horse momentarily giving Mr. Christy time to sketch the barest essentials of the portrait. "I can invent the background using the natural growth of a spring day, but there will have to be another sitting a few days hence, as I will be leaving for New York soon." Martha agreed and they arranged to meet the following Monday. After one more sitting that week, Mr. Christy told her, he would complete the work in New York and ship the portrait to her, but not to expect it for several months as he had other commissions to complete before he could get back to hers.

"No need to hurry," she told him. "I don't need it until late August."

By the time the sittings were over, she had paid him half of what he charged. The last half was to be paid on delivery. Will would have to be informed, as Martha no longer had money of her own.

Even though she still had the sidesaddle for riding in town, she had bought a new English saddle for straddling, and this purchase had further depleted her funds. The sidesaddle would make her appear somewhat awkward, for it was a struggle to keep a straight back with one leg wrapped around the horn. She didn't want to appear slouched, but grand like those English women, so the new saddle gave her a more elegant bearing. After all, she was English herself. Hadn't her father's ancestors and mother's too come directly from there, settling in Connecticut before going to Marietta?

"I wouldn't push her to go too fast now; sometimes a two-year-old can become spirited," Adam cautioned, when they saddled the horse for what he thought was the first time. He watched as Martha rode cautiously back and forth in the circular drive in front of the house. You sit the horse well," Adam called out to her as he tried to dismiss the sight of those laid back ears, now standing straight up. He guessed the horse had reacted to the newness of the situation and had finally settled down. I was foolish to be so concerned about such a simple matter as ears, he told himself.

"Don't forget I was practically raised on a horse. Riding was once what I liked to do most," she said as she cantered around the driveway.

Some said it was the cold weather that had lingered that year; she had gone out too early before the frost was out of the ground. Others noted that she had been riding the horse for at least a week before it happened, but generally on those rare days when the temperature went up, it would plummet again at night. A neighbor remarked that possibly she had gone too far away and was unfamiliar with the terrain.

But whatever it was, Dixie came trotting home riderless that afternoon. She was near the carriage barn when Bridget spied her, and thinking it was not like Mrs. Springer to leave the horse untethered, she went to investigate. Martha was nowhere to be seen.

Nellie, had gone to visit her family and was not expected home until the next day, so Bridget got the draught horse, harnessed him to the buggy, and set out for town to locate Will. "I can't find your mother; she went out riding about two hours ago. Dixie returned to the barn without her. I have looked about the neighborhood, but see no sign of her."

Will, solid and steady as a ship at sea faced with an impending storm, patted Bridget on the shoulder. "Be calm now. I'll go and tell Mr. Weber that I must leave. Wait here for me. I'll ride with you in the buggy."

At home there was still no sign of Martha. "If she fell from the horse, I would think she could have walked home unless . . . unless she is badly hurt," Bridget ventured, as the two walked to the end of Orchard Avenue, where cobblestones ended and the packed earth road began. They looked for hoof marks, and saw there were many in both directions.

"You head that way and I'll go this way." Will pointed in a southerly direction. Bridget tried calling out from the buggy, but she got no answer. Will picked up a stick and began beating at the brush beside the road. If the horse had thrown his mother, she could be lying within the thickets. He walked nearly a mile but found no sign of her. When they met again, Will's former tranquil manner disappeared, and he wore a desultory look. Bridget started to cry. Will made no effort to calm her; he had his own tears to choke back, for now he feared his mother had encountered foul play. Evening dropped over them early this late March day, and as the penetrating chill of twilight stiffened their bones, it was Will's turn to panic. "I'm going to the hose house, the firemen will help."

"But it will soon be night."

"We can't leave her to endure a chilly night, alone and hurt. If we only knew which direction she went."

"We'll take Ted," Bridget said. He might be able to track her scent."

Will grabbed the reins as the two climbed into the buggy. At the house, Bridget ran into the house where she got a blouse of Martha's and took it to the dog to sniff. Then she went next door to ask Mr. Brooks if he could bring along a lantern.

By the time Will returned with the firemen, it was already dark. They rode up and down the dirt road ringing bells and calling out. Toward midnight one of the firemen heard a whimper in the grass. Ted, who had sensed his mistress, took off toward a ditch bordering the road. Down in the scrub-filled valley, where a stream coursed in warm weather, the rescuers made out the dark form of a body along the sandy shore. Ted ran over the hill and lapped at her face as the men walked through the thickets to reach her.

She was barely conscious.

"Back's probably broke," one of the fireman ventured. "Bring some blankets down here," he called to his men on the bank, "also some matches. You over there get some firewood. She's already been in the cold too long."

They built a roaring fire and covered her with the blanket. Afraid to move her lest they cause more damage, two firemen and Will remained with her through the night. Bridget went home to get some warm broth, which she packed in a jar and placed in a kettle of hot water, then returned to the scene lit by several lanterns. "Mrs. Springer, Martha," she said softly. "Please take a sip; it will warm you inside. Mr. Brooks has gone for the doctor, but you may have to remain until morning, so we must keep you warm. And don't raise your head, just open your mouth." Martha formed an 'O' with her lips. Bridget spooned the warm liquid into her mouth, as best she could, but much of it dribbled down Martha's chin.

"She seems to be passing in and out of consciousness," Bridget gave the fireman kneeling beside her a worried look. "I don't want her to choke."

"Let that go," Will finally said. "We musn't move her—not even her head—until the doctor arrives."

A half-hour later Dr. McAuliffe came down the hill carrying his black bag in one hand, a lantern in the other. He knelt beside Martha. "Where do you hurt?" he asked gently.

"My back," she murmured.

He leaned closer, "Can you tell me, my dear, who is the president of our country now?"

"Mr. Roosevelt," she answered, her voice growing weaker.

"And the governor of our great state of Ohio?"

"James E. Campbell."

"I think we can move her now," the doctor said.

Six men carried their burden by stretcher up the hill and down the dirt road onto Orchard Avenue and into the house. With great effort they maneuvered their burden up the wide staircase to the first landing and rested briefly before going up the last six steps toward the bedroom. Bridget had pulled back the covers on the massive bed, and she helped lay her mistress down and arranged the blankets over her.

"I fear she is paralyzed," Dr. McAullife told Will and Bridget after they got her safely into bed. "Where is Mr. Springer?"

"Last I heard in Illinois," Will said. At least that's where his latest order came from about two days ago. Now he may have gone on to St. Louis."

"We need to get in touch with him," the doctor said. "I don't think there is much we can do for her but make her comfortable."

Martha groaned.

Dr. McAuliffe leaned over her. "Are you in pain?"

She nodded.

"In your upper back?"

She nodded again.

"I'll give you some laudanum. I have a bit with me. Then I'll leave some opium to be mixed with water and seventy-six percent alcohol. The pharmacist has both, but this will tide you over."

"I'd be grateful," Martha mumbled.

"At least you're conscious," Dr. McAuliffe remarked, "but we need to get Mr. Springer here."

"I'll go to the courthouse. There is a telephone there, and I'm sure the store where he goes in St. Louis will have one too," Will said, before leaving in the buggy to make the call.

Adam returned three days later.

247

Forty

"Is there to be no end to the tragedies that stalk me?" Adam peered dejectedly at his desktop.

Will stared out the library window toward the carriage barn. His face reflecting the turbulence he felt in the wake of his mother's tragic accident, he turned toward Adam. "Dr. McAuliffe says we can't hope for much more than to make her comfortable, but she is alive and expected to remain so. Can't we be grateful for that?"

"I don't see how. Your mother was an energetic woman; now she fights pain and immobility, and the laudanum will soon offer no relief unless we keep increasing the dosage. Men at Shiloh and Vicksburg, indeed at all the battlefields begged for morphine, and I know what these painkilling drugs can do. She will be crying for them; we will give in to her because we can't stand to hear her cries, and before our very eyes, she will become a raging dope fiend. No, I hope every day for her early death, but in the meantime each of us must do what we can for her. She can't be left to lie alone with only her thoughts for company."

"Dr. McAuliffe suggests a full time nurse. I think that might be wise. We can't expect Nellie and Bridget to do it all, and you will soon have to get back to work, as I will. I'm already on shaky ground. Mr. Weber is bringing one of his sons into the business. He's going to expand into the next building, add a line of women's clothing, jewelry, and the like, but if there's a question about who eventually takes charge, I don't think old man Weber will choose me."

"You're probably right about that. I had already begun to figure how we might get out of this costly house, perhaps go back to Putnam, which would put you and Nellie out on your own. It's time for that anyway. She is so used to being waited upon by Bridget that she has developed no homemaking skills and is content to live the refined life. You pay me no rent, nor do I expect it since you handle my accounts, allowing me to go further afield, but there is just so much business I can wangle out of four pottery companies. If we stay here much longer, I see myself going further into debt. I didn't like to get into this with your mother. She was so broken up by Ralphy's passing."

"I've been saving my money and hope to get a store of my own someday."

"A fine thought, but right now, we have to think about the best way to care for your mother. I wonder, could Nellie take over as nurse?"

"I asked her, but she was appalled that she might be asked to do, you know, private sorts of things for Ma. She would wash her face and feed her, but you and I know that is not enough. Dr. McAuliffe told Bridget to tear up some sheets so Ma can be diapered. We can use sheets until we can purchase some more absorbent flannel."

"Good God!" Tears welled in Adam's eyes. "We can't expect Bridget to do that. I still don't see why Nellie . . ."

"Forget it, Pa, she isn't going to do it. Not today. Not ever!"

"Who's doing it now?"

"Bridget, but she's got enough to do with the house, laundry, and the cooking. I think we should do as the doctor suggests and hire a nurse."

"Hire one then; I'll put another mortgage on the house if I have to."

The following week Mrs. Daugherty came to live in. She was to remain five-and-a-half days each week, returning to her home Saturday afternoons and coming back Sunday evenings. Bridget said she could take care of Martha Saturday nights and Sunday mornings before leaving for mass and an afternoon visit with her family.

Unbeknown to Adam, Bridget had long ago taken Ralphy's toys and his clothing from his room. She had packed the toy soldiers and carried the battlefield board and saw horses to the attic storeroom. Having removed every trace of the little boy's possessions, she was not surprised that no one noticed, since the doors to both rooms remained closed, and to her knowledge no one ever entered either the attic playroom or his bedchamber. "Unpleasant memories are best kept where they belong—tucked away," she told Adam when the subject of where the nurse would sleep came up. "We'll put Mrs. Daugherty in Ralphy's old room."

Adam did not object. He relied more and more on Bridget and recognized her hard work. She was bereft of material needs, unlike Martha in her prime and Nellie in the present. Adam studied his finances more closely and decided that Will would have to pay something for rent and board. "A modest sum is all I ask," Adam told him.

"Then what about Ben and Alma? Do you charge them for the farm?"

"No, but I'm going to. I had a letter from him a few weeks ago asking that I come out to see him. Some oil and gas people have been lurking about and now want permission from me to drill test wells on the property. When I go there in the next day or two to talk to them, I'll also tell Ben he will have to begin paying rent. Then I'm going on to Pineville, where I'll try to arrange for the sale of the mine property. These days what the pottery takes in clay is minimal. I have forbidden them to tear up the topsoil looking for more clay deposits, because a stripped landscape would make it less valuable."

Adam also rearranged his work schedule. Some of his orders renewed automatically precluding the need for a friendly call more than once every six months. The country was now nearly settled, and cities and towns on the prairies and in the western extremes were growing. There was business to be had in those communities, and he should be about getting it, especially now when his expenses were mounting. But he put off going further afield until he was certain the nurse was settled in and a routine for Martha was established.

During his two-night visit with Ben and Alma, Adam not only talked with the oil and gas people, but also called upon his aged Aunt Mary Jane, now in her late eighties. Feisty as ever, she lived in her own house with her niece whose husband farmed the land. They had been looking out for the old lady since Uncle Jake's passing a few years before.

Ben agreed to pay a small stipend monthly. He arranged a meeting with the oil and gas men, who asked Adam to sign a paper indicating he would accept a four-percent royalty on any gas and oil pumped out.

Adam was poised to sign when Ben interrupted.

"That's not enough; either eight percent or we don't go along."

"That's rather high," one of the men countered.

"I've been in the oil business," Ben remarked. "and we are not giving ours—or I mean my father is not signing for any less."

"Not only do we have do the test bores, but if we find oil and gas, our company sinks the casings and puts up the derricks. You people encounter no expense at all. Your terms are not fair."

"We own the land and the mineral rights. You can't get to them without our permission, so that's the way it's going to be. Do you agree, Pa?"

Adam did not want to cross his son in front of the men, but he was sorely troubled at this turn of events. Didn't Ben realize that he needed the income? "Why don't we let them go ahead and bore the test wells, then we can decide. Isn't that a fair compromise?"

The men studied Adam and must have concluded they would eventually be dealing with the older man, so they agreed.

While Adam watched them go, he considered that he could contact them later without Ben's meddling. But just as this thought was forming, Ben said, "I don't want to hear of your dealing with them for less than eight percent."

"What about the other farmers?"

"Some of them have already settled, but they are ignorant of this business, which, believe me, has its own charlatans. My father-in-law across the way settled for twelve dollars a year for each well, no matter how much they produce, simply because he's ignorant about the business. And he has no idea how much he's being cheated should the wells prove productive."

Adam decided he would leave the bargaining to Ben.

With the arrival of the nurse, Martha's medicinal dosages were established, and a certain routine took hold. Nellie fed her mother-in-law and read to her from the books kept on the library shelves. Adam also read to her in the evenings he was home. And after a few weeks, some of the neighbors came to call. Satisfied all that could be done was being done, he arranged his first long trip past the Mississippi River boundary and St. Louis. Feeling he could leave for longer periods, he looked forward to life on the road away from the stress of the household. In truth, he could barely wait to get away from the dreary house and his invalid wife.

Adam was in excellent physical condition, a handsome man with thick snow-white hair and white mustache, who met strangers as a man to be admired. Few knew that inside he was in turmoil. He missed the young Martha, not the one in the bed, to be sure. That woman was withering more than she was dying. Only her face remained mobile; she had to be raised and lowered to eat, and this usually took two people. To relieve the pressure on her back, they devised a hammock for her to lie in.

Adam and Nellie read to Martha from the works of Henry James, Mark Twain, Sir Arthur Conan Doyle, and Stephen Crane. He subscribed to McClure's Magazine and instructed Nellie and the nurse to turn the pages for Martha, so she could peruse the articles, serials, and short stories. At considerable expense, he had one of those new-fangled telephones installed in her room. "Unheard of" most of his salesmen comrades commented. Everyone knew telephone calls were reserved for commerce and emergencies, not friendly conversations. Adam told them the expense was worth it if their talks interrupted the tedium of her uneventful days and weeks. Usually, he could barely hear her, as she had to be lifted toward the mouthpiece while someone else held the slender column that supported it. And her voice was weak. He took to shouting so that anyone else in her room or in the hotel lobbies, from which he called, could hear. Conversations were stilted; they had little to say to one another once they got past remarking on the weather at home or wherever Adam happened to be.

He began to venture in different directions going to Detroit, Grand Rapids and Kalamazoo in Michigan, and to cities and towns in Iowa, where he stopped off to visit his brother's children. John had died ten years before leaving his property to his eldest son, but also providing his two other sons with spreads of their own. A successful farmer with a three-hundred-twenty acre spread near Marshalltown, Adam's nephew, James, was the prosperous middle son. Adam stayed on for three nights and marveled at the up-to-date farm equipment and well-appointed house. Their eldest daughter was planning to go off to exclusive Stephens College in Missouri in September.

Adam was impressed by the lush Iowa soil, black as pitch, and the flat land unspoiled by trees and brush. Every acre was productive, not like the Morgan County farm where hills and ravines cut into the fields and meadows. James could employ a crew of hired men when it came time for threshing. During corn harvesting, some twenty men sat down for the noontime dinner prepared by James's wife and a hired girl. Adam joined them and marveled at the efficiency of this Iowa farm operation and the ease with which the women handled the food for the group of hired hands.

Forty-one

As the train neared Zanesville, on the return from one of his month-long trips, Adam recalled how desolate he had felt riding over those same tracks after the war. That despair rose in him even more now when he thought what a visit home would entail. He could barely look at Martha; she was small, birdlike, and as the days and months wore on, her body twisted grotesquely. She could converse, but the laudanum had turned her dreamy. Adam thought she was going slightly fey in the head. She tired easily and frequently fell asleep while he was reading to her. Their conversations were limited. Her presence made him uncomfortable. Adam hated himself for these feelings and sought the company of other salesmen and dinner companions he met in hotels and taverns. And even as women of the night appeared always available and ever tempting, he remained faithful. Occasionally, when he chanced to meet one in the hallway going to or coming from a liaison, they greeted him with come hither eyes and tilted heads while leaning bosomy bodies temptingly his direction. Still Adam resisted even as thoughts of the wizened body in his bed seemed to release him from husbandly obligations.

Having never appreciated the ostentatious house on Orchard Avenue, Adam liked his homes away from home. New hotels had sprung up in every town, where the railroad station was not only a means of escape but the route people took to see new sights. Salesmen with their valises and trunks filled with temptations for an eager public were welcomed into the towns, even as mothers warned their daughters to steer clear of them. These hotels were finer hosterlies than Adam had been used to just a few years earlier. They boasted fancier furnishings, carpets thick enough to sink into, indoor water closets and bathing facilities. Wide hallways had davenports, chairs, and tables, where salesmen meeting with buyers could display their merchandise. There were elegantly appointed dining rooms with flocked wallpaper, white table clothes, and finger bowls graced with white doilies, all conducive to striking deals over excellent meals. The bedrooms were frequently spacious enough to set up shelves on which merchandise—everything from hardware to clothing—could be displayed. And in some hotels for the price of a quarter, a shower was available for unregistered itinerant travelers.

By fall, the Ohio household seemed to be running smoothly with the exception of the mounting costs for medicines. The nurse told Adam that Martha was too much work for the fee they had settled upon, and she would need more money. He complied and told Will to manage the best way he could. Nellie and Bridget did as asked, although Will's wife seemed reluctant when she was summoned to help the nurse with any lifting. "I fear for my back," she told Will, who told her to help regardless.

Martha's wedding band hung loosely on the fourth finger of her left hand, but she refused to remove it. So Bridget rapped string around the loop to secure it. "Make sure you use enough," Martha said. "I wouldn't want to lose it. I've had that ring for thirty-two years. Adam gave it to me on my wedding day. I never could figure out how he had enough money to pay for such a heavy one. Of course, then I didn't know how scarce his money really was. I married him thinking he was a well-to-do landowner like the farmers around Marietta."

"It's a lovely ring," Bridget said. "Mr. Springer must love you very much to have spent so generously."

Neighbors called frequently at first and less frequently as the months wore on. All went as well as could be expected until late mid-December when Will, carrying a package that had arrived via post, confronted Martha.

"What's this for?" He waved a piece of paper at Martha.

Adam thought he spoke a mite too sharply.

"I haven't opened the package, but this bill was enclosed in an envelope on the outside, along with an apology for the package being four months late."

Adam was seated in the rocker reading from *Treasure Island*. Annoyed by the interruption, he frowned at Will who stood waving the paper menacingly close to Martha's face. Will, who had to live every day with his disabled mother, was growing impatient. Adam would speak to him later about his attitude. He wanted no harsh words used around Martha.

"Two hundred dollars from someone named Howard Chandler Christy, for a painting. Ma what is this? You haven't been out of that bed in nine months. How could you have incurred a bill for two hundred dollars?" He glanced at his father. "There is no two hundred dollars to spare."

Martha, growing ever smaller among the bedclothes, looked stricken. "I don't want to see it; don't open it."

"Then I'll send it back."

"You can't send it back. He won't take it back," she shouted with more fury and animation than she had exhibited since they first brought her to the bed that would become her prison.

Will began to tear off the wrapping paper.

"No don't. I can't bear it. Please Adam make him stop."

Will dropped the paper from the large flat package. "We can't go on with these bills," he shouted. "Isn't it enough that you have a costly nurse and all those medicines? You buy paintings too? What did you do? Respond to an ad in McClure's Magazine?" The jagged wrapping paper fell to the floor. Adam was unnerved by the confrontation between mother and son: Will had always been a mild mannered boy, polite and respectful. As though he had caught her in some dastardly deed, Will held up the unframed portrait and thrust it toward the bedridden Martha.

Her long graying hair lay tangled against the pillow, Martha screamed and shut her eyes. With what little life was left in her bony arthritic hand, she clawed at the coverlet. "Take it away, take it now," she wailed.

"Do as your mother says." Adam rose from the rocker and went around in front of Will to look at the picture. Sitting tall upon a horse was an elegant Martha clothed in a black riding dress. Full of life and verve, her face a rosy glow, her back was straight with shoulders taut so that she appeared younger than her fifty years. She wore glossy black riding boots and a black derby cocked in a debonair manner. The horse's coat, a burnished chestnut, was glistening as though some attentive groom had wiped it down with oil. Dixie's ears were up, her head was high, her tail arched. Horse and lady were stark against the best of Ohio's foliage: oaks in full jagged leaf, maple and walnut trees forming a canopy behind the elegant subjects. The sky was azure softened by fluffy, snow-white clouds, and there was a meandering brook in one corner, its greenery-laden banks low against the water. Watercress, Adam thought, as he tried to avert his gaze from the elegant rider.

"Do as your mother asks and take it away this minute," Adam said. "She need not be reminded of what is past. And neither do I."

Martha died in 1902. Adam sold the Orchard Avenue house, with the never displayed portrait still in the attic, and moved back to Putnam. He retired in 1906. Shortly after Martha's death, Nellie and Will moved to St. Clairsville where he opened a store. In the summer of 1907, Adam treated himself to a grand railway trip west. He stayed three months with Frank and his wife on their fifteen-hundred acre California ranch. When his grandson, Ralph, turned five that July, Adam bought him a pony and took great pleasure in teaching him to ride.

Returning to Ohio in late September, Adam settled into the Putnam house alone. Ben realized that his aging father would need some looking after, so he and Alma and their two children left the farm and moved in with him. Ben found employment with the state supervising a work crew on the old National Road.

With its oil and gas wells supplementing the family income through the Great Depression and beyond, the farm remained in the family until 1968, when Adam's grandson, Charles, finally sold it one-hundred-fifty-one years after his ancestors first wrenched it from the wilderness in 1817 through back-breaking toil and tenacity.

Ted and Ralphy

Afterword

Fact and fiction blend in this story of a star-crossed family...

Continuing the saga of the same family of Muellers and Springers that appeared in *The Good Wife*, this story *Broken Country—Broken Soldier* takes them into another generation. Both stories, based on my family's experiences in America, are highly fictionalized thus, the family name has been changed.

My great grandfather (Adam) was a Civil War soldier. I don't know for certain that he was traumatized, but some of the family lore made it seem so. In 1868, at age twenty-seven he married eighteen-year-old Martha. They parented four sons, one of whom died in his crib. Supposedly, the hired girl threw a blanket over his face, and he suffocated.* The surviving sons, including my grandfather, are represented by fictitious characters. As in the story, their parents divorced, and Martha took her sons to the nearest town, where she ran a hotel. Several years later the couple remarried, and another child, Ralphy, was born. As a four-year old, he did march in the Fourth of July parade, contracted spinal meningitis, died, and was buried in his blue Civil War uniform.

Although my great grandfather never sold pottery, he moved his family to Putnam, where he worked as a mill superintendent. Proceeds from oil and gas wells on the Ohio farm supplemented the family income. His eldest son did work in the Bakersfield, California oil fields, where he was sweet on one of the Jewett sisters. Returning to Ohio in 1893 to see his little brother, his dreams of being an oilman on the cusp of a new industry were shattered by marriage to an Ohio farm girl who refused to leave her roots.

The story also stays true to what happened to Martha. Thrown from a horse at age fifty, she spent the last two years before her death in 1902 as a bed-ridden invalid. Alone and retired, my great grandfather traveled to California to visit his son, Frank, on his sprawling ranch where he took considerable interest in his grandchildren, Ralph and Marian. He died in 1922, and was buried in Black Oak Methodist Cemetery in Deavertown, Ohio.

*In all likelihood Sudden Infant Death Syndrome (SIDS)

Sources

Eric T. Dean, Jr., *Shook Over Hell, Post –Traumatic Stress, Vietnam, and the Civil War,* Harvard University Press, Cambridge, Massachusetts, 1997

Donovan, Hatrak, Mills, Shull, *Thirteen Colonies Cookbook,* Montclair Historical Society, Montclair, New Jersey, 1975

Shelby Foote, *The Civil War, a Narrative (Fredericksburg to Meridian)* Vintage Books, a Division of Random House, New York, 1963

W.P. Gault, Sergeant, Company F, 78th Ohio Volunteer Infantry, (Secretary to the Commission) *Ohio at Vicksburg, Report of the Ohio Vicksburg Battlefield Commission, 1906*

Robert B. Gordon, *Ohio Biological Survey,* College of Biological Sciences, The Ohio State University, Columbus, Ohio, 1972

Sharon and Robert Huxford, "Artware to Commercial Lines," (Roseville Pottery*) The Collector's Encyclopedia,* a Division of Shroeder Publishing Company, Inc., 1980

Merritt Ierley, *Open House, A Guided Tour of the American Home, 1637-Present,* Henry Holt and Company, New York, 1999

Merritt Ierley, *Traveling The National Road, Across the Centuries on America's First Highway,* The Overlook Press, Woodstock, NY, 1990

Merritt Ierley, *Wondrous Contrivances, Technology at the Threshold,* Clarkson Potter/ Publisher, New York, 2002

Marc McCutcheon, *Everyday Life in the 1800s,* Writer's Digest Books, F & W Publications, Cincinnati, Ohio, 1993

Charles H. Richardson, *Sherman and His Campaigns*, Press of Geo. C. Rand and Avery, 1865

Charles Robertson, M.D. *History – Morgan County, Ohio*, L. H. Watkins & Co., Chicago, 1886

Rev. Thomas M. Stevenson, Chaplain of the Regiment, *History of the 78th Regiment, O.V.V.I. Ohio Infantry Volunteers, Its Organization, Marches, Campaigns, Battles and Skirmishes*, Hugh Dunne, Zanesville, Ohio, 1865

William E. Woodward, *Years of Madness*, G. P. Putnam's Sons, New York, 1942

A. E. Youman, M.D., *A Dictionary of Every-Day Wants, Healthy Living and Successful Farming, 1850-1870*, Frank M. Reed, New York, 1878, Reprinted in Annotated Transcription by Katie F. Hamilton, Metheglin Press, Phoenix, Arizona, 1996 and 1998

About the Author

Mary Anne Butler has been a journalist with a metropolitan newspaper, a radio news reporter and a public relations executive with a national firm. Her writing has appeared in *The New York Times* and in an anthology published by Warner Books. She began writing fiction twenty years ago and now concentrates on researching and writing historical novels based on her own family's experiences in America from 1750 to 1920. Although all characters are fictitious and both books stand alone, *Broken Country—Broken Soldier* is the sequel to *The Good Wife* previously published. Both follow four generations of one family as their fortunes in America grow and change. A graduate of Penn State, she and her husband live in Tucson, Arizona.

Printed in the United States
20941LVS00003B/58-255